UNFIT
TO PRACTICE

Also by Perri O'Shaughnessy

Move to Strike
Writ of Execution

PERRI O'SHAUGHNESSY

UNFIT TO PRACTICE

PIATKUS

Copyright © 2002 by Mary O'Shaughnessy and Pamela O'Shaughnessy
Endpaper maps copyright © 2001 by Hadel Studio

First published in Great Britain in 2002 by
Judy Piatkus (Publishers) Ltd of
5 Windmill Street, London W1T 2JA
email: info@piatkus.co.uk

First published in the United States in 2002
by
Random House, Inc.

The moral right of the author has been asserted

A catalogue record for this book is available from the British Library

ISBN 0 7499 0608 1

Printed and bound in Great Britain by Biddles Ltd, *www.biddles.co.uk*

DEDICATED TO
ALL THE DESPERADOS OUT THERE TRYING
TO PRACTICE LAW ALONE

UNFIT
TO PRACTICE

PROLOGUE

AFTER BEING DROPPED OFF at a filthy parking lot underneath a gloomy concrete overpass, Nina Reilly stopped in for coffee at the Roastery on the corner of Howard and Main streets. A river of chilly air flowed through the tunnel-like streets around the skyscrapers of the Financial District. The buildings seemed to lean in at her, threatening. She had her pick of caffeine oases, not that it mattered. She was not here by choice. Any black bile would do.

At the bottom of Howard, the Embarcadero and Bay Bridge buzzed unseen, angry hives of energy. The tall buildings' glass reflected the sun's intense beams right at her. People glowed like aliens, or so she projected. San Francisco wasn't her city anymore. The town of South Lake Tahoe had sheltered her for the last few years after she left the Montgomery Street law firm where she had begun the practice of law, and the city had become a stranger.

Nina sank into a rattan chair. A young man at the next table, his Chinese newspaper close to his nose, blew steam across his cup.

Women like her, wearing expensive jackets and gold earrings, waited anxiously in line, then carried their medicine right out the door, swallowing on the run.

Where was Jack?

She watched a boy from some cold country, bearing a heavy backpack, lounge against the counter, waiting for his espresso. Next to him a balding man, not very much older but with the suit and briefcase of one who has settled into his life, took an apple from a bowl while the woman behind the counter heated up a muffin. The scent of cinnamon moved through the room, smelling of home, its effect immediate and painful. She thought of Bob, who was staying with her brother, Matt, back in Tahoe. She needed her son beside her but she didn't want to put him through this. It would hurt him too much.

She looked around. Jack should be here by now.

What a strange and terrible day, she thought, taking in the sounds of traffic and the city through the open doors.

Here she sat waiting for her ex-husband, a man she had never expected to see again, but as a result of this six-month-old legal case they had a closer relationship now than when they were married. Jack as a colleague was a savvy, reassuring presence beside her—a much better lawyer than he had been a husband.

Jack blew through the door from Main Street, tossing a raincoat on the chair next to hers. "Sorry I'm late."

"I just got here myself. We got stuck in traffic coming off the Bay Bridge. How much time do we have?"

"A few minutes. What time did you leave Tahoe?"

"Four-thirty." A long, long time before the dawn. She tried to smile back, remembering that attitude is everything. Reinforcements had arrived and she should straighten up.

Jack looked spiffy in his suit, his square jaw scraped clean. Fresh from the blow-dryer, his ginger hair stuck out as if fired by electricity.

Smoothing his hair down with one hand, he read from the green boards. "I'll be right back," he said, getting up and walking over to the counter.

Nina watched him sneak in front of a pale office worker, apologizing as if he hadn't seen her, offering to wait in line behind her, but the girl was already bewitched and said, oh, no, you go ahead. Jack had charm, that rare quality that eased the tensions in the courtroom as well as in life. Good. He would need that magnetism over the next few days.

He returned and slurped, careful of his white collar. Then he took her hand. "Relax, now. It's just another day in court." His eyes moved over her in a mix of personal and professional interest. "I like the suit. You could pull your hair back."

Nina considered the measure of control Jack now had over her, found a barrette in her purse, and pulled her long brown hair back.

"We should go in a couple of minutes. We'll be more comfortable if we have a minute to settle in before the judge shows up. You look worried. No, you look mad. Mad and worried. What's up?"

"I'm ready to fight, only who are we fighting? I can't stand this feeling that we're being manipulated."

"So we use the hearing to find out. We focus on that. Meanwhile, don't get weird on me."

"I'll look confident. But don't tell me how to feel." His eyes moved to her hand, where she had bitten a nail down to the quick. She rubbed her lips with her finger, opened her briefcase and withdrew a delicate mirror, then looked herself in the eye. The eye was still brown and showed no panic. Amazing.

"Why didn't you come down from Tahoe yesterday? I can see how tired you are, and we're just starting. You should have stayed with me in Bernal Heights last night, saved yourself that drive. What did you think I would do? Jump you?"

She didn't answer, telling herself, this is not the time. Lack of sleep and the months of tension building to this moment were unfettering them both.

"Sorry," Jack said after a moment. "The shoes are nice. You look remarkably respectable today. Like someone I might marry." He smiled, and the smile invited her to play along. He always wanted to brush the edge off, smooth things over with humor. Life is folly, his eyes told her. When she didn't smile back, his face hardened and he turned back into Jack the Knife, his lawyer-self. She preferred that. She believed it to be the real him.

His eyes flitted to his watch. "Time to go."

They left, hustling although they were still early.

Nina's new briefcase felt heavier with every step. Its contents, tagged paper exhibits, represented months of work. This was the most important hearing of her career. Still, she was not ready. She could never be ready for this.

They moved through a warren of skyscrapers into a dank alleyway. At an outdoor stand, more coffee shot into impatiently jiggling cups. The whole city seemed to be fueled with caffeine, hyper, irritable, on the move. Pushing through double doors, they walked up to a security desk. "Good morning. Do we need to sign in?" Jack asked.

A friendly black woman eyed their attachés. "You going up to the court?"

"That's us. Is the judge in a good mood?"

"You tell me when you see him. Sign in up there," she said. "Sixth floor."

The elevator gleamed bronze and silver. They rode up in silence, exited toward a sign that read QUIET, PLEASE. COURT IN SESSION, and laid their nail clippers, keys, and coins on a brown plastic tray before passing through the metal detector. As Nina walked through, the alarm sounded. The attendant, a young man in a starched white shirt, motioned her back. He looked down at her feet. "Hmm. No buckles," he said.

She removed her watch and walked through again. Again it rang. By this time other people in a small waiting area to the left, several that she knew, were staring at her. She swallowed and tried to think what in the world she was wearing that would make the thing go off. An underwire bra? No, she'd gone for the soft athletic one, invisible under her suit jacket and more comfortable for a long court day. She was already ridiculous. She felt an urge to flee.

"Your barrette, Nina," Jack said.

Nodding, she removed it. Her hair billowed out, but she walked through soundlessly this time. The guard smiled at her and handed her the barrette. "Sign in here." He pushed a lined pad toward her. "Put 9:22 as when you checked in. You don't have to sign out if you leave for a few minutes. Just at the end of the day."

"Can we go on in?" Jack asked. "We're scheduled in Courtroom Two, I believe."

"The clerk is already in there. Go ahead."

Nina felt the eyes on her back as they walked inside.

"Your hair," Jack reminded her.

"To hell with it." She slid her barrette into her pocket.

Small and windowless except for two lengths of frosted glass that ran alongside the door to the waiting area, the courtroom formed a long rectangle. On the right, the trial counsel, Gayle Nolan, sat at an L-shaped table behind two large black notebooks. Nina and Jack took seats at an identical table on the left, Jack seated on the outside, Nina tucked into the L, feeling the unnatural chill of an overactive ventilation system, grateful for a warm jacket.

Jack put papers on the table and handed her one of two bottles of spring water that were sitting there. She unpacked the briefcase swiftly and efficiently as she had done so many times before in her legal career, getting into it, appreciating the tight organization resulting from so many hours of work.

A study in neutrality, the courtroom walls were brown, white, and gray. The chairs they sat in bore innocuous stripes. The furnishings were affectless, designed to suck moods right out of the air. Details like the clock on the wall, circular, simply numbered, the judge's podium, and a large digital clock, right now showing dashes instead of numbers, were strictly functional. Behind them a dozen chairs for observers or witnesses lined the back wall of the court.

She could be in Chicago or New York. She could be back in her home courtroom in South Lake Tahoe, the room was so stylized. It reminded her of the set of a play she had seen not too long ago at a little theater, Sartre's *No Exit,* a black place presumably surrounded by the Void. Purgatory, timeless and eternal.

But this wasn't Tahoe. The mountains outside beyond the gray were tall buildings. The dreamlike element, the clash between the bland courtroom and the often terrible events that brought people there, gripped her. What am I doing here? she thought. Who has done this to me?

Jack reached over and ran his hand along her arm.

"Okay?" he whispered.

"Totally freaked out," Nina whispered back.

"How you can feel that way and still look so Darth Vader–tough I'll never understand." Jack fingered an empty Styrofoam cup, a scraping, ghastly wakeup. Gayle Nolan got up, ignoring them, and wheeled in a cart marked Chief Trial Counsel weighted down with thick notebooks, folders in file boxes, and code books. So many papers. Nina tried to enjoy the sight of her struggling with the load. No eager law clerks helping here. Light gleamed off Nolan's specs as she stacked the paperwork onto her table. Finally, she sat back down.

"Hey, Gayle," Jack said. "And how are you on this fine morning?"

"Hello, Jack."

"You can still back out."

"Don't make me laugh."

"This whole thing is a laugh."

"Yeah? I notice she's not laughing."

"She wants the last laugh."

The judge entered from one of three doors at the front of the room behind the podium. They all stood. Extra tall, with a full head of gray hair he had brushed back, he sported a small, neat mustache, not bushy like the one Jack used to wear. He didn't look at them. The file engaged his attention as he sat down, allowing them to sit, too.

A placard at the front of his desk read JUDGE HUGO BROCK. "We'll go on the record," he said. Sitting on his left with headphones over her ears, the clerk clicked on a keyboard. The digital clock at the front flashed to brilliant red life. It was the brightest spot in the courtroom, and they all stared at it as if the day had exploded.

"California State Bar Proceeding SB 76356. In the matter of Reilly," said the judge.

BOOK ONE

SEPTEMBER

The Grove, Nina's mother called her school, and whenever she thought of that name later on she naturally thought of rows of ripe apples and oranges, as though when she was six years old she had lived a country idyll. But it was only a hilly neighborhood in California, and the elementary school was really called Pacific Grove Elementary, a functional name without romance. Nina had gone to first grade there.

On the playground, little girls swung around a long metal bar about three feet off the ground. Little boys were not allowed to do this exquisitely exciting thing. One leg pushed off from the ground, the other draped over the bar, hands holding the bar, over and upside down she went, at every recess and after school when she could swing all alone. When she got her rhythm right she could somersault ten or twelve times continuously, and get dizzy and watch the hills and trees turn upside down, becoming other forms in an ever-changing world.

The first important thing in her life happened at The Grove. One day, all alone after school, she swung around and around on the bar, and after a while a thought swung into her head: I am me.

She had never had this thought before. As a matter of fact, she had never been aware of her thoughts before. I am me. My name is Nina and I live down the street. I swing on the bar. I am me! Wildly excited, she turned furiously upside down. The hills were the same hills now, just upside down.

Once this thought entered her head, she was never the same. She became aware of things she had never noticed and that was a loss, because she had been mindlessly free before, but there was also the joy of seeing how things fit together. She made discoveries about where she fit into this new orderly world, into her family especially, Mommy and Daddy and baby brother Matty.

And at school her teacher taught her rules. Follow the rules to keep away confusion. Follow them to keep things in order. Line up when the bell rings. Raise your hand to go to the bathroom. Little girl bathroom, little boy bathroom.

The second important thing happened toward the end of the year, after school again. Nina should have been heading home, a block away, but the heat made her thirsty, so first she had a long drink of water from the girls' water fountain. Little girls' fountain, little boys' fountain over by their bathroom, that rule was clear.

While Nina watched, a mother and a little boy came up to the little girls' water fountain.

And to her horror, the little boy started to take a drink from the little girls' fountain. Nina ran right up to tell him he couldn't do that and tried to explain. But the mother, ignorant and uncaring, brushed her aside and told him to go ahead. And he, who must have felt confused, decided to do what his mother said, but Nina now blocked the way, arms out, defending the fountain. It's the rule! she said, but the tall grown-up bent down and told the boy to drink up, and he gave Nina a little push to get her out of the way.

So Nina slugged him. That stopped him. He sat down on the concrete and cried, holding his hand over his eye. Nina breathed a sigh of relief and satisfaction, but then along came a big teacher with the mother and made her go into the office and called Mommy and said she did a bad thing! And no one got it, that her defense had saved the fountain and the rules and maybe the orderly world itself, that she was a champion of the girls' fountain. She had done the right thing and was punished for it.

To be so completely sure, and then have the system go topsy-turvy on her! She decided, and this was the most significant decision of her life, that from what she knew, she was right to defend the fountain and they were wrong because rules had meaning and purpose. What meaning and purpose, she didn't know yet. But rules made sense out of her blurry world.

• • •

In high school about ten years later, Nina went to Monterey with her class to watch a trial. The scruffy-looking, confused man on trial had done something very bad, maybe. Everybody was against him. But one person stood up for him and held them all off, making sure the rules were followed. And as she watched, she understood. This champion was not just defending that poor underdog but a system that kept the world sane.

How do people with different values, religions, economic status, and hopes coexist in peace?

Law provided a method.

And so at age sixteen she decided to become a lawyer.

1

THAT THURSDAY in early September billowed up blue and white, as breezy and innocent as a picnic, the air filtering through shimmering sunlit leaves. But during the afternoon, the true Sierra atmosphere showed its face in a ferocious summer storm, ruthless, unpredictable, and dangerous.

And because the storm dislocated all sorts of human arrangements that night, or because life is a mist of error, or perhaps just because she had been working too hard and couldn't deal with one more thing that day, Nina Reilly made a small, critical mistake that changed everything.

The day began at eight-thirty sharp with the Cruz custody hearing, now in its second day and going fine, if anything could be fine about a family splitting up. Lisa Cruz, Kevin's wife, took the stand, and she loved their two kids, no doubt about that, but she had some very strange ideas, too.

"I'm a full-time mom and a professional with a deep spiritual side," she said from the witness box, gazing at Jeffrey Riesner with large, earnest, liquid eyes that seemed to beg for further help. "I depend on the great philosophers for guidance."

Kevin began an astringent, whispered commentary. "Moving right along from Jim Beam, to pills, to marathons, and onward into religion," he muttered.

Lisa had a pale, heart-shaped face and a tentative, breathy voice. She wore a structured jacket and creased slacks and looked fragile, but Kevin had told Nina that Lisa could run five miles without breaking a sweat; had no compunctions about kicking him when he was down; had an extensive, X-rated vocabulary; and bore unswerving allegiance to nothing and no one except their kids.

Lisa adjusted her body, as she had frequently during Riesner's questions, raising one leg over another, then deciding against it. She was not a woman who enjoyed sitting still. "I studied philosophy at the community college," she said.

"She took one course, and quit before the final," Kevin whispered to Nina.

"I consider myself a truth-seeker and scholar. Of course, I work hard to impart the right values to my children: hard work, healthy diet, goal-setting." She had a lot to say about vitamins.

More whispering. "She'd use a cattle prod if she thought she could get away with it. She's fanatic about physical fitness. Those kids don't get a moment's peace, between the death marches up and down mountains and the bogus mind crap she feeds them." Kevin had arrived at court very emotional, as always. Nina had to watch out for him when she should have been giving all her energies to watching Jeffrey Riesner, the attorney representing Lisa. She shook her head sharply, her eyes closed, and Kevin understood and stopped.

Nina and Riesner went way back, but not to good places. They had a long history of conflict, which had begun almost the day she had arrived in the town of South Lake Tahoe and set up an office as a sole practitioner. A partner in Tahoe's most prestigious law firm, Caplan, Stamp, Powell, and Riesner, Riesner viewed her as an out-of-town upstart who had barged into his territory and seduced away several good felony defendants. Nina saw him as a relentless greedhead who held grudges and hated women, her in particular.

She watched him playing Lisa now, playing the judge, playing the court, as homey in a courtroom as you could be without moving in a couch and pillows. How he warmed their hearts with little stories of Lisa's generosity and kindness. The smallest smile was calculated, a warm nod to the judge, practiced. She could never understand his reputation for success in the courtroom. Apparently, judges and juries could not see through the tall, smooth-talking, Armani-clad exterior to his squirming, wormy insides.

Under Riesner's careful handling, Lisa went on for quite some time, modestly recounting her achievements as a parent and a volunteer firefighter with several exciting stories to tell. Slowly, Riesner built up his Wonder Woman. Her mother, who lived nearby, watched the children for her during fire emergencies, when volunteers were called out. She attended church, raised money for good causes, met with teachers for conferences, and loved her children.

What interested Nina most was not what she said, though, but how, whenever Lisa started to show real emotion by raising her voice or letting a little vehemence enter, Riesner gently steered her back to calm, like a fairy-tale hero sparing her the scary, dark woods. After several minutes, having wrung all the good he could from his client, he turned back to his table and sat down, but not without first casting a victorious sneer Nina's way.

Nina stood. She had thought a long time about how to cross-examine Kevin's wife. Lisa wasn't a bad mother, just as Kevin wasn't a bad father, but both parents couldn't have the children. Many had tried to split custody, and the only parents who succeeded were parents who respected and liked each other after the divorce. Lisa and Kevin didn't like each other anymore.

Emotional volatility was Lisa's weakness. She sat in the box, hands neatly folded, like a female Buddha. Nina needed to get around that pseudoserenity.

"Mrs. Cruz, you describe yourself as a seeker," Nina said. "Could you tell us a little more about what you mean by that?"

Riesner cleared his throat, considering an objection, probably. The phlegm went no farther than his esophagus and lodged there, to judge from its sudden halt. He didn't like the question, but must have decided to let it ride.

"Well," Lisa said, any ease she had developed during Riesner's questioning now gone. She hesitated, tongue-tied, staring at Nina with a half-fascinated, half-repulsed expression on her face, drumming her fingers on the rail in front of her.

"Mrs. Cruz?" Nina said.

Lisa finally spoke, although the words sounded forced. "Life has a deeper meaning than just—this," she said.

A few observers in the audience looked around the earth-toned, windowless courtroom and chuckled.

"I don't mean just this moment," she said defensively, "although every moment is significant. And this one certainly is, since it involves the future well-being of my children. But to answer your question more broadly, I would say I'm interested in the big picture. Taking responsibility for your actions. Accepting blame when you do wrong." Flat brown eyes followed Nina's every move as if she expected Nina to jump her at any moment.

"You are a religious person, I understand."

"Yes," she said.

"You take your children to church every Sunday?"

"Yes."

"I understand your religion forbids blood transfusions?" Nina asked.

"I haven't lost my senses just because I joined my church," Lisa said. "I'm open to advice from conventional medical doctors, and would take Kevin's wishes into consideration even after our divorce is final, as I always have before. You know, I don't limit myself when it comes to a personal philosophy to live by. I've spent a lot of time thinking about how we should live as well as why we live and I've drawn some conclusions."

"What conclusions?"

Lisa sat back in her chair, considering the question seriously. "Oh, there's a level we operate on in this country—hey, I'm not knocking anyone else, okay? But I don't want my life bogged down by trivia and reduced to a long series of tasks to be done. I try to keep my life spiritual, focused, and tranquil."

Nina knew Lisa had balked and complained bitterly for years about the changes in her life since having children. She had no more time for her personal pursuits, felt limited in her important volunteer work, and unduly burdened by the dragging weight of child rearing. Some of Kevin's resentments percolated around his wife's stubborn refusal to contribute to the normal running of their household.

"You have two children," Nina said. "Surely there are many chores that need to be done? Surely there is a great deal of trivia?"

"Of course. Children make messes. That's their job."

"And tranquility isn't really a normal state of affairs in a young family, is it?"

"No. Tranquility is an aspiration. It doesn't come easy."

"Isn't one of the big surprises about becoming a parent finding out how little we control the dynamic in the household and how quickly the most basic things can get out of control?"

"I've adjusted," Lisa answered dryly, understanding the direction Nina was taking. "Of course I do chores. Big ones, little ones. Petty ones. Many, many chores."

"You make sure your children have clean clothing?"

"Yes."

"You have a regular laundry day?"

"I do it when the basket is full."

"Whenever the basket is full?"

Lisa had begun to fidget. The questions about her domestic routine bored her. "Yeah, whenever," she said, looking at Riesner, who treated her to some serious eyebrow action. "Because what's the difference if I do it on Monday or Friday as long as it gets done eventually? You know, people don't realize how they try to re-create Victorian standards of living without the kind of help people had then. Yes, our standard of living is higher than ever, but just because you have a dishwasher, does every dish need to be done that minute? Just because you have a vacuum, should you be expected to vacuum every day?"

" 'Eventually' you do the laundry?" Nina persisted. "Would that be once a week or twice a week?"

Lisa rolled her eyes. "Probably once every two weeks, if you were to average it out."

"Do you feed your children regularly?"

Her eyes narrowed. "Of course I feed them regularly."

"How would you define the term *regular*?"

"Well, breakfast, lunch, and dinner," she said, lips curling with disdain at this truly degraded level of conversation. "Am I missing anything? Oh, yes. Snacks after school."

"What did you make them for breakfast this morning?"

She shifted in her chair. "This morning I was in a rush. Look, Joey and Heather are seven and nine, plenty old enough to get themselves cereal. The days of a home-cooked breakfast are pretty much gone."

"Why is that, Mrs. Cruz?" Nina asked.

"Who has time?"

"Do you like to cook?"

"I wouldn't say it's my favorite thing, but I know how to put together a healthy meal."

"Your petition says you are at home full time, except during fire emergencies, because your children are young and need you there."

"That's true."

"What did they eat for breakfast this morning, Mrs. Cruz?"

Stony silence.

"Do you know?"

"No. Although they ate for sure. There were dirty dishes in the sink."

"Did they get up before you?"

"No. I'm the first one up. I run in the mornings."

"You always run in the morning?"

"Most days."

"You don't make them breakfast."

"Not when I run." Again she adjusted herself in her chair, found a position, changed it, and frowned.

Nina had never seen a witness so ill-suited to spending a long time idle, although her excessive energy might serve her well as a mother and in her work, Nina had to admit. "Did your husband make breakfast for the children when he was still living with you?"

"Sometimes, I guess."

"Isn't it true he always made breakfast?"

She sighed. "You know, I'm a mother, but I'm also a professional who needs to stay fit and strong for my work as a firefighter. I'm in the business of saving *lives.*" She glared at Nina. "I don't think it hurts my children to get a meal for themselves once in a while. And low-sugar cereal with milk is a fine, healthy breakfast for children, anyone can tell you that.

"I only run five miles. Half the time they don't even know I'm gone. And my mom lives really close."

"And when you come back from the run, you take a shower?" Nina was reading from the deposition of Lisa Cruz taken some months before.

"So what if I do?"

"Who dressed the children for school? When you and Kevin were still together?"

"Kevin basically got them off to school. Okay? I have to run."

"Who gets them off to school now? Now that Kevin isn't around?"

"They're older now. Jeans, T-shirt, grab their books, out the door. They don't need me."

"And after school?"

"My mother. I told you. I spend every single evening with them."

"Except, let's see, Tuesday, Thursday, and Sunday all day."

"Those are my prayer-meeting evenings."

"Mrs. Cruz, how often do you do your housecleaning?"

"Regularly," Lisa Cruz said, mocking Nina's earlier line of questioning, this time enjoying the reaction she got.

Nina laughed along with Judge Milne, dropped her smile, and repeated her question.

But as time went on, as Nina continued grinding at life's petty concerns until the small issues had been hammered to dust, the atmosphere of the courtroom changed. Lisa didn't care about the trivial details of her children's lives, however much she cared about their salvation. She got bored. Her answers became careless. Her composure slipped into irritation.

The judge listened to the boring, trivial questions, the fidgety answers, giving no clue about his thoughts. Riesner objected as often as he could, but Nina's questions, while mind-numbing, were relevant to Lisa's mothering skills, so Judge Milne continually ruled against him. Lisa looked to Riesner for help, squeezed her lips tightly, and exposed an utter lack of interest in or skill at house-keeping, a preference for her own needs over her children's needs when it came to school activities, a chronic inability to pick the chil-dren up on time after school, lack of knowledge about her children's current schoolwork, and adamant opposition to any organized sports for her son, Joey, who really, really wanted to play soccer.

After nearly an hour spent on trivia, petty concerns, and the most mundane, rude mechanics of life, including toilet-scrubbing, Lisa was visibly fuming. Her hair had unpoufed and her crisp suit jacket looked wilted. Five miles couldn't make her sweat, but Nina's long journey through life's ordinariness had worn her to a frazzle.

"I'm good in the ways that matter," Lisa said in answer to a ques-tion about Joey. "I care about helping my kids grow up right."

"Does that include punishment when they do wrong?"

"I discipline them, of course." Nina heard tightness in her voice.

"What methods of discipline do you use?"

"That depends on what they do. How bad they've been. Like, say they talk back or use bad language, well, I might explain that's not allowed, that we respect each other and I must be respected as a parent. Then I might send them to their rooms."

"You don't like them to use bad language?"

"No."

"You don't use bad language?"

"I don't condone it, no."

"You don't use it?"

She had to answer honestly or risk impeachment, although her reluctance was palpable. "Very rarely. It's a poor way to communicate."

"Do you spank your children?"

"No."

"You don't 'smack them on the butt'?" Nina asked, quoting from the deposition.

Lisa remembered what she had said. She answered carefully. "Rarely, and only if they intentionally disobeyed me in some major way. Crossed the street without me, or did something dangerous. But never hard, never to cause pain. Only to get their attention."

"Does your husband smack or spank the children?"

"He's pretty poor at discipline."

"Does he smack them?"

"No."

"Spank them?"

"No. In my opinion, he lets them get away with way too much. I have to go back and do the correcting he doesn't bother to do. I have to be the bad cop, while he's Mr. Fun."

"Do you yell at them?"

"I don't think you should yell at your kids."

"Do you yell at them?"

"I'm sure I have. I'm not going to lie. But I try to be patient and thoughtful."

"Does your husband yell at them?"

She thought about the question. "No, he doesn't, not at the kids. Like I said, he plays the nice guy and I get stuck with the trouble after."

"Can you really describe yourself as a patient person?"

Anyone with eyes could see the restless, jumpy woman in front of the courtroom this morning was anything but.

"I try to be."

"Would you describe yourself as a happy person on the whole?"

Lisa looked down at her hands, then back up. She refused to

meet Nina's eyes. "I don't see life that way. Life is a vale of tears. There are such sorrows—" She stopped herself, changing direction. "Happiness is not an end in itself. If you're lucky, it comes along now and then."

"Mrs. Cruz, you've stated in your deposition that you were very close to your father and took his loss hard. Do you think that has affected your parenting since his death last year?"

Lisa stared at her, and Nina saw what she had been looking for, pushing for, serious anger flickering behind the shadowy brown eyes. She did not like this question. "No."

"You were seeing a therapist?"

"Yes, but I've done that for several years. That's part of the growth process."

Nina consulted her notes. "After he died, you took to your bed for three weeks?"

Lisa struggled, then said in a voice fat with distaste, "Yes."

"Who watched your children during that time?"

"My mother. And Kevin."

"How long before you recovered from your father's death?"

"I'll never get over my father's death. That doesn't stop me from functioning. I may not be a barrel of laughs every day."

"In fact, yesterday on the stand the mediator in your divorce case described you as a 'restless, troubled person, who blames other people for her unhappiness.' Do you think that's accurate?"

"That's not me." She shook her head. "I've had plenty of joy in my life. Plenty. Just not lately."

"Your own doctor said you've had ongoing problems with depression."

"I've got that licked now," she said. "I'm off the meds. Joining my church has helped with that a lot."

"There was another time you took to your bed, wasn't there?"

"I don't like that way of putting it."

"Went into your bedroom and locked the door for several days, wouldn't talk to Kevin or the kids, ate very little and didn't feel able to cope?"

"I don't remem—"

"In Seattle? When you and the family lived there?"

"That was a long time ago. Kevin got in trouble at work. The kids were little, screaming all day. We lived in a small, noisy apartment. I didn't have a decent stroller that would hold both of them. No washing machine, kids to drag everywhere I went, every single thing I did an ordeal. So, yeah, I've had some hard times. I'm stronger for getting through them."

"Your husband stayed home to take care of you that time, didn't he?"

"A few times," she said grudgingly.

"He went to work late and left early?"

"I don't remember."

"And lost his job as a result?"

"He lost his job because he screwed up at work. My problems were caused by his problems, not the other way around!"

"Mrs. Cruz, what happens the next time a problem comes along that you can't solve? Who will be there for your children?"

"My mother helps me a lot. I'm not perfect. I need support, just like anybody. Anyway, right now, my life is going just fine, if I could only settle this thing with Kevin." Lisa's arms crossed into the classic defensive position, almost as if she were trying to rein in all the nervous tension she exuded.

Nina decided the time had come.

"Mrs. Cruz, you don't like to cook, you don't like to clean, you don't like chores, yet you admit children are messy; when things get tough you take to your bed; by your own admission, you haven't gotten over your father's death; you're moody, changeable, unpredictable in your discipline—"

Riesner stood up. "Objection!"

"Ms. Reilly, what's your question?" the judge said.

Nina's attention never veered away from Lisa Cruz. "—can you really, in good conscience, describe yourself as a good mother?" She held Lisa's gaze, made her want to open her mouth, made her want to answer, to tell her off, to stop Nina from nipping at her like a bedbug. The fire Lisa had been trying to hide burst into her dark eyes.

Riesner stood quickly. "Your Honor, I—"

But Lisa would not be gagged anymore. "Who do you think you are," she said, directly addressing Nina. "You—fucking—hypocrite. Are you home with your kid today? I hear you have one. Shame on you. I do my best to have a life and do well by my children. But your job is to distort truth to serve your purposes. If you were defending me, I'd be your golden example, wouldn't I? It's so sickening."

All the time she spoke, Riesner tried to speak louder to shut her up. He waved his hand as if to dissipate the aggression she was finally hurling at Nina.

"Mrs. Cruz! Control yourself," Judge Milne said finally, taking up his dusty gavel and pounding it once. He looked startled at the noise.

But Lisa ignored him. "Instead I come off here as a selfish bitch, a creature you invent out of some weird bullcrap about my housekeeping, for chrissake. None of that shit matters when it comes to kids, and you know it! They need someone with something more on the ball than a Gestapo-tidy house and three servings of beef a day, which is what Kevin seems to think is required. They need somebody who cares about their souls!" She slapped her hand down on the railing in front of her. "You dare to talk about my father. About my grief. I know all about you. I see right through you, right down into your rotten heart that doesn't care who gets hurt!"

She stopped, her mouth still open, breathing hard, as though she'd just come in from one of those big runs.

"Do you lose your temper like this with the children, Mrs. Cruz?" Nina said.

"Get off my back!"

"I'm going to adjourn this court for ten minutes," Judge Milne said as Lisa fell into her chair, shaking, pushing her hair back. "Mr. Riesner, get your client under control. You hear?" He stepped down. Chairs scraped and voices rose behind Nina. The bailiff, Deputy Kimura, had appeared at Lisa Cruz's side. He took her arm and helped her step down and walk past Nina's table and didn't let her slow down for a second. Riesner followed her out.

Kevin's eyes followed his wife. He turned back to Nina. "You did it," he said. He didn't smile.

"I'm sorry," Nina said. "It had to be done." And she was sorry, too. Lisa may have had a foul mouth and some weaknesses as a parent, but Nina sensed the depth of the love she felt for her children in every intense word. She was fighting for her life.

"She's going to have a rough night. You hit hard."

"Kevin," Nina said, "something's going on here. Why was she attacking me? Is this something about her father?"

2

DURING THE BREAK, Nina tried to get Kevin to talk, but he needed to make a nervous trip to the rest room. On her way to the ladies' room, she ran into Stamp, a senior partner in Riesner's firm. A tanned, fit, superb-athlete type, a man who would always be more comfortable with a tennis racket or golf club in his hand than a brief-case, he did not brush past her in his usual fashion. "Hey," he said, coming to a dead halt. "Nina Reilly. It's been a while. Haven't seen you since that casino-gambling case." He pushed a hand into hers for a firm handshake.

"Well, hello!" The artificial enthusiasm she rallied was designed to obscure the fact that she wasn't entirely certain of his first name and wasn't about to call him Mr. Stamp. Wasn't his name Michael?

"Yeah, you banged us up good in that one. Rumor is, Steve Rossmoor was impressed, so impressed he approached you to repre-sent his casino. Rumor is, others might follow."

"You know better than to listen to rumors."

He liked her answer, but wasn't ready to let go yet. "You'd have to pass the Nevada bar," he said thoughtfully. "But I venture to guess you're too busy for that, trying to keep a solo practice afloat."

"That's so true," she said. So Stamp was worried she wanted the casino business. That would cut him where it hurt, right in the wal-let. Might as well put him out of his misery. "California's big enough for me at the moment."

He had his hands in his pockets, and seemed ready to settle in for a nice chat.

"Listen, I'm sorry," Nina said. "I've got to run."

"Sure. Good to see you. Give me a call sometime when you're not so rushed." She felt his eyes crawling over her back as she continued down the stairs. In the bathroom, she looked in the mirror for any signs of femme-fatality and found none. So, take the man at face value. He was worried she was after the casino business. She wasn't. Now he knew, which was the purpose of their conversation. She decided to like him for having the character to compliment her for winning against his firm, and for flattering her by worrying about rumors that reflected well on her. Riesner certainly never would.

After the break, Riesner took a crack at rehabilitating Lisa Cruz, who apologized to Judge Milne for her outburst and regained her poise, but the damage was done. He was brief, then returned to his table. Riesner, who did not like watching his nicely crafted case sink to the bottom of the ocean, stared down at the table in front of him. This time, when he finally looked toward Nina, fury glistened in his eyes like oil slick.

Nina had really worried about Kevin, who had temper problems of his own. But Lisa's example had taught him something. When he finally took the stand, he made an excellent witness. Nina had hoped he would have the advantage of plenty of experience testifying because of his work as a police officer, and it seemed he did. He looked relaxed and low-key up there, a nice guy, his legs splayed comfortably, his big body relaxed. Handsome, clean-shaven, with fuzz for hair and even white teeth that he used to good advantage, he spoke warmly about his children, his job, what fatherhood meant to him.

He told Judge Milne that he loved his children. His changing schedule wouldn't create problems because he had a good support system of local family and friends. He loved to cook, was a methodical person who was trying to teach his kids organizational skills. He had coached his son's soccer team until Lisa made Joey quit, saying he did not have enough time to finish homework.

"Did you agree with your wife?" Nina asked.

"Sure sounded like he had a lot of work, and she really talked it up. On the nights he was with me, I didn't see so much, but she told me it was much worse the nights he was with her. Made me wonder what the world is coming to, when a seven-year-old has too much homework to play sports."

He netted several sympathetic looks at that.

"I wanted to talk to Joey's teacher, but Lisa asked me not to."

"Why?"

"She admitted the homework wasn't as bad as she made out. She doesn't really like Joey playing soccer anyway, or any sport. She's afraid he'll get hurt, and doesn't want the extra driving. I offered to do more of the chauffeuring, but she didn't want that either."

Although he was not a churchgoer himself, he wanted the children to go to Sunday school at his church instead of Lisa's. "They ought to know what's right and wrong, and the Bible's a great resource and comfort to some people. What I don't like is too much talk of hell and damnation. That just scares kids, does them no good."

He knew every subject his children were taking in school, knew their teachers well, and could quote from their report cards. He showed pride, pleasure, and a caring attitude.

When Nina finished with Kevin, Riesner got up and brushed off his lapels, as if he'd already started the dirty work.

"You're a police officer, aren't you, Mr. Cruz?"

"Yes."

"A risky job."

"It can be, but I'm well trained in my work, Mr. Riesner. I work hard at defusing potentially dangerous situations before they get serious."

"Uh huh. Yet this is your third position as a police officer, isn't it?"

"Yes."

"Why did you leave those other two positions?"

"The first one up in Seattle—I was fired. I was young, we had two little kids, I felt pushed and pulled in a lot of directions. There were family demands, and my family came first."

"And then there was that little trouble about an old man who ended up in the hospital after you beat him and left him in the gutter?"

Kevin looked at him calmly. "You make it sound like I put him in the hospital. I didn't. I also didn't beat him. And I left him propped against a building in a seated position, to set the record straight."

"You were accused of using excessive force while attempting to arrest a known, chronic alcoholic who was seventy-two years old."

"He was belligerent. I used the force I needed to use to stop him from attacking me. Then I left without arresting him because I felt sorry for him. He ended up in the hospital because he was drunk and fell down after I left him."

"You were fired for that?"

"Mr. Riesner, I did nothing wrong. An internal investigation exonerated me but the damage was done to my reputation. Every time I came in late, it was noted. I was held to higher standards than the other officers, and because of the demands I had on me, with two young children and a wife that was having some emotional problems at the time, I couldn't keep up. It was decided that I should go."

Very respectable, the way he didn't blame Lisa for his problems. Nina liked that, and she thought Judge Milne would, too.

"Records show that the internal investigation did not exonerate you. They merely did not find enough evidence to prove the charge," Riesner went on.

"That's right," Kevin said. "It was never proven because there was nothing to prove."

"So you went to work in Marin County."

"Right."

"It says here"—Riesner waved a paper—"you signed on for a permanent job but only lasted six months."

"We discovered pretty quick we could never afford to live

decently there. Lisa would have to go to work and Joey was still very young to leave during the day then. I was offered a good job here, so we moved up to Tahoe."

"You quit without notice, didn't you?"

"I had to think of my family first. Tahoe wanted me right away."

"Not very responsible, was it, leaving your old job without notice?"

"I explained that," Kevin said.

"It must have been hard on your family, moving around all the time?"

"We didn't move all the time."

"Three times in the past five years?"

"The kids were too little to care much, although it was stressful at times, yes."

"You don't stay in one place long, do you?"

"I was looking for the right place. I've found it now."

"You know that after less than a year?"

"That's right."

"You think this one's going to stick when the others haven't?"

"I've been promoted once already. I think I'm doing well."

"Not all that well, actually. I understand you failed the detective exam when you took it this summer?"

"I put a lot of time in with my kids. I guess I just haven't put my energy there."

"Are you going to take it again?"

"I'm planning on it."

"You'll have to study nights for it?"

"I'll make sure Heather and Joey come first."

"Of course, if you happen to pass it this time, that will mean you spend even more hours on the job, is that correct?"

"Probably, but now the kids are in school, that should work okay and the extra money will come in handy."

"Or you'll flunk it again and move on to some new town?"

"No. I'm settling here."

"Now, you say that money would come in handy, Mr. Cruz?"

"Yes."

"Do you resent the child support you've had to pay pending this hearing while the children were with their mother?"

"No."

"You've paid late three months out of nine months. Is that what you call being financially responsible?"

"There was some kind of foul-up. It's corrected."

"The kids didn't get the money they needed, and it's just a foul-up to you?"

Kevin's face hardened. "I love my kids."

"You'd rather spend the money on, let's see, new bowling shoes the first month you were late, and, oh, in August there was that trip to Vegas."

"It was one weekend. The child support was only ten days late."

"So what comes first?" Riesner said, taking a long step toward the witness box and sticking his chin out.

"I'm not sure what you mean."

"You know, bowling shoes and Vegas seem to come first. The kids can wait."

Kevin put his hand up to his mouth. "I—"

"Move to strike that last malicious comment by counsel," Nina said.

"I'll withdraw it, Judge. How's your temper, Mr. Cruz?"

"Well, I think I'm holding on to it pretty good, considering how you're talking to me right now."

That got a relieved laugh from the audience, and Nina thought, he's going to get through it.

"Tell us more about your schedule, Mr. Cruz. How do you intend to put in the time it takes to raise your children when you're never home?"

Kevin kept his cool, got a few more chuckles, even one from Judge Milne, kept smiling, and looked confident.

Nina was satisfied. Aside from the vague and unproven trouble on his first job, which did not reflect badly on his abilities as a parent, and the late child support, Kevin had the edge. He was never violent with his kids. He wouldn't even spank them. Even Lisa had admitted that.

At lunchtime, Judge Milne adjourned the hearing until the next day. Kevin made a mumbled excuse and ran out ahead of Nina before she could speak with him.

Feeling like she'd had all her teeth yanked out of her jaw, the usual feeling that the court clerks, the other attorneys, and the witnesses milling around her in the hall probably shared as they made their way toward the exit at noon, Nina hurried out. As she left the courtroom in the crowd, Jeffrey Riesner sidled up behind her, brazenly close, brushing against her, walking in step, mimicking her short, swift stride for a few moments. She forced herself to ignore him. Thinking back to the case, hustling away, she refused to dirty her mind with rank images of what lurked underneath the gray silk slacks he had pressed so noxiously close.

In the hallway, where the other courtrooms were adjourning for the break, she felt a hard push to her shoulder and whirled around, prepared to confront him. But instead of Jeffrey Riesner, Officer Jean Scholl now stood behind her, uniformed, a skyscraper to Nina's low bungalow, six feet tall if she was an inch. "Ms. Reilly," Scholl said, her voice a slow drawl. "So sorry to jostle you like that, but you got right in my way."

"I don't believe I did," Nina said firmly, standing her ground. "Look, if you have something you have to say, why not just spit it out?"

"Okay," Scholl said, a hand on her hip. By now several other police officers had paused to watch. "Stay out of my face. I don't appreciate the way you handled the Guitierrez case. You made me look bad, when I was just doing the best job I can. I like to think we both serve justice, but when it comes to someone like you, I wonder. Now, you and I both know he stole that T-Bird and wrecked it."

"The judge saw it differently," Nina said. "Obviously, since he let the man off."

Scholl leaned in until Nina could feel the heat of her breath. "We didn't read him his rights because the rotgut he was drinking left him comatose. He wouldn't have understood them anyway."

"He has the right to a defense. He got it."

"Technicalities be damned," Scholl said. "Did you ever think about the kid who spent six years restoring that car? He came into our offices crying. But you don't give a damn about that, do you? You don't think about all the harm you cause, setting bad guys loose."

"Are you done?" Nina asked.

Stepping back slightly, Scholl nodded. "Look forward to seeing you in court again real soon, Counselor."

Nina fled for the outdoors.

Caught in a rush of wind, her friend Betty, a deputy clerk, sighed, "A big one coming up." The trees around them rattled and Nina watched clouds massing over the Sierra Nevada to the east. Betty ran for her car. Clutching her blue blazer around her, Nina ran for Paul's new Mustang, parked in a no-parking zone right out front.

"Let's blow, otherwise you'll get a ticket for sure," she told Paul as she climbed into the passenger's seat. "There were at least ten police officers in the hall with me. Some big drug case. Jean Scholl was in there. She's a real old-timer in the department, been there eight years at least and also has a lot of support in the sheriff's department. She blew up at me in front of everybody. She'd love to lay a ticket on us."

Paul backed out.

"I don't know why, but lately it seems like she's involved in every case I defend. I think she's taking it personally." Nina consulted her watch. "I'm exactly four hours into my day. I had to take a witness apart and it was damned unpleasant. Jeff Riesner was opposing counsel. I had to sit passively through his nasty cross of my client. Then Officer Scholl gave me a push and a warning. A morning like this makes me wonder why I do it."

"Hello to you, too, Beautiful," Paul said.

She exhaled the breath she had been holding and all the poisons of the courtroom went with it. She smiled, shook her head, said, "Sorry."

The man deserved her full attention. Ah, how she adored him. Tall and blond and hers at the moment, Paul van Wagoner worked for her as an investigator now and then. She had spent the past several weeks at his home in Carmel playing house, making love, and jumping ocean waves with him. Now they were back to their real lives, his in Carmel and hers in Tahoe, and, although the geographical separations hurt, Nina felt more tightly bound to him every day.

Using his left hand, he pulled out of the lot. His right arm circled her, pulling her close to him.

Taking in the fresh smell of his leather jacket, she kissed his cheek, letting the physical tensions of the morning slip away in his comforting presence. "The farther we get from the courthouse, the better."

"Good. Let's go all the way out to the Y and eat at Passaretti's. You have time?"

"Kevin Cruz's hearing was adjourned for the day. We start up again tomorrow."

"Trouble?"

"Besides what you'd expect in a full-scale custody battle?" She paused, reviewing the morning, which chugged through her mind in a blur of questions, answers, and lightning judgments. "Riesner's odd lately."

"What do you mean?"

She shrugged. "I really don't know. Just more at me than ever."

"Family-law cases are the worst," Paul said. "Give me a good old corporate dispute, partners gouging out eyes, stabbing each other in the back, but, hey, it's just business. Next week they'll be toasting the next great joint venture." He turned left onto Lake Tahoe Boulevard.

"Anyway, it's over until tomorrow and I'm going to put it out of my mind. And concentrate on you."

"I like that," Paul said. He ran a finger down her cheek. "Love me right and I'll love you right back."

She kissed him again. "It's so great when you're here. I wish you could stay forever."

"Come live with me in Carmel. You know that's what I want."

He popped that out as casually as popping a beer. It was the on-going struggle between them. How could they possibly create something strong and permanent living 250 miles apart?

"I know."

"Luck was with me this morning," Paul said. "I got the two witness declarations you wanted signed. Wish you had been able to drive Highway 89 with me up to Tahoe City. Whitecaps starting up, the sky that sensational transparent blue that you only see when it's swept clean and a storm's blowing in. Fall announcing its imminent arrival. The file's in the backseat."

Nina disentangled herself and twisted back, retrieved the file, and set it on the floor in front of her. Otherwise she'd never remember it. Curling herself against Paul again, she said, "I hate it that you have to leave."

"Job's over," Paul said. "I've got an office in Carmel crying for my attention. You could always come down again this weekend."

This reminder that he led a life complete and separate from her gave her a pang. The nights without him were hard. She missed the rise and fall of his chest, the rhythm of his breath. "You know I want to, but I've got an office in Tahoe crying for my attention too, and Bob needs new shoes and the house is a wreck." They drove along the lake under a lowering sky. Wind flattened the water way out and threw up ruffled whitewater closer in. One last sailboat tacked into the Keys harbor, the sail taut and the two people inside pulling hard at the ropes, their yellow life jackets bright in the half-light.

"We better get you on the road fast," Nina said. "You should just drop me at the office."

"No way will I miss lunch with you. It's too early in the year for snow. What's a little rain?"

"You've seen the mountain rainstorms," Nina added. But she didn't really want him to leave so she didn't ask again. While they ate at Passaretti's, the light rain turned into a downpour. By the time Paul kissed her good-bye in the parking lot of the Starlake Building, the skies were delivering a four-star one-for-the-books drenchfest.

Inside, she barely had time to fold up her umbrella and prop it in the corner of her office before the afternoon steamrolled her. Her assistant, Sandy Whitefeather, was in and out on errands, leaving Nina mostly on her own to answer the phone and handle emergencies. Two old personal-injury clients soaked up time without resolving anything. An interpreter slowed down a complicated phone call to the Vangs about a settlement offer in their insurance case.

Then, to cap off an already crowded afternoon, sisters named Brandy and Angel told her a harrowing story about witnessing something on a camping trip that had ended with a suspicious death the next site over.

She took notes, thought fast, kept her eyes on the tasks at hand, tried to keep track of everything. Between the phones and the thirteen other cases that needed attention in the interstices of the main appointments, she drank her bottled water and hung in there. She let the rough morning go and decided she had had a good day because Paul was in it.

Outside, dark came early and water flowed down the street. The lights flickered once or twice. Inside, Nina kept right on trying to fix people's problems and bring order back into the chaos that afflicted them. She thought once or twice about the Cruz custody case. Paul was right. Custody disputes between two more or less competent parents who both loved their kids were the most painful cases for the lawyer as well as the parents, because no just solution existed. You couldn't saw the kids in half. They had to spend most of their time somewhere.

She felt bad for Lisa Cruz, for what she had done to her.

•   •   •

When the last client had left and she was finally alone, she washed most of the hardened crud off the coffeepot, turned out the lights, packed her briefcase, and slung her purse onto her shoulder. Umbrella in hand, she headed down the hall not feeling anything at all except the desire to get home. She made it only a few steps at a normal pace from the office door before immense raindrops, ballooned into drunken saturation, reduced her hair to string and her boots to sodden. A gust of wind turned her umbrella inside out.

Abandoning all dignity, she ran for protection. She threw open the Bronco's door with such force that it seemed for a second it might break off. Safely inside, she tossed her briefcase and broken umbrella to the floor of the backseat and waited. The sky could only dump so much water. For a few minutes, she watched heavy branches ripping and scattering like twigs in the force of the storm. Freshets of water cascaded down Highway 50. Cars pulled over to the side, wipers going like mad, as the street became a brook, a river, a lake.

She let the drumming on the roof occupy her consciousness. Bob had probably made it home from school by now, and Sandy should be safe at home. Paul would be over Echo Summit and down in the Sacramento Valley by now. The briefcase on the backseat floor held her most pressing client files, the ones she would take to bed with her to read and consider.

Sharp pellets struck the roof. Hail. People on the streets scurried for cover like mice escaping a marauding cat. "Just ducky," she muttered as the streetlights blinked out all at once. Across the street, the neon flicked off on the Mexican restaurant's sign.

The whole town went dark, and this time the lights didn't come back.

A mountain town without power isn't a town at all, but an animal hideout under the trees, like a deer nest or bear cave. They saw it all the time up here, the facade of civilization casually torn away by snow, wind, storms, not to mention the raw human emotions uncovered after losing everything at the all-too-civilized casinos on the

Nevada side of town. Scylla and Charybdis, and humanity reduced to headlights in the din.

Now what? She gave it another minute, pulling for civilization, but nature had the town firmly in hand. No lights, rain lashing the windshield. She fumbled for her car keys, which were supposed to be clipped with a metal carabiner to her purse strap, but they weren't there. She must have dropped them somewhere. She clicked on the overhead lights, which ran on the battery, and looked through her keys on the ring. House key and office key, check, mystery key, check, Bob's spare bike-lock key, yep, but no car key.

She hadn't seen the doggone key since she'd parked at the office at eight that morning. Sandy had dropped her off at the courthouse and Paul had picked her up.

She should go back into the building and look for the key, a very daunting thought right now, but she was already half out the door again when she remembered that she had an old plastic key in her wallet, which the auto association had sent her for use in an emergency.

The fan on the heater at home wouldn't work without electricity. Bob would be making a fire and enjoying the process entirely too much. She should hurry before he burned the cabin down.

She would find the key tomorrow. Tonight she couldn't go back in there. She fished out the plastic key and turned it in the ignition, hoping the flimsy white plastic wouldn't break.

The Bronco started up with a mighty roar.

She crept down Pioneer Trail in four-wheel drive, sending up fin-shaped, watery plumes and jouncing over the forest trash. A few stalled cars surprised her in the middle of the road, one with the driver's-side door hanging wide open, its driver too concerned about getting home to care about water damage.

A branch from the sugar pine next to the porch sprawled across her downsloping driveway. She crunched over it, ran up the steps to the wooden porch, and unlocked the front door, noticing a pair of mountain bikes pushed together under the eaves. Two bikes, not one.

In the entryway, stripping off her boots and socks, she could see just a corner of the orange Swedish fireplace, and all she could think about was dinner.

A muffled commotion in the living room and scrabbling paws over the wood floors gave her warning of Hitchcock just before the big black dog rushed her. "You're supposed to hear me before I come in the house, you silly animal." She kissed the dog's head and pulled gently on his ears. "Bob!"

In the living room, the floor-to-ceiling window overlooking the backyard was inky—no one had pulled the curtains—and the wood stove was cold. She groped for the lights, and when that didn't work, she reached above the refrigerator for matches and lit the big candle on the coffee table.

"Right here," Bob said from the couch a few feet away. In the flickering light, another tangle of jeans and hair emerged next to him. Nina recognized Nikki, Bob's bandmate, three years older and three centuries wiser, she of the sly brown eyes. Nina knew Nikki well, well enough to distrust her. An ex-client, sixteen years old, she had the anarchy-of-spirit thing down pat. Nina did not like her sitting there on the couch, feigning innocence, or the skinny hand clasping Bob's.

"Hi," Nikki said, then, as if cued, disengaged her hand from Bob's. She picked up a can of cola and drank deeply. Bob watched her drink.

To cover a spasm of alarm, Nina turned her back on them, went to the fridge, and uncorked the half bottle of Clos du Bois, forcing herself to pour a glass instead of taking the swig she so fervently desired at that moment.

"We were trying to do homework, but the lights went out," Bob said.

"I see," Nina said. She took two sips and two deep breaths, walked back into the living room, and drew the curtains shut. While Bob and Nikki sat primly on the couch, she crumpled newspapers, tossed them on the grate, and dug out some kindling from the basket.

"I'll do that, Mom," Bob offered. He got up.

"Good idea. Nikki, there are more candles in the kitchen above the dryer. Would you mind getting a few? It's still too dark to see." And unwelcoming, to say the least, she thought.

"Cold, too," said Bob, who had apparently not previously noticed. He took the poker from Nina, jabbing the burning sticks in the wood stove. Nina sat down on the carpet, held her glass, and waited for the fire to flare up and send warmth her way. The sleeves of her blouse were wet, her very soul was wet, but she was damned if she was going to go into her bedroom to change and leave these two alone.

Nikki's bony knee came and went through a gaping hole in her jeans as she set candles around the room. The forlorn face and familiar defiant, ready-for-rejection expression inspired Nina's pity, exasperation, and righteous motherly fear.

"We were just going to practice a new song I wrote," Nikki said. "I brought my guitar. It was all very structured. But you can't play without electricity."

"Uh huh," said Nina.

"Well. I'm outta here," Nikki said, heading for the door, reading Nina's mind. "Have a good night."

"It's pouring out there. Does your mother—?" Nina started.

"I left a note, but she's not home anyway." Nikki found her parka on the floor. With the hood pulled tight around her face, she looked like an orphan boy.

Bob said, "I'll ride you home." He got up.

"Not necessary," Nikki said.

"Back in half an hour," Bob told Nina.

"I can take care of myself," Nikki said.

"Don't be stupid. When are you gonna get a good offer like that again?"

"Then I'm stupid."

"Wait. I'll drive you," Nina said.

"No. It's not that far. Stay here and enjoy your supper."

Nina almost invited Nikki to supper right then, she looked so much like a starving hound dog who hasn't eaten for a week, but there were limits. She wanted Nikki to go home, Nikki was heading out the door, and Nina wasn't going to stop her.

"Later," Nikki said, strapping her guitar on her back. She flipped a hand at Bob and went out the door.

Bob went to the window and looked out. "We should have made her stay," he said.

"Haven't you got homework? You're not supposed to—to—"

"To what?"

"Never mind. Do me a favor, honey. Just let me sit here for a second and drink my glass of wine in peace."

Bob shrugged, went into the kitchen, and came out with a turkey sandwich and a Gatorade. "Supper is served," he said, then went into his room and shut the door, not too loudly.

On an ordinary night, at this point in the course of events, she would cook, then tackle the files she had brought home, but the fire continued to burn, Bob had his sandwich, and the rocking-chair pillow lured her with its softness. She sat down to stare into the orange and red, listening to the whine and howl of wind outside. The briefcase was in her car. She was in no mood to stuff her warm feet into stone-cold boots and throw a coat on so that she could fight her way back through the damp, freezing night. She could allow herself to spend an hour this Thursday evening dozing here, stroking her dog.

She yawned and flashed to a memory of Bob as a toddler. They were still living on the Monterey Peninsula, where she worked as a law clerk during the day and studied law at night. His preschool teacher called her in the middle of a meeting. "Bobby won't lie down for naps," she said. "We've tried everything, Ms. Reilly, but I'm afraid you'll have to come and get him and take him home. He's a disruptive influence on the other children."

She hadn't known what to do with him then, and she didn't know what to do with him now. But for now he was safe and warm, and she didn't have to worry.

She woke from a doze and checked her watch. Already nine o'clock! Down the hall, holding a candle like a Victorian to light her way, she opened the door and saw Bob retired safely under his covers, flashlight glowing, his French textbook open beside him.

Hungry, she made herself a grilled-cheese sandwich and poured herself another glass of wine, telling herself that up to twelve ounces actually helps your heart. Scanning the newspaper by the last of the firelight, she yawned again and pushed it into the brown recycling bag in the kitchen. A hundred small tasks in that room drew some spotty attention. She wiped, closed cupboards, listed groceries needed. It was late and too dark to work, but she still should go get her papers out of the truck.

The kitchen lights crackled and died again. She hunted in the cabinets for the big flashlight for a long time, even exploring the dreaded laundry area. Giving up, she felt her way upstairs and down the hallway. Once in her own room, she tossed her clothes on the floor and climbed into bed, pulling the comforter up to her neck. Her files would be safe enough in the Bronco until morning.

But they weren't.

Routines. The first slap of cold water on the face, the scalding-hot shower. The lick and promise of lotion over rough spots on her feet; the peppermint of toothpaste. Bob rummaging for cereal, the clink of his spoon as he ate. The radio flipping from pop to talk and back again.

Friday morning rushed along, the storm over, the world outside steaming and sparkling, Bob late, Hitchcock barking for a walk before she had shaken off her nighttime coma and having to settle for a trip into the backyard, eggs needing to be cooked. The power had been restored and a multichrome rainbow of sunlight drenched the kitchen.

She loved the part where she walked out the door in the morning, loved the blowing leaves, the smell of wood smoke, and heart-piercing mountains all around. Another day awaited, full of large frustrations and small triumphs and more fresh coffee, if she was lucky. Her office was her second home, and Sandy and Sandy's son, Wish, were her second family. Her heart felt full; she felt sharp and cool; her son was ready for school; she had a full day ahead.

But that morning when she went out to the driveway all dressed up in navy blue for morning court she stopped cold in her tracks. Two long seconds of unreality struck before she could collect herself and make sense out of what greeted her.

An empty driveway.

Her car wasn't there.

Stupidly, she walked up the driveway to the street and looked left and right as if it had somehow moved itself in the night. Had it rolled into the backyard? No, she had let the dog into the yard earlier. No Bronco there. She tried to think. Yes, she had definitely driven it home last night, she remembered clearly.

Nikki? Her mountain bike was gone. Anyway, although she bemoaned the fact, Nikki didn't have a license to drive last time Nina heard. Neither did Bob.

The key! The white plastic key still sat in her wallet. But—

A lost vehicle isn't like a lost dog. You can't run around the neighborhood calling for it. Some jerk had stolen her truck right out of her own driveway. Nina went back inside and got Bob, who came out to stare in disbelief at the spot where the Bronco usually sat. Then she called the South Lake Tahoe Police Department and her office. Then she remembered the files.

Her heart fell to her shoes. She had definitely locked the truck, she remembered what a hassle it was with that stupid plastic key. . . .

She counted the files in her mind. Three: the Cruz custody battle, the Vangs and their insurance claim, and—oh no, the new one, the campground-murder case, with the sisters, Brandy and Angel.

Confidential files. Her most sensitive cases, the ones with information no one should see, stuffed inside her briefcase on the floor of the backseat of the Bronco.

Out there somewhere, in someone's sweaty, thieving paws.

3

WAITING ON THE DRIVEWAY for the police, Nina walked up and down rubbing her neck, and when that didn't take the rigidity out of it, she rotated it a few times. She had made the mistake that everybody makes once in ten thousand events. Nine thousand nine hundred ninety-nine correct decisions, one mistake, and with any luck at all, you don't get called on the mistake. You leave something important in the car, smack your forehead in the morning when you realize it, run outside, and find all is well.

Across the street, her neighbor climbed up a steep ladder to his roof and fiddled with green shingles.

He could fall, she thought. He could die. Every day presented new opportunities for catastrophe.

She decided not to wave at him.

A mud-spattered patrol car pulled up in front. Gleaming pines and firs dripped all around, but the asphalt steamed in the morning sun, rapidly drying. Bob, ready to take the bus, ran up behind her begging for money, lunchless because she had been hunting for the extra copy of the Bronco registration and the title. She shoved several crumpled dollars she had in a pocket toward him, leaning out for a kiss on the cheek as he passed.

"Good luck, Mom," he said, running down the street to the stop where his school bus was already loading.

Two officers, a man and a woman looking like carpenters with all the tools hanging from their belts, hauled themselves out of the car, leaving the police radio on loud to make sure all the neighbors would know there was trouble at the Reilly house. "Counselor. How you doing," said the tall woman.

"Officer Scholl. Thanks for coming." Great, Nina thought. Of course they would send Jean Scholl. She didn't feel thankful, she felt annoyed at her rotten luck, but she had no choice but to accept the help on offer.

Scholl stared at her for a minute, tightened her lips, then looked away. She didn't offer to shake and neither did Nina. Her gray eyes raked the empty driveway, looking for traces, suddenly all business.

"Good morning," Dave Matthias said, introducing himself. Newer in the department, he was narrow-jawed and short on hair.

A major drawback of doing criminal-defense work in a small town was that sometimes Nina had to try to discredit the work and the motives of local cops for the sake of her clients. Some cops lied and some were biased. Whatever the negative attitude, they didn't appreciate being called on it in court. Scholl's outburst on Thursday showed that. The best Nina hoped for from these two would be wary reserve, so she was pleasantly surprised when they listened intently and worked the information like pros. To her relief, Scholl had apparently decided to put their differences aside for the time being and do her job.

Nina spent an hour with them, retracing her trip home the night before, where exactly she had parked, handing over copies of the truck papers, which she had made on the home fax copier. They all went down to the driveway and looked for bits of glass, footprints in the still-damp pine needles in the cracks in the asphalt, anything. The driveway had no conspicuous clues to yield.

"You're sure you lost your car key sometime during the day yesterday," Officer Scholl said at least five times.

Nina had spent the past few minutes reliving the night's activities in excruciating detail. Her car key was gone. That was a fact. "I can't find it in my purse or the pockets of the clothes I was wearing."

"But you don't think the key could have fallen between the seats. Or something."

"I don't know. What I'm saying is that I locked the doors of the Bronco last night with my spare key. So nobody just came up and was searching through an unlocked car and just happened to find my key. Either they broke in and hot-wired the Bronco or they somehow have my lost key."

"No one could have used your spare key. The plastic one." The monotonic, carefully nonjudgmental voice made Nina feel worse.

"It was in my wallet in the living room. I always lock the house up tight and turn on the alarm. It was right there. This morning I found it in the wallet where I left it."

Officer Matthias gave the gate an experimental kick, as though this might make it give up a hint.

Nina went on, "It was the storm. It's a quiet neighborhood. I meant to go back out right away but I got distracted." Thank God, the house and office keys hadn't been on the same keychain. Nina closed her eyes for a moment, recalling a recent conversation with Paul in the Long's Drug Store parking lot as they had watched a man get out of his car and go into the store, leaving his motor running. "If someone drives off in that car," Paul said, "he's doing that ass a favor. They oughtta arrest him as an accessory, teach him a lesson."

The officers wrote down what Nina told them about the three files. "Legal files," she said.

"Client files?" Scholl asked, scribbling on a notepad.

She bit her lip. "Yes."

"Names on the files?"

"Yes. The files were labeled."

"I get that. But what were the names?"

"I can't tell you that."

"You won't give us the labels on the files? How are we supposed to identify them if they're found in a trash can behind some house in Meyers?"

"Call me and I'll come down and look at any legal-sized manila folders you find."

"And what if one of the people in your files decided he wanted them back? How are we going to question him if we don't even know his name?" Scholl asked, putting her pad down for the moment, letting only a glint of irritation enter her eyes.

"I can't help you there."

"Kind of a drawback to our investigation."

"Yes. It is."

"What's in the files?"

"Pleadings." Those she could reproduce, with copies from the clerk's office. Those were public documents. The Decree of Dissolution with the attached Marital Settlement Agreement in Kevin Cruz's case, for instance. "And business correspondence," mostly boring. Innocuous or technical lawyer letters from the other side. Transmittal memos to the court.

"And?" asked Matthias. Both officers now stood side by side waiting to hear the rest. They already knew, but they wanted her to say it.

"Confidential material."

Officer Scholl wrote. "That would include what?"

"My attorney work-product, including my legal research notes, my notes of consultations with experts. Confidential."

"Uh huh. Like what?"

"Like my client-intake notes. I can't give details. Most of it is protected by the attorney-client privilege."

"Written documents?"

"Right," Nina said, picturing the client-intake forms in her mind. Addresses for people who did not want to be found. Figures for a hefty insurance settlement that would make some people sit up and take greedy notice if they knew about it. Kevin's secret.

The ramifications rushed at her like a Roman phalanx. Kevin Cruz was a local cop. He would hear about the auto theft and the files and would want to know if his could be involved. He would be concerned.

The custody hearing continued at eleven-thirty this morning.

How could she manage this catastrophe? She had to get into the office, talk to Sandy.

"Because what I'm wondering..." said Officer Scholl, digging around in a pocket and putting on expensive-looking mirrored sunglasses against the glare of sun. She faced Nina directly: "Is the auto theft ancillary? You know? Did this thief want your files?"

"How could anyone know I'd be taking them home last night? I don't often do that," Nina said.

"You don't take files home?"

"Well, yes. But these particular files—"

"Could someone have seen you leave and followed you home?"

"I didn't notice anyone, but I wasn't looking either."

"This young lady, Nicole Zack. She left after you had arrived."

"I'm sure she had nothing to do with it."

"Maybe. But it's raining, it's dark, she's supposed to be biking home. Maybe she opens the Bronco door—"

"It was locked. I locked it."

"Maybe. But maybe she sees a key on the seat. You dropped it there. Maybe she decides to borrow the Bronco just to get herself home."

"She'd have to break in, because as I keep telling you, the Bronco was locked with my spare key."

"You were tired. Maybe you just thought you locked it," Officer Matthias put in.

"Talk to her if you want," Nina said. "But it wasn't her. I locked the doors. I didn't hear anything."

"Well, but, you know? Nikki Zack, right here last night, walking along this very driveway on a noisy, stormy night. We know her. You defended her once."

"I know what you're thinking, but she was acquitted. She was proven to be innocent of that crime."

Scholl sighed. Here police butted heads with defense attorneys daily. "Maybe she was proven innocent of *that* crime," she said. "But, speaking generally, involvement with the law, meaning us, gets to be a bad habit. Like cigarettes." She smiled in an overly friendly fashion. "People get hooked before they know it. They can't quit." Below his own sunglasses, Matthias's pale mouth wiggled in response to her joke.

"That may be the opinion around the good old police department," Nina said, knowing better but unwilling to conceal her disdain, "but she's a friend of my son's, and I trust her." She didn't, but they didn't have to know that.

"She know any of the people whose files got stolen? Any people who might be mentioned in the files?"

Nina thought about her cases. "No. Look. This is simple auto theft. I believe that, but it's an emergency for me because of the briefcase. The files. This is urgent, Officer."

Scholl snapped her notebook shut. "We'll give it the same urgent attention we'd give any theft of property." She delivered the news in that same controlled officious monotone that made Nina think paranoiacally of all sorts of things: whether she was more unpopular than she knew with law enforcement, whether they might actually put the theft on the back burner to cause her further discomfiture, whether Scholl was laughing at her problems behind those unfashionable glasses, for starters.

"I have to get to my office," Nina said. "I have to call a taxi. I—"

"Call me if you find your files at your office," Scholl said, handing Nina her card.

"I won't. They were in the truck."

"Check anyway." Officer Scholl asked for Nikki's address and phone number and Nina gave the information. As soon as the two officers pulled out, Nina got on the phone to the taxi company. Another half hour passed before she arrived at the Starlake Building and rushed down the hall to her office, feeling naked without her briefcase, stripped, vulnerable, mad, and frightened all at once.

"Three questions," said Sandy as Nina came into the office.

"These points and authorities on the summary-judgment motion..."

"I have one for you," Nina said, tossing her things into her office
and turning back to face her secretary. "Did I by any chance leave a
pile of files on your desk last night?"

"You always leave a pile." Sandy pointed to a stack of paperwork
Nina had left. Sandy Whitefeather, a member of the local Native
American Washoe tribe, had been working with Nina ever since
Nina had left her marriage and job in San Francisco and moved to
South Lake Tahoe several years before.

"Not those." But she rummaged through the papers on Sandy's
desk anyway.

"Whoa, Nellie," Sandy said, putting a smooth brown hand with
short nails and a heavy silver wristband down on the stack of files
just in front of her. "You lost some files?"

"I lost the Bronco."

"What?"

"I lost the entire Bronco, and my briefcase happened to be in
it." Sandy's eyebrow rose perceptibly as she tapped her fingertip
against the tip of her nose, listening while Nina told her in a few
words what had happened. "I know, I know," Nina said. "I never
should have left them sitting there on the floor of the backseat. That
was foolish. I can't believe my rotten luck. The Cruz case. That's up
in the air, and there's something strange going on with Lisa Cruz,
who went nuts on the stand yesterday. The third day of Kevin's
temporary-custody hearing is in two hours. He wants those kids
and she gives him a hard time about letting them visit."

"He's been waiting a long time. He's not gonna let you put it
over."

"No, he won't. He shouldn't have to." Interject a massive guilt
attack into the hellish clash of emotions she was feeling. "But Kevin
told me something in strictest confidence. It's on the client-intake
form, information that could ruin his chances to get joint custody of
his kids if—if—"

"If his wife finds out. Can you handle the hearing without the file, that's what I wonder."

"Of course that's my biggest concern at the moment. The basics—most of the prep work for the hearing—we have the computer file."

"I'll make you a printout." Sandy started hitting the keyboard keys as they talked. The printer clicked and hummed and sucked in a sheet of paper. They watched the paper fill with words.

"What about the exhibits?" Sandy asked.

"Kevin was bringing the originals to court. I only had copies in the file. This hearing I can manage."

"What about the others? Kao Vang and the two sisters?"

"All those files contained were my client-intake notes. But they are crucial. Oh, this is such a mess. It's the same as with Kevin's file. Those notes contained material that can't get out."

Sandy heaved herself out of the tight black swivel chair. "Well, before we get all panicked, let's look around here. Car key. Briefcase. Three files." She moved around the two rooms, sandals light-footed, long blue cotton skirt swaying, long glass earrings tinkling.

Nothing showed up in Sandy's stack or on Nina's desk.

Sandy searched through the cabinet behind her. Nina moved over to the client area and restacked magazines, checking for anything that didn't belong. They let the voice mail pick up the ever-ringing phone.

"Where'd you see the briefcase last? Maybe we can apply the eighteen-inch rule. Whatever you lost is almost always within eighteen inches of where you saw it last."

"I saw it on the floor in the backseat of the Bronco."

"And the key?"

"That's a tough one. I keep it on a separate keyring and keep it handy because I use it all day long. I know I used it when I drove to the office yesterday morning."

"Yesterday, during the day, when it was out in the parking lot, was the Bronco locked?"

"No. The CD player broke six months ago and we just took it out so I've been a little lax about locking up."

"So. Could you have left your main car key in the Bronco yesterday?"

"It could have fallen just as I got out. You're saying anybody could have been nosing around out there and found the key. But why not steal the truck then and there? Why wait until I drove it home?"

"Okay, then maybe you lost the car key somewhere else while you were running around town. Where were you?"

"At the courthouse. In Paul's Mustang. Passaretti's at the Y. The office. That's it."

"I'll call the court administrator and get hold of the janitors. I'll call Paul and have him search his car. And the owner of the restaurant. Have him search the place."

"Yes. Thanks, Sandy."

Sandy straightened up, turned, and put her hands on her hips. "Guess we'll have to get out the old eighteen-inch ruler another time."

"Check the library for the files one more time before we give up, will you?" Nina searched her office again. She went down the hall to the bathroom and looked around, or maybe she just went in there to catch her breath, regroup, because it had acted as a haven from turmoil so many times in the past for her. She walked outside to the parking lot, analyzing every step even though by now she was positive the briefcase had gone home with her and the car key was in someone else's pocket.

The files were gone. Might as well quit wasting energy. She felt the cold edge of panic.

Nevertheless, a half hour later Nina was examining the closed files for the third time when Sandy touched her arm and said in a softer tone than usual, "They aren't here."

Nina sat in one of the orange client chairs. "Well, I'll be doggoned. I will be doggoned. I have been robbed, Sandy."

"Now what?"

"Soldier on. The Cruz hearing is in exactly"—she squinted at her watch—"one hour and fifteen minutes. Before you do anything else, Sandy, would you please call Kevin and ask him to bring his entire file? He's got copies of all the main stuff. Dog-eared, coffee-stained, scribbled-on, ask him to bring it. I'm going into my office to try to reconstruct my closing argument."

"You can take my car when you go."

Nina got up.

"It's an oldie but a goodie," Sandy said. "Watch out for the transmission, though. It doesn't like shifting gears."

When she arrived at the courthouse, Nina called Sandy on her mobile phone. "Did you call Kevin Cruz?"

"He'll meet you by the rocks."

"Good."

"His wife's lawyer faxed us a supplemental witness list three minutes ago. You know who."

Sandy had worked for Jeff Riesner once and loathed him so much she refused to say his name. In agreement with Nina about the insidious poison of the man, she even kept some compromising material she had on him in a safe place for self-protection, like an antidote to snake venom.

Nina had been trying not to think about Lisa's attorney. Once again, his routine consisted of violating normal ethical standards, his version of a walk in the park. "He can't do that! The hearing's in an hour. Who's on this list?"

"Just one new witness. I never saw the name before. A woman. Name's Alexandra Peck. I just looked her up in the phone book and checked some Net directories. There are some Pecks in Tahoe, but her name is not listed."

Nina said, "Oh, boy," and rubbed her forehead. "This is not good. This is bad."

"I figured it might be."

"Does Riesner share even the barest bones of testimony he expects her to give?"

"What you'd expect. Matters relating to the ability of Respondent Kevin Cruz to care for the minor children."

"I'll talk to Kevin about her before court. Riesner has such diabolical instincts, Sandy. He knows Kevin won't wait another day to get this settled and won't let me ask for a continuance."

"Who is this witness?" Sandy asked.

"I'll deal with it."

How could Riesner know about Ali Peck? Had he known for some time? Was he pulling a Riesner special, trying to kill her case with a last-minute, high-voltage shock? Or had he somehow learned about Ali within the past twelve hours, from her client-intake notes? Anything was possible. Riesner had means that put Nina's to shame, and ends that would shame a squid.

A fantasy bloomed in her mind—Riesner following her home in the storm in his sleek black Mercedes, creeping around the Bronco, his dapper Italian loafers squishing through the puddles, stealing her car like a street thug. Almost funny, if you left his face out of the picture.

Or what about Lisa Cruz? She had been very, very angry at Nina in the courtroom the day before. Did she pick up Nina's car keys?

Nina put aside her suspicions. She couldn't find her vehicle right this minute. She needed to move on to a more immediate problem, discussing the unfortunate reappearance of Ali Peck with an overwrought client who was heading into the courtroom to face one of life's decisive moments.

"That man better not be pulling something," Sandy said, referring to Riesner.

"Our old buddy," Nina said to Sandy. "Never far from our hearts."

Sandy's wrathful snort carried over the miles.

4

BECAUSE SIXTY-FOOT-TALL FIR and pine trees towered over the two-story structure, the familiar brown and rustic El Dorado County Courthouse building sat in what seemed like perpetual shade, the better to cast a muted mood over its denizens. In the same building were housed not only the courtrooms and clerks and judges' offices, but also the jail. Next door was the plate-glass window of the South Lake Tahoe Police Department. Across the courtyard another low building held various offices connected with county law enforcement, health, or the judicial system, including the Tahoe offices of the El Dorado County district attorney and the public defender's office.

Locking Sandy's car carefully, Nina tramped across wet grass to reach the mass of granite boulders erected to honor two Tahoe pioneers. Kevin Cruz sat in a tiny patch of sunshine on one of the large rocks smoking a cigarette.

"Hi, Kevin," Nina said.

"Hi."

They sat down on the bench and talked, Kevin firing up every two minutes, Nina wondering how to approach the bad news she carried and full of questions for him about Lisa.

Kevin had bulked up since his wife left him six months before. Like Officer Scholl, in perennial cop fashion, he wore impenetrable shades over his eyes. He didn't look good today. He must have been to the barber, because his hair was so aggressively trimmed Nina could see pink scalp under the fair hair. His court clothes, a sport coat and slacks, looked unfinished without his usual nightstick appended. One of those men who look hopelessly phony in a necktie, he had settled for an open shirt under the jacket.

"You were brilliant yesterday," Kevin was saying again.

"Kevin, there's something you haven't told me. Lisa's got something personal against me."

"Hey, you got what you needed to get out of her," he said. "She got mad. She looked bad. She showed what a witch she can be."

"Kevin. C'mon."

"Okay, okay." He stamped out one cigarette on the ground and rummaged for another. "I didn't see any point in telling you," he started. "Ah, shit. Okay. She holds you responsible for her father's death."

"What?"

"It's a long story, but I'll give you the short form. Her dad ran a small logging company that did a lot of cutting up near Wright's Lake. Sound familiar?"

"Maybe."

"Remember Richard Gardener? Client of yours? Guy who lost his leg in a logging accident."

She remembered.

"You helped his worker's-comp lawyer get him a big award, then you went after the company for shoddy safety practices and won a bunch more. Well, her old man ran the logging company, and that lawsuit wiped him out. He died shortly after it folded, heart attack. She blamed you."

She remembered the bankruptcy, the notice she had received of the death.

She was silent for a moment. Then she said, "Why did you hire me, Kevin?"

He flushed, embarrassed. "She was always on about how tricky you were in court, how smart-ass. I didn't know you, Nina, I just knew I wanted a damn good lawyer. You fit the bill. I never liked her dad. He was such a sleazeball, and to be honest, it always sounded to me like your guy deserved the money."

Nina thought about that for a while. Realizing she was in the situation too deep to climb out, she decided to accept it. "It's a big day for your case," she said finally. "We're winding things up. Are you ready?"

"I'm not ready for any of this. You know, I never hit Lisa, never scared the kids, always supported the family, always came home after my shift. But I know I made mistakes."

"We have to talk about that," Nina started, but Kevin rushed on.

"I think you were right yesterday, when you pointed out that her dad's death hit hard. He cherished her and spoiled her. She isn't as close to her mom." He shrugged. "Who knows why? But she was never a happy person. Since her dad died she's in a permanent state of, I don't know what to call it. Confusion? Despair? She's like a speed freak out to find a cure. She grabs at anything that might give her a moment's peace. Heather and Joey are so confused, they forget how to tie their shoes right."

"Kevin, listen."

"But the firefighting will go the way of all her other fads. She's probably already losing interest, talking about throwing it up to train as a nurse. Or an optometrist. Or a dancer. Or a skydiver, maybe." He sighed. "She'll never be happy. She's a terrible influence. Thank God I'm going to get those kids away from her before she wrecks them."

"Kevin—" Nina put her hand on his arm.

Reading something in her expression, he shut up.

"They know about Alexandra Peck."

Only two weeks before, during one of two panicky, weepy, middle-of-the-night phone calls to Nina, Kevin had told Nina a secret. After a big argument with Lisa, she had kicked him out of their bed and he had started sleeping with a seventeen-year-old police cadet.

In one of those programs that are nobly conceived but loaded with hazards, high school students rode around with patrol cops on evening shifts to observe, learn, and assist. Like police officers, they wore uniforms and looked like adults, but these were kids, half of them girls, while the cops they rode with one-on-one were almost all adult men.

Kevin, raised in a small Catholic New Mexico town, had married Lisa at twenty. When he met Alexandra Peck, he didn't know what hit him. "It just happened," he said, and the shame in his voice over the phone only magnified the banality of his words. "We rode together for three months before I touched her. I fought it for a long time, but—Ali had no compunctions. She said she had fallen in love with me, and God, how that girl came on to me. I was so lonely. Nobody cared about me but her. In the end I couldn't resist."

Next he would be telling her that the girl was very grown-up for her age. Nina didn't want to hear it. "How did it end?"

"She bolted," Kevin said, "right after I asked her to marry me."

"How is she now?"

"I don't know. She dropped out of the program. She lives with her parents, so I don't feel right about calling."

No, Nina had thought. He wouldn't. As he talked, she thought about affirmative action, about bringing women into male-dominated professions, about human nature, about the victims of this particularly ill-conceived experiment in social engineering. Disgusted and disappointed in her client, she allowed a few cynical thoughts about the naiveté of the police-department human-services staff who had dreamed up this program, but she kept her opinions to herself.

Kevin's confession rearranged the balance of blame for the failure of the marriage, if Nina had cared to think about that, but she was Kevin's advocate, not his judge. Kevin had assured her during that late-night phone call he had been very careful and that no one knew, not Ali's parents, not his chiefs, and especially not Lisa.

Up to now, the story had stayed hidden in Kevin's file, existing only in Nina's scribbled notes on yellow legal paper.

· · ·

Now Nina put a hand on the cold granite rock and told Kevin that Alexandra Peck had been discovered.

"Of course we can object to the late notice," she said. "But Kevin, suddenly the case is complicated. The recommendations might change."

His latest cigarette had burned down his finger. He dropped it.

"There's more." Steeling herself, Nina told him her Bronco had been stolen the night before and that his file had been inside it. "It's possible—I mean, we have to consider whether whoever took my truck read your file and somehow, for unknown reasons, informed your wife or her lawyer about the contents."

"Wait a minute. How'd you find out they know about Ali?"

"I got a fax in my office just a short time ago."

"You think this has something to do with your lost files?"

"I just don't know. It's suspicious. On the other hand, they could have known about her for some time and waited until the last minute to spring it on us."

"But how else—" Kevin stopped. "Is she going to testify?"

"Yes. She's been subpoenaed. She may be here today."

"Then they knew about her yesterday, right? Before your files were gone."

"Possibly. But it's also possible they got her in on very short notice."

"My God. The kids. We've got to stop her!"

"I will object, but if the judge decides to let her take the stand, I'm afraid we can't," Nina said. "All we can do is hope she's fair, Kevin, and hope the judge can put the relationship into perspective, as part of who you are."

"Lisa did it," he said. "You saw her yesterday. She's pissed at you, and believe me, she doesn't hold back when she's got an issue. She can't stand to be criticized, and you really let her have it. They can't steal my damn file and use it against me, can they?"

"I will object," Nina said again. "It's wrong. But I have to give you the heads-up."

"You let them take my file from you?" The news finally reached him.

Nina said, "I don't know who took my truck. I don't know if they found out about Ali from my file."

"Don't try to defend yourself," Kevin said. "Don't put a spin on it. Don't give me a song and dance. Jesus!" His mouth contorted. "I'm gonna lose the kids over this! You have to fix this!"

"Listen, Kevin. We can continue the hearing, give ourselves some time to sort this out. If they want to put Ali Peck on the stand on this notice, we have a right to prepare for it. Let's continue the hearing. That's my advice."

"Continue it? For how long?"

"It depends on the judge's calendar."

"I waited nine months for this hearing, which is only a temporary-custody hearing anyway. It's almost over. Today's the last day. So you tell me. Can you keep Ali out if we continue the hearing?"

"I don't think so," Nina said. "The purpose of the continuance would only be to allow us to prepare for her testimony, you see?"

"She'd definitely testify?"

"Yes."

"We wait God knows how long and then she takes the stand anyway? Why are you suggesting this to me? Object today. Stop it."

"I can try. But if we don't ask for a continuance—"

"My kids are growing up! A continuance is only going to drive me crazy, you understand, Nina? Nine months I've waited, while Lisa jacked me around on the visits. Ali or no Ali."

"It's time. We should go. Can you stay calm, Kevin?" Nina didn't feel very calm herself. Riesner's missile had launched and now zoomed through the air toward their flimsy bunker.

5

NINA AND HER CLIENT entered the familiar doors of the courthouse, passed through security, and turned right, taking the stairs up, Kevin moving fast. With her heavy bag in tow, Nina had to struggle to keep up with him. Setting it down for a moment to rest her arm at the top of the stairs, she looked around, seeing no sign of a girl in the hall. She allowed herself a happy thought: Maybe we'll luck out and Ali'll evade process or fight it. Sometimes the lawyers kept the cases right on track, and sometimes the cases oozed in unexpected directions, along with the witnesses.

Inside the courtroom, Kevin took his place at the table beside Nina, his face set and his eyes averted from her. She smiled first at her good friend Deputy Kimura, the bailiff today, who was on the phone as usual, then nodded at Judge Milne's clerk. Praying for the glint of a car key, she sneaked a quick look under the table. Nothing there.

Just to their right, Jeffrey Riesner took his place alongside Kevin's wife and whispered into her ear. Lisa Cruz inclined her head toward her lawyer, listening. When he finished, she turned toward Nina and stared, holding still, all frantic activity ceased for the moment, almost frightening in her cold disgust. Eventually, she turned back to the table. She had a stiffer look today—her long hair sprayed into a twist, tiny pearl earrings, smooth white skin.

Lisa's long-fingered hands eventually settled down on the photo of her children on the table in front of her that had kept her company throughout. Riesner finished his intermittent whispering, then got up and approached Nina. She stood to meet him, tensing her muscles to prevent herself from flinching.

Of course he noticed. Stretching to emphasize the whopping height difference between them, he plastered on a fake smile for the onlookers. "We should chat."

Kevin excused himself to go back into the hallway momentarily for some water, leaving the two lawyers alone at Nina's table.

"Why?" she asked.

Riesner nodded. "Outside." Seeing her expression, he chuckled a nasty chuckle. "In full view of the glass front door of the police department. That way there's no chance you'll lose control. Get violent. Or something." Although he overtly referred to an actual physical altercation they had gotten into during another case a few months earlier, the subtext was, as always, sexual.

"No," Nina said. "I don't think so."

They both kept their voices low so the conversation, already bursting with tension, held an intimacy that made Nina recoil.

"Am I supposed to coax you? Don't worry, I only eat what tastes good. You're too sour to bite."

"You already bite," Nina said. She gave herself an immediate, silent tongue-lashing about not giving him the satisfaction. A cringe, a flinch, a flash of anger—he lapped up her emotional reactions like Dracula lapped blood.

The slightly upturned corner of his mouth twitched with pleasure. He had shaken her already. Success. "My client has a settlement proposal."

"You better be serious." Nina looked at her watch. Court convened in seven minutes. She indicated the back of the courtroom with her head. She wasn't going to get out of Deputy Kimura's sight this time.

Riesner followed her to the back wall and leaned against it, arms crossed. His eyes were green, the same color as fungus on the rotting stump in her backyard. "Well?" she asked.

"Mom gets sole physical custody. She'll agree to joint legal custody. Under the circumstances, she's being generous. Supervised visitation. He can have Christmas. She doesn't celebrate it, so she doesn't give a shit. And the kids go to her church."

Sole physical custody meant the kids would live with Lisa. Kevin would have visitation rights. Joint legal custody meant Kevin would have to be consulted regarding important issues such as the kids' educations and health.

The offer wasn't much. Lisa couldn't get a better deal even if she won in court. Plus Kevin had already rejected the whole idea of Lisa taking physical custody of the kids.

But Ali altered the topography of the case. Could Kevin lose even joint legal custody? Nina thought about it briefly, then decided. When in doubt, give nothing. "Too bad," she said.

"What do you mean, too bad?"

"You weren't serious." She began to walk away.

"Last chance," Riesner said. His celebratory tone stopped her. "Personally, I'd just as soon drag this thing out, rack up fees, and end by humiliating you. That would be a pleasure."

"Why should my client consider this offer?" Nina said. "Give me one good reason."

"Don't you remember sweet Ali?"

"Go on."

"I faxed the notice in advance, as you well know."

"Too late under the rules."

"Just learned about her myself. Ask for a continuance if you want. Heck, let's both make more money on this thing."

"How did you learn about Ali Peck?"

Riesner blinked. "Such an attractive young lady. Such a young, young lady."

"If you don't answer my question right now, this discussion is over."

An innocent look. "As I will be happy to tell the judge, I received a call about six this morning at my home."

Nina steeled herself and asked, "Who called you?"

"Ali Peck, stricken by a guilty conscience?"

"I don't believe you," Nina said. "I'm going to object."

"Of course you will. I told my client you would."

Nina didn't know if Riesner already knew her files had been stolen and she recognized her need to tread extremely carefully. Just keeping her face straight stressed her out at the moment. "Where is she?"

"Oh, she's here somewhere, trailing her subpoena, rarin' to go."

"If she came forward, why is she under subpoena?"

"I don't have time right now to get into all that. Suffice it to say that Lisa now knows all about her husband's adultery. Suffice it to say that she's not taking it well."

Adultery. The word recalled red letters, pulpit-thumping, and that old-time religion. Nina tried for a noncommittal expression.

"Cruz folds. He pays my fees," Riesner said, moving away from the wall and putting an open hand out as if making a generous gesture. "He can even have a payment plan."

Nina said through gritted teeth, "I'll speak with him."

"Do that." He smiled at her, one hand in his pocket, projecting suave. "Save the little girl from the witness stand and all those sordid details about that big bad cradle-robbing client of yours."

"Is that it?" Nina said. She looked at the clock on the wall.

"He looks chipper today," Riesner said. Again he laughed. "He puts on a good front. Maybe that'll make it easy for him to do the smart thing."

"Don't concern yourself with my client."

"Now, there's some damn good advice."

Back at the table, in a hurry now, she leaned down to give Kevin a brief rundown of the conversation. He fixated on one thing. "Where's Ali?" He looked around the court.

"Probably waiting outside by now. Riesner's keeping her out of sight until the last second so we can't talk to her."

He ran a hand across the fuzz on his skull. "She worried that it might come out more than I did. I'd hate for her to go through this. Oh, man."

"Kevin, joint legal custody gives you a lot of say, and I would make sure the visitation was generous. But it's not the result we wanted."

"I'm sick that this is going to happen, but I'm not going to give up. Like you said. Maybe the judge can see past Ali. I have to get Heather and Joey away from Lisa." He shook his head. "No, we have to win. We have to fight."

"Of course the choice is yours."

He turned to look at Lisa and Riesner, then looked back at Nina. "I'm the better parent."

"We still have a strong argument," Nina said. "We'll work around Ali. We have to."

"Good. Thanks for not telling me to give up." Nina felt a pang. He sure shouldn't be thanking her when she might be part of his problem.

Nina looked over at Riesner and gave her head a sharp negative shake. He shrugged and bent to Lisa's ear.

They all stood while Judge Milne entered the room and took his seat. Judge Milne, a tall, imposing man, had a deep golf tan and an untroubled brow. He trusted himself, that was his secret. He made his decisions and then never thought about them again. Luckily, if you appealed to his pragmatic side, his judgment was pretty good.

And luckily, he seemed to have a soft spot for Nina. She played to that. There were limits to high-mindedness.

After the preliminaries, Riesner, straightening an imaginary bend in his faultless tie, stood at his table.

"I would like to call a final witness," he said.

"Objection, Your Honor." Nina leafed through the pitifully small pile of papers relating to the case just to give herself another second to construct her reaction to this unsurprising news. "There are no further witnesses on his list, Judge. It's improper and should not be allowed."

"I see that," Judge Milne said. "What's going on here?"

"Your Honor, I have provided the court with a copy of a supplement to the witness list, duly faxed to counsel as soon as the witness was discovered and filed this morning. I just received some information about Miss Reilly's client that has bearing on his fitness as a parent. I apologize that I was unable to give reasonable notice to his attorney, but this information came to me through a third party early this morning. I took Miss Reilly aside just before court and advised her again of the circumstances, so I hope we aren't going to have a show of disingenuous surprise."

"Inadequate notice, Your Honor."

Judge Milne found the supplemental document. "Oh, here it is. A supplemental witness. Affidavit in support thereof. Ms. Reilly. You are requesting a continuance?"

Kevin shook his head. No.

Credit the judge for giving her a full ten minutes to argue her objection for the record. She realized from his expression almost from the beginning that he would allow Peck to testify. Finally he raised a hand to stop her. "I'll continue it if you need additional time, Counsel. Otherwise, we'll proceed."

Nina sat down, already moving her mind on to the testimony. No sense letting this lost skirmish knock her off-balance. Judges were notoriously lenient about allowing evidence when it came to custody hearings. There was no jury to confuse and they wanted as much information as possible.

As Riesner escorted a young woman into the courtroom, Kevin no longer looked the confident father. He murmured something unpleasant and started to get up. Nina clamped a hand on his shoulder and shoved until he sat. "Settle down," she whispered.

"I can't just sit here and let them screw me!"

"Shh," Nina said.

The buff-looking girl clumped up to the stand in jeans and hiking boots, her pink cheeks complemented by shiny black hair. Kevin clearly favored athletic women, Nina thought, as Ali swore to tell the truth. Riesner got right to it, rushing through the boring preliminaries and dallying in the salacious details.

An older version of the girl sat in the back of the courtroom, wincing. Ali's mother.

"We went together for about three months," Ali said in answer to a question.

"How often did you engage in sexual relations?"

She lowered her head. "A few times a week."

"And you were seventeen at the time."

"Yes."

"Not even old enough to vote or drink a glass of wine, were you?"

"Objection," Nina said. "She was seventeen. We get it."

"Sustained."

"And where did you have these sexual relations?" Riesner asked, steepling his hands on the table.

"Different places." Her voice had a note of anger in it. Resentment at being hauled over here today? "Sometimes on a blanket in the woods."

"Anywhere else?"

"In his car."

"His patrol car?"

"No, his regular car. Never in the patrol car. We had a rule."

"Anywhere else?"

She flushed a deeper red and didn't answer.

"Did you ever have sex with Mr. Cruz at his home?"

Although Kevin seemed ready to explode, Nina put her hand on his arm and sat calmly. No point in objecting. Riesner would insist on this one and the judge would allow it.

"Yes."

"Please tell the court how that came to happen."

"We had finished for the day."

"You mean, the youth cadet program?" he asked, with the emphasis on *youth*.

"Right. We were done for the day. We stopped at his house on the way to my house and, uh, we got carried away."

"Where did you get carried away?"

"Uh, in their bed?"

" 'In their bed.' "

"Your Honor," Nina started.

"We can hear, Mr. Riesner. No need to repeat," said the judge.

"And where were the children?"

"Where do you think they were, asshole?" Kevin whispered. "Standing there watching?"

"I think they were gone somewhere. Yes, they weren't there. We just got carried away. Kevin wouldn't have—Kevin kept me away from his kids. I never met them."

"Were there any other such incidents?"

"You mean did we do it in his house again?"

"Yes."

"No. We didn't. Except kissing once out front on the porch."

"Where were the children that time?"

"Oh. They were supposed to be asleep but that one kid, the boy, he woke up. Kevin had to put him back to bed."

Kevin jabbered into Nina's ear. "Joey never saw anything, I swear it, Nina. We had no privacy—things got out of hand, but we were so careful. The door, that one time at our house, it was locked and the kids weren't even home. I would never harm my kids, never expose them to anything like that."

When Nina's chance came to cross-examine the girl, she took only enough time to clarify the issues. The girl had entered into the relationship willingly and had, in fact, initiated it. The Cruz marriage had already broken down. Kevin Cruz had always shielded his kids from knowing anything about Ali. Nina kept her questions short. The longer she stayed up there, the worse things would be for Kevin.

Although Kevin tried to talk her into it, she decided not to put him back on the stand. Refuting the details of Ali's statements might work just to etch sordid details of the relationship into the judge's mind. And anything Kevin said now might be used against him in the further complications that were sure to develop due to Ali's age. She had to protect him from incriminating himself.

Besides, what could Kevin say in his own defense?

Riesner made a powerful closing argument, holding forth on the virtues of Lisa Cruz, pooh-poohing the doctor's report on her ongoing depression except to say that she was "striding toward a healthy future with her children." He spoke glowingly of his client with zeal and warmth Nina knew was affected but seemed absolutely real. Now that he had Nina back where he wanted her, in the weaker position, he seemed assured and smooth, his old self.

"Your Honor," he continued, "there's been some effort on the part of the respondent to use religion as a factor in this case. Doctrines that have to do with the celebration of Christmas and birthdays or participation in voting or military service have been held to be outside the realm of religious views that could be considered as a danger to a child's mental or physical health when it comes to deciding custody in a divorce proceeding."

"I have your citations, Mr. Riesner," said Judge Milne.

"Mrs. Cruz has stated that she does not know what she would decide in the sad event that a blood transfusion was recommended for one of the children but that she would be open to the input of medical professionals in addition to the opinion of Mr. Cruz. Her community activities as a firefighter and fund-raiser for good causes should be seen not as a distraction from her mothering, but as a shining example to her children, and must be considered in the light of her overall excellence as caretaker to these precious children. She's a superior mom and commendable human being, that is clear.

"Mr. Cruz, on the other hand, with his spotty work history and reprehensible immorality, brought his adulterous behavior right into his home. The best interests of these little children are to remain with their primary caregiver. Not to cast this as a morality play, Your Honor, but consider the character of the players. Consider Mr. Cruz.

Moral turpitude, Your Honor. Sexual misconduct. A crime. Mr. Cruz may end up in jail, jobless. He committed statutory rape. I will of course be compelled to turn this information over to the district attorney's office."

Nina's turn.

She started her own list, a list of Kevin Cruz's practical virtues. "A careful review of the testimony given in this case shows that Kevin Cruz would make the better custodian of his two minor children.

"Lisa Cruz's religious activities, while admirable, are extremely time consuming. To make up for the time she spends away from home looking for converts, she told the court she would take her children along with her door-to-door. We have previous testimony that this activity, while not necessarily harmful in itself, can in time generate painful conflicts between her and the children."

At this point, she skidded hard into the mental-health problems suffered by Lisa Cruz, recapitulating the testimony of Lisa's own doctor, hammering home his words "chronic depression," and reminding the judge that her own doctor said Lisa Cruz's chronic condition was likely to come and go for the foreseeable future and could be considered a lifelong disability.

"Now, as to Ali Peck. Mr. Cruz was in fact worrying about his children and did keep her away from them, as she testified. The point is, his children were not affected in any way by this affair. His marriage was in trouble. He was lonely. He made a mistake. What's important, Your Honor, is that this affair lasted only a short time and is long over. A single misstep should not in any way overshadow the mediator's recommendation and finding that overall Mr. Cruz is better suited to have physical custody."

After she sat down, she caught her breath and, by chance, caught another unsettling glare from Lisa Cruz. After Lisa turned away, Nina scrutinized Judge Milne, trying to read him.

The judge was looking at Ali, who had taken a seat in the back row, probably picturing sweaty embraces observed by little kids. Nina almost saw the decision forming like a cloud over his face. He turned back to his notes. He had decided that an excess of spiritual seeking was better than an excess of lust.

They had failed. Ali, the trim little cadet, had dispatched Kevin directly into the lonely hell reserved for loving fathers without custody.

Okay, that wasn't fair. Kevin had put himself there.

Her client had also spent the past few minutes studying the judge. One glimpse of his white, balled knuckles was enough to tell Nina he knew what she knew. After court adjourned, he stood in the doorway shaking, curling and uncurling his fists, apparently waiting to punch somebody out. Nina nudged him through the door safely, but once they got outside he ran after Lisa, who was walking with swift steps toward the parking lot.

"Wait right there. I want to talk to you," he said.

Nina ran up behind him. "Kevin, no."

"Leave me alone, Kev," Lisa said. "I'm warning you. Stay away from me."

"You stole my file, didn't you? You talk ethics night and day, but you know what? I know the real you under that sanctimonious bullshit. You'd do anything to keep Heather and Joey. You'd lie, cheat, steal—anything. But now hear this. I won't let you have those kids."

"You have no choice, do you? Just had to have your little girlfriend. You cheated on me, and you cheat your kids, behaving that way, like an animal. You have nerve even talking to me today."

Her composure pushed Kevin right over the edge into the abyss of his fury. "Watch your back, Lisa!" he yelled, shaking a fist at her. "Those kids are mine!"

Nina held his arm. "Don't touch her. Please don't," she said.

"Don't threaten me, you loser," Lisa said. "I'm not afraid of you or your dipshit lawyer. I'm the one in control now. And you'll be living with that for the rest of your days."

Kevin looked at his fist, put his hands at his sides.

Lisa turned to Nina. "As for you? I'm not surprised you crawled out of the woodwork, that's bound to happen with vermin. Maybe it's a good thing. I finally can tell you exactly what I think of you. You disgust me. You're a disgrace as a human being. Why am I not surprised you get your jollies out of hurting another mother?" With that parting shot, she pulled open the door to her car and drove away.

6

"THREE FILES," Sandy said back at the office. "Our trickiest cases."

Five P.M. The end of the day had arrived. Unlike every other day, when they would leave the door unlocked until they actually left, this Friday they had locked the door promptly and turned on the voice mail. The public business of this calamitous day had ended.

Nina had already reviewed Kevin's hearing and its probable outcome with Sandy, who had reacted with initial restraint at the news that Nina had probably lost. Now Nina stood beside Sandy's computer and pointed to a sheet of lined yellow paper. "These weren't complete files, so I've tried to outline what I know was there in some detail over here."

"What's this?" Sandy said, her beringed finger hovering over a small dark blob on the sheet.

"Jelly," said Nina promptly.

"Is not. You cried."

"I never. But I know I shouldn't worry so much. My files are as dry as dead beetles to anyone but another lawyer. They're in a trash can somewhere, dumped by the delinquent who stole my car. The courthouse is always swarming with criminal defendants. If you tried to think of the worst place to drop your car keys, try the place where car thieves spend half their lives."

"Whoo-wee." Sandy examined the list.

"The client-intake notes are my biggest concern. People are

forthright with me, and of course, like a good schoolgirl, I write it all down. And as I'm listening, I'm scribbling my thoughts and impressions."

"Not to mention doodling all over the page. Let's start with Kevin Cruz."

"The secret's out. Ali Peck testified. The result isn't going to be pretty."

"Quite a coincidence, her showing up at the last minute. Her name's in the missing file."

"I know. They might have found Ali without the file, but the time frame—"

"Anything we can do?" Sandy asked.

"Not about the hearing. It's too late to do anything about that," Nina said.

"That man's gonna win," Sandy said, referring to Riesner. "And we were five and O!"

"I wasn't keeping score. This isn't about—"

"You can bet *he* was."

Nina stuck to the point. "Kevin was having a relationship with a young girl. Milne isn't a prude, but, boy, she looked young up there."

"Well, don't sound so guilty. He slept with her, not you, for Pete's sake," Sandy said. "How'd they say they found out about her, anyway?"

"In court this morning, Riesner said he got a tip at home early this morning. Implied she called him."

Sandy frowned. "He claims he just found out about her but it's my policy never to believe a word he says. Maybe he knew months ago and sprang it on you. However. Maybe he did get a phone call. From a car thief."

"Exactly what I'm afraid of." Nina noted with clinical interest that her throat seemed to be closing up. She went over to a client chair and sat down and knew she was finished for the day. Time to go home.

"Wish knows Kevin. Says he's seen him around the community

college. Says Kevin comes down hard on the druggies." Sandy's son, Wish Whitefeather, helped around the office, studied criminology at Lake Tahoe Community College, and now drove Paul's old van. He idolized Paul, and made a good sidekick when Paul needed help on his Tahoe work for Nina. "So. Moving right along. Number two— the arson case—the Hmong. The Vang family."

Nina went to the window. The purple mountains' majesty didn't soothe her as much as usual. A Sunfish with its tricolored sail hoisted high glided into view on silver water toward the Tahoe Keys Marina in the distance. False tranquility, Nina thought. Too beautiful to be true. She remembered someone telling her once there might be bodies lingering on the bottom of Lake Tahoe, perfectly preserved in the melted snow.

She said, her back to Sandy, "The Hmong. Nobody, but nobody, knows about the insurance claim I filed."

"It's a pitiful story. What was the worst thing in the file?"

"Kao Vang's address. He didn't want to give it to me but I insisted. Kao said, he warned me, that his family would be in danger if the news got out that he might recover a settlement from the fire. People might get angry."

"Angry enough to do what?"

"I don't know. The Vangs won't talk about it."

"What should we do?"

"I don't know."

Nina's voice must have told her assistant to leave things at that, because the usually exhaustively thorough Sandy moved briskly forward. She scribbled a note in pencil, then went back to the list. "Brandy Taylor and Angel Guillaume."

"Witnesses to a murder. Deeply buried, until I wrote it all down for our thief. I have to get Brandy and Angel to the district attorney and get them protected. How I hate unknown quantities. Those two are about as unpredictable as my cooking, especially the younger one, Brandy. She got dragged here by Angel in the first place. They could get hurt, Sandy. My intake notes—I listed Angel's address here in Tahoe, and maybe even Brandy's in Palo Alto. Along with the whole story they told me."

"Yeah, it's bad. I read your notes while I was making up the file."

"Anyway. The weekend is starting. I'm taking a run down to the Monterey Peninsula tomorrow morning, and I plan to ask Paul to come up here as soon as he can next week."

"Wish could help out in the afternoons."

"We could use his help. Could he come in next week?"

"You kidding? He'll make time."

Nina already felt better.

"The A-Team," Sandy said. "Back together again. Last time was, I think, the Nikki Zack case."

"You know, Sandy," Nina said, "believe it or not, I saw these cases as a symbol of our success. We were helping ordinary people in the worst trouble of their lives who heard such good things about our work, they trusted us to do a good job." She found herself unable to continue with the thought. "Let's finish here quickly and go home. I have to see everyone on Monday."

"Maybe you should wait longer."

"I can't. I'm not feeling good about even taking the weekend. I have an ethical duty to tell these clients promptly that there's been a possible breach of confidentiality. Monday's as late as I can wait. If the files turn up, great. Maybe the police will find the car with the files intact. But I have to give myself the weekend. I have to think and talk to Paul, and the insurance company. And—" She stopped.

"Two days to pray."

"Exactly."

Sandy said, "Things were rolling along so great. For a minute there we had so many clients we almost had the money for bigger offices. If this gets out, we'll be lucky to keep the fig in Miracle-Gro." They both looked over at the plump-leafed tree, which, in spite of the misfortune of living in a law office, thrived in its sunny corner. "Look. Let's get some perspective here. Some skunk is banging around in your Bronco, having a whee of a time. He has zero interest in a briefcase full of papers lying on the floor in the backseat under his empty beer bottles."

"The Bronco bunged up and the papers ignored—that would be the ideal outcome, and I never thought I would feel so casual about my truck. I love my truck."

"Question."

"Yes?"

"You pay that legal-malpractice-insurance bill I put on your desk a couple of weeks ago?"

"Sent it out last Thursday."

"Good." She punched her lip with a pencil, thinking. "So we went down today."

"It's not a football game, Sandy. Like I said."

"He makes a lot of money."

"Yeah, he does." Nina had had the distinct displeasure of visiting Riesner's leather-swaddled, mahogany-bedecked offices a few times in the past.

"I'll tell you something about him and money. He's also a cheapskate. When I used to work there, he gave the most pathetic Christmas presents. Instead of bonuses. Stuff he makes down in the basement at his house. Spice racks, lazy Susans, wood bowls." She made an impolite sound. "We'd have to admire his talent. What we would have really admired was a big gift certificate from Macy's. His ego is the size of Cave Rock. I still have one of his bowls. The dog admires it when he drinks his water. Yeah, he's a prick, no way around it."

"Sandy, you're going to have to find another description for Riesner. I find that term objectionable."

"You offended? You never said that before."

"I'm not offended. It's just objectionable."

"Huh?"

"I'm going to make a couple of quick calls before I go." Nina opened the door to the inner office and went in, leaving the door open.

After a few minutes, Sandy called, "So what's your objection? Why's it objectionable?"

"It's not offensive enough," Nina said, and was rewarded by a dusty chuckle from the outer office.

Sandy said, "I'll call Angel Guillaume tomorrow morning to set up the appointment. How do I get hold of Brandy Taylor?"

"I think she's still at her sister's."

"And Kao Vang?"

"Call his friend Dr. Mai. He gave me his phone number in Fresno."

"If it's okay with you, I gotta go right now. Joe and I are on the committee to organize a powwow down by the lake two weeks from now. So far, lots of discussion and nothing getting done."

"Sounds like my life. Go get 'em, Sandy."

"Yeah, we'll ruffle some feathers tonight. Don't forget to lock up. And."

"And?"

"Stay cool."

"Yeah."

As soon as she heard the outer door slam, Nina punched in the number of her malpractice insurer, Lawyer's Fidelity. No answer. The company had gone home for the weekend. She should have called earlier.

She called the Lake Tahoe Police Department and asked for Officer Scholl or Matthias. The officer on duty took her message and told her the Bronco hadn't been found yet.

She called Paul.

"Van Wagoner Investigations."

"Hello."

"Hi!" She always forgot his voice, so warm and full of life.

"Paul, I changed my mind. I have a big problem up here I need to discuss with you. And I miss you. I can be there about four to-morrow. Okay?"

"Sure. I was just on my way out the door. Big football game

tonight at Carmel High School. Can you tell me what's up right now? Are you okay?"

"I'm okay. It'll wait until tomorrow."

But Paul made her give him the outline, and from the long silence on the end of the phone when she finished she knew he, too, was grappling with what to say.

"You go on," she said. "You'll miss the game. And I have to get home."

"Wait, Nina. Here's what I'm going to do. I'm going to call an old buddy of mine who happens to be certified to practice in the state-bar court. All he does is lawyer-discipline cases. He can help us sort this out."

From the new relief she felt, Nina knew he was on the right track. She needed information. "That sounds great. But is this attorney good? You know this person well?"

"He's been around. Left private practice two years ago and does this exclusively now. Lives in SF and loves to come down to the Monterey Peninsula. Big talker, big ego, but you see plenty of that in your business."

"What's his name?"

"Let me call and see if he's available first. Meanwhile, pack light. My big plan for the evening won't involve dinner clothes."

Nina's bed did not offer its usual comforts that night. Instead of resting, she journeyed bleakly through times she had screwed up or swerved into the windy side of the law. Green sunglasses—two years ago, she had hidden this evidence of one client's presence at a crime scene. Hypnosis—she had assured another client it would remain private. She had been wrong and Misty Patterson had almost been convicted of murder because of it. Bob's No Fear cap, recognized by her at another crime scene—she had never told the police about that. And then there were the pieces of a dead man out there buried under the pine trees of Tahoe—a murder had been committed to protect her and Bob.

She had thought of herself as a good lawyer, good enough to look for the spirit behind the letter of the law sometimes, looking for the real rule that ought to govern the situation, trying to be brave about applying it.

She had been accused of recklessness many times, but she had always managed to pull the right result out of the situation before. Sometimes, she had to admit, she had taken risks that were more suitable to a horse track than a law practice. All in the service of the clients, she told herself.

Last night? She hadn't even identified the risk in advance. She had been careless and lazy.

How hard would the clients get hit?

How hard would she get hit? For the first time, she let her most private, selfish fears loose, and the thought came:

Fuck! I could get disbarred!

And then what would I be?

She opened a bleary eye to the green clock light at 2:30 A.M., then rolled and tumbled until dawn in the twisted sheets. Gut-wrenching self-doubt, the whole night long.

7

"YOUR BAG?" Paul said, peering into the backseat. He must have been watching for her, because he had appeared the moment her car pulled up. Paul lived in a neighborhood called Carmel Heights at the top of the hill high above the ocean. Dry fir trees around his town-house condo whistled and creaked in a hot wind. Behind them lay the hills that led to Carmel Valley a dozen miles inland from the central-coast community of Carmel-by-the-Sea. Beyond the trees of his parking area, the Pacific twinkled in the sun. Even in the shade the air felt heavy with heat.

"This is it." She shouldered a small duffel. She had stuffed it with her weekend needs early in the morning: a toothbrush, a nightie, swimsuit, and a few other items, imagining herself as Grace Kelly in *Rear Window,* reaching into her minuscule designer case to pull out a fluffy negligee, making Jimmy Stewart's eyes bulge. She unzipped a corner and showed him a bit of transparent chiffon.

"Ah."

His eyes didn't exactly bulge, although he gave her a squeeze that made her jump. "You won't even get a chance to put it on," he promised.

"No, no, I insist that you tear it off me." Satisfied, she stuffed her nightie back into the bag. "Is your friend coming?"

"We're driving down to Big Sur with him for lunch tomorrow."

Inside, he pulled the door shut behind her and did exactly what she had imagined he might do during the long drive from the mountains to the ocean, lifting her off her feet until their faces matched, kissing her with the passion she found so moving.

She licked his neck, lounging in the spot where his hair curled slightly, and ran her hand down the dip in his back as far down as she could reach. They swayed in the doorway for some time before he set her gently down.

"I have a bottle of Veuve Clicquot in the fridge. Do you know that you can take the cork out of that thing and let it sit all night and the next day it's still fizzy? It's a wonder. Let's get started. Even if it is four in the afternoon."

"I'm hot. Long drive."

"The towels are clean in there."

She went into the bathroom, stripped down, and jumped into the shower. Paul's decor followed his stated principle about himself: What you see is what you get. Simple and direct with a touch of whimsy in the forties' posters of guns and molls, the room had white walls, a black-and-white-tiled floor, and white towels.

She heard Paul pop the cork off the balcony deck. He had put on the Michael Hutchence CD they both liked and was humming along. He was happy to see her. The evening would seem to stretch on forever, and that was how she wanted it: dinner, drinks, talk, lovemaking, a swim in the condo pool, late night on the balcony, his arms around her as she fell asleep.

She needed this night away from everything. Just this one night, she told herself. So it always went with Paul. "You're already married," he would tell her. "To your briefcase."

As she hung the damp towel neatly on its rack, she admitted something to herself: Their relationship had changed forever on the day, just a short time before, that she realized that Paul had saved her life by killing a man who was trying to kill her. She trusted him now in ways she didn't trust anyone else, even her brother and father. In the face of his extraordinary act, she had surrendered much of her resistance to him. She felt bound to him in some primitive way that she had better sort out fast. Coming to him now, when she was so vulnerable, felt natural and right.

She needed him. Before, he had needed her. Her need for his solidity, his loyalty, was beginning to overwhelm all those other conflicts between them.

This feeling is new, she thought to herself, looking in the mirror. Was weakness driving her so urgently to him now?

Did it matter?

Sun poured through the window. She looked at the black teddy. It wouldn't do. The 1950s were dead, R.I.P. Grace Kelly and Jimmy Stewart, but viva the new century! She would at least skip the underwear.

Pulling her shorts and tank top out of her duffel, she dressed swiftly, giving one final glance to the woman in the mirror, the physical one that seldom communicated with the cyborg of the office, the one with nipples obvious under the thin material of her top, the one with tangled brown hair and bare feet. This woman could be irresponsible without dire consequences because she knew it— Paul would never hurt her. She could relax into a blur of sex and pleasure with him, if just for tonight, sleep dreamlessly in his arms, and store up power for Monday.

Out on the deck, Paul grilled teriyaki tuna and steamed asparagus with butter. She fed the blue jays, letting them do the chattering. They ate at a patio table covered with a red cloth, the candle flame flickering in the breeze. As the sun moved west across the ocean and the moon revealed herself, splendid and yellow, Nina ended up on Paul's lap. They moved right along into the bedroom and Paul finally revealed the rest of his big plan.

As she walked toward the living room late on Sunday morning, she heard the low rumbling of masculine voices. His lawyer friend must have arrived. The man stood up when she came in and took a step toward her, his hand coming up and then hanging in the air, along with his mouth.

She stopped, her mouth frozen in the polite smile.

"Oh, no. No, Paul," she said.

"What's she doing here?" her ex-husband, Jack McIntyre, said at exactly the same time.

They both turned to Paul, who sprawled in his chair, long hairy legs stretching out from his khaki shorts. "You both would have said no. You'll both thank me later. Get you something, Nina?" he said.

"I'll get it," she said, retreating into the kitchen, trying to figure out what in the world she felt, seeing Jack again. Shock, definitely. They hadn't met since before their divorce, not since the day Jack walked out on her and their place in Bernal Heights.

She walked slowly back out, holding a soda. Apparently not a word had been spoken. Jack held a beer to his mouth and appeared to be draining it. Beer on Sunday morning. That was new.

"Well," Paul said. "Ha, ha. Jack, Nina. Nina, Jack."

"Hello, Nina," Jack said. He raised his eyebrows, shrugged, smiled slightly. "Believe me, although I should have suspected he was up to something, I didn't."

"Hello." She sat down on the couch, keeping her legs together, and crossed her arms. "What're you doing here?"

"I was invited," Jack said. "It's been a couple of years now, hasn't it? Amazing. I meant to call Bob more often."

"He's been busy. Like you, I'm sure."

"You always did fit into a T-shirt just right," Jack said.

Nina crossed her arms.

Jack broke into a broad smile. "Paul, you old fox."

"Don't get the wrong idea, buddy. This is business," Paul said.

Jack ignored him. He did look fine, if pale from the years in high-rise San Francisco and away from the beaches. Shorter than Paul, he was brawny, although leaner than he looked, something you only saw when he took his shirt off. He had reminded her of a teddy bear when they met, a hairy Big Sur guy who brooked no shit but had a ready smile and a kind word for everyone.

Nina was remembering her last phone conversation with Jack. He had urged her to hurry up and sign the papers so he could marry his girlfriend. She had reacted, well, with a certain lack of gentility. The old anger hadn't had time to rise up yet and all she felt was nervous and curious. She looked again at Paul, who cleared his throat, stalling, as if waiting to see how she would react.

"He's the state bar defense lawyer?"

"I hear he's good," Paul said. "Of course, I hear that from him."

Jack said, "Ah ha. The pieces begin to come together."

Odd, to be in a room with two men she had slept with. She had no urge to compare them, then suddenly found herself doing exactly that. Apples and oranges, she thought. Onions and leeks. Cucumbers and bananas. She giggled. Nerves.

"What's so funny?" Jack asked.

"Nothing. Sorry."

"I haven't even started my song and dance yet, and you're smiling." He turned to Paul. "Did you tell her about Eva? Is that why she's smiling?"

"Tell me what?"

"She dumped my ass," Jack said. "Two months ago." He looked hurt when he said it.

"Really," Nina said.

"I didn't even see it coming. She moved out and served me the next day."

"She does move fast," Nina said. Jack's new wife had also been the attorney who represented Jack in his divorce from Nina.

"Go ahead. Tell me I deserved it." After a pause pregnant with Nina's silence, Jack said, "Well. You get a gold star for restraint. Here I am, battered and blue. So, Paul, you going to tell me what's up?"

Paul got up. "Let's save that until we're on the deck at Nepenthe. It's a forty-five-minute drive and I'm already hungry."

Jack and Nina continued to sneak looks at each other. She decided he was as intense and brash as ever but he had a new aspect today. He looked wounded, maybe. Chastened.

Improved. Definitely improved.

"Okay," Jack said. "Sure."

They took Jack's green Chrysler Sebring, top down. Paul sat in the rear seat, his legs digging into Nina's back. The fog had drifted out to sea around the Highlands Inn and the twisting road revealed glimpses of deep blue sea on their right around every turn. Vacationers blew past them as Jack stuck to the speed limit. When the houses grew sparse, the road hugged a cliff that stretched high above them on their left and down a thousand feet, to the crashing surf far below.

"Awesome!" Jack shouted over the noise of the engine. "I always forget."

As they crossed the Bixby Creek Bridge, Paul leaned forward to touch Nina's shoulder, because she had a very bad memory of that place that had to do with her mother's death many years before. They swerved past the Point Sur Lighthouse, where the navy was on the lookout for terrorists these days. The world had changed since Nina's childhood, when VW vans full of bell-bottomed kids had traveled this beautiful road.

At the thick redwood forests of Pfeiffer Big Sur they dipped into shadow. Jack told them about how his wife had taken their hamster with her and how he had seriously considered filing for custody. Solemnly, he laid out his legal strategy, even citing some cases, probably invented but nevertheless credible and detailed. Some people in trouble turned to counseling; Jack turned to storytelling. His disasters always evolved into deadpan comedy skits, which was his way of controlling and reshaping his psychic traumas.

They parked in the driveway at the foot of the concrete staircase that led to the Phoenix Shop and Nepenthe. "Haven't been here in years," Jack said. "Lots of good times here. Remember that Halloween party in, let's see, I forget the year. Who was it wore the pumpkin head? Probably Paul."

Paul took Nina's arm as they went up. They both puffed, but the hike was worth the wait because Nepenthe possessed a spectacular view. Under the enormous, shifting sky, miles and miles of ragged cliffs collided with the ocean.

"There are seven wonders, but are there seven wonderful views?" Jack said as they arrived at the top. "There ought to be. Put this one at number one."

They sat on the outside deck and ordered burgers and margaritas. Paul and Jack had fallen into the old banter Nina remembered from years ago when she had first met them. She had been a law student clerking at Jack's firm in Carmel, and Paul—incredible! Paul had still been a cop. Bob was a toddler then. Her mother was alive.

So much had happened since, too much too fast. Another marriage, another loss...

"I was sorry to hear about your husband, Nina. What a sad way to die. How terrible for you and Bob."

Jack had wormed his way into her heart, just like old times. She never knew what to say. "Thank you."

"How's the law practice up there in the mountains? I look east sometimes outside my window on the thirtieth floor in the Financial District and I think of you in your cozy town and I think, you finally figured it all out—"

Nina gave a short laugh. "Right."

"She needs to talk to you professionally," Paul said. "So straighten up. Go ahead, Nina, dive in."

"I'm still thinking about it," Nina said. "Jack, are you really a certified specialist in state bar matters?"

"At your service, fair lady," Jack said. He stood up suddenly and pretended to sweep a cap off his head and bowed. "I've been hoping Paul dragged me down here just to get us talking again, actually."

"I didn't even think about that," Paul said. "Actually." He put his hand over Nina's.

"So you guys are lovers?" Jack said, Jack-style, no pussyfooting around. "She's with you?"

Paul pulled Nina close. Jack's eyes flickered.

She felt vaguely like a sack of flour being weighed by two merchants. "Paul and I aren't your business," she said.

"Maybe. Still, I find myself absorbed by the implications, and just a little aggravated. Paul, you could have said something. I've talked to you on the phone many times. We went climbing this summer at Pinnacles. We hit Vegas last month. You never once mentioned Nina."

"No time like the present."

"Well, well, well," Jack said. "Coffee for me," he told the waitress. "Nina? Anything?"

"I'll have the chocolate mousse," Nina said.

"That's right. Chocolate in times of stress. I remember that. You have need of my services, I take it," he said. "I'm sorry to hear it. That's the first thing I always tell my clients. I also tell them it's inevitable. Happens to every one of us sooner or later. Complaint from a client. Ceiling caving in. It's the grand old practice of law these days."

"I'm looking for some advice. Some information. About malpractice," Nina said.

"Okay," Jack said. He folded his hands. "You get a complaint against you? Malpractice?"

"Not yet."

" 'Not yet.' A wallop awaits behind those two little words. What happened?"

Nina told him. She didn't spare herself, telling about the missing key, her stolen truck, her sleepiness, the fact that she often brought files home. Jack shook his head and Paul narrowed his eyes. Then she got to the worst part.

She talked about Jeff Riesner's new witness in the Cruz case and her fear that Kevin's file had been read. "These particular files—they are seriously confidential. The ones where—the clients could suffer severe harm if the files are read by the wrong people. That may already have happened in the Cruz case. I don't know for sure."

"Hard luck," Jack said. Putting his hands behind his head, he expelled a long breath.

"Well?" Nina said.

"You want to know, are you going to get into trouble with the California State Bar? You could get sued, too, in a civil action, but let's put that aside right now. It's your license you're worried about right now, not your fortune. Or have you got a fortune these days?"

"I'm paying the bills. I put a down payment on the cabin where Bob and I live. I'm not rich."

"You talked to your malpractice insurer?"

"Couldn't reach them. Monday."

"Talked to the clients?"

"Not in the other two cases. Monday."

"Current status of the police investigation?"

"I called this morning before I even got out of bed. No Bronco, no files, no progress. They're already tired of hearing from me, and I wasn't popular before."

"Hmm. First. Paul did right, coming to me. I do this stuff all day long."

"Thanks for listening."

"No problem. Pick up the tab and you can write the whole dinner off. It's a legal consult now. Hire me."

"What?"

"Okay, I'm hired. Pay to be worked out later. This is now an unassailably privileged conversation."

"What about Paul?" Nina said. "He's not a lawyer."

"You're not here, buddy. Never forget that."

Paul nodded.

"Okay. Second thing. I have never heard of anybody getting disbarred for losing some files, for a single act of carelessness. You have to work at it to get disbarred. A pattern of dipping into the trust funds, sure. Conviction of a felony. Taking off, address unknown, with the retainers and leaving the clients twisting in the wind. Mostly it's money stuff."

"There was—a complaint some time back."

"Oh?"

"Jeffrey Riesner got annoyed with how I was handling a case. The bar slapped me on the wrist, verbally, of course."

"No harm done, then. Tell you a big secret." He leaned his head close to Nina's. "They'll reinstate just about anybody after a few years. There's no such thing as disbarment for life. You can always lay low and do community work and try again later. But I'm getting ahead of myself."

"I can't imagine that happening to me. I've been a lawyer for years, Jack, and for that privilege I slaved for four years in night law school, working days at Klaus's firm. It's all I know and all I ever wanted." There was a catch in her throat.

"So you've never heard of a disbarment for lost files," Paul said, prodding him.

"I'll tell you what concerns me. The state bar prioritizes, you know. They get more complaints from the public than they could ever start to handle. So they look at the complaint, and the main thing they want to know in almost every case where it isn't just summary disbarment, where you killed your wife and you're out, buddy, the main thing is the extent of the harm to the client. That's the criterion. And that's my concern here. It's not just, ah shit, I lost some paperwork, I'll just run down to the courthouse and get duplicates. Or incorporation documents or even a contract dispute. Right?"

"Not these cases, no," Nina said.

"These are people who have something privileged they have told you, and it's gonna shake their world if somebody reads your notes and talks to the right people?"

"Exactly."

"Anybody gonna commit suicide if the story comes out?"

"Oh God, I hope not!"

"There's that potential?"

"I can't say."

"Extortion?"

"Could be."

He tilted his head. "How bad is it? Is it possible one or more of these people might be physically harmed by someone else if the news gets out?"

She didn't trust herself to speak.

"So, you feel seriously compromised. If the worst happens, that one innocently careless act might result in irreparable harm," Jack said slowly. He thought for a while, scratching his thumb back and forth along the wooden table. "My advice to you is, when you get back think about what you can do to prevent the clients from getting hurt."

"The first thing I'm going to do is disclose everything to them," Nina said. "My indefensible carelessness. The whole thing."

"No, no, no. No sackcloth and ashes. They don't need that. Just tell them somebody stole your truck with the files in there, and definitely tell them immediately."

"I might be able to maneuver better if you don't tell them right away, Nina," Paul said. "Tiptoe in there and find a few things out before they're warned."

Jack didn't get it at first, then he said, "I don't know, Paul."

"What's not to understand?"

"Looks to me like you're personally involved here," Jack told him, frowning.

Nobody said anything for a moment.

"A job like this requires extreme subtlety, quiet smarts. Maybe—"

"I'll quietly smart you," Paul said, grinning. "I'm on to you. You're jealous."

"Well, she is my wife."

Nina interrupted. "I *was* your wife, Jack. Past tense, over, and let's not forget it because so far, that has worked for me."

Paul's smile grew.

"Of course I want your help, Paul," Nina said. "Thanks."

"Obviously," Paul said.

"But I plan to take Jack's expert advice. I'll tell them tomorrow, if possible."

Now Jack smiled.

Paul shrugged. "I can live with that."

Jack steamed forward. "Okay. That was the good news. It's not the usual disbarment situation. Also on the plus side, Nina, your truck might still be found with files intact. Or nothing comes of this for whatever reason, and nobody complains to the state bar, so no process gets initiated. Now let's talk about the bad news. Let's assume a client does complain."

"Okay," Nina said, bracing herself.

"Let me lay some startling statistics on you. Solo practitioners are about twenty-three percent of the lawyers in California. That's sizable. About one out of four out of one hundred seventy thousand lawyers. Now. Fifty-four percent of complaints, which are called inquiries, are filed against solos. You get twice as many complaints filed against you, you solos, proportionately. You get that?"

"Yes. Why's that? It doesn't seem fair."

"I'll get to that in a minute. You think that's unfair, listen to this—seventy-eight percent of the cases the state bar takes through the disciplinary-hearing process to completion are solos. Damn near four out of five, although solos only constitute a quarter of the lawyers. What does that tell you?"

"It tells me something's wrong with this picture," Nina said.

"Now. Let's skip the small-firm practitioners with fewer than ten lawyers in the firm. They don't get off easy, but don't do nearly as badly as the solos. Let's compare what I just said about solos to the big-firm lawyers. Lawyers in firms with more than ten people. About forty-four percent of the lawyers in California are big-firm lawyers. But guess what percentage of inquiries concern them."

"I won't even try," Nina said.

"Only twenty-eight percent. And guess what percent of the cases the state bar prosecutes to completion are big-firm lawyers."

"What?"

"Two point eight percent. Less than three percent, compared to seventy-eight percent for the solos."

"No," Paul said. "You're kidding."

"No lie. Of you solos, four out of five are going all the way. If you're big-firm, one out of forty is going all the way."

"That's got to be illegal," Paul said. "Targeting the little guys."

Nina sat there, stunned.

"So you don't, repeat, don't, want to get close to the system. It's a whale. Sucks in the little krill, avoids the sharks."

Nina gathered her wits. "But that's discrimination. Deliberate or institutional, I can't believe my colleagues would allow it."

"Who knew?" Jack said. "There were rumors for years, and we finally got a law passed to force the bar to keep the statistics and make a public report. It's called the State Bar Report under Senate Bill 143. Read it and weep."

"But what are they going to do about it?" Nina said.

"Not a goddamn thing. They report the stats because they have to, then they apply a thick coat of whitewash. The whitewash goes like this: It's the fault of the solos because they don't make as much money, don't have lots of clerks, don't have other lawyers around to make appearances when they're down, operate under more stressful conditions. They say the solos are more dishonest, basically, more likely to dip into the trust account. I say bullshit to that. I don't think that's what happens. I've represented enough lawyers in these proceedings that I've got the real picture."

"And?" Nina said.

"It's two things," Jack said. "First, when one of their own gets in trouble, the big firms pay off the client. Poof, the problem goes away. And second, the state bar disciplinary procedure is totally different from regular courtroom procedure. The mines are buried in different places. The solos in trouble often can't afford a lawyer. They start thinking well, shit, I'm a lawyer, I'll represent myself. Boom, they make a minor technical mistake and they've lost their profession and their livelihood and incidentally their reputation and often their marriages and they don't even know what hit them. It's ironic. They're babes in the woods just like the *pro pers* who get slammed around all day in regular court because they don't have lawyers."

"I see," Nina said. She stared at her plate.

"But you've got me," Jack said, smiling. "You want me to represent you beyond this consult? I'm willing."

"I could represent myself," Nina said. "In spite of what you just said. I'm a good trial lawyer. It can't be that different. If it comes right down to it."

"No. No, you can't do that. Let me give you just two reasons among many why that would be a big mistake."

"I'm listening."

"First, here's a small thing, subtle. If you represent yourself, you don't get to be called Counsel. You're Ms. Reilly, and the other guy, the state bar lawyer, she's 'Counsel.' You're a second-class citizen. You don't get any respect. You argue your brains out, the judge is looking at you thinking, well, it's her ass on the line, can I trust this citation she's giving me? See?"

"I'm still listening."

"And second, much bigger. You're your own lawyer, you're on double trial. You're trying to make a point, and the judge is watching you, saying, she did all right with that one, or she's an exaggerator, or she's all over the map on that one. You see? You incriminate yourself every time you open your lovely mouth. Your every flaw is blown up for the judge's viewing pleasure, as big as in the movies."

"That's a good point," Nina said.

"And I didn't even mention the xenophobia. These people are as ingrown as my right big toenail. You sound like an outsider, you can't help it, you don't know the right approach, the lingo. The judge's nose twitches, you give him a headache with your foreign ways. You need me."

"What would you charge, Jack?" Nina said.

"Half price. One fifty an hour."

"I do want the benefit of your counsel even if this goes nowhere, Jack. But it has to be at your regular rate."

"I'm trying here," Jack said. "Will you please let me make nice? For old times' sake."

"Don't overdo it," Paul said.

"I'm on to you, too," Jack said. "Who's jealous now?"

Paul held Nina's shoulder in a death grip and scowled at Jack. Jack leaned across the table, practically snarling back. Nina nestled into Paul's arm, furtively enjoying the posturing of these two rival males. The primitive female in her felt hugely gratified.

But back to business. They were all professionals. This hormonal dustup would settle down fast.

She reached her hand out and shook with Jack. She had a lawyer, even if everything he had told her so far discouraged her.

They moved on to topics that didn't piss anyone off, heinous murders, extortions, securities fraud. Paul gave them the rundown on his latest conquest, locating an in-house theft ring at a local restaurant that included a stockpiled warehouse of fine wines and frozen gourmet pizzas.

Six o'clock came and went, and the waiters went around lighting the candles. Beyond the redwood railing the faraway cliffs softened as evening fog rolled in here and there. Suddenly feeling anxious, Nina thought about the long drive home, Bob waiting to be picked up, the dog at Matt's, grocery shopping to do before starting her week. "I have to hit the road, gents," Nina said, rising. Both men stood up, too.

They drove back to Carmel, Paul in the backseat again, Jack holding forth in the driver's seat. The waves below reflected the gold of the setting sun and Nina lowered the sun visor in a useless effort to stave off its assault on her eyes. She wouldn't be home until ten and she would be tired, but she felt better. She knew there were others supporting her. Like a general, without precisely realizing it, she had spent the weekend mobilizing that support.

This time she accepted a hug from Jack in the driveway, feeling some of the tension ooze away as she hugged him, but pulling away quickly.

"It's been so wonderful to see you, Nina. You're more beautiful than ever," Jack said.

"Give it a rest," Paul said. "I'll see you in a couple of days, Nina. Call me."

"Better yet, call me," Jack said. "Or I'll call you. See how it's going with the clients."

Her kiss good-bye to Paul was perfunctory because she didn't want to precipitate any more dissension in the ranks. She left the two men standing side by side, her soldiers preparing for war, she hoped not against each other.

BOOK TWO

The mail came late, at four in the afternoon. Nina had just grabbed her purse and was running out the door to pick up Bobby at Tiny Tots when Anne, the lead secretary at Klaus Pohlmann's law firm, rushed down the hall toward her.

"From the state bar," she said, handing Nina the white envelope.

Her bar-exam results. Only half the law-school graduates passed on their first try.

Nina returned to her cubbyhole law-clerk's office, shut the door firmly, and leaned against it. She had taken the bar over a grueling two-day period in July and now, five months later, Santa and his reindeer decorated her window. Outside, the dark had begun to crawl over the cottages, shops, and shiny cars, bringing on the twinkling Christmas lights of Carmel.

During that long wait for the results, as she toiled through her daily life, she had thought so many times: Will I make it? She had never felt sure that the years of work would pay off. She never had enough time for the home-work, and she had sometimes fallen asleep during the endless night classes. The devilishly difficult bar exam had seemed like a plot to keep out as many people as possible. She sat down in her worn chair, taking the load off her weak knees, swiveled back and forth, and stared at the envelope.

"The time has come," she thought, "to believe impossible things." She tore the thing open.

"...pleased to announce...welcome you to the bar...ceremony in San Francisco..."

"I passed! I passed!" She emerged into the hall again, where Anne waited inches from her door and threw her arms around her.

"Good work!" Anne said. Nina ran down the hall to Klaus's office. The old man had heard the commotion and was already hobbling toward her across his fine Isfahan rug, his face wreathed in smiles. He held her tight, his slight bony body seeming to send waves of strength through her.

"Congratulations, Counselor," he said, and hearing this word, which meant everything to her, Nina realized it was true at last. She was a lawyer.

Handing her a handkerchief, Klaus sat her down on his leather couch. From his desk drawer he produced a big bottle of scotch and a tray full of etched shot glasses. The rest of the lawyers and staff of the small firm had streamed into the room, beaming, nobody talking yet while Klaus poured the shots with a hand that trembled only slightly.

"I would like to propose a toast," he said quietly. *"To our new member of the bar, who I know will bring honor to our difficult and rewarding profession."*

Then they were drinking to her and clapping her on the back and hugging her.

When everyone else had left and only Nina and Klaus remained, she asked, *"Klaus?"*

"Yes, my dear?"

"Do you think—that is, can I—"

"Of course you can. You may turn out better than any of us. Perhaps because you have had the hardest struggle, working, studying, raising your little boy the whole time."

"I'll never let you down. I promise," Nina said. *"You gave me my job and helped me all the way. I'll always look up to you as my example."*

"Don't think about me," Klaus said. *"I am the past and you are the future. Just try to relieve a little of the suffering in this world with your skills. I know you'll never disgrace us. Now, go get your little boy and go home."*

"I'm so happy. But also afraid."

"You can handle it."

Before she left, she bent over and kissed his withered cheek.

"I'll make you proud of me," she said.

8

ON HER WAY OUT of Tahoe again on Monday morning in the white subcompact the insurance company had laid on her, Nina drove past the lot on Highway 50 where the Vangs' Blue Star Market had once conducted business: ragged wooden fencing, a chipped construction sign, and disturbed dirt had reclaimed their space, as though the dreams of the Vang family had never existed. On both sides of this neat emptiness, small businesses—a hair salon, a video store—carried on as though arson and death didn't exist and the world remained a just and benign place.

She had an appointment to meet Dr. Mai at the Strawberry Lodge, a half hour from Tahoe on the highway to San Francisco, a meeting place that would preclude the worst part of his drive. The Vangs wouldn't be there, he had explained on the phone when she called him at his home in Fresno on Sunday night. She became insistent. He became gruff. No Vangs. He would drive up to meet her alone. She would have to take what she could get on this Monday morning: the Vangs' elderly adviser.

Just before Echo Summit, at the famous place in the road where the cliff drops a couple of thousand feet and tourists coming the other way catch their first glimpse of the lake, she pulled over at the lookout and stood by the edge, wind whipping her hair, a few drops of rain hitting sideways. September snow had fallen the night before on the granite summits all around the lake, which appeared only as a vague gray line far away. From her seven-thousand-foot vantage, she looked down at Christmas Valley, a solid green forest with a hint of the single main road that snaked through it. Eighty miles west in the San Joaquin Valley where Dr. Mai lived, people would be complaining about the heat of late summer, but up here she needed her warm jacket.

Nina had first met Kao Vang about a month before, in early August. He came into her office for a free consultation.

He and his family had fled from the middle hills of Laos as refugees in the early eighties. Nina had never heard of his hill people. Later, after she took the case, she read up on the subject, learning that the Hmong were an ancient people who had supported the U.S. during the Vietnam War. For this assistance, the Communists punished them after taking over the country in 1975. Every year, the Hmong came before the U.N. to request that observers be sent to the remaining refugee camps to investigate reports of systematic arrests, beatings, and murders, but with so many trouble spots in the world, this was a backwater that had receded into history.

Still, in recent years life had improved for the Hmong, and many longtime refugees returned to their homeland. The lucky ones returned with American money in hand for themselves and their extended families, which went a very long way.

What Nina saw on that first day was a small, slight, youngish man in new jogging shoes who spoke very little English and didn't crack a smile. Kao Vang's shy wife, slightly built, with bright, intelligent eyes, sat lightly on the edge of the chair beside him. Her name was See, she told Nina, but after that she didn't speak at all. Their young son, Boun, and another fellow had come with them, a gnarled older man wearing some sort of tribal vestments, who said he was from Kao's church.

Later she learned that Dr. Mai, the older man, had connections to no church and no normal medical practice. He was some sort of shaman. The culture was simply so different that they had tried to put her at ease by presenting themselves in terms she could understand.

They arrived early for their appointment and sat up straight in the client chairs, speaking in low tones to one another. Sandy went back to her filing. The Hmong language sounded very, very foreign. When Nina came out to greet them, she felt the hesitation before her hand was grasped by the older man. She brought them into her office and shut the door. They emanated a simplicity and formality that made small talk impossible.

Dr. Mai talked. Often he asked Kao a question and translated Kao's response. See Vang listened, her hands in the lap of her long skirt, crossing and recrossing delicate feet that ended in rubber thongs.

Nina looked over her sheet. The Vangs wanted to consult her about "insurance." Kao had given no street address, listing his residence just as South Lake Tahoe. No phone either. Nina insisted and explained that the address, along with the entire conversation, would remain confidential. Finally Dr. Mai gave her the address of an apartment near the casino district.

In answer to her first questions, Dr. Mai told her that the Vangs owned a convenience store in the tiny shopping center anchored by the Grand Auto Store, about a mile from Nina's office. He showed her a lease made out to Kao and See Vang. She had never been in there, but something tugged at the edges of her memory.

"How long have you been in the U.S.?" she asked Kao.

"Twelve years," answered Dr. Mai. "Very difficult. No money. Two children. These are very hard workers. Work all day and night."

"I am curious as to why you came to see me," Nina said with a smile. "There are many lawyers."

"You were recommended."

"By whom?"

"By others in our community." He gave no names.

Nina felt absurdly flattered. Apparently her recent notoriety was paying off. She picked up her pen. "How can I help you today?"

Dr. Mai talked with Kao for a moment, then said, "An insurance claim. A business policy. You can help with this?"

"Is it in litigation? Has someone been sued?"

"No. This is—this is private."

Kao launched into a short speech, talking to Dr. Mai rather than Nina. Energetic and quick-moving, he was what some people might call the mercurial type. A big Fossil watch, sunglasses peeking from his pocket. All-American in some ways. Nina had trouble reading his mood. Was he nervous? Worried? Afraid? Anyway, smiles were miles away.

"Kao would like to know if you would be able to work quickly. Can you begin immediately?"

"I have some time, I'm not in trial at the moment. But how much is the claim amount?"

"He doesn't know yet. You will help him decide."

"What is the reason for the claim?" She began her habitual note-taking, copying down fragments of sentences, making a few of her own observations.

"A fire."

"You brought the policy?"

"And other papers. Police reports also." Ah, Nina thought. Police reports equal a crime. Again, memory nagged at her. A crime involving a liquor store. She had overheard one of the deputy D.A.'s talking about it. She couldn't pull it back into consciousness. But the emotional content of the memory remained. Something chilling.

She pushed back her chair, crossed her legs, balanced the pad across her lap, and said, "Tell me about it."

Their story was all the more wrenching because of the matter-of-fact way in which Dr. Mai spoke.

Kao and his family had worked and saved for a number of years to earn the start-up expenses to open a store. When they had found a well-placed business for sale eighteen months earlier, they were overjoyed. The purchase took everything they had. After much happy discussion, they named their new venture the Blue Star Market.

Their original plan called for a grocery store, but liquor sold better, so they stocked liquor, but they also sold imports from Southeast Asia—canned food, spices, toys, candy, clothing and hats, magazines and newspapers from Thailand and Vietnam. The store had been modestly successful from the start. People came from Reno and Fresno, where over twenty thousand Hmong lived, to find familiar items unavailable outside San Francisco otherwise. Tourists from all over enjoyed stopping in to look at the exotic items and usually left with something.

Their twelve-year-old boy, Boun, worked there after school with See Vang. Their daughter did not, for unexplained reasons. Kao worked two shifts, from ten to two in the midday and again from seven to midnight.

Dr. Mai explained that the Northern California refugee community viewed Kao Vang as a big success story. The family bought a Jetta. All the Hmong people in the area knew about the store.

One night, about a year earlier, a man—"A Hmong man?" Nina asked, but got no answer—entered the store. Waiting until the other customers had gone, he put a six-pack of Budweiser on the counter, pulled out a gun, and told Kao to open the cash register. As this story unfolded, Kao sat tensely beside Dr. Mai. Now Dr. Mai paused and Kao spoke his first English words: "I say, 'Go to hell!' I reach to take gun—" He spoke in a thick, garbled voice.

The robber shot Kao in the face and sauntered out, leaving Kao bleeding but still conscious on the floor behind the counter. Showing unusual presence of mind, the robber had hung the CLOSED sign and locked the door behind him.

Kao came close to dying. But minutes later, Boun found him and called 911. While they waited for the medics, the boy wrapped his father's head in his shirt and held it gently in his lap.

Immediate surgery took care of the initial repairs to Kao's

shattered jaw. Some weeks later, surgeons inserted pins. Two months after that, he underwent further surgery designed to rehabilitate his speech. Unfortunately, that didn't work very well, but at least now Kao could make himself understood.

Then Kao went back to work. But he had a new attitude.

"Could you identify the robber?" Nina asked. "Did they make an arrest?"

Dr. Mai shook his head impatiently. "No identification," he said. Nina wrote on her pad, "Knows the guy? But closed society, these people don't want to go outside." She was guessing. She couldn't tell what Dr. Mai was thinking or how a Hmong would handle being shot in the face.

"That must have been very painful," she said gently to Kao. Dr. Mai translated. Giving his injured jaw a smack with his own hand, Kao shrugged to show his obliviousness to pain. Nina wrote, "Brave guy."

"Go on," she said.

For the sake of his wife and son, Dr. Mai said, Kao bought a gun to keep under the counter. Several months passed. In early June, just before closing, a man came into the store, keeping his face hidden under a cap. But Kao Vang, alone behind the counter, knew immediately who he was.

"The same man?"

"Yes. Back again."

This time Kao was ready. When the man pulled out a gun, Kao already had his hand on his own gun. No time to think. He pulled out his gun and shot the robber point-blank in the chest.

This time Kao punched in 911. Then he called his family.

"Yes," Nina said. "I remember this story."

The Tahoe police detectives made out the report, clapped Kao on the shoulder, and recommended no further action. The dead man had thirteen previous felony convictions including two assaults with a deadly weapon in the course of a robbery. But the police also took away Kao's gun. Two days later he got his first E-mail. The one-word message, a sort of declaration of war, came in his own language. "Revenge," it read. Family or friends of the robber probably wrote it.

Dr. Mai said, "Kao couldn't sleep anymore. His jaw hurt all the time. He was afraid to leave his wife alone in the store. He didn't know what to do."

Nina wrote all this down. She looked up to see Kao adjusting his jaw again as though it had slipped off its track. Dark, intense eyes studied her. When his hand came down she noticed that his jaw was not symmetrical.

"Kao and his family came to me. We decided he must continue. Friends came to the store to help. Kao worked hard."

The July fourth holiday brought tourists and heat to Tahoe. Kao woke at four o'clock the next morning to a phone call from a fire marshal who yelled that his store was on fire. By the time they got there, the interior of the store had been gutted by quick and successive plagues of flame, smoke, and the rescuers' water and foam.

Everything was ruined. All the Vangs' stock had been reduced to rubble. Cash register, counters, display shelves, bottle glass, melted candy pieces, and ashes jumbled together in blackened heaps.

"Destroyed," said Dr. Mai, putting a finger to the bridge between his glasses and pushing delicately upward. "So much hard work for nothing."

"I am sorry," Nina said, moved, knowing her words were inadequate. She felt the urge to apologize for all Kao's bad experiences in America.

Kao said something curt. "But this is America," Dr. Mai translated. "Kao had a small-business loan."

Nina nodded. "So he was required to carry casualty insurance," she said.

Now Kao nodded. "Casualty insurance," he repeated.

"No one knew," Dr. Mai said. "No one thought of this when they destroyed Blue Star Market. Kao was supposed to crawl away. But he brought me the policy. And I wrote a letter to the insurance company." Dr. Mai laid two much-handled documents in front of Nina. She picked them up but did not look at them yet.

"When was this?"

"I wrote the letter on July twelfth and sent it certified."

Almost a month ago.

"They sent me this letter quick." The letter bore a July 18 postmark and the imprint of Heritage Insurance's office in Reno. The company was sorry to hear of his loss. Kao had ninety days from the date of the event to file a claim.

Nina flipped open her calendar. "Today is August eighth. October third would be the deadline. We have plenty of time. Good."

"Kao and his wife would like to know if you wish to help them."

"Yes," Nina said. "Yes, I wish to help."

"No one must know of the claim."

"No one will know. But why does it matter?"

"If anyone learns that Kao is not destroyed—that he will have some money even—then his family will be in very great danger again."

Nina said, "Why? Who is threatening Kao? Are the police being told everything?"

Dr. Mai consulted with Kao. "There are no suspects."

"If you know who these people are," Nina said, "you have to tell the police."

"You don't understand. Kao does not want revenge. He does not want justice. He wants his family to live. Kao wants to take his family back to Laos. For that he needs the insurance money. Whatever you can obtain for him."

Nina wanted to tell the Vangs to stay here, fight the good fight awhile longer, do it our way, put 'em away. Again her eyes met Kao's. Maybe now she understood better what she saw in them. Kao was brave for himself, but he was afraid for his family. He had no fight left in him. He wanted only a dignified retreat.

"Okay," she said. "All right."

Dr. Mai nodded. "Thank you. Also I do not know what is charged for these services."

Nina considered this. To take a percentage of the Vangs' recovery seemed wrong to her, like another nick at them, and it would probably result in an overpayment to her. She adjusted her sliding scale lower than she had in a long time and said, "I would charge forty dollars per hour for this work." She drew a retainer agreement out of the drawer.

Another short consultation. This time, See Vang spoke to Dr. Mai, too, although she said only a few words in a soft voice. "That is fair," Dr. Mai said.

That same night, at her second office on her bed at home, Nina read the documents Dr. Mai had laid in front of her, three different sets of police reports, news accounts, medical bills, the insurance policy, the loan documents, and the lease agreement for the store. Every detail matched. For her, the sad and notable reality was how little attention had been paid to Kao's tragic experience. The *Tahoe Mirror* buried the incidents in single-paragraph back-page items: "Shopkeeper Shot in Robbery." "Police Seek Arsonist." Nina wondered if the lack of coverage reflected public apathy about poor, foreign people and their worries, or if it reflected a bigger picture—such grievous events had become frequent enough to be commonplace and therefore unworthy of newsprint.

A determination grew in her to have one thing go right for Kao. The family, traumatized, wanted to return to Laos. So be it. She would help them get the insurance money. They had followed the rules, paying the premiums each month. Examining the policy again, she saw that the maximum insurance payout could go as high as $250,000.

The next day she called Heritage, locating the adjuster assigned to the claim, a woman named Marilyn Rose, who seemed startled to hear that the Vangs had hired a lawyer. Nina gave her an overview of the situation and promised to submit a detailed claim shortly. She tried to communicate the urgency of the Vangs' problems by going on at some length about their difficult adjustment to a new country, how hard they had worked, and what their trials had cost them personally. She felt she connected. Her contact at Heritage sounded sympathetic by the end of the conversation.

A few days later, on a hot mid-August Sunday, Kao, his wife, his son, and Dr. Mai returned to her office. They brought every business-related scrap of paper they possessed with them in white plastic trash sacks.

They all sat down on the beige carpet in the outer office and started making piles. The documentation consisted of hundreds of paper scraps—mimeographed, penciled, faded, half-legible, in the writings of half a dozen Southeast Asian languages—and most of it was legally irrelevant. Many of the actual receipts, the inventory list, the bills, had burned in the fire. This would be no ordinary insurance claim.

"Many times no receipt," Dr. Mai explained. "Mrs. Vang went to Salvation Army, houses of friends, farmers' market in Fresno to buy items for Blue Star. Paid cash. Many items burned up with no receipts."

"Can we get a list of those items?"

Dr. Mai spoke to Mrs. Vang, who first shook her head and then shrugged.

"Things came from Cambodia, Vietnam, Laos. Refugee items. Records burned up. Wrong language anyway." Dr. Mai squatted comfortably on the floor. They all drank Sprites. Although Kao's wife looked much younger than he did and was more traditional-looking with her turquoise bracelets and black braid, she too bore the careworn look of premature age. She could have been twenty-five or forty.

"Don't worry," Nina said.

"But we cannot—we just cannot prove all the lost items."

"Just make me a list. In English. Everything you remember. Can you help with that, Dr. Mai?"

"But—we do not know the money paid."

"Estimate. Here." Nina made a heading on a fresh legal pad and picked up a scrap. "What does this say?"

"Four pairs sneakers. No amount."

"What kind of sneakers?"

Shrugs all around. Kao's shoulders sagged. He and See looked at each other.

They could have been Chinese and worth five bucks a pair. They probably were Chinese.

But they could have been Nikes.

"Estimate forty dollars a pair," Nina said. "We'll make sure the insurance company knows it's only an estimate."

At the end of the week the family trekked back to the office. This time Nina managed to persuade them to accompany her to Sato's for dinner. Dr. Mai wore his usual oxford-cloth shirt and sandals. Kao somehow managed to look debonair in spite of everything. Boun, their son, came, too. Their daughter, Dr. Mai explained, was ill and couldn't come. See smiled here and there, and Nina got the feeling that she had a sunny disposition in better times and understood English fairly well. After dinner, Dr. Mai presented Nina with the list. Estimated $54,000 in inventory lost.

She gave it back and said they must have missed a lot.

By the following week the loss amount topped $175,000. Nina had gone over almost every item. Almost twenty pages long, with several hundred paper scraps pasted onto ink-jet paper as exhibits, the list had been generated out of thin air, the same thin air that the inventory had burned into.

Nina spent a whole office day, phone off and door shut, dictating the claim letter. She gave a lengthy summary of the violent events and attached all the documents she had along with photographs of Kao's face after the first shooting, creating a package both heartrending and intimidatingly thick. A solid week passed before she and Sandy had all the exhibits organized completely to her satisfaction.

Kinko's had to keep the package overnight to make the copies, and the final hefty original had to be carried in a box.

After completing all this labor, Nina drove the claim over to Heritage personally, staying for a long chat about the need for discretion and speed with Marilyn, who did not overreact to the large claim amount and continued to flash hints of a beating heart.

Sandy took the first call from the insurance company on the first Tuesday morning in September. She came into the office, where Nina was stuffing pleadings into her briefcase for court, and said, "Heritage's first offer is in. They're starting at a hundred fifty thousand dollars."

"Glory be," Nina said.

"It's like the miracle of loaves and fishes."

They experienced a rare moment of perfect harmony. Sandy approved. Nina was elated. Sandy liked Nina to win for the less powerful in the community, and Nina liked to imagine that occasionally she actually helped to alleviate some human suffering, her way of giving back to the planet. Even more important, she felt that justice would be served. Wrongs would be compensated. The system was working.

"They've decided to work with us," Nina said. "Call the court and tell the judge's clerk I'll be a few minutes late." Picking up her own line, she called the adjuster, thanked her, and refused the offer.

"But we can't even read the receipts. As you well know," Marilyn Rose said.

"Did you see the medical photos?" Nina said. "It makes me ashamed. They come all the way here to start a new life in the land of freedom and—"

"All right already. I'll get back to you."

Thursday brought another call. "Two hundred ten thousand," said Marilyn. "That's the best I can do."

"What's the point?" Nina said. "Why not pay out the limit?"

"Because that puts some new procedures in place with some different oversight. Trust me, you don't want to go for the limit. Look, you've probably only got about sixty thousand that actually meets our documentation standards. This is it, Nina. I'm not holding back a nickel of what I got approved."

"I'll get back to you tomorrow. Thanks." Thrilled, Nina called Dr. Mai and the Vangs and told them about the offer. "I think we should sleep on it," she said. "Maybe I can squeeze out another ten thousand."

"It is wonderful. Wonderful," Dr. Mai said. "Kao calls me every day. He never expected so much, I know."

"Does the family still plan to return to Laos?"

Dr. Mai hesitated. "It is complicated. Everything in Kao's life is complicated." He seemed unwilling to explain further. Again Nina had the feeling that no amount of reading about Hmong culture would give her much useful insight into the family's American experience. Dr. Mai seemed unnaturally restrained to her, as if he felt shy about sharing the extent of the family's suffering.

Maybe they were just the kind of people who disliked having to ask for help of any kind. Or perhaps Dr. Mai's reluctance arose out of embarrassment that the people who had snuffed out Kao's livelihood and who would come after any money he might possess came from his own hills and his own culture.

"I will call you tomorrow," she said.

That last call to Dr. Mai had occurred on Thursday, September 6, four days earlier.

And that night, that ill-starred night, wanting to take one more look through her notes to decide whether to try for a larger claim or just shake hands with the princess of generosity who had adjusted the claim, Nina had taken Kao Vang's file home in the Bronco. The file had been right on top in Nina's briefcase in the backseat—not the enormous claim file, which was safe, but the client-intake file with her notes of her interviews with Kao and the notes regarding negotiations.

Just the notes that could tell Kao's enemies just how much money was involved, and contained her speculations that he knew exactly who they were.

And the Vangs' home address, which they hadn't wanted to give her. Gone.

Nina hadn't called Marilyn Rose at Heritage that Friday. She had waited until now to meet with Dr. Mai. Today she had to tell him. Taking a deep breath of cool mountain air, she strapped herself back into the rental car and drove on.

The Strawberry Lodge was a big, beat-up, green-roofed, barn-like edifice alongside the highway. Usually you could stop for a cup of coffee there, and the place bustled on weekends, even in fall. In winter there was cross-country skiing and sledding down the hill, but today, an off-season Monday, the weekend fun-lovers had deserted. A few rebel stragglers had parked SUVs out front. She parked the rental and went inside.

Dr. Mai waited for her on the wooden deck outside the coffee shop in back. In the near distance, the American River, low in September, more like a creek in this spot, swished along. Dr. Mai wore the same suit, a bit thin at the knees, the same shirt, the same dusty sandals, and that somber visage, the look of the priest who can't understand how the world could have sunk so low. She wondered for a moment what his story was, what persecutions he had endured, what had driven him from his homeland.

No time to find out today.

Sitting across from him at a rustic table, drinking from a glass of water, she gazed out at the scruffy dry grass and trees beyond. "I need to speak with Kao," she said. "He is my client. I'm concerned about confidentiality."

"I am his agent and adviser in all legal matters," Dr. Mai said, not moving.

His demeanor toward her had changed indefinably, and she felt even more uncomfortable, but she had no choice. The information had to be conveyed today.

"You have accepted the offer?" he asked. "The money will be available when?"

"I haven't called the company back yet. The offer is still on the table. Dr. Mai, I—I'm afraid another matter has come up."

Dr. Mai unfolded a piece of paper in English with the signature *Kao Vang* and a date. "Kao Vang instructs you to accept the offer immediately," he said. "This is what you call a power of attorney. I can sign for them."

"Kao Vang didn't write this himself," Nina said. The paper appeared to have been copied by hand from a legal form book and was correct in form.

"He asked me to write it. He signed. He dated."

"All right. We'll get back to this in a moment. May I please speak to you about the matter about which I contacted you?" They had moved somehow to a very formal basis.

Dr. Mai pushed up his glasses. "Speak, then," he said.

"Kao Vang's file has been stolen," she said. Keeping the story short and straight, she explained the circumstances. As she spoke, not sparing herself, Dr. Mai's face fell into a grimace of pain and disappointment.

"I am very sorry. I want to say that directly to Mr. and Mrs. Vang," she said.

He waved a hand at her, his face still screwed up with that awful expression.

"What is wrong?" she said.

"Sad how one ill leads to another," Dr. Mai said.

"Where is Kao?"

Dr. Mai closed his eyes.

"Where is he? What's going on?"

"Just get the money to me," Dr. Mai said. "As soon as possible. Kao cannot talk to you right now. Just do what you have promised."

"Does someone know about the insurance? Please tell me."

"I love this family," he said. "Kao is my wife's nephew. My wife died in one of the camps. Kao is all the family I have left. I must support him, but it is sad." He looked out the window, and she caught the same weary expression that she had seen in Kao's eyes.

"Dr. Mai?" She reached over and touched his hand. "Dr. Mai!"

He turned his head toward her and said, "We mean nothing to you. Nothing at all. Just get the money."

"It's not true. I do care. And—and I fear I have—from your reaction I am very concerned. I must know if the Vangs are safe."

"Just get the money. Please do your job. Get the money. Have your secretary call me when you have the money. That is all I have to say."

"Let me help to protect the Vangs. I have a friend—"

"No more of your help." He walked out on her, shaking his head.

9

NINA PICKED UP A SANDWICH in Meyers at the deli and ate it while driving, wondering how long a long Monday could last. A margarita might have temporarily eased her own misery, but that would only lead to more trouble, so she settled for a V8. Although Dr. Mai's reaction had not been entirely unexpected, his vehemence unsettled her. To prep herself for her next appointment with the girls from the campground, she turned into the Starlake Building parking lot, mentally rehashing the meeting she had hosted in her office with Brandy and Angel four days before, on Thursday.

The two women had shown up at Nina's office for an emergency appointment late in the afternoon. Although they refused to say why they needed to see her so hastily, Sandy squeezed them in before leaving to run an errand. "The girl that called sounded scared. Terrified."

"An abusive husband?" Nina asked. Sad that that would be her first thought, but experience taught unhappy lessons.

"I don't think so."

One wore her peroxided hair short in rough layers, the other had swinging shoulder-length brown hair, but Nina needed only one look at their wide gray eyes. "You're sisters," she said, rising to greet them.

"Angelica Guillaume and Brandy Taylor," the blond said, shaking her hand. "Call us Angel and Brandy. Thanks for seeing us on such short notice."

They flopped into the orange client chairs, but Nina could see their casual ease was a pose. The muscles in their identically wiry legs remained tense, as if ready to propel them right back out the door. To give them a minute to orient themselves and calm down, Nina waited while they commented on her view of Lake Tahoe and admired the Washoe baskets on the wall. Nina quickly figured out that the blond, Angel, acted as leader. Twenty-three to Brandy's nineteen, she wore a hip-hugging skirt and a tiny black cotton shirt that stopped just below the rib cage. Her face was in sharp focus: red lips, each lash carefully highlighted with mascara. Brandy, considerably taller and vaguer, wore a cotton floral skirt and loose sweater. She drooped behind her sister.

"What can I do for you?" Nina asked.

"Brandy saw a murderer," Angel said.

Nina pulled out the legal pad. She took notes while they told their story in fits and starts with constant sisterly interruptions. The trouble had started right before Labor Day weekend, the week before.

"Brandy. You can't just leave Bruce and run away to our house every time you have a fight," Angel's husband, Sam, said. "If you're going to marry the guy, you've got to learn to work things out—"

"This wasn't a fight. It's over."

The phone rang, Bruce again. Sam wanted to talk to him but Brandy snatched the phone away, slamming it into the cradle. "This is none of your business!"

"Like hell it isn't!"

At that point, baby Jimmy and two-year-old Kimberly began to bawl. Sam, heading for the bathroom, the Tahoe cabin's only refuge, tripped on a bag of groceries and let loose with a string of shouted curses. The children cried louder.

Angel turned off the kitchen faucet and saved the day, bustling in and plopping the kids in front of cartoons with crackers.

"We haven't had a minute to talk, Angel," Brandy complained. "I have nowhere else to go. I'm sorry if I'm getting on Sam's nerves, but I'm hurting!"

"Don't worry about Sam. He likes you, but he gets cranky when we're all crammed in here like this. Listen, Bran, let's do like we used to when Mom and Dad got weird on us," Angel said. "Let's split. It's a long weekend. Just give me an hour to arrange the kids and someone to cover me at the salon."

Unfortunately, by the time they had located two musty sleeping bags and properly provisioned themselves with graham crackers, chocolate, wine, marshmallows, and sweet rolls from Raley's, the campgrounds at Richardson's, D. L. Bliss State Park, and Nevada Beach were full. The ranger advised them to try the Campground by the Lake, right smack in the middle of South Lake Tahoe.

"Damn," Brandy said. "Why didn't we think of this? It's Labor Day weekend, the worst time in the world for camping. We're stuck in the center of town—unless you want to drive some more?"

"We're not likely to find any vacancies for miles around here and it's actually a really nice campground. Let's see if we can find something. I'm sick of driving around and we still have to put the tent up."

They amused themselves surfing the radio until they got to the campground at the corner of Rufus Allen Boulevard and Highway 50, finding it also full. "Let's take a look anyway," Angel said.

"Oh, forget it. It's getting so late. Let's just go back to your place and try again in the morning. Shoot. Sam's going to hate it if we come back tonight. Did you see what he did when we drove away?"

"He has got a silly way of waving good-bye."

"That was his victory salute, Angel."

"He's just kidding. He loves me madly," Angel said. "I'm so hot he couldn't do anything else. Watch this." She leaned out the car window and gave the ranger on duty at the entrance a sexy smile and a long look down the front of her tank top and they were through the gate without paying the day-use fee in about a second, giggling like when they were kids.

Sure enough, around a bend toward the back, they found a family of five pulling up stakes on a large dome tent. "Ze miracle she is arrived," Angel told Brandy, then, out the car window, "You leaving?"

"Sure are," said the wife, tossing a picnic blanket and cooler into the back of an old blue minivan. The kids were stuffing bags of chips and cookies into brown bags, handing them off like a bucket brigade toward the car.

"Any chance we could grab your spot?"

The wife laughed. "Believe me, you don't want it."

Angel put the car into park. She and Brandy both got out of the car and approached. "Why not? Is it haunted or something?"

"You could say that." She jogged her head in the direction of the next camp over. "Coupla lowlife rowdies."

"They come over here and cause you any trouble?" Brandy asked.

"No. Nothing like that. Drinking, carousing. Using foul language. People like that are trouble, just being alive."

Brandy reached into her purse. "Here," she said. "Here's thirty bucks for your campsite. You already paid, right?"

The woman's face brightened. "Yes, we did. Only for the one night. But not this much."

"We'd be so grateful if you'd just let us camp here tonight."

"Just so you know what you're getting into. You've been warned."

While setting up the tent and bags, they had a good laugh over old farts who couldn't take a joke or a little profanity now and then. Luckily, setting up the tent turned out to be a snap. They saw no sign of the so-called troublesome neighbors and decided the people in the orange tent next to them must have zoned out early.

By ten o'clock, they had a fire crackling, had stuffed themselves full of sweet goodies, and started in on the wine. So fun! Trees and stars surrounding them like comforters, and all of it totally safe, just like summers at camp.

"I hate drinking wine after I eat. You waste the full effect," Brandy said. "Harder to get to that pleasantly blurry, sentimental stage."

"Hasn't stopped you. You have definitely reached that place."

Brandy leaned back against a log and twisted her hair into a bun in back. "What a relief to be somewhere quiet. You know I love your kids," she said, taking a swig from the bottle, "but it's nice to get away."

Angel took the bottle. "I'll drink any chance I get, mainly because I never get any. Two kids put a crimp in your style. You have to be a grown-up all the time."

"Hey, next week's sign for the salon! Don't put a crimp in your style!"

"I like it. Maybe you should try to get a job with that advertising agency you worked at while you were at college—"

"Out of business. I called before I left Bruce."

"Ah, and so we arrive at the night's topic," Angel said. "Why you left. What happened? He's got another girl?"

"Nope."

"You've got another guy?"

"I never!"

"He works too much?"

"I don't mind that. He's trying to gather a nest egg for both our sakes."

"Mom's driving you nuts with wedding plans?"

"Yes, but no."

"So tell, before I slap you silly out of frustration."

"I went off sex."

"What?"

"I can't make love with him anymore," Brandy said. "So how can I marry him?"

"Criminy, Bran. This is serious. Is he kinky? Does he want you to wear rubber strappies and a head thing with studs or something?"

"No. He's a little—old-fashioned. That's one big reason I fell in love with him, you know? It's simple with him. Roses, candles, naked bodies, beautiful music. All the love you want when you want it. You know, Angel, he's my real love. That's why this is so hard."

"Well?"

"Let's just say it's me."

"Did you see a doctor?" Angel asked, really concerned. "Maybe you could take testosterone shots or something. I've heard they make you horny."

"You're the geezer. You're closer to running out of hormones than me."

The flap over the door to the tent came loose in the wind and Angel got up to tie it back down. "Here I come out in the night and I'm forced to drink wine and eat chocolate and listen to insults from my punk sister. Life so sucks." She walked back over to throw a log on the fire just as two faces peered out from inside the orange tent about fifty feet away—a yawning girl with long black hair and a man, unshaven and ragged-haired but a muscular hunk nevertheless. He said, "Get a fire going, woman," but in an affectionate, relaxed voice.

Brandy and Angel broke chunks of chocolate off their Ghirardelli bar as they watched the girl next door pile sticks haphazardly into the fire pit. She saw them watching and gave them a wave. They waved back. She started to sing. "She sounds like a sick cat," Angel decided after they had a chance to listen for a few seconds.

"I did see a doctor a few weeks ago," Brandy said a few minutes later. "A head doctor. He was such a dork. I felt like he didn't take me seriously."

"Bran, don't you love Bruce anymore?"

The wine hit, or something, because Brandy started crying then, big jagged sobs. "That's what really stinks. I love him as much as ever. I just don't want him to, like, touch me."

"Have you told him?"

"Are you kidding! I can't hurt him like that!"

"Aw, Bran, go on, cry awhile. Here, have some more wine." And that was about it, Brandy polishing off the rest of the bottle and crying and saying she loved Bruce, who must be a quickie Dickie, that was Angel's instant speculation, but she was going to wait awhile to tell Brandy.

They went to bed shortly after, just as the fire next door got hot. After another half hour or so, loud music started up at the next site over. They peeked out, seeing a boom box and two floppy figures dancing by the fire.

"How nice for them," Brandy groused, "but isn't the routine you dance first, then crawl into a sleeping bag together?"

"Oh, ease up. It's amore."

Campers from across the way got involved at this point, telling the couple to please turn the music down. They did, and a temporary hush descended upon the campground. Then a motorcycle with an engine like a 747 pulled up. The biker joined the couple. The music went up again, as did, after some time, the voices. Back and forth, something about money paid out, money owed, money not paid out, love and sex and other personal realms. Angel and Brandy listened avidly. Other campers complained again, but gave up when the boisterous campers ignored them. After a good half hour of arguing, a fistfight started between the biker and the camper guy.

"You goddamn lying, cheating, scum-sucking piece of—" *Thwack.*

"Where do you get off coming here with an attitude like that? Phoebe chose me, Cody, not you. C'mon, baby."

"Phoebe's been two-timing them," Brandy guessed. "I think the one who spent the evening tucked into the tent with her is named Mario."

The thunk of a fist contacting skin was followed by a shoving match.

"Round Two, I guess," Angel said wearily. "Well, we were warned. Should we do something? Get the ranger?"

"A hundred people are listening to this. Someone else will get him eventually."

They sneaked a look through the netting, hiding in toward the edges.

"She looks scared," Angel said. "You know what? I don't like the way this looks at all. We should do something."

The studly camper, Mario, shoved by Cody, the biker with long hair, landed against their tent, almost crushing Brandy's leg. "That's it," Brandy said, as he lurched back to the fray. "I'm going for the ranger!"

"They'll see you," Angel said. "I don't want them to know anything about us. Use your mobile phone and call."

Brandy dug around in her bag while the fistfight escalated into a free-for-all just a few feet from their tent. Incoherent screams and cries rent the night. Only Phoebe made any sense at all.

"Help!" she screamed. "Help!"

After the ranger came to bust it up and Cody thundered away on his bike, things settled down at last, the dogs quit howling, and the kids stopped crying, but now neither Brandy nor Angel could sleep. They lay in their bags for the next couple of hours checking their watches and chatting quietly.

"I have to pee," Brandy said.

"So, enjoy. You know where the bathroom is."

"Come with me."

"What?"

"C'mon, Angel. Don't make me go alone. Remember that story Sam told about the night the bears came to your cabin and broke into that refrigerator you keep in your garage?"

"There was only one bear and he was dinky."

"Sam said that dinky bear knocked the refrigerator over, broke open the door, and ate all the frozen meat. When you came out in your nightgown to scare him off, he chased you across the yard. You screamed, too."

"Oh, chill, Brandy. I haven't heard a peep from anything or anyone since the ranger came."

"Please? I'm scared."

They pulled on flip-flops and sweaters, examined the road carefully for shadows, and stepped outside into the stinging-cold night.

Brandy waited for another latebird lady to finish washing up, then used the bathroom in private while Angel stomped the concrete to heat up her toes, keeping a watch outside for bears or strangers or anything at all, but the dark made it hard to see much except lights reflecting off the lake in the distance. Hard to believe they were right in the middle of the city of South Lake Tahoe.

"Gag me," Brandy said, when she finally came outside. "It smelled like vomit in there. That poor woman partied too hearty for her own good."

"She did look terrible, except that I loved her hair," Angel agreed. "Should have stuck to chocolate and wine like us, huh? No ill effects, except maybe that we're jumpy as little bunnies." They walked through the darkness toward their camp.

"Wait!" Brandy whispered suddenly, putting a hand out to stop Angel. She pulled her sister back toward the side of the road.

"Is it a bear?"

"Shh!"

"Let's go. You're not three years old anymore. No need to be so damn scared of the dark."

"Shut up!" Brandy hissed.

Angel shut up and looked in the direction Brandy's nose pointed, seeing nothing.

"It's so dark," she whispered. "What are you looking at?"

Brandy's finger shook as she pointed toward the orange tent next to their site. "There's enough moon to see."

Angel stared but saw nothing special.

"He's gone now."

"Who?"

"I saw someone leaving that tent."

"So what?" Angel said. "When you gotta whiz, you gotta whiz. You're living proof."

"But, Angel, didn't Cody—the biker—leave after the ranger came around?"

"Yeah."

"How come he's back, then?"

"No idea. You sure you saw Cody, Brandy?"

"Unless Mario suddenly grew his hair long, has lost about fifty pounds and gone all ugly, and looks just like Cody."

"Where's the bike, then?"

"He knew he'd wake up the whole camp if he came in on that thing so he parked it out on the street?" Brandy guessed.

They puzzled about it for a minute or two, but the camp remained silent and peaceful, so they went on back to their tent, slept for the few remaining hours of the night, and got up the next morning, deciding to strike out early for a hike up to Beauty Lake and a new campsite at Wright's, out of town and out of the whole city campground B.S.

"They found her body in her sleeping bag, dead, the next morning when the ranger tried to roust them out of the site," said Brandy. "Mario was still asleep, right next to her!"

"You seem sure Cody is responsible for the woman's death," Nina said. She had paused in her note-taking. The office door, slightly ajar, told her Sandy was probably listening.

They stared at her. "Well, heck, I don't think there's much doubt," Angel said. "Cody came back, Brandy saw him. And even a drunk wouldn't jump back into his sleeping bag and pass a peaceful night next to the dead body of his girlfriend like Mario did. If Mario had done it, he would have run straight across the state line, across Nevada, and all the way to Colorado before he stopped to breathe."

"Ms. Guillaume, Angel, you mean to tell me your husband didn't mention a murder at a campground to you over the weekend? We don't get many up here."

"He never saw the story or he would have freaked."

"Why didn't you go straight to the police when you got back to town on Tuesday?" Nina asked them.

"I'm ashamed to say, we don't always read the papers," said

Angel. "We just saw an article about what happened this morning. It's so sad! It's just terrible! That poor girl. Cody must have snuck back and strangled her in the night. Mario was so drunk, maybe he didn't even wake up."

Nina picked up the phone. "I'll arrange for you to speak with the police or the D.A.'s office as soon as possible. They should know what you saw."

"Hold on. Did you read about these people?" Brandy said. "The camper, Mario Lopez, the one they arrested, had just gotten out of prison that day! He's a violent felon. He was in for assault for years. The other guy, Cody, he was in for drug trafficking last year, plus he has a whole bunch of other convictions. The truth is, we're scared to death to tell anybody."

"If I have your story right, no one, except for the tourists you replaced, even knows you stayed at that campground that night," Nina reminded her.

"Which is the one reason I can still sleep at night," Angel said.

"I just don't want to talk to anyone about this until I've had a chance to talk to my fiancé," Brandy said. "So we came here today for your free consultation. Besides, Angel told me all about how you kicked butt in the Misty Patterson case, even though you got hurt in the process. You're tough."

"I'm lucky," Nina said. She touched her hand to the scar on her chest. Did anyone realize how superstitious even the most pragmatic lawyer could be?

"Will it make any difference to Mario if we don't come forward today? I mean, is he in some horrible place where he's going to get brutalized or something?" Brandy asked.

"No. Remember, this man just got out of state prison. The jail in Placerville can't compare to that. But, Brandy, you have to tell the prosecutors what you saw as soon as possible."

"What about the chances of Cody leaving town before I say anything?" Brandy said.

Nina said, "The article mentions the fight, then it says Cody

Stinson has a local friend who says he spent the rest of the night with her. She's his alibi. He's also on probation. Probably isn't allowed to go far. Although I'm sure the police will be questioning him, since they have a suspect in custody, he has no reason right now to worry about getting arrested."

"He will when he hears what Brandy has to say," said Angel.

"We'll explain our concerns about your safety. The D.A.'s office won't reveal your names or anything about what's happened until you're well protected."

"I won't talk. Not until I reach Bruce," Brandy said. "Tomorrow, first thing?"

"You can call him from here," Nina pushed.

"Like I told you, we're at a rough patch," Brandy said. "Bruce and I haven't been speaking, so it makes everything more complicated. After a week of calling me nonstop, he quit answering his phone. Just give me some time. Meanwhile, don't worry. I won't let Mario go down without telling the police Cody came back that night. I just can't do it yet."

"The longer you hold off, the more complicated your situation becomes," Nina warned. She got names, addresses, and phone numbers for both the women. After they left, she tucked her intake notes into the manila file she planned to take home in her briefcase that night. Maybe Brandy would decide she was able to go first thing in the morning. Nina wanted to review her notes and prepare for anything.

The whole story was scribbled on yellow legal sheets and sitting in that damned file, the one she took home that night.

And here in front of her on Monday afternoon sat the sisters, Angel with her platinum-tipped bristles, Brandy with her dimples. But there were no smiles. They said they hoped Nina wasn't too upset that they didn't get back to her on Friday. They had their reasons. They knew she might insist that they go talk to Henry McFarland, the assistant district attorney for El Dorado County based out of Tahoe, right away, but they hoped that wasn't necessary.

Well, they did have to go right away, Nina told them.

"We can't go," Brandy said, tearing up. Nina got up and shut the door.

Angel spoke up, her tone very serious. "Brandy's fiancé has taken off. We have to find him first."

"Taken off?" Nina said.

"I mean, I know he was upset at me, probably, but why would he leave home like that? Angel drove me home to Palo Alto over the weekend so that we could maybe work some things out, but he was gone!"

"We talked about it on the way over here," Angel said. "Bruce took his wallet, but he didn't take his mobile phone. He doesn't exist without that phone. Brandy says he starts yakking on it when he brushes his teeth in the morning and doesn't let up all day long. He took some clothes, but stuff Brandy says he hates." Her voice dropped. "So we had this thought. We're thinking him being gone is suspicious. We're scared. We're thinking, maybe Cody found out somehow and went over to the house and did something. To Bruce. You know?" She put her arm around Brandy. "You know what I'm saying?"

Now Nina had to speak. She said she understood, but unfortunately had to add to their fear. She told them that someone had the file with all their information, the names, the addresses, the phone numbers. She told them that she was worried, too. Their concerns about Bruce just added to the all-around bad news.

Two sets of frightened gray eyes stared back at her.

"I'm going back to Palo Alto tonight," Brandy said. "I have to try again to talk to Bruce."

"Not alone you're not," Angel said. "I'm coming. Sam's taking some time off. He's taking the kids to Oregon to visit his mother. I'm supposed to join them, which I will when I get around to it."

"We can stay at Maria's. Cody won't have that address."

Angel turned to Nina. "We'll make you a deal," she said. "We'll drive back up first thing in the morning. I'll make some arrangements at the salon. We'll meet you there."

"Don't go," Nina said. "Let's talk to the D.A. today. It's not safe."

Brandy's jaw set. Angel looked at her, looked at Nina, and shrugged. "That's the deal," she said. "We'll be careful."

They looked unbudgeable. "My investigator, Paul van Wagoner, will pick you both up at your beauty salon at ten tomorrow morning," Nina said.

"Okay," Angel and Brandy said together.

"Give me Maria's address and phone number."

"No offense," Brandy said, "but you've already got my mobile phone number."

Only after they left did Nina realize what she meant. They didn't feel safe entrusting her with the information. They didn't, in fact, want to pay much attention to her advice at all.

She had lost her credibility with them and they were spending another night on the road. She could only hope they wouldn't look back and find Cody's motorcycle on their tail.

10

AT FOUR-THIRTY that Monday afternoon, while stumbling toward the rental car with the large gift she had just picked up for Matt's wife Andrea's party that night, Nina saw Officer Jean Scholl in the parking lot outside her office. The policewoman stood by while Nina strained to open the trunk of the rental car and ended up dumping the big gift box on the asphalt while she fooled with her key.

Scholl watched, detached, while Nina stuffed the present into the trunk, adjusting it into several positions before it would fit. Only then did Scholl say, "We found your truck. Let's go get it." She led the way to her patrol car, clanking and clinking all the way.

Behind a chain-link fence, the pockmarked, lava-colored sea of asphalt that constituted South Lake Tahoe's impound lot was not far from the police station and courthouse. Officer Scholl, driving Nina in her patrol car, waved to the security man on duty, got out, and used a key to unlock the gate.

"Where did you find it?"

"In the Heavenly parking lot." Heavenly Resort was only a few miles away, straight uphill from where they stood at the foot of a ten-thousand-foot mountain, the highest ski resort this side of the Rockies.

"I spotted it in a nicely painted parking spot at the base of the

World Cup run, not that anyone's skiing this time of year. Lots of hikers and gondola riders leave their cars up there. Logical place to dump a joyride if you don't drive it straight out of town. And then it's pretty easy to catch a ride down Ski Run Boulevard back to town. Or just walk. It's only a mile or so."

The big, dirty SUV looked foreign to her, but the Hawaiian-print seat covers told her that the Bronco was her old familiar mountain buggy.

"Not too much harm done," Scholl said, her finger inserted into a long scratch on the left bumper. "That's old." She reached into her pocket and tossed Nina the metal key. "We found it on the front seat." She sounded bored as ever, but Nina sniffed out the contempt in her words. Officer Scholl didn't bother to conceal her antipathy.

Nina walked around the Bronco, noting the nicks and scratches.

"Any new dings?" Scholl asked.

Her truck led a visibly hard life. Nina couldn't distinguish new dings from old. "I don't know. Can I get in?"

"It's your truck, or so the registration says." She opened the driver's-side door.

"You didn't lock it?"

"The barn door's already open."

I'll say, Nina thought. She climbed in, bent toward the backseat, and began to hunt.

Scholl let her look awhile, then said, "No briefcase, if that's what you're hoping."

Nina sat up, disappointed, rubbing her forehead. "My files?"

"No sign of them."

"Did you dust for fingerprints?"

"We did our jobs."

Nina straightened up wearily.

"What I wonder is, were they ever even in the truck?" Scholl said.

"I told you they were. What do you mean?"

"Maybe you lost the files some way you don't want to talk

about. Maybe they've been lost awhile. Maybe one of your crook clients took them from your office and you invented this cute cover story." She came over to Nina, looking down at her through those anachronistic reflective sunglasses, and said, "Maybe you're lying."

"I resent that. I told you the absolute truth," Nina said.

"Yeah, like you tell the judge the absolute truth about your clients."

"Like you never exaggerated a word in your police reports. You seem to have a problem with me, Officer," Nina said. "But whatever you think of my work as a lawyer, what's happened here is that my truck was stolen and I'm grateful to you for finding it."

Scholl didn't answer. The police radio blasted out a call and she went to answer it.

"I represent police officers, too," Nina called after her.

Nina called Sandy. "No files in the Bronco. But the truck's okay."

"So the files have been stolen," Sandy said. "I never would have believed it. The briefcase?"

"Gone. Thanks for staying late tonight."

"I would sure like to know what is going on," Sandy said. "Wish is coming in tomorrow morning. I cleared the decks for an hour."

"Paul and I will be there. He's driving up from Carmel as we speak."

"Bring doughnuts. Cinnamon-sugar and glazed. Good for thinking."

"Anything else?"

"There's a Minute Order in the Cruz case."

Much too fast. It should have taken ten days for the judge to rule. "Damn," Nina said. "Physical custody to the mother?"

" 'Fraid so."

"Damn," Nina said again. Defeat struck hard. "I'll call Kevin."

"Call later. Andrea called. She says it's okay to come late. You go on over and visit with your family."

•   •   •

A compulsive demon took hold of Nina. After finishing her call, she stopped at the first gas station she saw to fill the almost-empty tank, then ran the truck through the automatic carwash twice. When she got back to the office, she transferred the big box from her rental car to the Bronco. Sandy arranged to get the white sub-compact back to the rental agency while Nina drove to Raley's for cleaning supplies.

After removing the seat covers and tossing them into the back for laundering, she used an entire roll of paper towels and nearly a bottle of ammonia-laden cleaner on the interior. Sandy left for home.

Nina was exhausted, but the Bronco was hers again. Dark descended, and the parking lot emptied. Dinner would be waiting, and she would sit on the old couch and visit with Matt and Andrea and the kids, and gather the strength to call Kevin—who dashed her plans to procrastinate by driving up in an unmarked police car just as she completed this thought.

"Hey," he said, leaning out the window. "Lisa called me to crow. I can't stand this. What can we do now? Where can we talk? Listen, let me treat you to something at that Mexican place across the street. It's true, isn't it? I lost?"

"It's true. I'm so sorry, Kevin, but I have to be somewhere. Of course we'll talk. I'll call you at about ten tonight."

"Just a drink," he pleaded.

"I'm sorry—people are waiting."

"Sure wish I could say the same for my son and daughter."

He had just had the worst news of his life. "I have ten minutes, Kevin," she said.

They crossed the busy highway together, Kevin's long legs in khakis progressing two steps ahead for every one of hers. Taking a booth by a window facing a side road with a glimpse of mountains, they were both silent for a moment. Kevin's emotional hell had hollowed his usually blunt, fleshy face. "I have to hit the head," he said suddenly and left.

She leaned back against the upholstery of the booth and drifted back to an afternoon she and Paul had spent across from his office in Carmel at the Club Jalapeño. He had work to do but blew it off in favor of a long lunch, later walking her down to the beach, removing her shoes, and spreading a blanket on the sand at sunset. She licked the salty rim of her margarita, remembering Paul's kisses, thinking she would see him in just a few minutes. Right now, she wanted him fiercely.

Anything to stop thinking about the files. And the loss in court.

"Bottoms up," Kevin said, returning. He downed half his beer in a gulp. She snapped back to attention. No way could she make this easy on him. "Kevin, I'm sorry. It's true, what Lisa told you. The judge awarded Lisa temporary physical custody of Heather and Joey."

Kevin leaned forward and jabbed a finger into her face. "There has been a huge mistake here," he said. "I mean, huge. They can't get away with it. I'm starting to figure out exactly how I have been abused by Lisa. And I won't be abused. Not by her and not by her stinking lawyer. You know, there is absolutely no justice in this stinkin' world."

"It's very hard, I know, but remember this was a hearing about temporary custody. The permanent-custody hearing is another opportunity."

"That doesn't happen for months. I already waited nine months for the temporary hearing. We both know how the system works. Mom gets temporary custody, the kids get used to her place, they get comfortable, they don't want to live with their dad anymore. They tell the county investigator they want to stay with Mom and the investigator sees, yeah, it's working okay. So now they have a known quantity, the kids are doing all right living with Mom, leave 'em alone, they don't need another move. I've lost, and it wasn't supposed to be that way. Now I don't have anything."

She patted his hand. But he spoke the truth. "I am also very concerned—" she said, then stopped.

"About the file you left in the Bronco? Yeah, I talked to Jean Scholl at the station today. She found your vehicle, no files."

"Yes." Nina looked at the tablecloth.

"You shouldn't have left them there. Easy to lift. Hey. We all make mistakes. I made my own mistakes in my time." He looked to the side, shook his head.

"That's very kind of you to say, Kevin."

"But my kids mean everything to me. You understand?"

"I know how hard it is for you. We'll make sure you get plenty of time with them, I promise. Kevin, I'm going to ask you to do something for me. You should know this could be risky, considering your possible legal problems, now that your relationship with Ali is public knowledge."

"Legal problems?"

"A potential statutory-rape charge."

He flushed red all over. "It won't come to that. It was consensual. She was nearly an adult."

"It doesn't seem likely," Nina agreed. "But you should be thinking about the possibility."

"What is it you want me to do?"

"Call Ali. Jeff Riesner said that someone contacted him. Was it Ali, and if it was, why did she do that? Why, at the very last minute? Would she talk to you about it?"

"Oh, geez. Call her? Her parents must be so pissed. Now that she had to go to court—" He took note of Nina's face and a puzzled expression came into his eyes. "Would it help me get my kids? Could Lisa have stolen my file? It's so complicated. I'm all confused. I get mixed up and I make mistakes."

He has a big heart and a small brain, she thought, then mentally kicked herself. "Never mind, Kevin. It's all right. I'll find out another way. I just want to know if her appearance in court was somehow related to the loss of my files."

"Why? Who cares at this point?"

"Well, there were two other files."

"Oh, right. Big problems for you. Listen. I'll talk to her. I want to talk to her. Don't worry, I'll be careful. I just don't want to make things worse, is all."

"Maybe I'm wrong to ask you, but I think it would really help," Nina said. "You're a police officer, Kevin. You can do this carefully. This might be useful to you in other ways, too. Maybe talking to Ali will help you find out whether the D.A.'s considering a charge against you. And we really need to find out what happened, how Lisa's lawyer learned about Ali."

"Why don't you just ask Riesner?"

"Because he and I have a history. We don't get along."

Darkness shrouded Kevin's face, and Nina thought, I have to be careful not to make Kevin any more angry. She knew it was tricky, putting him in contact with Ali. But she wanted to start fighting back, and Ali was a lead.

Kevin was settling in. He waved at the waitress, who swooped down in a flash.

"Ready to order?"

Nina checked her watch. "I told you. I have to go."

"Don't leave!" Kevin said. He sent the waitress away. "I'm so alone right now. Please don't leave me." He gave her those sad eyes. She could see how he might look in ten years. He would age fast, the slight pouches under his eyes and chin would coarsen his face, the sad expression would harden to bitterness, the extra bulk would lead to a big belly, and too much smoking would lead to wheezing breath and coughing spells when he woke up in the morning.

She hoped she was wrong, that he would find happiness with someone new, that he would see the kids regularly and develop a sane visitation schedule with Lisa. That he would quit smoking. She wished that she could fix all that had gone wrong for him.

But some people never got past the divorce. It cleaved their lives too deeply.

"Call me tomorrow. We'll talk some more," was all she could say.

"I'll walk you back across the street. It's dark."

"Don't bother. It's the middle of town."

"It's no bother."

When they got to the truck, Nina said, "Good night. Try to get some sleep." She touched his arm.

Kevin fell onto her like a drowning man hugging a life preserver. Bending his head down, he broke into heavy sobs. The big cop cried on her shoulder. After a few seconds, she patted his wide back. She got into the truck, putting distance between them, reminding him that they still might turn things around later.

After giving the dog his dinner, she and Bob drove straight to Matt's house, spotting Paul pulling up in his Mustang right out front. Bob ran for the house as she walked up to greet Paul.

He opened his arms and she rushed into them. Her arms went around him and she held him tightly, kissing his slightly stubbly cheek, smelling the leather he wore on cold nights. His mouth was warm and as she pressed against him she felt his instant readiness. He was attuned to her physically, and she, melting against him, was helplessly responsive.

"Paul," she said. She buried her face in his shoulder.

"What is it, honey?"

"Just a hard day. I missed you."

"Me, too."

"I'm afraid I'm starting to depend on you."

"Is that so bad?" He caressed her shoulder and whispered in her ear, "I want you to depend on me."

"All right, then," she said, holding his face in her hands and looking into his eyes. A few droplets fell on them, and she released him slowly.

Paul smiled at her, then turned to the Bronco. He walked all the way around it, kicked the tires, patted its hood. "Good to see you again," he told it as Nina described the impound yard and her words with Jean Scholl. The drizzle turned to rain, and Nina began to shiver. "In we go," Paul said. "There's some kind of party going on in there."

"Wait. Can you help me with this thing?"

He pulled the big box out of the truck and they ran up the steps. Paul gestured toward the mailbox. "Mind explaining the box? And those balloons?"

"You're crashing a baby shower."

Inside the house, they found Matt and Andrea holding court in front of the fireplace, a fire burning, a dozen other people floating like confetti around the room along with wrapping paper, paper plates, and yellow-cake debris.

"Sorry we're late," Nina said, helping Paul to arrange the box within Andrea's reach.

Her younger brother, Matt, and his wife, Andrea, were expecting a third child. Andrea had been married once before and had a child during that marriage, so this would be Matt's second biological child. Since they already had Troy and Brianna, they didn't require one sex or the other, feeling free to root for a different sex each day depending on where whim led them, although Nina imagined Matt probably wanted a son of his own. Wasn't that hardwired, wanting a child of your own sex? When dreaming about another universe, Nina occasionally imagined a sister for Bob, a daughter for herself.

Matt ran a tow business in winter and took tourists parasailing in summer. Nina made sure he carried heavy insurance. He made sure his equipment met tip top safety standards and groaned about the bureaucracy.

Andrea worked part time at the local women's shelter. Matt and Andrea were Nina's best friends. Complicated, loving, loyal people, they had built a true marriage. Matt disapproved of Nina's profession even more than her father did, but most of the time he kept his mouth shut about it.

Matt put a beer in Paul's hand. Paul sat beside him and drank thirstily.

Andrea pointed at Nina's large box. "What did you bring baby?"

"This is more for the parents."

Andrea pushed her curly red hair back from her face and went at the present with a pair of scissors. "I know I should save pretty paper but screw it," she said. "Oh, Nina! Wow! Wonderful! You remembered how I used to rave about these things." She went over to Nina and gave her a kiss.

"I remembered it was the most-used present I ever got."

Someone turned on some music, Burl Ives singing "The Little White Duck." Someone popped champagne and someone else sang along in a pleasing baritone. Children shouted, marauding through the room in bursts.

While Paul, Andrea, and Matt took turns making a mess out of assembling the automatic rocking baby chair, Nina squatted on the floor, remembering baby Bobby swinging away in the dead of night all those years before, his bright eyes wide open, his soft-spun hair, silent as long as the rocker moved. During those long nights of his infancy, she had sat up with him, looking out her window, at peace.

Her mother had given her the baby chair. Funny she had forgotten that. She thought more often of her mother lately, maybe because lately there was always that idea about moving to Carmel with Paul oscillating like static in the background of her mind. The thought came: She would be closer to her aging father if she lived with Paul in Carmel. She would be closer to her mother's grave.

Later, Paul headed for his hotel room at Caesars alone and Nina and Bob drove home at eleven o'clock, beat. "Uh oh," Bob said as they swung onto Pioneer Trail. "I forgot something."

"What?"

"I have an essay due tomorrow."

"Oh, Bob, no. You shouldn't have gone to the party."

"A bunch of kids were gonna be there, Mom. Aunt Andrea asked me and Troy to play games with them and keep them out of the living room."

"I'll write you a note."

"Ha, ha. Make me laugh. 'Bob had to go to a party.' How long since you were in school, Mom? I'm dead. Forget it."

They argued about this until Nina gave in. Back at the cabin, they dialed into the Internet and looked for anything they could find about Thomas Dewing, a nineteenth-century artist.

"He paints women to look like pieces of furniture, Mom."

"How insightful of him. I feel like a broken-down footstool at this very moment. Can we go to bed now?"

But Bob's research had woken him up. He had other ideas. "Mom? Sometimes I miss my dad. I wonder what it would be like. To have two parents in the same place. I mean, that party. A new baby and everything and all of them together."

Instantly, a gap opened in her heart. She thought of the men in her life. Kevin Cruz, the father about to lose his children. Jack, Bob's absent ex-stepfather, and Kurt, his biological father, so far away in Germany. How confusing it must seem to him. How lonely. "Call Kurt," she urged. "It's morning in Wiesbaden by now. You'll probably catch him at home. But make it short, it's late."

Bob made the call, spending nearly an hour on the phone. He would be so tired in the morning. She would set her alarm early to make sure he had enough time to wake up and get rolling. Listening from her bedroom to his pauses and happy laughs, she reminded herself that rates after eleven were the best they would be.

When she heard the thunk of the phone returning to its cradle, she went into Bob's room to say good night to him and kiss him on the cheek. "Thanks for letting me call him," he said, his voice thick with fatigue. "Sometimes I get low."

The words struck like a whip. She said, "Everyone does, honey. You know that, don't you?"

"Sometimes I feel alone. You work so hard."

"Is there anything special you want to talk about?" She thought of Nikki. She hadn't had time to think about Nikki and Bob. "Is everything all right at school?"

"Same as usual."

"Are your friends doing all right? Taylor? Nikki?"

"Screwed up, as usual."

"Then what do you feel low about?"

"Don't worry about it."

"Paul and me? Is that bothering you? Do you want to—"

"Things were easier before. It's more tangled up now. I want to get to know my dad better, but he's so far away and I live here with you. I want to stay on your good side, but you don't like my friends. You need me, so does he."

"I do need you, Bob."

"But he needs me in a different way. You need me to stay your little kid."

"But, Bob, you *are* still a kid."

"Sometimes. Sometimes I'm a man."

"What?" Nina said. She was too tired to deal with that one.

"G'night." He closed his eyes.

"Good night, honey."

She managed to brush her teeth and throw water on her face before climbing into bed. Could it possibly still be Monday? She checked her watch, the modern curse, again.

No. Tuesday had arrived. Maybe she'd get a chance to breathe.

But then she remembered what T-Bone Walker said about Stormy Monday:

   . . . Tuesday's just as bad . . .

11

PAUL PROPELLED A LEG from the Mustang and then a small Styrofoam cup full of espresso he was holding, lid askew. Then the rest of him slid out and straightened up. Not one drop spilled, not that the asphalt of the Starlake Building parking lot would have suffered. The air had that peculiar late-summer Sierra quality of being both crisp and warm at the same time. He checked his watch, saw that it was one minute to nine, and leaned back against the car, planning to spend the entirety of that minute with his face turned to the sun and his eyes closed.

A large indeterminate-model brown car—who made brown cars and why did anyone buy them?—pulled up sedately beside him. Wish Whitefeather was in the driver's seat and Sandy sat in the passenger's seat, spine straight, purse in her lap. Paul saw with a small start that both Wish and his mother had the same profile, strong brow ridge and nose, beetling brows. As Wish turned off the ignition, they both turned toward him. Sandy said, "It's you."

Paul bowed and opened the door for her. "And how is my favorite Washoe maiden?" he said.

"Don't think that's gonna gain you any points." Sandy gathered her coat around her. Paul had noticed that she often wore her coat outdoors, even on warm summer days. Heaving herself out of the car, she brushed out the coat crinkles and adjusted herself while Paul shut the door. "Well, speak up," Sandy demanded. "How was the drive?"

"Long. I wish a big earthquake would come and cram the coast against the mountains so I wouldn't have to drive so far."

"You could always move here," Sandy said. Paul smiled and thought he detected a faint thawing of her expression in return.

"How you doin', buddy?" he said to Wish, who had carefully locked up and was following them toward Nina's office. Wish was still a sloucher, too tall for the rest of the world and trying to blend in. He wore his straight hair longer these days and a loose black sweater contributed an illusion of broad shoulders. At age twenty, he was starting to settle into himself without any of the jaded irony of his fellow MTVers. Paul liked that, liked his straight-up enthusiasm and naiveté, but had to stay watchful when Wish rode with him.

"Real good. Been hiking a lot. Goin' to school. Gave the van a paint job."

"You did? What color?" The van had once been Paul's.

"Brown."

"Hmm."

"Then you don't have to wash it so much."

"So Nina talked you into helping out for a few days?"

"I only have three classes this semester, and a pretty flexible schedule. I wouldn't miss out for anything. Mom says Nina needs help."

"I never said a thing," Sandy said.

"You don't have to say it, Mom. I knew it the minute you told me to get up early and come to the office with you. Don't worry, Paul, you got backup now."

"I feel better already," Paul said.

They went into Nina's office and Nina called from the conference room, "In here." She shut the law book she had been reading when she saw him, looking relieved. New strain lurked in her eyes and she'd forgotten the mascara that morning, a sure sign that the night had not gone smoothly.

She got up. Paul came around the table to give her a hug and a kiss while Sandy and Wish hovered back in the outer office. Nina's soft brown hair swung around her face, smelling like a rain forest, and he rubbed her back through the silk blouse and inwardly cursed her high IQ. Once in a guilty while, a dull-normal version of Nina who didn't have any significant problems or complexity held real appeal. He was not proud of these thoughts; they were as involuntary as the sexual response she aroused when she brushed her hair against his cheek. Lucky for him, she couldn't see into the dull-normal corner of his mind or she wouldn't be looking at him so kindly.

"Thanks a lot for coming," she said. "I know it isn't easy for you to get away."

"Couldn't let you down."

"Hey, Wish. It's good to see you."

"At your service," Wish said, stopping just short of a courtly bow. "I can't wait."

When they were all settled around the long table with their notepads, instead of launching into discussion, Nina did a strange thing. She picked up the cordless phone and punched numbers, a finger touching her lips.

"Dr. Mai?" she said a moment later. They could only hear her side of the conversation. "How are you? Uh huh. Yes, I have some news. We are settling the insurance amount at two hundred ten thousand as Kao instructed through you. Yes." She paused, then said, "That's why I'm calling. Right. I'll have the check this afternoon. But there's a problem.

"A problem, right. I can only turn the money over to Kao Vang and his wife. I'm sorry, but you'll just have to find him and bring them up here. Well, you'll just have to. No, I won't turn the money over to you. I know you have the power of attorney. I can't accept it. I regret that I am unable to accept it."

Her pause this time lasted quite a while. Then she said, "I'm sorry, but that's the way it is. I am not going to go into my reasoning at this time. I'm going to hold the check until my clients are available. Dr. Mai? Dr. Mai, listen to me. Where is Kao?"

She raised her eyebrows and set down the phone. "He hung up. He's angry. I wanted you all to hear me withhold that check," she said. "It may be legal malpractice, but I had to do it. Now let me back up and tell you about the Vang insurance case. Then I would like to know if you think I just did the right thing."

She told a succinct story of Kao Vang in five minutes. For once, she had not prepared the usual written case summaries for them, she just laid things out, ending with, "And that's the first file that's missing. I have two hundred ten thousand dollars that belongs to Kao Vang that I am picking up from the insurance company this afternoon, and I am not going to go through an intermediary like Dr. Mai no matter how many powers of attorney are thrown at me. So. I'd like to hear your thoughts."

"I don't get why," Wish said immediately. "Dr. Mai wouldn't steal the file, would he? He already knew everything because he was there with your client all the time. So why don't you trust him?"

"Good question. I only know one thing. Over the weekend, I lost touch with my clients and that doesn't feel right. I have to know the Vangs are all right. I have to see that for myself, not take anyone else's word for it. And once I hand that check over to Dr. Mai, I will never see him or the Vangs again."

"How do you know that?"

"Because they never wanted to come to a lawyer in the first place, Wish. They aren't comfortable with this system and they don't particularly trust me, I would guess. They want to fade into the woodwork, maybe leave the country. That's fine, but with the file missing and Kao unwilling or unable to talk to me, I have reached a degree of discomfort or concern that is going to prevent me from handing over that check even to an authorized representative."

Wish scratched his head. "You mean you have a gut feeling things aren't right?"

Nina said, "You got it, cowboy. Did someone call someone else with information that was in my file? The guy who robbed his store, the one Kao shot dead—did someone in his family steal my file to get at Kao? Is Kao in danger? Is Dr. Mai legit?"

"What do you think is wrong?"

"I don't know. I've been doing some reading about the Hmong. They've had a hard time adapting to this country, and with California cutting off welfare benefits after two years, Hmong people are going hungry. The violence in their own country left many of them with depression and post-traumatic stress disorder. Hmong men sometimes just die in their sleep for no known reason. It's called sudden adult death syndrome, and the medical guess is that severe and unremitting stress causes it. The women have their own set of problems. They usually take care of big families and do the whole second-class citizen thing, walking five steps behind the men. That doesn't work too well when there's no man to walk behind, for instance."

Sandy said, "But they need that money. And withholding a client's money is an absolute no-no, isn't it? I thought Dr. Mai was all right."

"Maybe he is all right," Nina said. "Maybe he's trying to help the Vangs. Maybe I'm causing them a big problem. I can't help that if they won't talk to me directly." She firmed up her jaw.

Paul said, "I hark back two days to our talk with Jack. Remember? He said the state bar problems usually have to do with money disputes. Have you talked to him about this? You could just pass on the check, avoid any question of malpractice, and flourish the power of attorney if Dr. Mai steals the money. You would be protected."

Nina waved her hand. "True, the power of attorney seems to be legitimate. Paul, would you pay out the money in these circumstances? Did I do the right thing morally? Totally aside from the fact that I'm exposing my own rear end."

Paul sighed and said, "Of course you did, honey. You have Mai's address in Fresno? I'll follow up for you." She smiled and gave it to him. Paul went on, "I need to look at this large claim you put together. Maybe there's some information hidden in a receipt or supplier's note about where the Vangs live."

"Very little of the supporting documentation is in English."

"Can we have it translated?"

"That'll take too much time, Paul. I can't hold the check for very long. Here are the police reports that detail the original robbery and shooting, the second attempt when Kao killed the robber, and the arson. These reports will tell you all I know about Kao Vang's enemies. But first, obviously, you need to try to talk to Dr. Mai."

"Okay. We begin with Mai, who you just jump-started. He's sitting in Fresno right now looking at the phone and realizing that if he doesn't cooperate, nobody will see that money. He ought to talk to us. What else?"

"The man Kao killed in self-defense. His name and address are in the police reports. The name was"—she flipped to one of the exhibits on the claim—"Song Thoj, age eighteen, a known gang member in Fresno."

"That brings up a new set of concerns."

"Exactly."

"I have to agree that I don't think we understand enough about this situation," Paul said.

"So I'll keep the check safe and you and Wish make sure I put it into the right hands, Paul."

"I realize that the main question right now is, where is Kao? But there is that other question hanging fire," Paul said. "Are the bad guys who torched the Vangs' convenience store also the ones who stole the files out of your truck?"

"I hope not," Nina said. She rubbed her forehead and went on, "But *if* they followed the Vangs to my office, *if* they followed me home, *if* they saw files and took them opportunistically, then they would know where the Vangs live. They would know about the settlement money. Which would make an extortion attempt possible."

Sandy stirred at this. "You're suggesting they kidnapped the Vangs because of the files? Then they call Dr. Mai and say, get the money to us and we'll let them go."

"Oh, my gosh," Wish said.

"It's the kind of thought that strikes at three A.M., yes, Sandy," Nina said. "Let's hope it's just another bad dream."

"But who *are* these 'bad guys'?" Wish asked.

"Let me know when you find out."

They took a break so Nina could deal with a couple of phone calls in her office. Wish walked outside.

Sandy sat down behind her desk, slammed an offending open drawer shut smartly, and looked at Paul, saying, "And that's only one file out of three. Now look. Why does she have to dredge so deep? How does a simple insurance claim turn into this? Is it her?"

"In a way, it is," Paul said. "Another lawyer would give Mai the money, make rapid washing motions with her hands, and move on."

"What about if these enemies stole the files?"

"Another lawyer would say, 'Let the police find the files.' And move on."

"She feels responsible," Sandy said.

"Yeah. The advice Jack gave her was, try to prevent harm to the clients. He was thinking about her. But you know, she's thinking about the clients. She does want to prevent harm. Reminds me of another lawyer I worked for once, a big-shot personal-injury lawyer. He'd work the claim for years, never give an inch, throw a thousand curves, wear down the other side until even the big insurance companies gave in and handed him the big recovery. Of course, by then, the client wouldn't need the money anymore, because the client would have gone insane from the endless delay."

"I get you. He won the case but he didn't do right by the client."

"You notice that she talked to Mai first, then asked us what we thought," Paul said.

"She didn't want us to feel like we had responsibility in making that decision not to pay out the money?"

"Yeah."

"Hmph."

Nina came out of her office. "Ready for the next round?" she said. "What are you looking at?"

"A pretty good lawyer," Sandy said.

"Let that be my epitaph," Nina said.

Five minutes later, back in the conference room with a half-dozen doughnuts piled on a plate in the middle of the table, Nina said, "And now we discuss the second file—the Cruz custody case. The players are Kevin Cruz, his soon–to–be–ex-wife, Lisa Cruz, and his ex-girlfriend, Ali Peck." She went through the background and summarized the hearing.

"Ali may be the best lead we have on the lost files," she finished. "How did Riesner hear about her? Did she contact him directly?" She wiggled a chocolate doughnut out of the middle of the pile and took a bite. As she talked, she had been doodling ducks and snakes all over the page in front of her.

"Check," Wish said. He made another note. He had pages full of notes by now.

"We have an address on this girl?" Paul said.

Sandy passed it over, studied the doughnuts, and picked out a glazed one, which she set neatly on a napkin beside her coffee. "Watch out. Alexandra Peck still lives with her parents," she said.

"But Kevin Cruz already lost custody," Wish said. "Aren't his problems too late to fix?"

"At the hearing last week, he only lost temporary custody," Nina told him. "I agree, now that Ali has been outed, the temporary-custody order isn't likely to change, and there's still the possibility of further damaging charges hanging over him. But let's speculate with what we know. Let's think further. How did Ali get outed?"

"Assume the files were stolen to find out Kevin's secrets, you mean," Paul said.

"Okay," Wish said. Relying on a genetically programmed aid to thinking, he was worrying his lower lip exactly like Sandy did sometimes. Paul looked over at Sandy and darn if she wasn't doing it, too. Nina's pen scribbled angular abstracts all over the nice clean page she had just exposed on her pad. Paul noticed that he himself had just polished off his second doughnut. So had Sandy.

They all felt the strain.

Wish finally let go of his lip. He raised a finger. "Mrs. Cruz."

"She hit gold there," Sandy agreed, tearing off another chunk of doughnut.

"Mom, are you sure you want that?"

A dreadful, anticipatory silence descended upon them. Sandy drew herself up slowly. "Sometimes I feel like hog-tying you and leaving you out in the field for the red ants," she said.

"But you said—" Wish blurted.

"Dip him in powdered sugar first," Paul advised.

"But she said I should stop her if she—"

"Nina?" Paul said hastily. "You were saying?"

"Lisa Cruz testified at the hearing on Thursday morning," Nina said. "She could have picked up my truck key lying on the counsel table during a break, or on the ground if I dropped it and she saw me. It's also just possible Jean Scholl, the patrolwoman who found the Bronco, had something to do with it. She was there that morning in court. I saw her."

"Yeah, but how could anyone know you would leave files in there that night?" Wish asked.

"You know what I think?" Nina said. "I don't think anyone deliberately set out to get my files. I think someone found or stole my key and then used it late that night with a vague hope that they might gain access to something they could use against me, or to win a case. Something balled up in the litter, even."

"Sometimes when you're looking for a break, you see a chance and you say, dingdong! This could be my opportunity!" Wish said, still casting a wary eye upon his mother.

"We'll talk to Ali," Paul said, "and do some checking on Scholl."

"I'll tell you who won that day. Lisa Cruz's lawyer," Sandy said, referring to Jeff Riesner. She did not look at Wish as she took a big bite of her doughnut.

"I like to think I would have noticed such a loathsome creature slinking around my driveway," Nina said.

"I still have a good friend at that man's law firm. She eats lunch with his secretary every day," Sandy offered.

"Wouldn't hurt to try to find out what Riesner was doing Thursday night," Paul said. "Check him out, Sandy. But quietly."

"Will do."

"Which brings up a point," Paul said to Nina. "Nicole Zack actually was in your driveway on Thursday night." He angled toward Wish, explaining. "Bob's girlfriend."

"Bob has a girlfriend?"

"Bob does not have a girlfriend," Nina said. "But you're right, Paul. You need to speak with Nikki. She's capable of a joyride."

She handed over a copy of the written statement Nikki had given to Officer Scholl. "The police found no fingerprints, nothing, in the Bronco."

"Impossible," Paul said. "Unlikely, anyway. They must not be looking hard enough. I'll also have a chat with Officer Scholl."

"Oh," Nina said. "I should tell you I told her about these three files."

"Got it," said Paul.

"So Bob has a girlfriend," Wish said. "When I was thirteen, I fell in love for the first time, too. She was a year ahead of me in school, on the track team. Sita, that was her name. She broke my heart and I've never been the same."

"He never could watch a track meet again," Sandy said. "It does something to you." She popped more of her doughnut into her mouth and chewed.

"Make fun of me if you want, Mom," Wish said. "You always put on this big act about not being sentimental. But I heard you crying in the kitchen the night Dad called and said he was coming home—"

Sandy's face began to turn purple and her eyes bulged. Wish watched the changes with an alarmed expression.

"What was that you said, Wish?" Paul put in hastily. Wish seemed unable to take his foot out of his mouth this morning. They all knew how much Sandy hated any mention of her private life. "I didn't catch it. Nina didn't either."

Nina nodded vaguely. Sandy said nothing. She was grimacing and seemed to be building up to something. Paul thought, oh brother.

"Oh, but before you say anything more, Wish, I have a question for Nina," Paul said, trying to deflect whatever was coming. "Um, so, returning to the issue of Bob's girlfriend, didn't you tell me once she doesn't have her driver's license yet?"

"Bob does *not* have a girlfriend," Nina said. "And not having a license isn't necessarily going to stop you from driving. I'd like you to talk to Nikki. Now can we move on? Wish? Sandy?"

Sandy's eyes were still popping. She made a gargling sound. Her hands gripped the edge of the table. Paul thought, this is it. She's gonna explode like Krakatoa. Wish finally did it this time.

"Sorry, Mom," Wish said. "Mom?"

"He's extremely sorry," Paul repeated. "Sandy?"

Nina watched Sandy. They all watched Sandy, waiting for the forthcoming eruption, ready to take cover under the table if necessary.

Sandy coughed loudly into her napkin. She coughed again. Her highly bruised color faded slightly back toward normal.

"Why didn't somebody clap me on the back?" she demanded. "Couldn't you see I was choking? None of you did a darn thing to help!" She glared at them. "Now, what's so funny?"

When order returned, Nina said, "People, File Number Three presents what I think are the most urgent problems. Let's go through this. These two young women, sisters, were staying here in South Lake Tahoe at Campground by the Lake, right off Rufus Allen Boulevard—" She summarized the facts of the campground homicide.

Paul struggled to assimilate it all. He wasn't used to having so much thrown at him at one time. Nina was going to run him ragged with all these people. But he had to agree, with the file gone and Nina's notes on the events of that night gone along with it, Angel and Brandy needed to make their report to the D.A. and the South Lake Tahoe police even if he had to drag them there by their crimped and moussed hair. He and Wish would have to roust them from Angel's beauty salon right after the meeting. Paul liked barbershops with their phallic striped poles and no-nonsense razor jobs where the tacit guy agreement called for lickety-split efficiency, and he couldn't understand why women had such a different take on the same operation. What exactly did women do to their hair that could possibly require an entire afternoon?

"Angel's salon is located in Harveys Casino, in the basement," Nina said.

Paul said, "I think Angel and Brandy have to come first. If this fellow Cody is the one with the files, he'll come after Brandy. It's possible. Telling it all to one of the deputy D.A.'s over at the courthouse may or may not get them adequate protection. Brandy shouldn't be at home alone."

"She's worried about her fiancé," Nina said. "He seems to have disappeared. It's another unsettling event of the weekend that may or may not be connected to the theft of the files."

"It's a lot, Nina. I don't think we can bodyguard Brandy plus look for the boyfriend and get the other work rolling, too."

Nina said, "I have an idea. I'll see if Andrea can put Brandy and Angel up at the Tahoe Women's Shelter. Brandy shouldn't go back to Palo Alto, especially if her boyfriend isn't there."

"Excellent," Paul said. "Give us a chance to try to untangle a few things. The sisters have to come first. There's some major exposure there, and I think it goes beyond speculation." He pushed his chair back.

"We'll crack it," Wish said. He got up and gave Nina a serious nod.

Paul and Wish went outside and slid into Paul's Mustang. Wish drew on his sunglasses and smoothed back his hair.

"Let's roll," he told Paul.

12

DOWN BELOW HARVEYS CASINO, through caverns measureless to man, amid the video arcades and Mexican restaurants and the boutique bursting with burlwood bears, Paul and Wish found a curtain of orange crystalline beads framed by an archway. Beyond that, a door with a glass insert advertised the salon. On the glass, painted in flesh-pink and sea-green tones, Cupid shot an arrow toward filmy clouds shaped into the words Angel's Heavenly Hair.

Wish shoved the beads out of the way and stepped through, followed by Paul, who took a battering as the beads, released by Wish, fell back into his face.

"Oops," said Wish.

The stench of primitive chemistry greeted them as they pulled open the door. A chime rang, unnecessarily announcing their arrival into the small room.

Several female faces turned to look at them, looking both intrigued and astonished. They had entered the forbidden precincts.

A young woman with brown hair, dressed in a long soft skirt, stepped up to a kind of podium. "Um," she said, flipping a notebook open and picking up a pen. "What can we do for you?"

"We're here to see Angel Guillaume and Brandy Taylor," Paul said, handing her his card. "Are they here?"

At the back of the room, a girl with white tips to her choppy hairstyle, a mouth full of pink tissue squares, and hands full of hair nodded so vigorously a few of the tissues flew. "Mmpf," she said. She wore a pale blue apron with a white badge in the shape of Gabriel blowing his horn over her breast. Angel, it said.

The girl who had greeted them said, "I'm Brandy. Why don't you sit down and wait here for a minute." Pretty and young, she curved sweetly enough to guarantee Wish couldn't take his eyes off her.

"My pleasure," he said.

She dimpled at him. Wish sat down on a prissy brass-legged bench in front of a window. He picked up a magazine with pictures of women with long hair, short hair, tall hair, wide hair, but he was distracted, watching Brandy walk away. Paul continued to stand while Brandy took the spike-haired blond by the arm and steered her through a pastel curtained doorway in back.

Angel's the punk star, he thought, making his quick classification. Brandy's the gentle dreamer. Another woman with an angel badge came rushing out from the back, brandishing a pair of scissors like a relay runner who has just been passed the baton.

"I'll finish you up," she told the lady in the front chair with twists of cone-shaped aluminum on her head.

"If I wanted you, Jill, I would have asked for you," said the lady. Jill smiled, bent over, and gave a vicious yank to a metallic cone.

"Hey!" her client said.

"Oh, I'm so sorry. Did that hurt?" She winked at Paul. "How do you know Angel?" she said a moment later. They could all hear the whispered voices rising from behind the curtain.

"I don't. Not yet, anyway," said Paul. "Mind telling me what you're doing there?"

"Frosting," she said, then laughed at his expression. "I'm streaking her hair. It brightens up a dull look. Helps transition ladies to gray."

"You saying my hair's dull and gray?" asked the client.

"Oh, come on. Would I insult you? You're one of our best clients," Jill answered without answering.

"Angel, I don't have all day," called the other woman in curlers. The whispers stopped. Angel came out first, smoothing her apron. She put a hand on the woman's shoulder, said a few words in a low voice, and walked up to Paul, followed closely by the girl in the skirt. "Follow me, okay?"

"After you," Wish said. They all squeezed out the door into the walkway right outside the salon. Slot machines pinged all around them.

"Nina's waiting. We have an appointment set up for you," Paul said.

The two women looked sick. Brandy said, "Mr. van Wagoner, I don't know if we can go through with this. We went back to my house in Palo Alto last night and there's still no sign of Bruce. I'm scared. I don't think we should tell anyone anything. Maybe Cody kidnapped Bruce!"

"And I'm worried about my family." Angel bit her lip.

"What should we do?" Brandy asked, agitated. "Tell the police Bruce's kidnapped? I don't even want to see the police. I want to stay out of this thing. Maybe he's fly-fishing somewhere in Alaska for a few days with some client of his who's got money to burn. That's more logical, more real. That guy, Cody, why would he go after Bruce anyway?"

"Right! He'd go after us!" Angel said. "He won't be thinking about my kids and my husband. They'll be safe because he'll want me or my sister. We want to hide until they all go away."

"Where?" Paul asked. "Where would you go?"

Brandy looked at Paul and Wish. "Somewhere only we know."

Angel shook her head. "I'm so confused. Oh, man, this is the point on TV where people don't tell the police what they know and get whacked."

"Nobody's going to get whacked," Wish said, horrified. "We'd never let that happen."

"You have no choice," Paul told them. "The police can arrest you as material witnesses if you don't come forward. Believe me. Talking to them is the wise thing to do."

"Can't Nina just tell them what we told her?" Brandy asked. "She knows the story."

"You have to tell the D.A. what you saw," Paul answered, tired of arguing. "Let's go."

"And exactly who are you, anyway?" Brandy asked Wish.

"She sent me to protect you," Wish said. "Don't worry."

"Oh. Wow." Brandy gave him a radiant smile and Wish dissolved into his high-tops.

Paul didn't think telling her they weren't leaving without them would improve the situation. "We're here to escort you safely to the police. Once the D.A. has your statement about what happened at the campground, you've done your duty," he said. "You'll be safer. It's like insurance."

"Angel, if you don't come back in here right now," said a voice from inside the salon, "I'm going to get up and walk out of here with one half of my head full of pink curlers, then I'm going up to Raley's and tell everybody there why I look so foolish."

"Coming!" she said. "Look, I have to finish Mrs. Gerdes before I can leave."

"How long will that take?"

"Let's see, finish rolling, then the perm, wash it out, dry it. Make it look outstanding. At least an hour, maybe longer."

"We'll wait," Paul said. "But you'll go?"

Angel looked at her sister, then back at Paul. "Yeah, we'll go."

When Paul's stomach began to rumble as loudly as Wish's, he sent him out for some food. Paul balanced himself on the flimsy bench in the salon and observed Jill's frosting of the coneheaded woman and the manufacture of artificial curls on the head of Angel's client.

Brandy sat with him. She spoke hardly a word to Paul, but she perked up when Wish arrived, slightly bent with the weight of bags full of quesadillas and nachos. They spread the food between them and ate and talked. Brandy asked Wish questions about his studies. Listening to them, Paul learned that she had been a philosophy ma-

jor at community college and that she didn't feel like she belonged in
Palo Alto. She didn't talk about her fiancé, Paul noticed. Wish
seemed to be making a conquest. Or he was being vanquished, Paul
wasn't sure which.

After a while, Angel finished and joined them. They all piled
into the Mustang.

"You know, we always intended to go to the police. We
wouldn't have let that bastard get away with killing her," Angel said
as they drove alongside the lake toward Al Tahoe Boulevard. "We're
just afraid."

"Sure you are," Paul said.

"Why did Cody have to kill Phoebe?" Brandy asked.

"You know why," Angel said. "Sexual jealousy. She was with another guy." Sitting in the front seat beside Paul, she pulled her feet
up on the car seat as if settling down for some titillating gossip. "This
is what we heard. Phoebe is sleeping with Mario but he gets arrested
and lands in prison for a long time, like maybe a whole year," she explained. "He and Cody were old friends from way back, and so
Phoebe and Cody're hangin' out together moaning about poor
Mario. And then one fine night they get—"

"Down and dirty," Brandy said from behind her.

"And Mario gets out of prison earlier than anyone expected,"
Angel continued. "He shows up out of the blue at Cody's house.
Well, it makes sense. He goes to see his best friend first thing—"

"Wanting to spend the night on the couch and collect the
money Cody's keeping for him," Brandy said.

"But Cody's surprised and not that happy to see Mario after all.
He's cagey. He doesn't want Mario to know about Phoebe hanging
with him, so he makes up an excuse and says, 'You can't stay here.'
He swears he doesn't have the money but promises to get it and
bring it to Mario the next day."

"They were in on a drug deal together and Cody held the
money for Mario while he was in prison," Brandy said.

"Taking the rap, I think," said Angel.

"So Mario asks, 'Well, then, where the hell can I go?' 'Cause you have to remember, he's got practically no money," Brandy added.

"So then Cody gives him twenty bucks or so and sends Mario to the campground with a ratty old tent and a bag. Some friend."

"Meanwhile, guess who's listening from somewhere behind the drapes?" Brandy asked rhetorically.

"Mario's old girlfriend, Phoebe, who's actually been missing him or maybe is just getting very sick of Cody, his second-rate stand-in," said Angel. "Mario was definitely the better-looking one."

"So Phoebe sneaks out and follows Mario to the campground. And initiates a rowdy reunion. If she'd only known. It's so awful. I guess that's what those other people who had our campsite before really objected to. Probably they were hanging all over each other," Brandy said.

"Indiscreet," Angel agreed.

"So Cody—he came back late at night. And he killed her! Angel, should we really do this?"

"It's for the best, Bran."

They fell silent, both with one arm folded, the other resting under a chin.

Paul turned up Al Tahoe, intrigued and moved by these two young women. Telling the story lightened their emotional load. Nina, the amateur psychologist, would probably say their reworking of these memories helped them to gain control over their fear. And then there was the relationship between them. They were like children of exactly equal weight on a teeter-totter, shifting back and forth in perfect harmony. He sighed, thinking of his own sister in San Francisco. The last time he saw her, he had been in the hospital with a broken leg. The moment he regained full consciousness and saw her there at the foot of his bed, all he could think about was how to send her scurrying home.

"Then Cody showed up," Paul said, prompting them.

"He's got this shattering motorcycle engine. I mean, you couldn't hear a china cupboard collapse over the noise of that thing," Brandy said.

"Or a house fall down, for that matter," Angel added.

"A Harley," Wish said. "Or maybe Kawasaki? They make some really powerful engines."

Brandy, sitting next to him, seemed startled at this sudden show of interest. "Who knows?" she said. "Just *really* loud."

"Cody hops off the bike," Angel said, "and the fighting starts. He's really pissed about Phoebe. He says she's already jumped in the sack with Mario, hasn't she?"

"Which is literally the truth," said Brandy. "I always wondered if those double bags were roomy enough."

"Mario says, 'F-off! She was mine before and she'll always be mine. And by the F-ing way, where the F is my mother-F-ing money?' "

Paul stifled a laugh. Mario's language had even the bold Angel cringing.

"So they got into a fistfight, and I called the ranger and the ranger came and ran Cody off," Brandy finished suddenly. "That's the whole story."

"Except that Cody came back and strangled Phoebe," Angel said.

This time, no amount of prompting could lift the sisters out of their silent funk.

They found Nina leaning against her Bronco in the parking lot at the county offices. She went into the D.A.'s office with Brandy and Angel while Wish and Paul waited outside for a long time.

When the women returned, Angel looked wrung out down to the ends of her bleached hairdo. Brandy had lapsed into introspective gloom. Nina had a court appearance in another fifteen minutes in the building across from the D.A.'s office.

"We have lined up a place for you two to go that's safe," Nina said.

"What?" Brandy said. "I thought you guys said talking to the D.A. was our insurance."

"This is just intensive short-term protection," Paul said smoothly. "The D.A.'s office agrees it's a good move."

"We'd like you to move into a shelter operated by my sister-in-law, Andrea Reilly, at least for tonight," Nina said. "The location is kept very private. They have excellent security, and it's just the spot for you two until the police can arrest Cody Stinson. It's my advice that you go there immediately. They have everything you need for an overnight stay."

"Forget that," Angel said. "I'm sleeping in my own bed tonight. We'll bar the door. Sam's still out of town with the kids, so they're all safe, and I am so tired of running around. We'll be fine at my house." She shook her head and twisted her mouth at the thought. "We're not going to some icky place for abused women!"

"You hired me for advice. Now take it," Nina said firmly. "This is a good, clean place with some wonderful professional people who know how to make you feel comfortable in addition to providing security you need. As long as Cody Stinson is out there, there may be danger for you both. The district attorney's office has placed people at the shelter before."

"No." Brandy folded her arms. Angel followed suit.

Nina and Paul both argued hard, but in the end, the two women, armed with their elbows and stony expressions, formed an impervious blockade against all imprecations.

When Nina had to leave, Paul and Wish offered to take Angel and Brandy back to the salon. Angel announced that she was ready to call it quits for the day. She and Brandy wanted a ride back to the Harveys parking lot to pick up Angel's car, then they planned to head straight back to Angel's cabin. Subdued, they said little about their meeting with the D.A. other than to report that he seemed like a fair man who believed them and now would go out and get Cody Stinson and lock his butt up.

With that hopeful analysis behind them, they clammed up. Wish rose to the occasion, suddenly voluble on several topics, beginning with motorcycle lore, skipping to detective lore, finally landing upon hip-hop music, which sparked some interest.

Paul dropped the sisters at the casino and drove around the corner. A few moments later he watched the two jump into Angel's car. The women drove off into the late-afternoon traffic. Paul followed behind a couple of cars.

"We'll escort them safely home," Paul said. "I'm thinking we'll sit on their curb tonight."

"Well, sure. They're in danger."

The sisters passed the turnoff at Al Tahoe that would lead to Pioneer Trail. At the Y intersection, Angel swung the Echo right. Brandy held a small purple mobile phone to her ear. Holding tight with one hand to the oh-shit bar above the door to keep herself steady against Angel's erratic driving style, she talked. Since Paul knew she lived on Blackfoot Avenue about two miles west of Nina's, he also knew that they were not, as advertised, going directly back to Angel's.

At Camp Richardson, the Echo swerved right. Paul narrowly avoided missing the entrance. The dapper little car jaunted all the way to the end of the narrow camp road, past the one-room cabins lining it, and stopped in a marked spot at the end where the asphalt broadened. Paul and Wish followed a few seconds later.

The girls had landed at the Beacon Bar and Grill. Paul heard them ordering espressos while he and Wish hunted for a table where they could observe without being noticed. They ordered iced tea, which arrived in wet, cold glasses. Wish busied himself with a multitude of sugar packets while Paul squeezed his lemon slice.

At this late hour, Lake Tahoe rippled in a steady breeze. Gulls coasted above. Even the narrow stretch of beach sand wore a glaze of tiny airborne granules. Umbrellas above the tables adjusted dangerously. Behind Mount Tallac the sun slipped low and the sky shifted from azure to indigo. The wind hushed, bringing that moment of quiet before the onset of evening.

The girls packed away two hot drinks each rather quickly, checked their watches for the time, and with what must have been a zinging buzz, left a pile of one-dollar bills on the table and set off down the beach at a near run. Paul and Wish established a slightly more leisurely pace but stayed close. "Getting some exercise," Wish guessed, "staying fit."

"They're meeting someone."

"Ah. The phone call. The time."

"Right."

The sisters walked west toward Kiva Beach, passed by a succession of joggers and bikes until Beach Road ended, then entered that sparser realm just a few steps past all public areas where only the intrepid ventured. Trees crept closer to the edge of the water, their long shadows casting triangles, blotting the beach.

"Who could they be meeting?"

"If I were to guess," Paul said, "I'd say Brandy's boyfriend, Bruce, is supposed to appear."

The women stopped suddenly, turned away from the lake, then stepped into a black patch of shade and ducked into the woods.

"You don't think he will?"

"Damn!" Paul said, breaking into a trot, then a run as a shout, then a scream rode toward them.

"Wish and Paul saved our lives," Brandy said, sobbing in Nina's office a half hour later. Nina had stayed late after receiving Paul's urgent call. "If they hadn't happened to be walking along the beach at the same exact time—"

Angel put a hand on her sister's head. "Bran, wake up, they didn't happen to be there." She looked up at Paul. "You followed us."

"Exactly what happened?" Nina asked.

"Brandy got a phone call while we were going home from a guy that said he was a friend of Bruce's, that he had asked this guy to call and let Brandy know he would meet her at Kiva Beach at a certain time."

"You weren't suspicious?" Nina asked.

"Of Bruce? He didn't have his cell phone. That's unusual, but not impossible. And I always thought he might follow Bran up here."

"Why the beach?"

"He said he wanted a quiet spot for them to talk. It's a public place, you know," Angel said. "I wasn't about to let her go alone, even though she told me not to come."

"We walked along the beach," Brandy said, "then we heard someone calling us from the trees. It was windy—not like you could identify a voice. Anyway, even if it hadn't been Bruce's voice, when someone says, 'Over here,' you go over there."

Paul coughed and shook his head in the direction of the floor.

"And he leaped out at us like—like a rabid dog," Brandy finished, "a wild creature. Angel tried to jump him, so he knocked her down right away, the entire time just jabbering. I screamed and tried to fight him. He grabbed me from behind but before he could do anything else, Wish and Paul ran up and pulled him off me. I—I—"

"She was screaming her head off," Angel said. "So was I. Paul wanted to know were we okay, but it took us a minute to realize there was no blood anywhere on us. Not even a nick. We were so lucky."

"That wasn't luck," Brandy said. "Wish and Paul being there wasn't luck at all."

"He got away," Paul said, and a world of disappointment underlaid his words.

"You recognized him?"

Paul nodded. "Same as the guy in the paper, Cody Stinson."

Wish said matter-of-factly, "It was definitely a Harley chopper. Heard it first, and glimpsed him taking off."

"I tried to get them to see a doctor but they refused. We have agreed they'll spend the night at the women's shelter. They wanted to come here first," Paul said.

"Yes," said Angel, turning her attention back to Nina, "because any way you look at it, Cody would never have come after us if you hadn't lost that file."

"It sounds mean, but yes," Brandy said, "a man attacked us today, and it's all your fault."

"He's out there, and you know what?" Angel asked. "He wants my sister dead."

"So our question is—"

"What are you going to do about it?"

13

THEY DON'T HANG PEOPLE in Old Hangtown anymore. They don't even call it that anymore; it has mutated into the innocuous foothill resort town of Placerville where they pop the accused into the sleek new El Dorado County Jail, all very civilized.

On Wednesday afternoon, Paul exited and drove uphill past swatches of red dirt to Forni Road and parked in the second parking lot. He followed a long concrete walkway inside to the blue-and-white-painted glass-walled entry of a brick building that resembled a college campus. Only a closer view to the left of the main building, behind barbed-wire-topped fencing, exposed slitted windows that revealed its true purpose.

He walked into a blue-and-white room on a color-coordinated white vinyl tile floor speckled with blue toward the reception area behind glass at the right, wondering what considerations determined decor for a place that housed criminals. Were these two colors thought to be neutral? Upbeat? Tranquilizing? He spoke into a metal disk-shaped speaker in the center of the glass, signed paperwork, and slipped it through the slot below. The clerk directed him first to a set of blue-and-chrome chairs permanently attached in rows balanced on one bent leg apiece where he waited for a few minutes. Then the clerk moved a hand toward him, allowing him through the door and into the windowless bowels of the building. A green stripe led the way.

A young man wearing a blue shirt that strained to cover a muscular build entered the visitors' room and sat down across from Paul. Paul introduced himself as an investigator for attorney Nina Reilly.

"She's not my lawyer," Mario said. "What are you doing here?" A shave and a haircut and a few days in jail had eliminated the unkempt drunk the sisters had described. This tall, strong ex-con had pale green eyes, a mouth with only a hint of meanness in its arc, and an intelligent expression. Paul classified him as salvageable, although he had a long record, a lousy education, and a public defender who didn't return Paul's phone calls.

"I need some information."

"I can't talk to you about my case."

"No, you shouldn't. I'm just looking for information about a friend of yours, Cody Stinson."

Mario sat back and laughed from one side of his mouth. "I thought you said a friend."

"I'm trying to find him."

"So?"

"So I'd like your help with that."

"So what?"

"Don't buck me, man. You talk to your lawyer lately?"

"She's coming in today."

"She's bringing good news. A witness in your case saw Cody come back to the campground the night you allegedly strangled your girlfriend. The D.A. took a statement that may just be your ticket out of here."

"Is this a joke or a trick? Because I don't take kindly to being jacked around."

"It's all true."

"Let me see your license again." He examined it, then said, "You got any cigarettes?"

"Sorry."

"Lay ten bucks on the guard and I don't even care if you are jackin' me."

"I always pay my way," Paul said.

"I'm getting out?"

"I don't know what the next steps are. But Cody's looking like the killer."

Mario leaned in toward Paul. "Somehow that doesn't surprise me. Because I never touched her. I've been saying it all along. How'd he do it?"

"Came back while you were sleeping it off that night."

"And didn't kill me?"

"Here you are."

Mario looked down. "I can't believe I was laying right there. I was royally passed out. Poor Phoebe. I ain't never drinkin' again. Now let's think. You all want Cody. I know old Cody, I sure do."

"Cody's made himself unavailable to the police. They can't question him; they can't arrest him if they can't find him. They'll be along, probably today with your lawyer."

"What's your interest?"

"I can't get into that. Going back to our original question, do you have any idea where he might go?"

Mario wiped a bead of perspiration off his forehead with the sleeve of his shirt. "I think I can help you there. Thing is, he's waiting on some big money, supposed to come in any minute. He won't leave Tahoe without that."

"Where would he wait?"

While Paul was down in Placerville visiting with Mario Lopez, Nina scooted out of an appointment to stop in and see how Brandy and Angel were making out at the shelter.

A roomy old vacation house within walking distance of Regan Beach, the structure for the women's shelter had been donated by an eccentric widow, Anabel Wright, a dozen years before. In those years it had provided a refuge for women and children with all sorts of problems.

At first it had been lacking in almost every modern amenity, but the earnest efforts of Andrea and friends over the past two years had wrought big changes. A new laundry area attached to the kitchen had been built with two washers and dryers. New donated counter-tops and cabinets had been installed by skilled women who had vol-unteered labor on the project. A forest-green trim on the windows spiffed up the wood exterior without making any statements except that this was a well-kept property. Inside, gracious Arts and Crafts–style wooden furniture, more donations from wealthy patrons and grateful former clients, gave the living room the character of a charming mountain lodge, and due to the goodness of a group of re-tirees, every bedroom now sported a homemade quilt.

Andrea had decided to work part-time months before she even knew she was pregnant and Nina knew she was loving spending more time at home with her children, but she was there today to greet Nina and show her where to find Brandy and Angel, in the basement recre-ation room engaged in a savage game of foosball. Insults flew between the two of them as they flipped and thwacked the sturdy plastic char-acters. While Andrea and Nina watched, Brandy, cheeks ruddy with concentration, finally edged Angel out. "Ha!" She threw up hands open wide with delight. "I beat you."

"Cheater."

"Loser."

"Flake. You blew three goals."

"Ingrate. You know I gave you all three."

Brandy noticed Nina and said, "Hey! You got him?"

"No, not yet. I'm just checking to see if you're okay here."

"Oh, we're fine. Andrea's very nice. The room is great. Every-thing's great except that life's on hold, Angel's husband's upset. She can't go to work. My boyfriend's missing and I can't go looking for him. We're twiddling our thumbs."

"Let's hope it's not for long," Nina said. Her mobile phone rang. With a quick good-bye to the two women and Andrea, she took the call on her way out the door.

. . .

"If there's any possible way, Kevin Cruz wants you to stop by," Sandy said.

"What, now?"

"That's what the man said. He and Lisa are fighting about exchanging the kids this afternoon, one of those he-says-she-says deals. It's his turn to take them for dinner. No, it's her turn. You get the picture. I think she's still there. He said please come to his condo. It's urgent."

From where she was parked, a slip of the blue lake glimmered in afternoon sunshine. "Everything's urgent," Nina said. "Where does he live?"

"Here's the address. You going?"

She unlocked the Bronco's door and jumped inside, checking the time. "I don't have anything else scheduled until three, do I? I'll swing by."

Since splitting up with Lisa, Kevin had rented a condo at Lake Village just across the state line in Nevada, no more than a half mile past the casinos. Perfect for a bachelor, the hilly clumps of two-story buildings offered a generous pool and tennis courts, along with some glorious views of Lake Tahoe, spectacular sunsets, and a green-gold golf course. He had an extra bedroom for Heather and Joey.

Nina remembered his comments on the new bunk beds he had found in Reno at Macy's, not even on sale. He seemed proud to have overpaid, as if he were making something up to his children by repudiating petty frugality.

Poor Kevin, she thought, understanding perfectly. Being a single parent sometimes meant that you did crazy things in the name of making your kids happy, which kept you from drowning in the bottomless well of guilt out of which you could never crawl.

Driving past Caesars, she thought of Paul and the nights they had spent together there, so romantic, in love, in lust, oh, God, she didn't know what to call it. Paul had never been a parent, and according to him, he would never be. If she stayed with Paul, or married him, she would have to resign herself to the fact that she would never have another child.

Why did she keep thinking about Paul? Why was he, a simple man by his own definition, suddenly such an obsession?

Anyway.

She located Kevin's place easily on Clubhouse Avenue, not too far from the pool or the highway, on the shady but noisy side of the street. Lisa stood outside shouting at him. Kevin yelled back. The language was not pretty. The children stood behind their dad, clinging to his legs. The little boy, tousle-haired and flushed with emotion, shrieked, eyes tightly closed, a siren without a fire on this clear, cool day. Silent tears ran down the stricken little blond girl's face. As soon as Lisa caught sight of Nina, she ordered the kids into the car. Kevin kissed them both, wiped their cheeks with a handkerchief, and led them to their mother's car, speaking softly to them, so softly, Nina couldn't hear.

"I'm not through with you!" Lisa said, slamming the door on her kids and jumping into the driver's seat. "I'm not through with either one of you!" Tires screaming, she took off with the children.

Nina parked in a visitors' spot in the lot beside Kevin's building and walked up a winding path through dirt and low bushes up to a set of shredding wooden steps. Kevin now stood on the porch looking at the spot where Lisa's car had been parked.

"You okay?" Nina asked, approaching.

He ran a hand over his short hair. A cigarette burned forgotten in his other hand. Hot ash fell onto the tinder wood of the porch. Nina forced herself not to move, but watched the ash turn from orange to gray before she breathed again. He lifted a Coke can from the ground, poured its contents out into the dirt, and smashed it flat with a fist. "I hate when we lose it like that in front of the kids. Did you see the looks on their faces?"

"Sorry. I really am. It's rough. I think you ought to have me arrange for a civil backup when you and Lisa are making trades."

"Have a cop stand by? I'd be a laughingstock. I know everybody. I don't know what happened, how we exploded. I picked them up from school. I thought Wednesday was my night this week to make dinner and then get them back to Lisa's by eight. But she came screeching over here insisting tomorrow was the night. I decided to let it go just before you drove up."

"I looked at the visitation schedule, and Thursday's your night for dinner with Heather and Joey."

"Guess I was mixed up. Schedules. Every day something different. It isn't good for them. And Lisa. I never saw her blow up like that. She's steamed about Ali."

"Shouldn't we go inside?" Nina asked, feeling the eyes of the neighborhood, but Kevin sat heavily down on the bottom step, and after a moment considering the damage that might be done to her suit skirt, but seeing no alternative except to stand officiously, she sat beside him. He tossed his cigarette into the dirt.

"Fuck it," he said.

"Kevin, before we get any further, did you get a chance to talk with Ali Peck?"

"I called her," he said. "I asked her what the deal was, with her spilling out the story of our relationship at the hearing. I mean, she knew how much that would hurt me. Well, she didn't volunteer anything. She said Lisa's attorney called and woke up her parents first thing Friday morning, then some guy showed up and handed her a subpoena. Her parents called their lawyer. She was told to come to court and she did. She had to tell."

Riesner. Nina's teeth ground. How did Riesner know about Ali? Did he really get a phone call? Where was Sandy when she needed her to say something objectionable?

"He suggested that Ali called him," she said. "He didn't come out and swear it."

His lips formed a hard line. "You're surprised? I thought that's what lawyers are famous for."

Nina said with heat, "Do I do that, Kevin? Do I lie and mislead people? I'm sorry to think you have such a low opinion of lawyers in general. As a matter of fact, I'm proud of what I do."

"Forget what I said, okay? I get those comments all day in my line of work, too. Sorry."

"Oh, well. Never mind."

"You know the upshot, and that's what matters. Lisa's got her teeth in my kids. You say it's temporary. I say, I have one more chance to get them back and I'm giving it all I got. Whatever it takes."

"Does Ali know whether the D.A. is pursuing a statutory-rape charge against you?"

"She said the D.A.'s office talked to her about it. She said she was real honest, and after they talked, they seemed inclined to let it go. She also told them if they went through with it, she'd leave the state. She would never testify against me. She thinks it's offensive that a mature seventeen-year-old can't make her own sexual choices without the law butting in." He shook his head. "Isn't she something? I believe her, Nina. Apparently, they did, too. So I think that gets me off that particular hook."

"That's good to know, Kevin. It must be a relief to you." This news wouldn't help him keep his kids, but at least they didn't have to worry about a wrench flying in from that direction to smash their case.

"Of course, things aren't looking too good at work now they know about Ali. They're investigating the situation before they decide whether to put me on probation or fire me. And there's still Lisa to worry about."

"Maybe Lisa stole the Bronco. Maybe she did," Nina said, half to herself, remembering the coldness in Lisa's eyes as she drove away. Paul had a lot to do but he was going to have to check Lisa out, and soon.

"Maybe she did. I don't know," Kevin said flatly. "It's a fight to the death between us." Hopelessness drained color from his eyes. "I would like to take back everything that's happened. I wish I could go back to those weekends. We'd take a paddleboat out of Zephyr Cove, or rent a motorboat over at the Ski Run Marina and take off with a bottle of wine and this sweet honey bread Lisa made. And peanut butter. Have you ever looked at her lips? So soft," he said. "Malleable. That's a word, isn't it? Maybe I thought that meant she was malleable."

He picked up a forked branch and began to break pieces off. "I thought Lisa and I were together for life. It's ridiculous, isn't it? I can't go on like this, watching my kids cry."

She saw hostility in his eyes. Representing him in his divorce and custody fight meant she represented all that was going wrong with his life. She took information from the alcohol on his breath. That couldn't be helping him with his problems. "Since I'm here," she said, "let's go over how the visitation schedule works."

"It's too complicated. I did crummy in math in high school." His arms crossed over his barrel chest, as if to defend himself. He must be getting cold out here. She thought, I want to leave. What good am I doing sitting here with this guy? He seemed to be working himself up to something. She hoped it wasn't another revelation.

"Would it help if we organized a simple calendar for you?" She tried again to find a practical solution to his insoluble dilemma.

"No."

"What would help?"

Kevin leaned in toward her.

"I guess only one thing," he said, his voice desperate.

"What?" At that moment, she would do anything to make him happy and get him out of her hair. She had never thought a cop would need so much hand-holding.

He answered by seizing her face between two meaty fists, pushing his face against hers, sticking his tongue down her throat, and moaning joylessly.

The whole thing lasted about half a second and she was so shocked it took her that long to fight back. Then she pushed so hard he fell back against the porch railing. He stood up. So did she. She moved away, putting several feet between them. Looking down, she saw that when she pulled away he had grabbed for her, ripping her silk blouse. Her bra was showing. She wiped her mouth with the back of her hand, never taking her eyes off him.

He took a step toward her. She carried a small can of pepper spray in her purse. She opened the purse and put her hand inside, found it, and took it out.

Kevin's face flared red. Apologizing profusely and abjectly, he backed toward his doorway. Making very little sense now, practically babbling at her, he insisted she wait while he looked for a pin for her blouse.

She had been assaulted by him. Had he gone crazy?

"Come inside," he babbled. "You can't drive around like that! Just inside for a minute. I can fix this." He was almost shouting. "Don't go! Please let me make this one thing right!"

"I'm leaving now," she said. "Don't come after me. Go inside, quiet down, and go to bed."

"I'm sorry. I didn't mean—it just happened. Don't look at me like that." He kept calling after her, but she didn't wait to hear any more.

14

After interviewing Mario Lopez at the jail in Placerville, Paul drove back to Tahoe in good time and picked up Wish at Nina's office. Nina listened without much comment to his report, passed on joining them for dinner, and examined her watch, saying she had to pick Bob up from somewhere. She looked upset, but she waved off his questions.

So Paul gathered Wish up from under the iron fist of his mother. On the way out of town, they hit the Coyote Grill in Round Hill Mall, a spanking-new shopping center just over the Nevada state line. Stuffed full, they drove along the eastern side of Tahoe toward Incline Village as dark descended and stars burst into the dark of a moonless sky. Moist lake smells floated around them until Wish complained of frozen ears and Paul pulled over and raised the soft top.

A funky bunch of wooden cabins that had been around for as long as Paul could remember, the Hilltop Lodge loomed over Truckee from a small hill southeast of town. The lodge rooms backed up to views of the town and curved around a central area. They pulled up to a spot not too far from the main building and parked. For several minutes, they watched groups in various stages of happiness laugh, reel, and lurch around the parking lot, in one case piling into a Jeep, deciding not to drive after all, and bumping out down the hill singing, arm-in-arm.

"Looks like a permanent party," Wish said.

Paul got out. "Wait here. Keep watch."

As Wish rolled down the window, Paul could see his breath in the air. In September the weather changed from moment to moment; a cold front must be rolling west from Nevada. Clouds spiraled up in the night sky and a few drops of rain fell on Paul's head as he went looking for the manager's office.

Not surprisingly, no one had registered under the name of Cody Stinson. A minor lie involving a special request for service from the girls in number eight that made the manager's cheeks flame and got him away from his desk briefly meant Paul could check out the register, but no name leaped out as an obvious alias.

He returned to the car. Wish stood next to it, arms wrapped around himself. "Must be under forty degrees tonight," Wish said. "You bring an umbrella?"

"No," Paul said.

"Shoot."

"Tough guys don't use umbrellas."

They watched from inside the car for a long time, using the defroster and heat intermittently to keep the windshield clear and their bodies from freezing. Cars from the highway below whizzed by, and the lights of the town turned cloudy in the mist.

Doors opened and closed. People came and went. No sign of Cody Stinson.

At midnight, Paul told Wish to take a nap. They would need to stagger each other. He had a chart marked, keeping a record of who seemed to belong to what lodging, and by now they had narrowed their field of interest to three doors. He hunched into his jacket and prepared himself for a nightlong wait.

By three in the morning, all celebrations ceased. The dull roar from the town stopped. No more trains flew by on the tracks below; the cacophony of different musical styles from bars on the main street faded. Wish snored in the backseat. Paul pulled his leather jacket tighter.

Door number two opened. Paul, half dozing against the steering wheel of the Mustang, first noticed the absence of light. Generally when someone opened a door, they left a light burning in the room behind long enough to see the way out. This time, only a qualitative change in the black of a shadowy doorway showed him someone was standing there.

Paul reached a hand into the backseat and tapped Wish on the shoulder. "Wake up, Sleeping Beauty," he said in a low voice. Wish opened his eyes with the immediate alertness of the young and slipped silently out of the car to watch with Paul.

The door opened wider and a man stepped out into the light rain, long-armed and lean, carrying a brown bag. Cody Stinson.

They both recognized him. "Now what?" Wish said.

"We call the cops as soon as he goes back inside."

Stinson stretched, and as he approached a pool of light from an outdoor post, Paul saw that he was fully dressed in heavy boots and a jacket.

"He's not going out in this," Wish said. "Not on a bike."

But he was. He pulled on goggles and a helmet, mounted the Harley, and, indifferent to the hellish commotion of its engine or, more likely, proud of it, revved a couple of times to warm it up and took off down the hill, leaving a drizzle trail.

Paul and Wish jumped back into the car. "Should we call the police?"

"And say what? Tell 'em to go looking for a guy on a motorcycle?" Paul asked, frustrated. "We need him back in his room tucked up tight in bed, or somewhere for more than five minutes so that they can swoop down and grab him without a slipup. Oh, great." Pea-sized hail pelted Paul's windshield. His wipers pushed futilely against the onslaught.

"You're not supposed to eat in bed," Nina told Bob, who balanced a bowl of tortilla chips and a plate of salsa on the sheet as he talked into the phone. He wore boxers and a towel draped around his neck.

Lately he had begun taking half-hour showers. As his teen years bore down on him, he had fallen into the grip of passions that he understood no better than Nina, passions about everything, from a certain kind of cereal to be eaten every morning for three months, to blue shoelaces ordered off the Net. He had suggested that he would like to dye his hair. His attention span for school subjects had dropped to about five minutes, but he could still surf the Net for hours with an intensity befitting a brain surgeon.

At the same time the blitheness of childhood left him, he began to suffer from a lack of confidence. He believed that he was ugly and socially maladroit, though he was strong and healthy with no particular drawbacks that Nina could see. In fact, she thought he might, with luck and a softening of his lantern jaw, grow up to be an attractive fellow.

However, there were a few years to go between now and then.

"So bye," he said to the phone, and hung up. He dipped another chip, which dripped onto the sheet. He gave Nina a look.

"Was that a glare?" she said.

"All I did was look at you."

Nina sat down on the bed. "Could I have some?" They ate a couple of chips. Bob wouldn't look at her. He picked up the remote and an ancient episode of *Friends* popped up on cable TV. Nina felt the usual pangs. If only she had forbidden TV, maybe Bob would be happy and outgoing and an Eagle Scout.

Clothes and CDs covered every surface including the floor. She tried not to notice. Her run-in with Kevin had left her fuse short and her nerves shaky. "Was that Nikki?" she said in what she hoped was a casual tone.

"Uh huh."

"How's she doing?"

"Fine." When she waited for more and the silence grew oppressive, he broke, adding, "Working on the Web site for that hard-core band from Sweden."

"Will you be seeing her soon?"

Bob didn't answer.

"Is she still doing home-schooling?"

"What do you care? Is that a problem for you?"

"I was just asking." She had many questions about Nikki but didn't dare ask them. She would have to find out somehow for herself without trampling further upon this mine-filled earth.

Bob munched on another chip. Hitchcock roamed over to his side of the bed and he patted the dog's back.

"So how's the band?"

"Defunkt."

"What?"

"That's our band name. Nikki finally came up with it. Like it?"

"It's kind of unusual," Nina said. "Hard to spell. But—"

"Defunkt with a *k*. Aw, you don't care. Admit it. You don't care about the band at all."

"I do want to encourage your interest in music." But not your interest in Nikki, she had to add to herself. "Any luck finding a bass player?"

"We'll find one. Why are you cross-examining me? I confess, I did it to Colonel Mustard in the library. With a drumstick." He scowled. "This isn't court, Mom."

"Bob, all I was trying to do was—"

Bob rolled off the bed. Hitchcock jumped up to meet him. "Think I'll take a shower. Lay there as long as you want, Mom. Eat all the chips you want." Mockery lurked in the words.

Why, you're getting damn disrespectful, she said to his back as he disappeared into the bathroom. But she didn't say it out loud. A bad influence was at work, no question, and this bad influence was cute, and maybe she'd be famous someday like Courtney Love, but Bob wasn't going to be part of Nikki's band much longer. Defunkt would soon live up to its name, she decided.

Hitchcock took a running leap onto Bob's bed and the salsa did the merengue all over the sheets. Nina pushed the dog off. She wadded the sheets up into a dirty ball and tossed them into the hall. As she remade the bed, Bob whistled in the shower "The Little

White Duck." The children's tune must have stuck in his brain from Andrea's baby party.

She followed along with the whistling. The white duck on a lily pad, visited by a green frog, and then a buzzing black bug.

And along came the hissing red snake to frighten the other critters away.

What snakes were they turning up?

Unable to answer that question, she went back to whistling the innocent children's song with its ominous undertone. Opening Bob's window, she looked out into a late-night storm. Hail battered the roof like falling pebbles.

Paul gripped the wheel, struggling in vain to see something through his windshield. "We have no enemy but winter and rough weather, and man, those are serious enemies." The hail splattered down like a million shards of breaking glass. He could hardly hear himself shout above the racket.

Wish shrugged. "When you live up here, you get used to it. It's almost always sunny, except when it's a blizzard."

"Look, Cody's motorcycle has just the one dim light fading into obscurity up ahead of us. He doesn't care if he lives or dies, and that's a dilemma, because I'd like to go on living at the moment. Where are we?" He gave the wheel a swift tilt to the right, narrowly avoiding a swimming pool in the middle of the road.

"Well..." Wish considered, then peered out the window to place himself. "We're headed east on 267. He skipped a couple of side roads and seems to be going fast—"

"No shit!"

"—so he's probably not planning to stop anytime soon. Anyway, there's no major place to turn off after Northstar for miles. He's heading for the lake."

"If I can stay up with him past the Northstar turn, we'll have a breather, maybe," Paul said, pushing the accelerator down. "Then if he gets ahead, I can catch up without committing suicide."

"Don't you just love a solid V-8," Wish said, smiling, approving of the Mustang's speed.

The speedometer crept up, and Paul used all the old tricks to keep himself from skidding off the road, two hands in proper formation on the steering wheel, cold sweat left unwiped on his brow.

"Most people don't go out on nights like this," Wish observed, arms folded calmly, "even if it isn't three in the morning. More roadway for us."

His nose as close to the windshield as he could get it, Paul cursed. "We lost him on that last curve. So quick-decision time. Turn right at Northstar or keep going toward King's Beach?"

"I don't gamble," Wish said, "not much anyway, but somehow I can't see any friend of his living at Northstar. Too ritzy. I bet on passing."

"Okay," Paul said. The sign indicating the Northstar ski resort area swept by in a blur. Paul stomped down again, the car swerved right, then left, then straightened itself on the road.

Wish flicked the radio on. A static howl filled the car.

Paul flicked it off. "Are you nuts?" he said. "I'm doing sixty on a dark wet road in the middle of a blizzard!"

"I just thought we'd see if there was a weather report on," Wish said reasonably. "Anyway, we have nothing to worry about. There he is."

Sure enough, there he was.

"Ooh," Wish said, as the hail stopped suddenly and a beautiful starry night materialized like magic. "I just got my first good look. It's a 1960s Arlen Ness chopper, customized in the seventies, I'd say. That's a California streetdigger or lowliner, if you're in the market. No wonder it's noisy."

This time, Paul jumped hard on the motorcycle's tail and didn't let go.

Once Cody Stinson's motorcycle reached King's Beach, he slowed down, scrupulously following the speed limit. They followed him through King's Beach to Tahoe City, expecting him to stop, but he never did.

"The scenic route around the west shore," Wish said. "He's heading around the lake the hard way."

"He's nuts. He must have a death wish to take 89. A road designed by Lucifer," Paul murmured, following as close as he could up and down the narrow, curving roadway above Emerald Bay, invisible a thousand feet below in the predawn. "He's going all the way back to South Lake Tahoe."

Stinson passed through the Y intersection at the bottom of the lake, riding along the boulevard.

"Where could he be going?" Wish asked.

"No idea." By now, Paul had been without sleep for a good twenty hours. His mind simmered grayly, like overdone pot roast. "What I know is, Nina wants us to find him and get the police on him, so that's what we'll do the minute he stops for more than ten seconds."

"Uh oh," Wish said, straightening up. Wish, a local, knew the streets better than Paul. Paul knew only that they had made a turn up the highway toward the bright lights of the casino district, wherein sat Caesars, wherein was his bed, a warm place he liked. What he did not know was what subtle confluence of geography in the small town that constituted South Lake Tahoe had prompted Wish to utter those portentous words, "Uh oh."

"So?" he asked as they turned off Lake Tahoe Boulevard toward Regan Beach.

"I thought Nina said this place was really, really private. Somewhere nobody knows about."

"What place?" Paul asked, turning to follow Cody down a small, dark, empty street on the left.

"I mean, he's definitely not the type I would expect to know," Wish said, voice heavy with disapproval.

"Know what?" Paul said.

"Maybe a girlfriend told him or something."

"Told him what?"

"About the shelter."

• • •

There wasn't any way to head Cody Stinson off before he got to the women's shelter, so Paul continued to follow.

"He must know I'm right behind him."

"If he does," Wish said, "he doesn't care."

This seemed accurate. Cody stopped the chopper dead on a side street near the shelter, setting off on foot.

Paul and Wish did likewise, ditching the Mustang at the corner of Berkeley and Alameda. Paul, who hated mobile phones for completely unoriginal reasons, had bowed to necessity and bought one. He flipped it open and turned it on. The phone began its start-up routines.

Hurrying up the street, he heard himself huffing. Every time he came up here, he had to make the adjustment to the impossibly high altitude. He was tired of feeling red-faced, dried out, and oxygen-deprived. He wanted Nina to land in Carmel with him, in the richly oxygenated air at sea level. He wanted her to evacuate from her mountains, her frenzy of trouble, her daily trials, and move into a place where there was the placid calm of ocean and good healthy light.

The women's shelter came into sight, Cody Stinson making headway up the steps.

"What's he going to do?" Wish asked, astonished. "Just knock?"

He did knock. Nobody answered. He wasn't brandishing a handgun, at least.

Paul punched 911 with great deliberation. "If some lamebrain woman has it in mind to answer the door," Paul said, "we take him out."

"Did you bring a gun?"

"No, I did not bring a gun," Paul said. He had, in fact, left his gun behind in the glove compartment. It was the mistake of an amateur, and it made him worry about his edge and lack of sharpness, but by now four in the morning was creeping up, and Paul did not feel at his best. He knew he could take this guy if necessary. He had thirty pounds on him, height, superior physical training, and a will to succeed, he reminded himself.

"How do we take him out, then?" Wish whispered.

"Any way we can," Paul answered.

Cody, at the door to the shelter, had started yelling. "Please, somebody let me in," he called pathetically, pounding loudly. "It's so cold out here."

"Where are these people?" Paul said, giving attention to his inattentive phone. "Why don't they answer?"

"911," a bright voice piped.

He gave brief details, starting right in with the fact that Cody Stinson was a wanted man.

"We'll be there asap," the lady said, *asap* all one word.

"They'll be here asap," he told Wish.

But by now, Cody Stinson, impatient with the lack of response, had decided to take matters into his own hands. He wandered back out into the yard in front of the shelter, picked up a loose limb, held it high in one hand, and broke the front window. "What does it take to get you women's attention, anyway?" he yelled.

A woman holding a rifle appeared in the window. Andrea Reilly.

"The police have been called," she yelled. "If you don't leave, you'll be arrested and charged. Leave now."

"I'm not here to cause anybody any trouble," Cody Stinson whined. "I just want to talk. Are Brandy and Angel here by any chance? I heard they might be."

Paul made his move. He ran up swiftly and quietly behind Stinson and pulled him down. Stinson didn't resist or say a word as Paul straddled him and searched his pockets. Wish came over and said, "We got him, buddy!" and Paul heard the welcome siren of the South Lake Tahoe police at his back.

"Drop the gun!" the police ordered Andrea. "You there, freeze," they advised Paul. He froze, the full weight of his body pressing down on Cody Stinson.

15

AFTER SOME PALAVER, the police arrested Cody and escorted him away, deaf to his protests. "I wasn't doin' nothin'! Hey, I got a right to come here, same as anyone else! Big deal about the freaking window! I said I'd pay for it!"

Back in his hotel room at Caesars, Paul left a message for Nina at the office, deciding not to wake her. He and Wish caught six hours of precious sleep, Paul on the bed, and Wish all over the easy chair. Then they got back into the car. After all the time they had spent driving recently, the Mustang felt about as comfortable as a camel. They wended their way six thousand feet lower in altitude to the city of Fresno, where the Vangs had recently moved, arriving just after the morning rush-hour traffic.

After the Gold Rush, not much had happened in Fresno for about a hundred and fifty years, except that tracts of ranch houses sprouted in place of orchards these days and strip malls lined the once-lazy country roads. Over the years immigrants from many lands had adopted Fresno. They found the pickings good in the agricultural central valley of California and didn't mind the long series of hundred-degree days from August to October. They came mostly from Mexico and Central and South America, as always; they came from Bosnia and the Ukraine; and they came from the villages of Asia, the brave and the desperate, to stoke California's goliath agricultural engine.

The Hmong had arrived during the mid-1970s and after, jettisoned by the war in Vietnam, which had spilled over into wars in Laos and Cambodia. When Laos went Communist, the Hmong went resistance. Preferring their traditional village systems, they distrusted the increasing centralization of power in the lowlands and generally became thorns in the side of the Pathet Lao government. After the U.S. lost the war, many Hmong fled to refugee camps on the Thai border and from there dispersed to new lives in California. Their people mostly practiced Buddhism, Paul knew. Hard-working and intelligent, they had been brutally rushed into the twenty-first century.

WELCOME CENTER read the wooden plaque on the wall of a small bungalow in the old part of town. Letters in a strange and beautiful alphabet just underneath must have said the same thing to those in the know. Paul pulled into the parking lot behind the building.

Inside a fan circulated air. Greenery filled the windows. Hardwood floors and a few straight-backed chairs left the front room austere. In the larger room beyond, Paul saw a large group of preschoolers sitting on the rug, singing a ditty to their teacher, a young lady playing the piano.

"Well, that's sure not Dr. Mai," Wish said, disappointed.

Paul noticed a door marked Kitchen and poked his head inside. A scanty-haired elderly man who met Nina's description of Dr. Mai worked at the sink, washing a huge aluminum kettle, rubber gloves on his hands and a dishtowel around his waist. When he saw Paul and Wish, he dropped the kettle, which bounced onto the linoleum, and looked around wildly for an escape as if confronted by thugs armed with AK-47s. Clearly, he had been through a war. Paul held up his hands, showing his palms in the universal sign that he came in peace. Then he reached into his pocket and presented the old fellow his P.I. card, telling him that Nina Reilly had sent him.

Dr. Mai sagged in relief, catching hold of the sink edge. "Just a moment," he said, and straightened up. He took off the apron and gloves, hanging them neatly over the sink. "She has regretted her decision? You have the check?"

"She has a few questions first."

"No check?" he mumbled to himself, shaking his head as if in disbelief. "After all this, no check. Why come here, then?"

"To find out about the family."

"She doesn't need Kao. She has the power of—"

"She's stubborn that way."

Mai shook his head. "Kao is safe," he said. "They are all safe."

Wish picked up the pan and carefully placed it in the dish drainer. Paul leaned against the wall, put his hands in his pockets, and said, "You know, sometimes when people come to this country it doesn't go smoothly. Sometimes they open up businesses that bad people want a piece of. Sometimes they still owe money to the agents who brought them here. Is something like that going on here?"

"No, no," Dr. Mai said. "It's nothing like that."

Hmm. The old guy dismissed the idea so easily, it had the ring of truth. Paul had developed his own private working theory, sure the urgent need for the settlement money came from a shakedown gone bad. It had crossed Paul's mind that Kao had shot one of the enforcement boys and had his store burned down in retaliation.

Then again, maybe not.

"What are you cooking?" Wish asked Mai.

"Vegetable stew," Mai answered shortly, while Paul wondered how to get the information he needed.

Wish nodded. "Want some help with the chopping?" When the old man didn't say no, Wish washed his hands and picked up the knife and skinned an eggplant with expertise Paul had never suspected he had. Also watching, Mai appeared to relax. "Your mother must be a good cook," he said to Wish.

"My dad taught me. You should taste my dad's chili. My dad, he used to run a store on the Indian reservation where he grew up. Sold everything you can think of, fishing gear—he lived by Pyramid Lake, you ever hear of it?—canned food, toilet paper." Wish finished the eggplant and took a big yellow onion and had the skin off it in half a second. Chopping rapidly, he added, "He never could make a living off it, though. He went into truck driving after that. Gets me thinking about Mr. Vang. I know he doesn't want to see us, but maybe Mr. Vang doesn't know Nina's awfully worried. If only we could tell her he's all right."

Dr. Mai seemed to be mulling this over. Paul decided to lie low and see if Wish could take this situation somewhere.

"You want me to put some water in the kettle?" Wish asked. Mai went over and started doing that. He was thinking, and Paul let him think. Mai let Wish put the heavy kettle on the stove, turn on the heat, and dump in salt. He picked up a potato peeler and handed it to Wish.

"I'm tired," he said.

"Sure." Wish started peeling potatoes into the garbage can.

Mai pulled out a step stool and sat down slowly. "Kao deserves peace. He has suffered gravely. I have stayed with him all this time, through the surgeries and the fear."

"We want to help him," Paul said.

"Kao Vang knew the men who robbed his store."

Paul grabbed the word *men* and filed it. The police reports had only mentioned one robber, Song Thoj, the man Kao shot during the second robbery attempt.

"What really happened, Dr. Mai?" Paul said. Mai shook his head with a look that said, next you'll be asking me to describe the here-after.

"Will she be satisfied if I take you to talk to Kao right now?" Mai asked. "Will she stop this stubbornness, this misguided attempt to help?"

"If he personally directs us to give him the check."

"All right. If we must do it this way. I have to finish the lunch. Come back in an hour." He didn't invite them to lunch, but that was fine, Paul wasn't into vegetable stew, he was into easing Nina's mind about this family so he could run down other leads on the lost files.

"It's a deal," Paul said.

He and Wish went outside to sit in the car, which by now had surpassed the temperature of Mercury's sunny side. The hood had been pocked by hail the night before. That would cost a pretty penny to fix. He turned the engine on and got the AC blowing.

"Nice job softening him up," he said.

Wish, leaning back with his eyes closed, said, "Huh?"

"The story. About your dad and his store. That worked."

"Well, my dad did have a store. But I did lie some."

"Which part?"

"Well, about him becoming a truck driver. What happened was, he fell in love with another lady—"

"You mean, besides your mother?"

"That's what I mean—and then they took off. My mom tried to run the business but she couldn't keep it going. It reminded her too much of him."

"Well, I'll be." Paul knew Sandy had divorced Wish's father, Joseph, years earlier, and remarried him only the year before. He had never heard the details.

"I was still pretty young," Wish said. He reached into his pocket, took out an apple, and bit a huge chunk out of it.

"Damn, I'm hungry," Paul said. Wish offered him the other side of the apple but Paul shook his head. He checked his watch, a Swiss Army Chronograph he had found on eBay. "We're going to have to wait on lunch. I don't want Dr. Mai to change his mind and leave. Did you catch what he said? He mentioned more than one man involved in the robberies."

"So—one is still alive!"

"And he's a good prospect for the man Kao's hiding from," Paul said. "We don't have much in the police reports, but one thing we do have, the last known address of Song Thoj." He consulted his notes. "He lived near the Chaffee Zoological Gardens on Palm. The Hmong have a tight community. The other bad guy might live there himself."

"Do you want to go there after?"

"Maybe we won't have to. Maybe Kao will be fine, and maybe we'll see him and go home and Nina will get him his check."

"Okay. So we wait for Dr. Mai. So I was saying how my mom had a broken heart."

"I always thought she did. I'm glad the story has a happy ending. She and Joseph found each other again."

"Yeah, they're happy," Wish said. "It's a love story."

Paul leaned back and dozed. He was trying to decide who could play the lead part in the movie of Sandy's life. Gertrude Stein would be good, but she was long gone. He thought of the Eskimo receptionist he had seen in recent reruns of the TV series *Northern Exposure*, who might even have hit the forty-something mark by now. Perfect.

His thoughts moved on to Nina, another love story, this one belonging to him. The question was McIntyre. Would he actually make a play for her again? Would she be interested? Jack had always liked women, many women, though Paul had enough collegial loyalty never to mention that to Nina.

Nina could never choose him over Paul. Jack was built like a kiln and as cynical as a bookie. However, she had in fact married Jack once, he couldn't imagine why. The clear thing to do right now was to take care of her problems, so Jack could recede back into her past where he belonged.

"Maybe we shouldn't leave Dr. Mai alone," Wish said. "Somebody might try to kill him while we're sitting out here. Aren't you nervous?"

"Nobody tried to kill him before we got here and nobody's going to try now," Paul said. "He's not a target, he's a go-between. He just needs to finish his cooking."

"But—"

"It's not always gonna be excitement and broken windows and getaways. It's mostly steaming in a hot car, starving."

But hyper as a greyhound right before the rabbit runs, Wish pointed. "Ah ha!" he said, which made Paul jerk upright.

"What? What's happening?"

"He's coming."

The elderly man in shirtsleeves and shiny pants right off the Salvation Army rack exited, holding tight to the rail as he came carefully down the steps. Nothing much was happening, it was just a hot, quiet afternoon in a sleepy town, but Paul felt a thrill, because this particular old man knew something Paul didn't know. Paul started to explain that to Wish, then thought, let the kid figure it out for himself.

That thrill kept Paul in the business, not the tension and aggression and the rush of adrenaline, but the pursuit, the persistent uncovering of the facts, the coaxing away of denials and obstacles, the buttons slowly unbuttoned, the murmured confessions, and finally, the moment of eye-widening, naked, sexy truth. He eyed Dr. Mai and thought, now we get down to it.

Wish climbed into the backseat and Dr. Mai, smelling comfortingly of onions, sat next to Paul as they turned onto the shaded street. Mai's face was thin and bony, the skin not much wrinkled. He led with a long, yellow-nailed finger to the freeway on-ramp, and they moved north on the highway. At the off-ramp he pointed again, and they moved onto the boulevard of used-car lots and strip malls. Paul didn't disturb the silence. He didn't want to accidentally offend, even though the KFCs and Burger Kings they were passing made him want to moan with hunger.

"Here." They turned onto a residential street and Paul stopped while a school bus let off some kids. They scurried in all directions, heavy backpacks flopping. Following the finger of fate one more time, Paul stopped in a driveway halfway down the block at a tract house just like the rest. No car rested in the driveway; the garage door presented a blank facade. Dry grass and a couple of thirsty-looking bushes flanked the front porch. Paul assumed they were expected.

The door opened. A lovely young girl stood there with long black hair, big almond long-lashed eyes, and a pair of brown legs with just that turn of the flesh, that absolutely perfect curve of calf and thigh that Paul had dreamed of every night from the age of thirteen to the age of eighteen. These firm, luscious legs thrust beyond ragged cutoffs, descending into sockless athletic shoes.

"Uncle Mai," she said, and pulled the door open, giving Paul and Wish hardly a glance, her mind clearly somewhere else.

"This is Yang." Mai slipped off his shoes before he went in, which caused a delay as Wish's hiking boots took awhile to unlace and pull off. The girl disappeared and they finally entered a barren living room furnished primarily with a low, round table and big patterned seat cushions. In the window alcove Paul noticed a red cabinet with a mirror and a Buddha statue draped with white scarves and flowers. White votive candles burned and the room smelled of incense.

"Kao!" Dr. Mai called. "Kao!" He said a few more words in his language, the warning tone unmistakable.

A small Hmong man came into the room, wearing shorts and a black T-shirt. He paused in front of Paul, then stuck out a hand.

"Hi," he said.

"As you can see, he's fine," Dr. Mai said.

Kao Vang did look fine, perfectly healthy, a sheen of light sweat over his scarred face, no signs of torture or duress, no cameras in the corners that Paul could see, no shadowy figures lurking in the kitchen. But tension entered the room with him.

"Can we sit down?" Paul said. He pulled up a pillow and found it wasn't so bad so long as he could lean his elbows on the table. "You know who I am?"

"I explained to him," Dr. Mai said.

"He said 'hi' just then. He doesn't speak English?"

"Only some. I will translate."

"Okay. How are you, Mr. Vang?"

"He says 'I am fine.'" As if to illustrate how fine he was, Vang pulled out a pack of Indonesian cigarettes and lit one, looking away from Paul. A moody customer, Paul decided, and not a happy one.

"How is your wife?"

He stiffened. He had understood that.

"Also fine."

"Is she here?"

"She is working so the family can eat while waiting for the check."

"Where does she work?"

"Not far away."

"I see that another young lady is staying here, too."

A few sentences went back and forth.

"Yang is their oldest child. Their son Boun is twelve."

"Nina hasn't met Yang yet, has she?"

"Yang is busy with school." Well, she ain't in school right now, Paul said to himself. "How old is she?"

"Fifteen. Why do you ask about her?"

"No particular reason. Well, Mr. Vang, thank you for seeing me today. We can clear up this problem once and for all."

"There is no problem," Dr. Mai said, although Vang hadn't spoken.

"Is there any special reason why you can't come up to Tahoe to go to the bank with Nina and get your check?" Paul said. The Hmong began talking and gesticulating. Kao and Dr. Mai didn't seem exactly mad at each other, but there was some disagreement.

Wish got up and went over to the altar to examine the statue. He started edging toward the hall door, which was ajar. Yang's listening to every word, Paul thought. An itch rode up his back to his neck and his scalp, and he thought, she's part of this somehow.

Wish pushed at the door. It opened. No one there now.

Dr. Mai said, "Kao has to stay here right now—"

"Why?"

"This isn't the Communists. You don't get to know everything. Kao is very disturbed that he hired this woman lawyer who is keeping his money from him for no reason. Now. The money is urgently needed. Kao is returning to Laos. If I must, I will return to Lake

Tahoe to receive it. Kao asks you to call your boss and ask her to deliver the check tonight or at latest tomorrow."

Paul thought this over. "Let me go outside and make a call to her."

"Yes. Get your instructions."

"I have to explain a couple of things to her when I call."

Dr. Mai's eyes rolled upward.

"This second robber, the one that got away. Has he threatened Mr. Vang?"

"Call your boss! Get the check!" Kao yelled. He had been frustrated into using English. "I will call the police on her! She is a thief!" He held his jaw, moved it back and forth, grimaced. "Look at me! Look what that money is for! It's my money!" He lapsed back into Hmong.

In the back room, Paul heard a sound. Crying.

"All right, I'll go out and call." He motioned to Wish and they walked out into the blazing sun. Paul stood under the garage overhang, far enough away from the house that he wouldn't be heard, and called Nina.

"Honey, this guy Kao is very annoyed," he told her. "Nobody's beating on him. Nobody's got a gun on him."

"Where's his wife?"

"He claims she's working. I could check that out. I could keep harassing this guy, checking everything he says. But you know, I'm not getting the feeling that the wife has been kidnapped. This is not a straightforward extortion. It's something, but I don't know what. And the thing is, they don't want us involved. We could be making things worse. It's his money, right?"

He heard Nina sigh. "If he turns that money over to someone who is pressuring him, Paul—it's his family's future. It's the difference between extreme poverty and college for their kids, a farm wherever they're going—"

"At some point you have to do what he says," Paul said. "I think we have to give him the check. Kao himself is asking for the money, that's clear. Still, there's the young girl. She's a beautiful kid, Nina, you should see her. She was crying in the bedroom. I got one of those flashes you always talk about. That she is involved."

"Where's his son?"

"At school, I think."

"Wonder why I never met his daughter. They brought their son to my office," Nina said, mule-like, still balking at letting the money go.

"By the way, there was more than one robber," Paul went on. "Mai let that slip."

"So Kao lied to the police. Why would he do that?"

"No idea."

"Someone dangerous is still out there and the police don't know about it."

"I would say very simply that Kao wants the money to return to Laos," he said, "maybe because of the second guy. But that isn't all of it. This young girl—"

He almost heard the decision being made during a portentous silence on the line.

"I'm not going to do it yet, Paul. I've got it deposited in my trust account, but I'm not going to write out the check yet."

"So how do I wrap this thing for you? Make you feel like writing the check? What do I tell this angry client?"

"Just one more thing, Paul. Talk to Mrs. Vang and make sure she and her son are safe, too. She's co-owner of the store. She's my client, too. Just do that. Jack wants to talk about all this some more. I'd like to get his thoughts on this before then."

"Find the wife."

"Sorry, Paul. It sounds difficult—"

Back in the house he tried to put a happy spin on Nina's decision. Yes, she would deliver the check just as fast as she could. Maybe even Monday, wasn't that a happy thought? There was just this one teeny detail, he had to talk briefly with Mrs. Vang—

Kao hit the roof. He started shouting again and this time Dr. Mai couldn't calm him down. Walking into Paul's face, Kao poked his finger in Paul's chest. Paul stepped back, telling Wish it was time to go, they'd be in touch. In perfect American English, Kao said, "Get out!" and herded them outside, hard fists at the ready. The door slammed, leaving the lot of them behind, the old man, the angry man, and the teenage Venus of Fresno.

"What now?" Wish said.

"Food," Paul said.

16

ABOUT FOUR-THIRTY ON THURSDAY, Paul's second call came in.
Driving back from court in the nice clean Bronco, Nina had just
passed the Swiss Chalet Restaurant on the left when she heard the
ring from the purse lying next to her on the seat. A warm breeze
pouring through the open windows made it hard to hear.

"Last report of the day," he said. "We're en route to the coast to
get a line on Brandy's fiancé, Bruce, so I thought I'd give you the fi-
nals. First, Cody Stinson has been arrested for the murder of Phoebe
Palladino, as I mentioned in my message this morning. Word is
Mario Lopez will be released sometime this afternoon. Then there's
the Vang file. Mrs. Vang wasn't too hard to track down. We met her
at a fabric store in the suburbs, where she works. She says she has a
new place."

Stuck at a red light, Nina said, "New place? She's not living with
her husband?"

"No, she isn't. That's the key to everything. She's moved out.
She looked fine, by the way. No sign anybody was trying to extort
from her. She says her kids are safe and well and I believe her."

"You got a lot out of her. It sounds like she knows English better
than I thought. But something major has happened?"

"Well, you were right and you were wrong about that. Before
we left town, we talked with a chatty neighbor who is not Hmong.
Found a few things out. The family has split up, but that doesn't

seem to have any connection with the lost file. It's the settlement money. Here's the story. Vang's beautiful young daughter took up with a gang member by the name of Song Thoj who lives down here in Fresno. The Vangs lived at Tahoe at that time, and he spent a lot of time up there."

"The man Kao shot!"

"That's right. Kao found out about the relationship and locked up his daughter. The boyfriend couldn't get to her, so he drove up to Tahoe one night with a gun and shot Kao."

"Why didn't they tell the police?"

"And ruin the daughter's reputation? She's only fifteen. She never could have married. They wanted to save face. That's how Mrs. Vang explained it to me."

"Poor Kao. And his poor daughter." Green light. She drove on toward the office.

"So the parents carried on as well as they could, but Kao started packing a weapon. Sure enough, the boyfriend, Song Thoj, came back again to the store with another guy. This time Kao had to kill Song Thoj or be killed."

"What was really going on in that store? Who was this second guy we're hearing about for the first time? They didn't tell the police about him."

"Apparently, they found it useful to claim these were simply attempted robberies. Then the store was burned down, and I have the impression the second robber was suspected, at least by the Vangs, but they refuse to talk about him and so the complete story about what happened remains murky. The store's burning broke Kao completely. All he wants is to get back to Laos somehow and save his daughter from this den of iniquity. Dr. Mai helped him make the insurance claim to get the ticket money.

"Meantime, Mrs. Vang has lived here long enough to undergo a revolution in her thinking. Turns out she's an excellent seamstress. Hmong women are not supposed to work outside the home, but with the Blue Star situation, Kao had to let her. She's been studying

English and made some new friends, particularly a lady from El Salvador who works with her, a big influence. In short, Mrs. Vang doesn't want to go back to Laos, and furthermore, she doesn't want her children to go back. She wants her son and daughter to be American."

"But Kao—"

"She says he's stubborn. He won't go to the cops for all the reasons mentioned, and he's paranoid. She loves him but she says she won't go with him. She says she'll die if she has to go back to the old life. I have the impression that there is even more in their past—did you know the men often have several wives? I suspect that there may be another wife in Laos. Anyway, there doesn't seem to be any solution except for the family to split up."

"What about their kids?"

"The final decision hasn't been made. Dr. Mai and a few of the senior members of the community are trying to mediate that. Mrs. Vang seems sure the kids will remain here."

Nina said, "It's tragic, Paul. It isn't fair. They have had to go through so much."

"One more twist," Paul said over the phone.

"The money?"

"Right. Mrs. Vang didn't know you had the check and didn't know Kao was trying to collect the money without her cooperation. She didn't say much about that, but I could see the information hit her hard. Evidently Kao figures he's the head of the family, so he'll take control of the money. Then he'll pressure his wife into doing what he wants her to do."

"But this is America," Nina said, "and Mrs. Vang owned half their store. Half the money is hers."

"That's right."

"Thanks so much for going the extra step, Paul. I never would have forgiven myself." Nevertheless, Nina felt sad. The family had cracked. The insurance money couldn't save them as a family. She couldn't fix that no matter how hard she tried.

"None of this has anything to do with the file," Paul insisted. "You had a gut feeling something was wrong and you made me look into it and we prevented a major injustice."

Nina pulled into the Starlake lot and turned off the ignition. "I don't expect to fix all the problems in the world. I just wish I could."

"Take a step back," Paul advised. "One more thing. I also went to the last known address of the boyfriend Vang shot during the second robbery attempt. It's a dump under a freeway overpass. I was looking for information on the second robber. The people who live there now are from Alabama and never heard of the kid or his family. I think, since you knew nothing about a second robber, whoever has your file doesn't know either, so there's been no contact. I don't think we need to worry that there's danger coming from that quarter, and I couldn't do any more on it today. We have two other files demanding attention, so I quit for now. Is that okay?"

Holding the phone to her ear, Nina walked into her building. She waved at the real-estate ladies in their office, walking all the way to the other end of the hall to her office, thinking: Was this new information enough to appease her gut-level worry about this case? How far could she go? She now understood Kao Vang's demand for immediate payment. She didn't like hearing that there was another loose end, a second robber even the police didn't know about—but this could go on forever.

She was satisfied that the Vangs were safe and unthreatened. Her duty now was to give them their money and provide them that resource as they flailed around trying to solve their other family problems.

"Go on down to Palo Alto and turn that eagle eye to the campground case," she said. "I'll tear up the joint check and issue two separate checks, half and half, from my trust account, then have a courier deliver them to Mr. and Mrs. Vang separately on Monday. I just want more time to let things settle in my own mind. They'll get their money. We can't get involved any further. It's already Thursday, so first day of business next week."

"Good plan," he said.

He knew she was delaying, but that was her choice. The jerky, sudden twists and turns of the case continued to make her apprehensive. She needed to sit on the information for the weekend and didn't want to rush into something she would regret.

"Vang won't be happy to be outfoxed by you and the wife."

"Tough," Nina said. "I understand. He's been hurt. He feels the money is his because of his injury. He's the father of the girl who precipitated all the problems and the head of the family. But the money can't make up for all that. The money is for the business, which Mrs. Vang put her toil into, too. So we do this our way. Give me Mrs. Vang's address."

He did.

"Now, there's a final issue. Who took the files."

"Right."

"Do you think, after you visit Palo Alto on the campground case, and after you interview Ali Peck up here on the Cruz case, that you could zero in on which of our three favorite people had means and motive, et cetera?"

"You mean Lisa Cruz, Jean Scholl, and Riesner. You want alibis for the night the Bronco was stolen?"

"We've been stamping out wildfires all over," Nina said. "But overall is this burning smell from the big question we haven't had time to address."

"I'll hang on to the hose until I keel over."

Nina heard the fatigue in his voice. "I'm sorry to ask so much," she said. "But nobody ever said I was easy, even back in the days when I was."

He laughed and she hung up, opening the door from the hall to to the outer office. No clients awaited.

Sandy, bent way over in her chair, filing, sat up when she heard the door. "Good," she said. "Mountain of messages on your desk."

"Anything important?"

"Well, Jack called twice. He said call him back."

Nina closeted herself and answered the other messages. She wrote out two Vang checks while Sandy got ready to go. At just after five, Sandy appeared at the door, saying, "So long."

"Have a good night, Sandy."

"Don't be takin' any files home, now."

After Sandy left, Nina picked up the phone message from Jack, put it down and started to get up and leave, sat down, and picked it up again. She wasn't sure she liked Jack's sudden devotion. He called her almost every day now with thoughts, advice, and reprovals. She had latched on to him in the first moments of panic, and she was grateful that he had been available and willing to help, but...

Putting her feet up on the desk, she thought about the three cases. The Vangs were under control. Brandy and Angel were safe and Stinson had been caught, although Paul still needed to find out where Bruce Ford had gone. That left Kevin Cruz, the desperate cop she couldn't represent anymore. She had cleaned up the harm as well as she could. She could do nothing more for him.

She flashed to the moment when he had grabbed her, to her disgust at his touch and the nascent fear she now felt. What he had done was an incomplete gesture, so fraught, like an obscene promise that must be kept. Why had Kevin gone so far? He didn't need her comfort as much as he needed her skills as a lawyer. He knew that. Then why? She searched but could not find a reason why. She didn't feel able to tell anyone about Kevin. Paul would overreact. Kevin was her client and she couldn't turn on him for one very bad move, go to the police or something. He was already in so much trouble.

She hugged herself, remembering. He could have hurt me, she thought. Then she topped that thought: It's not over with Kevin.

She called Jack. Predictably, he was still at his office. She imagined him on a high floor of the Transamerica Pyramid, at a wide mahogany desk, an Italian lamp's hot halogen rays broiling his Harvard blotter.

"I'm just checking in," Jack said. "What happened with Taylor and Vang?" The depth of his interest extended beyond his casual words. "Did Paul find everyone?"

"Vang is under control," she told him, and explained, then went on to tell him what had happened at the women's shelter with Cody Stinson.

"Paul could have handled that better," Jack said. "Should have held on to the guy at the Hilltop and called the cops."

She knew Paul wasn't happy with the way things had gotten away from him either. "So easy to second-guess people, isn't it?" she said.

He laughed. "No need to defend him, honbun. He's capable of a mean left hook if I get too rough with him."

She couldn't believe he had resurrected the hated nickname of their married days. Through her teeth, she said, "As for the Cruz file, Paul plans to interview Ali Peck tomorrow to try to find out how the secret came out. Kevin's asked her but I need Paul to cover that ground again."

Jack asked more concise questions and Nina responded concisely.

"You still have no idea who took the files?" he said.

"For purposes of discussion, we've narrowed it down to three potentials, Jeffrey Riesner, Jean Scholl, and Lisa Cruz, but you know, Jack, I have stepped on many toes up here. It could be someone I can't imagine."

"Are you putting Paul to work on it?"

"I think—I hope the damage is already done when it comes to those files. But I would like to know. So, yes, within limits."

"The police aren't moving on it?"

"They figure getting the Bronco back is all they can do," Nina said. "The files have no tangible value and I couldn't explain why I was so worried." She told him some more about Officer Jean Scholl and their problematic relationship, but fended off Jack's offer to get emphatic with the local police.

"You sure you have enough help? I mean Paul is good, no question, but Wish, he's not a trained investigator—"

"He doesn't work independently. Paul supervises. And Wish is a friend."

"Loyal, honest, idealistic," Jack said. "When will you grow up and get with the dead dust of this cynical, postapocalyptic world, girl?"

"The day I get cynical is the day I know I'm done. No offense."

"None taken. I think it's essential to be a cynical bastard in this profession, but that's just me. No, actually, I want to say this. I've always been so impressed by you as an attorney, Nina."

"But not as a human being?" she asked, unable to resist the provocation.

"Well," he said, "now that you mention it, there was that kid plumber. That definitely colors my perception of you. You half-dressed on the couch, legs spread. Him on top."

So he had materialized at last, the bugaboo plumber of Bernal Heights, the invisible man that stood motionless between them, undiscussed and misunderstood. "You know, Jack, we should have had this conversation a long time ago. I can't believe you still hold that guy against me. We were kissing. My legs were not spread. We never even—"

"You only stopped because I showed up and scared him off. That stupid earring he wore. You ten years older than him."

The disgust in his voice drove away all her pretense of composure. Her voice rose. "So? What about the fact that you were sleeping with another woman at the time? Huh? I mean, talk about lonely. I was in hell, and I never knew why. I couldn't think what I'd done wrong, except maybe work too hard."

"People ought to restrain themselves, under the circumstances. Maybe you could have talked to me. We were still new together, only two years into it. Maybe our marriage was salvageable at that point, if you hadn't—"

"You cheated. You lied. You blamed me for everything that went wrong—"

"Nina," he said softly, "did you ever love me? Did you ever really love me?"

The question brought her up short. She couldn't think of an answer. She had married Jack for a million reasons: his sense of humor, his passion for his work, his devotion to her and Bob. They had such fun fantasizing a life together in San Francisco.

Bob needed a father.

She needed someone.

"Yes, I loved you. But you made me so lonely."

"I was lonely, too," he said. "What a shame neither one of us had the guts to deal with the problem without all that drama."

Emotion swept over her. "Worse than that. It was melodrama."

"We both screwed up," he said.

Admitting her role in the breakup was hard. The time had come to make peace. Maybe she knew from the first time she set eyes on Jack again they would arrive at this moment, the chance to nail down the coffin lid on their marriage. "Yes," she said finally, "we both screwed up."

"I regretted it right away, you know. I married her, and I knew it was a mistake from day one. I wish you and I had tried harder."

Did she regret the end of her two years of marriage to Jack? The answer came quickly. Not anymore. If she had stayed with Jack, she would never have married a man she had loved with all her heart. After his death, she would never have found her way back to Paul.

"While we were drinking margaritas at Big Sur," Jack continued, "I had a fantasy that you and I might fall into each other's arms again."

"Then you saw me and thought again," she teased, ready to lighten up.

"I saw you and I saw him. I saw the whole damn thing."

"Jack, I'm sorry about the way it ended."

"Me, too, Nina-Pinto. Me, too."

Papers shuffled over the phone on his end as she closed her eyes and sighed deeply.

"So," he said, in one of those rapid turnarounds that made him so successful in his work, "moving on."

"Oh, sure. Of course. We have work to do."

"What were we talking about?" he asked thoughtfully. "Oh, yes. Your abilities as an attorney. To go on, I'm sorry you're running into the usual snags, and I know you won't let it get you down. 'Cause you're one of the good ones, Nina. Destined to debate. Well-intentioned. The old-fashioned, go-for-real-justice kind of person our profession needs. Unlike me."

Not quite as fast to recover from their earlier exchange, she said shakily, "Oh, you're not so bad."

"I am. I am proud to be bad. Luck or talent, I don't care what helps me win, as long as I do. And I'm not afraid to get dirty just for the sake of winning. It's detestable, but it's me."

Suddenly the compliment looked less complimentary, as if Nina had a weak, feminine side that prevented her from dirtying her skirts.

"That's why people are smart enough to hire me and I'm up to my neck in lucrative trouble," Jack went on arrogantly. "P.S., did you know Paul considered law as a profession?"

"What? No."

"Yes, indeed. We took the LSAT at the same time, but he blew it. Hates tests, our Paul. Won't be judged by people he doesn't admire, and those he admires are few and far between. So, keep that in mind when he begs you to join him in Carmel to live a life of leisure as his concubine. He flirted with the law and it slapped him down. Don't let him sabotage you. You're too good to fritter yourself away like that."

"You are so out of line."

"I love the guy. He's my best friend. He has many fine qualities. His relationship with the world isn't one of them. He's brilliant sometimes at his job, but partly that's because he never follows any rules but his own. He made a lousy cop because of it, and I don't trust him as a P.I. because of it."

"Shut up, Jack. I don't want to hear this."

"Be wary and be smart if you insist on hanging with him. That's all."

"Do me a favor. Stick with the legal advice. I don't need you for personal advice."

"Okay. All right. Live with him and be his love, but call me if things don't work out, deal?"

"Enough!"

"Sure. Back to business. All right? Put all that aside for now?"

"Back to business."

"Give the Vangs their money. Potential exposure is that Mr. Vang will be so pissed off that his wife got half that he'll file a complaint with the bar that you withheld the money by a couple of days. He won't look good and you will. I say you have no problem there."

"I'll send it on Monday."

"Don't wait. Do it right away," he said. "As your attorney, I advise you to get this one out of your hair immediately."

She opened her side drawer, looked at the checks, shut it, and opened it again. "Okay, Jack," she said, angry. She should never have mentioned that she was waiting to courier the checks. That had been an unconscious slip, a desire to get his stamp of approval. Predictably, he had picked up on her delaying strategy. He knew her too well. He didn't want to know why she wanted to put it off, he didn't want justifications, he just wanted a clean slate. Was this what it meant, having an attorney? Taking unwelcome advice? Doing things that made you queasy?

Yes. She put the checks on her desk. She would get them on the road before she left today, like an intelligent client following the expert advice of her attorney over her own instincts.

"The sisters. Brandy and Angel," Jack said. "There's more exposure. This suspect, what's his name, Stinson, assaulted the girls on the beach. An argument can be made that Cody heard from the possessor of the files that the girls saw things. But who knows why Cody got on 'em? Maybe some other camper told him something. I can't see a complaint from them going anywhere."

"I know the timing makes it look that way. But let's just stop right here. Listen, Jack. I want you to tell me what you really think. Did the theft of my files cause these innocent people to be threatened?"

Jack gave his answer some thought. No lawyer likes to tell what he really thinks. "Frankly, I don't believe it. I think old Cody found out some other way, from a fellow camper, maybe. I think Kevin Cruz's wife found out about Cruz's girlfriend on her own, too. And I see no evidence any outsider has made any mischief in the Vang case."

"You're not just trying to make me feel better?"

"I think you can rest easy. I don't mean that. Don't rest easy. Be vigilant. Take care of business. But I don't believe you're being set up. Which doesn't mean you shouldn't stay in close touch with me. Every lawyer in California ought to be in close touch with me. You're all gonna get complaints sooner or later."

"But not this time."

"It'll fade. You lost some files. You had to run around. There was worry, but nothing is gonna develop. You know what Mark Twain said. 'I've been through some awful worries, and some of them actually happened.' "

His tone comforted her. He always could comfort her. She had always relied on his strength, his assuredness. "Thanks," she said. "It's a relief to hear you say that." She wanted to believe him.

"Only the Cruz case is still a concern. We'll stay on it. We should get together and have dinner alone sometime, Nina."

"What for?"

"What for? You have to ask? We're old friends back in touch, aren't we?"

"Ex-spouses back in touch," Nina said. "There's a world of difference."

"Let's erase that old garbage, okay? We're past that now. Let's not discuss it again. I'm curious about your life, how you're getting along. I'd like to see old Bob. How about if I come up on the weekend? We'll go for a bike ride."

"I don't think so."

"You'll be astonished how much fun we can have. Come on. Don't be that way."

"Jack—"

"Is Paul jealous of me? Because obviously he has no reason to be jealous," Jack said, sounding irritated. "I think I've made that clear."

This jarred her, and she thought, I also remember how he used to drive me crazy, cutting from one emotion to the other like now, confusing me, never really listening. All she said was, "Gotta go."

She left the office and drove home, thinking about the men passing through her life. Kurt Scott, Bob's father. Jack. Collier Hallowell, her husband for a very short time. Paul. All of them incomprehensible, when you looked deep. Every one so alike on the surface, so impossibly complex within.

What does Jack want with me? she wondered. To get my defenses down, then take revenge? Show me what I missed because we broke up? Wile his way back into my heart for sport?

17

LYING IN BED at the Menlo Park Inn early on Friday morning, forty miles south of San Francisco, half-dreaming, Paul came to a conclusion. He had reached that sensitive state in which a man has to do what a man has to do. An entire workweek had passed, five days, and he and Nina had met like professional cohorts, on courthouse cement, in offices, in rapid-fire telephone conversations that did not contain his preferred content and did not usually end in a satisfying manner.

His frustration was not bearable and, worse, was not necessary. He needed to touch her, to hold her, to smell her shampoo. He needed to see her tonight and convince her to love him forever, to marry him, to run away with him, to make a life with him. He wanted to make love with her and open up a new universe.

To start with, he opened an eye.

To cartoons. Rocky, high-pitched voice of reason, and Bullwinkle, idiot savant, cavorted through an episode loaded with Cold War innuendo three feet away.

"Turn it off," he told Wish distinctly. He might have to share a room, but by God, he would not watch cartoons first thing in the morning.

"Okay," Wish said, wandering off toward the bathroom, toothbrush foaming in his mouth, the television untouched.

In this episode, Boris once again plotted Rocky's downfall. He knew who held the real power. Natasha, as always, went balefully along. Paul pulled a pillow over his head, otherwise powerless to resist. He and his sister used to watch this same cartoon. She played Natasha and he was always Rocky, the intelligent do-gooder, although something perverse in him identified more closely with Boris. "I said turn it off," he shouted through the flimsy brown door.

"Uh, okay," said Wish, returning clean-shaven and freshly scented to press a button on the remote.

After Paul took his turn in the bathroom, they asked at the reception desk for a recommendation and ended up at Ann's Coffee Shop on Santa Cruz Avenue for breakfast.

"So old-fashioned," Wish pronounced, lighting into an impressive pile of pancakes. "People don't hardly eat like this anymore."

"No, they don't," Paul said, making headway through his plate of deliciously greasy potatoes and eggs.

"Great to get a decent night's sleep for a change," Wish said, yawning. "Remind me again why we had to go rushing off to Palo Alto instead of back to Tahoe last night?"

"To find Brandy's boyfriend," Paul said.

Spearing a pie-shaped chunk, Wish nodded. "I guess over the weekend I'll have time to make up some assignments before next week starts."

Paul grunted, not knowing. Of course, Wish's classes were important, but what came first for him was the current pressing issue of the day: Bruce Ford, fiancé manqué.

"Where are we meeting Brandy?"

Did Paul imagine it, or did Wish's ears seem redder than usual?

"I told her we'd meet her on University Avenue. Her boyfriend works near there."

Wish had never, in the two or three years Paul had known him, shown anything but enthusiastic curiosity for any subject at hand. This time, Wish frowned. "You think we'll find him?"

"That's the plan."

Wish sipped orange juice. "Yeah."

"Funny," Paul said. "I get the impression maybe you don't want to find him?"

"Yeah."

"Brandy is pretty, isn't she?"

"Yeah."

They paid for their breakfast and went out into the warm fall weather, directing the car toward Palo Alto, the next town over. "Why couldn't we stay there?" groused Wish as they passed the grand, landscaped Stanford Park Hotel. "Too expensive?"

"Full," Paul said. "Some name-brand politician is giving a lecture at Stanford."

"Oh."

"Plus Brandy said Bruce's mother always stayed where we stayed and that maybe Bruce Ford would think of the place. Too bad we didn't get to try the Hotel California over on California." Wish's oblivious reaction to the suggestion told Paul that he did not even know the song. Paul remembered that Wish was twenty and he was twice that. His good mood evaporated.

"So did you talk to the manager at the inn?" Wish asked.

"I did. No sign of Bruce. He said he'd get in touch if he saw him."

They made a left off El Camino onto University and drove down the tree-lined street until they crossed over Hamilton and parked. They walked south until they came to a three-story building that looked like a church. Wish checked the address, nodded, and in they went.

Brandy sat on a concrete bench near the pebbled stone entryway. She stood up to meet them, all pink and cream and gentle languor. "Bruce wasn't at home, and I already checked his office," she said. "He isn't there either. By the way, thanks for coming." She seemed subdued.

"You're welcome," he said. "Can we see his office?"

"Okay." They took an elevator to the fourth floor. Bruce Ford shared a receptionist with four other loosely associated professionals. The receptionist hadn't seen him in days and had nothing more to report than that "a man came by" before Bruce left. As to the identity of this man, she couldn't say. She described him as "rough" looking, a description that certainly fit Cody Stinson.

"What exactly does your boyfriend do?" Paul asked as they walked the long hall toward a front office.

Brandy sighed hard. "Didn't you know? He's a tax lawyer." Sticking a key into the lock, she swung the door open.

A flatscape of houses with the San Francisco Bay beyond unfolded outside Ford's office window. A walnut desk piled with folders sat in front of the wide window, waiting to be rifled. Brandy went to a small photo on the desk and showed it to Paul and Wish. "Our engagement party." She had worn pink. He had worn a white tux. The man, who was much taller than Brandy, had curly black hair, too long for someone in serious business, and grinned like a winner. His hair blew out in strawlike tendrils from under the breezy arbor.

"Look wherever you want," Brandy said. She sat down on a chair across from the desk. "I don't expect you to find much. Bruce is careful."

Paul started on the tabletop while Wish picked through the contents of the drawers. While Brandy sighed and stretched, Wish's eyes straying her way every minute or two, they conducted a thoroughly professional search of the office.

In the bottom right-hand drawer, exactly where you might expect to find it, Wish unearthed a day diary and started to read it out loud, but as Brandy's brows furrowed, Paul took it away from him and shut it. "We have what we need. Let's see where your boyfriend has gone."

"My fiancé," Brandy corrected, looking conflicted. "We're supposed to get married in June."

"Right," Paul said, tucking the photograph of Brandy and Bruce into his pocket.

He let Wish slip a picture of Brandy from the credenza into his pocket without remark. In the photo, she wore a demure red bathing suit, not a bikini, but the effect was obviously irresistible. Well, what harm could it do? Wherever Bruce was, he didn't care at the moment, and neither did Paul.

They walked up to Il Fornaio for caffeine, coming out slightly brighter-eyed. "Shouldn't we go through his diary?" Brandy asked. "I figured that might tell us where he would be. If he's got another girlfriend, I might as well find that out right now."

"On the relevant day," Paul said, looking at the right page but keeping it well out of her line of sight, "he planned to attend a lecture at Stanford, then go to a French film at someplace called Aquarius."

"He studied French in college. I never did."

"Where did you go?" Wish asked, his notebook and pencil poised.

"Why does that matter?"

"You never know what might be important," he said.

"I went to Mission College down near San Jose. He went to Santa Clara University and got a law degree. Now, are you going to tell me or not? Was he alone?"

"He was meeting someone," Paul said.

"A woman?"

"Someone named Kirby." That sounded safe. That was a male name.

The lines in her forehead cleared. "Oh, Kirby! Let's go talk to him! Of course, I called him already when I called all Bruce's friends. He said he didn't know anything, but he's a pal. He'd lie for Bruce. He's from back when they used to make student films and Bruce was planning to become an auteur."

"I thought you didn't know French," Wish said.

"I only know one line," Brandy said. *"Aimez-vous les pique-niques?"* She said it artlessly, with no awareness of the impact of her words. Paul propped Wish up to make sure he could get out the door without fainting.

Kirby lived only a few blocks away, on a wide residential street lined with soldierly groups of luxuriant trees, in a compact thirties bungalow with a sky-blue-painted porch and generous front yard. Brandy led the way. "Kirby works nights, so he should be home."

"Nice little place," Wish observed. "I might like living in a neighborhood like this."

Brandy laughed. "After you've made your first five million. This house would set you back at least a million."

"How do people make that kind of money?" Wish asked, staggered. "And why would they spend a million of it to live in a house that's half the size of my mom's?"

"Kirby owns a chain of twenty-four-hour printing shops and he lives here because—oh, this is a great location. Between two major airports, beautiful weather, money growing on trees." She sounded tired. "What more could you want?"

"Bruce likes this area?" Wish asked.

"Yeah."

"What about you?"

"Where we live isn't the problem between me and Bruce."

"Then what is it?"

Brandy cast a cold eye on Wish, then Paul. "It's personal." She pressed the doorbell.

A small, sandy-colored man on the sunny side of thirty answered the door after several minutes, his eyes opened only halfway. "Brandy?"

"Sorry to wake you up, Kirby, but it's important."

He opened the door to let them inside, but didn't move past the entryway. Brandy made introductions. After inspecting Paul's license at great length and asking Wish a longer-than-polite series of questions about his role in all this, Kirby invited them to sit in the living room. "You're still looking for Bruce, I take it."

"Do you know where he is?" Brandy asked. "Because I really need to find him."

A white-paneled door to the right of the fireplace opened. "Hi, Brandy," said Bruce.

•   •   •

Bruce Ford, wearing thin black–rimmed glasses and hair trimmed and tamed since his photograph, was taller than Paul, which made Paul want him to sit down. Kirby excused himself shortly after Ford's arrival, which left Bruce at one end of the room, Paul in a chair by the dining-room archway, and Brandy and Wish aligned in chairs by the fireplace, which held an ornate iron grille and tall candles instead of a fire.

Paul couldn't figure out a way to get Bruce down, so after a moment or two, he stood and leaned against a squat pillar.

Bruce seemed to be waiting for something from Brandy, who finally realized it and got up to kiss him at the same time as Wish seemed to find something mesmerizing about his shoelace.

"As you can see, I was worried about you," Brandy said, disengaging from Bruce's grip.

"You hired a private investigator to find me?" Bruce asked.

"Not exactly."

"Well, are you going to tell me why you took off like that, without a word?"

"I'll get to that," Brandy said. "Let me just tell you how we got here first, okay?"

He folded his arms and listened. When she got to the campground story, the agitation began. "Brandy, you owe me an explanation."

"I know but..."

"You run out on me, then waltz in here and tell me you've been mixed up in a murder!"

"I'm not waltzing." Brandy folded her arms, too. "And I tried to reach you but you left your phone at home!"

"My phone's broken, so I left it behind. And, in case you're wondering why I'm here and not home, it's because your campground friend came around to my office and scared the hell out of my staff."

His staff? Paul thought. She must be some dazzling part-time receptionist. "Cody Stinson came to your office?"

"That's the name he gave."

"What did he say?" Paul asked.

"First off, he was loaded on something and didn't make a whole lot of sense. Second, he's not the type we get in our offices usually. Not an easy man to talk to. He said that we were trying to get him thrown in jail for something he didn't do. Well, when he got to the part about not strangling someone, I cut the conversation short. I got him out of there and came to stay at Kirby's until things settled down. That seemed like a logical response, considering a very strange person with a scary story had shown up in my office." He turned back to face Brandy. "I called Angel's, assuming you were there, but I got the machine."

"Sam's out of town with the kids," she said.

"Then I called your mobile, and got more mechanical messages. You need a decent message system! You've got to keep that thing charged up! I've been frantic, worrying about where you were and what was going on!"

"Bruce, I've been trying to call you everywhere! I went to meet that guy, thinking it was you!" By now, Brandy was in tears.

"Brandy, this is awful," Bruce said. "No more fighting. C'mere." He held out his arms, and she walked into them. "I'm so glad to see you."

"We need to talk in private," Brandy said, sniffling, to Paul and Wish.

Paul and Wish returned to the car to wait.

Wish took out his notebook and took his lip between his thumb and pointer finger. "So what have we learned so far?"

"We found him. I guess that makes her glad."

Brandy stayed inside for a long time. Through the glass of the Mustang's front window, Paul and Wish could easily follow the overall thrust, if not all the details, of the argument.

"Brandy is saying that she hasn't been fair with him," Wish reported, leaning his head out of his open window to hear better.

"Bruce wants her to come back, but she's not willing to live there again unless—unless they don't sleep together anymore. Bruce hollered when she said that."

"What does she say?" Paul had jazz on low, trying to obliterate the background brawl, which reminded him of moments in his two past marriages he preferred not to revisit.

"She says—she says she just won't do it."

"What does he think of that?"

"He says he's not clairvoyant. He wants to know what the heck does she want from him? She says—ah, it's pretty private."

"Come on, Wish, spit it out. Nothing's private to a private investigator."

"She says she never wanted to hurt him, she loves him, but she thinks they better cancel the wedding. She won't tell him why. That makes him insane, basically."

Oh, that girl, Paul thought, hoping for Wish's sake she reconciled with her man, and fast. What a handful.

"Now he's really mad," Wish said unnecessarily. He turned the music up. "I'm going to buy you some new music," he said. "Something newer than thirty years old."

"This stuff never ages, Wish. It's classic."

"A fancy word for *obsolete*. By the way, what was so private in his date book you took away from me?"

"Appointments."

"There is another woman?" Wish guessed.

"He's working like a dog. He lives at the IRS office and tax court. There's no other woman. Listen, I think it's time we bow out on Bruce and Brandy. There's been enough intemperate sharing of information in this case already."

"He's young to have big sex trouble, isn't he?"

"I hate to speculate."

"Yeah, it is pretty disgusting, thinking about another man's sex problems."

"Right."

"On the other hand, I'm going to sleep good tonight, hoping that. What could be wrong with his approach, do you think?"

"Settle down, Wish."

"She could like me, if she dumped Bruce."

He was such a messy mix of mournful and hopeful, Paul almost laughed. "She's almost a married woman. You ain't got no business there, to misquote Sippi Wallace."

The blue front door to Kirby's house flew open. Brandy stepped outside, pulling the door shut hard behind her.

"Things didn't end well," Wish almost chortled.

"I reiterate, we don't get involved with clients," Paul said. "It's unprofessional, plus it could get you in real trouble."

"Okay, Rocky," said Wish.

"I'm going back to Tahoe," Brandy informed them.

Wish, grinning broadly, jumped out to open the back door for her.

Around Vacaville, Brandy finally started talking again. "I told him I'm going back to Angel's for a few more days. He's very mad at Nina for bringing all this trouble our way."

"He's mad and he's a lawyer," Paul summarized.

"Beeg trouble for Moose and Squirrel," said Wish.

Friday-night traffic up the freeway to South Lake Tahoe made the long trip an infinite exercise in stop-and-go and imposed patience. The usual four-hour drive took them six. For dinner, to appease Wish and Brandy, Paul stopped in Placerville. They carbo-loaded at Mel's Diner, a chrome-trimmed restaurant on the main drag. Paul left them to it and went out to the car to use his phone. Reaching Nina at her office, he was happy to hear Bob had been invited to sleep over at a friend's house, which meant they would have the four-poster bed and the yellow comforter to themselves for the entire night. Elated, Paul hung up and went back to the table.

Watching Wish as he talked with Brandy, Paul stuck to iced tea, amazed that the gawky kid's social gaffes and big elbows did not seem to register with her at all. Brandy ate like the hungry girl she was, oblivious to the effect she was having on the big lunk. Meanwhile, Paul did what he could to urge things along. He wanted to get to Tahoe.

Unfortunately for him, there was an unavoidable delay. In a ritual that probably originated with the first language, Brandy and Wish needed to exchange life stories. Brandy talked first. I'll show you mine if you'll show me yours, thought Paul, exasperated, trying not to study his watch too openly. But Wish, Paul observed, was having the time of his life, listening intently as Brandy talked about her childhood, flirting in his oddball Washoe way. After she reported extensively, Wish told his own story in fits and starts, glossing over college, launching into asides about Sandy and Joseph, their marriage, divorce, and remarriage, their ranch near Markleeville, their activism in Native American causes.

"Your life is so exotic, Wish," Brandy said after he finished his narrative of his vital legal investigations for Nina's office.

"It is?"

"You know, Native American people and heritage, such fascinating roots in a culture struggling to maintain dignity and identity in a new, complicated era. Your mother sounds cool, too."

"Oh, that describes Sandy to a T," Paul said, slipping out of the booth, meditating upon the mincemeat Sandy could make of a Wish-Brandy alliance. "And on that ominous note, I think we'd better hit the road again."

Back in South Lake Tahoe, Nina prepared for Paul's arrival. After packing Bob off to Taylor Nordholm's—driving him there herself just for the reassurance that he was, in fact, exactly where he said he would be—she ran through the cabin with stern determination, shoving kitchen piles into drawers, kicking loose shoes and laundry into Bob's room and shutting the door, and cutting stems off three bunches of flowers she had bought to splash around the place. Roses in three-colored bunches, yellow, pink, and red, were arranged loosely in vases, placed and replaced on tables and in corners.

Then she examined her handiwork and decided things looked unearthly neat, so she messed a few magazines around on the coffee table. As if Paul cared. But the work was automatic and inexorable, as important as a court appearance to her on this night. She wanted everything beautiful and harmonious.

She missed him every night. She loved him so much! She wanted to be with him forever. Or something!

In the kitchen, she laid out ingredients as directed by Andrea to be swiftly boiled, blanched, and assembled later: fresh rigatoni, Swiss chard, toasted crumbs, anchovies, newly grated Parmesan. She tossed sliced tomatoes, slivered carrots, and two kinds of lettuce into a bowl, covered it tightly, and put it into the refrigerator. She would add homemade tomato-basil croutons and dressing, her specialties, later. A frosty bottle of champagne rested on the middle shelf, lonesome. She inserted a second beside it.

After lighting a pyramid of orange and blue candles on a side table in the living room, she threw a fresh log on the fire.

She took Hitchcock out for a brisk trot up the road, and then, murmuring words of apology, she tossed a big bone into the laundry area and shut him up inside for the night.

Upstairs, she changed the sheets on her bed and gave the yellow roses a pat. Checking the clock, she stepped into the shower. Hot steam forced her to shut her eyes. She stayed under the waterfall for a long time, until her skin was pink and shining, all the sins of the days and weeks drained temporarily away. Back in her room, she settled on a silk nightie with a matching silk robe loosely tied at the waist. She brushed her long brown hair, despaired of controlling it, and let it fly.

The phone rang. She started toward the bedside table.

The doorbell rang. She let the phone go to the message machine, racing downstairs to answer the door. Paul walked in the door, grabbed her, and trundled her into the warm, vanilla-scented living room, his mouth all over her neck, shoulders, and breasts, lips cold with the outside. Within minutes, he removed his shirt, her fine silk.

Everything.

Bliss, or fatigue, or mutual satisfaction must have knocked them both out, because a strange sound woke Nina, the sound of a key jiggling in the front door.

But how could that be? Why wasn't she in bed, with this long, hairy arm across her breasts covered demurely by a down comforter? Why did she feel so exposed?

The fire must have kept them warm, she thought groggily, realizing they had never made it to the bedroom. Paul, who lay all over and around her in an intimate clutch on the living-room rug, snored softly. Before she had time to heed the situation further or form a plan to stave off impending disaster, the front door opened widely.

Bob stepped in. "Mom?" he said. "Taylor's grandma's sick. I tried to call—" His voice fell away.

Closing her eyes, Nina played asleep, trying to keep her breathing regular, just like Bob used to do when he was little and was caught late at night reading by flashlight.

"Mom." This time, Bob said the word more softly. He stood there in the entryway for what seemed like months, then tiptoed past them and crept up the stairs to his room.

"Wake up," she whispered to Paul when she felt convinced of the thoroughness of Bob's absence from the room. She tried to lift Paul's heavy arm off her, but the arm, awakening slowly, had other things in mind. She repeated herself a few times, watched the lazy hazel eyes open wide at last, and fended off his hands, which had gone exploring. "I have to get up. Let me go!"

Something in her voice worked. He removed his arm. "What's the matter?"

"Bob came home," she whispered.

"So?"

"Are you awake? He caught us lying here." She moved her leg out from under his leg and stood up.

"God, you are so pretty from this vantage point."

"Paul, get up!" She took his hand and tried to get him to his feet. "Put something on." She handed him his shirt, which he obligingly put on. She handed him his pants. He pulled them over his legs. "Now button that shirt," she commanded.

"What's the rush?" He fumbled with buttons. "He's on to us. There's no going back now."

Trembling, she picked up her nightgown and robe. She put the robe on and climbed the stairs to her room. "Shh. I'll be right back."

She returned fully dressed in a sweater and long knit skirt. Paul sat at the kitchen table in front of a beer and half-empty glass. Nina went directly to the refrigerator and pulled out the champagne. "We might as well open a bottle of this," she said, and she knew how she sounded, sick at heart, horrified.

"Sure," Paul said, ignoring all that. He popped the cork. She handed him two crystal flutes, which he filled.

"To us," he said, clinking. "Bob will take it all right."

She nodded and drank.

"Dinner?" Paul said, pointing his glass toward the full countertop.

"Yes, except Bob hates anchovies. You mind if I leave them out?"

"I don't mind."

"You can't stay over tonight," she said. "Taylor's grandma's sick."

Before Paul could respond, Bob's door opened. "You guys decent now?" he called down the hall. "Can I come out?"

"Come on out," Paul said.

"What will I say to him?" Nina asked.

"Say it's time for dinner. You're delighted he decided to join us after all. Say you're sorry about all that. Ask him if you can put anchovies in my half of the pasta."

Lacking a better idea, she did.

18

On Saturday morning, despite the pressure Nina and Paul felt to work, they both dropped everything when Bob extorted his way into their plans.

"The only thing that's going to make it up to me is a hike up to Cave Rock, Mom," he told Nina slyly, after she offered awkward apologies for the previous evening's living-room debacle. "I've been wanting to go there all summer, and now winter's coming and we still haven't gone."

Nina called Paul to tell him. Paul invited himself along. "Let me check with Bob," Nina said.

"Sure," Bob said, "let's invite Paul. He's *such* good company. But I guess you know that." Chuckling, he took off to find his boots.

Although Nina was clearly still worrying about Bob, he seemed untraumatized enough to Paul when he picked them up. They drove past Zephyr Cove to Nevada State Park, parking in the lot below the tunnel, Bob talking nonstop about why he needed to see the famous cave. "Wish told me there are spirits here and if we don't make any noise we'll hear them."

When Bob let up for a few seconds, Paul listened to Nina tell about her conversation with Jack, and how Jack felt she was in the clear. She watched him out of the corner of her eye, as if daring him to say something different. He kept his skepticism to himself. He also kept himself from making one single crack about Jack.

The parking lot abutted Lake Tahoe, ending at a boat ramp, and the two or three other cars all had empty boat trailers. Flights of gulls punctuated the delicate sky, which looked as if it might destabilize into a storm during the afternoon, but the lake lay passive and cool beneath.

In a triumph of functionalism over history, Highway 50 had been blasted through the bottom of Cave Rock as a WPA project. Cars roared through the tunnel as they climbed up the hill in light scrub. Bob sat on the edge of a wall overlooking the lanes until Nina, nervous, called him back.

"The Washoe used the waters below this cave for their sacred burial area," Bob lectured, climbing on ahead, Paul behind, Nina on his heels. "I asked Wish to come along, but he said he has too much homework, which is too bad, because he knows a lot more than I do about it." They came very quickly to a flat area marred with concrete and broken glass with an enormous natural archway entry into the rock. Within the gloom they made out a hundred years of graffiti on the walls. Stacked bits of granite, feathers, and twigs, offerings of mysterious origins, decorated the large slabs of granite at the far end, where the rock narrowed into a V.

"There is a cave like this on Oahu," Nina said. "Bigger, but with that same narrowing at the back. It's still an opening, but it seems to continue down into the earth at that point. The Hawaiians say it's where their race was born."

They walked back into the light and poked around. Bob set off, climbing beyond it onto a hillside of loose shale. Nina, who had been sitting cheerfully on a rock overlooking the lake getting her picture snapped by Paul, got up grudgingly to continue on with him.

"I'll wait here," Paul said, checking out the steep rock walls, noting the places where climbers had attached fixed holds. After they left, he walked around until one particular line on an outside wall of the cave attracted him. Cave Rock might be a sacred place to the Washoe, but to the profane rock-climbing community it was a vertical park.

Pulling his climbing shoes and some chalk for his hands out of his pack, he quickly readied himself for some free climbing, scoped the line out some more, eyeballed some handholds, and pulled himself into the ascent.

How he loved to climb. He loved the stretch of muscle under his skin, the adrenaline rush, the cold edges of rock that nicked him as he felt for handholds. He ignored the pitons left by more cautious roped-up types. After a while, he settled into a slow rhythm, taking no chances on the holds, which were, true, not too reliable, just enjoying himself in the moment, doing what his body was meant to do, his eyes six inches from Mother Earth, his hands holding her tight.

He reached the top fairly fast and sat down to enjoy another fantastic view of the lake and surrounding peaks, clouds massing in the east, a sliver of moon ghostly in the thin morning air. His reverie was interrupted by a shout, followed by a second shout, followed by his name.

He scuffled down the gentle backside of the rock face, toward the voices. There he found Nina kneeling over Bob, who was sitting at the bottom of a long rockfall, blood gushing from his knee. A bruise was beginning on one cheek, and scrapes on his arms told Paul he had taken quite a tumble.

"You all right, Bob?"

"It's not broken. I can walk." Nina started to help him up, but he shook her off. "Leave me alone, Mom."

They walked, or in Bob's case, hobbled, down the hill to the car, where Nina found her first-aid kit. By the time she bandaged the wound, Bob had established a policy of silence, which he somehow maintained through the stinging, painful cleansing regimen.

They rode back without even the soothing effects of music. Nina turned on NPR, and they listened to Bob Edwards telling, in his earnest round voice, the latest disheartening world news. By the time they reached Caesars, Paul was happy to say good-bye, although sorry for Nina. They got out while Bob stayed in the car, and walked a short distance away.

"What happened up there?"

"He was fine until I told him he couldn't go to 'band practice' this afternoon at Nikki's. I made up an excuse but he saw through me, which upset him. He suddenly decided to leave the trail and climb a steeper part of the hill. I told him to stop, it was too steep. Then he fell, which humiliated him."

"Humiliated?"

"You can't imagine how much he looks up to you, Paul. He didn't want you to see him."

Touched, Paul said, "I'll take him out sometime and teach him a few things."

"I don't want him rock climbing."

"He's getting older, Nina. It's a safe sport if he learns right. I started at about his age."

"Sure. He can spend the nights with Nikki and the days risking his neck. Why not? He's a big thirteen years old!"

Paul said gently, "He's going to grow up with or without you, honey."

"You don't understand," Nina said with that fierce note in her voice, and Paul did understand that he'd better back off or she might kick him out of the stepfather competition. He was feeling a certain solidarity with the kid, and she didn't like that. Did "stepfather" mean being a yes-man for the mother? He experienced a moment of doubt about Nina. She was too driven and too protective of the kid.

She made a good boss, though, and unfortunately he was in love with her. He had wanted to do some serious talking about their future the night before, and it didn't look like the opportunity would come again soon. "I'll call you after I speak with Ali," he said.

•   •   •

He set out up the road toward Meyers, the next town over on the California side of the lake.

The Peck family owned some acreage on a side street off South Upper Truckee Road. Consulting his map and watching for a crooked wooden sign Ali had described, he arrived at the house at a few minutes after noon. U-shaped, with an open grassy courtyard in front, the house stepped down a hill on the backside and must have had some expansive glass in back for admiring the craggy landscape beyond. He looked forward to a peek inside, but as it turned out, he had no opportunity.

Ali Peck waved him over to the side of the house. She had a split stack of wood beside her on the left, a few short logs to the right, and a two-foot log set up lengthwise on a low stump. As he walked over, she gave it a smack with a long-handled ax. The log fell open like the O.E.D. She threw the two pieces toward the split pile, then started in on another one. "Hang on," she said, "I'm almost done."

She wore jeans and a V-necked T-shirt that read One Tequila, Two Tequila, Three Tequila, Floor. He watched her shoulders work. He could see her appeal. Youth, pep, spirit—she had it all, and if he could see that in a few strokes of the ax, imagine what riding with her day after day must have shown Kevin.

She stopped, set the ax against the stump, removed gloves, and wiped her hands on her jeans. "I won't shake," she said. "Blisters."

"You know who I am."

"Yeah. You can call me Ali if I can call you Paul."

"Okay."

"I don't know what you expect to get out of me. This mess with Kevin has been such a pisser." She pushed hair away from her face, and Paul noticed she had not broken a single nicely manicured fingernail.

"Your parents around, Ali?"

"They do a big grocery shop on Saturday afternoon. I don't want them involved."

A careful and mature young lady, Paul thought. And it made things easier for him. "Looks like you do a lot of that."

"Two cords a season. My father chops the other two cords. He's a karate instructor. Do you want to sit down? How long is this going to take? I'm willing to do this one last thing for Kevin, whatever loose ends you're here to take care of, but tell Kevin I won't be taken by surprise again. I'll be out of state when the permanent-custody hearing comes around. I'm not going to go through another court scene. So embarrassing. I don't specially like hurting my first lover, you know."

"Where are you going?"

"To spend the spring at my aunt's ranch in Arizona. It's too hot for me here in the mountains at the moment. I'm a scandal." She laughed. "I just hope all this doesn't ruin my career in law enforcement." She sat down on a smooth rock in the yard and Paul sat on a log beside her. The yard, Tahoe style, had been left natural. The well-spaced pines and the soft lawn of needles made it look like a nature preserve.

"You may still get subpoenaed," Paul said. "Even in another state. There are ways."

"I'll get a better lawyer if I have to. Can we get this over with? I heard that Kevin lost the hearing. He really loves his kids. It's too bad."

"How did it happen? You and him, I mean?"

Her eyebrows went up and she smiled. For once she looked her age. "It just happened. We were alone a lot. I was helping him right down to assisting in the apprehension of suspects. I know cadets aren't supposed to be put in harm's way but things happen fast. We became like real partners who trust each other totally. Sometimes we went on stakeouts and we'd tell each other all about our lives. Kevin was miserable with his wife. He finally broke down and told me." She glanced at Paul.

"I'm sorry, I forgot how old you are. I need to make a note," Paul said.

"Yes, legally I was underage. Kevin worried about that all the time. We had to be incredibly careful. He might be fired. Has he been disciplined?"

"There's an investigation."

"He has to be in trouble. Everybody knows about us now. At least I fended off that statutory-rape garbage. My father wanted to go to the police but I wouldn't let him. After it came out, they decided not to prosecute, because I wouldn't cooperate. The fact is, we were in love. We were two adults and what we did was our own business." She had a clear, intelligent way of talking. Maybe someday she would become a police officer, but she had some work to do on her judgment first.

"I'm confused," Paul said. "Did Kevin and his wife split up because of the affair?"

"No! Absolutely no way could she know about it. They were living together the whole time. This custody issue hadn't come up. But we were in love. Kevin was everything to me. I planned to marry him."

"So the two of you talked about marriage?"

"Sure. He wanted to marry me, too, but he wanted to be sure he'd get the kids. I wasn't sure what I wanted except that I wanted him."

"So did Kevin tell his wife he wanted to separate while you two were still, ah, in the relationship?"

"No. We almost got to that point. We had plans. Go to Alaska, if you want to know. I was there two years ago on an Outward Bound kayaking trip. It was an excellent place. My parents wouldn't like me going, but they would respect my rights. But it never got to that point."

"Why not?"

"Well, we had been together about three months. We were patrolling the condo area up at Ski Run around eleven at night in a snowfall. We had a big talk. Kevin told me, okay, Ali, this is it, I'm going to tell her tomorrow. And we're going to go to Alaska and start over, and I'll bring my kids and we'll get jobs and live in a cabin and do some hunting and trapping. He had finally come around to what I wanted. We had sex in the patrol car. I fibbed in court when I said we never did it there, incidentally. Then I went home and went to bed."

"I see," Paul said. He checked her face again. Was she truly eighteen, or some hard-nosed mama of forty?

Ali did that smile again, the smile with the eyebrows up that made a sort of facial shrug. "Yeah," she said, "that's how close I came. But then when I went to bed I couldn't sleep. I thought stuff like, we don't have any money, how do we get to Alaska? And I don't like doing dishes or anything, so do I want to take care of kids? All of a sudden, you know, this lightning bolt hit me and I fell out of love. Like this." She snapped her fingers. "All of a sudden I couldn't understand what I ever liked about Kevin.

"He has no ambition. He's actually kind of passive except when it comes to his kids. The truth is that I initiated everything. He liked being dragged along. And the sex was good but he was only my second boyfriend and there was this cute exchange student from Sofia—that's in Bulgaria, in case you were wondering—at school who I was starting to think about, like, you know, what a shame. He's soulful. He wants to be a writer. You know?"

"I know." He thought back to a beautiful artist he knew once.

She shook her head wonderingly. "I felt like I had been sick with flu and just suddenly got over it. I searched my soul that night and I realized I didn't want to go to Alaska. I knew it was over. Has that ever happened to you?"

"Not since I was seventeen," Paul said.

"Are you saying I'm immature? Because—"

"No, no. I have no problem with that."

This magic sentence always worked. Ali's defensiveness dissolved and she said with a trace of boastfulness, "So that was my love affair. Is that all you wanted to ask me about?"

"Not exactly. Although you have been very frank and helpful."

She nodded and said, "Anything I can do."

"What I need to know is how you ended up getting subpoenaed."

"I explained that to Kevin when he called. And incidentally, tell him not to call again. I'm with somebody else."

And I bet that somebody else writes beautiful love letters in Cyrillic script, Paul thought. "Explain it to me one more time."

"Simple. The phone rang last Friday morning about seven. My parents talked to this lawyer named Riesner, Lisa's lawyer. He told them he'd heard Kevin and I had been involved in a serious sexual relationship. They didn't believe it at first. It shocked them quite a bit when I admitted it. I hated it coming out that way. I felt bad that I hadn't told them before on my own, so that wasn't fun. There was some shouting, you know how it is. Then a little later someone came to the door, a grungy-looking man wearing a wrinkled flowered shirt looking lost. At that point, my parents weren't in any shape to answer, so I did. He said, 'Ali Peck?' I said, 'How'd you know my name?' He handed me some papers and I said, 'Listen, pal, I'm sorry, I already go to the Lutheran church,' and he said, 'It's a subpoena, dollface. Read it and weep.'

"My parents read it and they called their lawyer. He said I was a witness in Kevin's hearing that same day and he could get the hearing continued if I wanted but eventually I'd have to tell the truth because now Lisa knew. I said I might as well get it over with even though I was plenty nervous. Then I needed to talk with my parents for a long time, explain everything until they understood. After that discussion, my parents said they respected my need to live my own life."

So sixties, thought Paul.

"So our lawyer talked to Lisa's lawyer and gave me advice on how to testify and what they were going to ask me. The whole experience was pretty gross. Very embarrassing, but the worst thing was knowing I was hurting Kevin. But I couldn't lie about the big stuff. That would be perjury."

Paul made some notes, looked at the healthy radiant girl in blue jeans with the bright future, and said, "Just wondering. Why didn't you call Kevin before the hearing? A little advance warning. That sort of thing."

"I had a *lot* going on! My parents upset. A trig test I might miss. Kevin would have cried, too. He wouldn't have even thought about *my* feelings. About how I, an innocent party, got sucked into this ugly custody hearing." She picked up the ax and ran her finger along the edge.

"This subpoena came as a complete shock to you."

"Yes. Kevin said Lisa's lawyer sort of implied that I called him and told him about us. That's a complete lie."

Paul closed his notebook. "Just one more little thing I need to go back to, Ali. You said that Lisa Cruz never knew about the affair until the time you were subpoenaed."

"No one knew. Kevin would never have told her."

"You're a woman of the world," Paul said. "Obviously you're no fool. Don't you think Lisa might have figured it out? Maybe from Kevin's attitude, or his lack of interest in her—"

"She kicked him out of her bed and for some reason expected him to stick by her. She drove him crazy, starting up one manic lifestyle racket after another, then, when it didn't fix her life or make her happy, she turned off like a run-down battery toy. I really think he tried to make her happy for a long time, but she's one of those people who's so self-absorbed, she barely registered him."

Paul nodded. He stood up just as a Ford Explorer rolled into the driveway. Paul passed the man and woman inside on his way to the Mustang out front. "It's okay, Mom," Ali called.

Like their daughter, the Pecks practically vibrated good health, but they looked nervous. He would be, too, if he had Ali for a daughter.

After his visit with Ali, Paul stopped in at the South Lake Tahoe police station to check out the Bronco theft investigation. As soon as he walked into the building, old, familiar sensations assaulted him, which quickly overrode his well-being.

He hadn't fit into the San Francisco Police Department from the beginning. Following a beer or two, when he felt insightful, he sometimes reflected that the cause of his unease there was not only a generalized problem with granting any idiot authority over him. His problem was also with *specific* idiots, the officious ones that seemed to have an almost military need to break his spirit and create the right kind of soldier. He irked them. They irked him. And one day, after a series of incidents, rather than granting him yet another promotion in Homicide, he was fired for insubordination.

Now, just over forty, entering what should be his maturity, he still got riled at the signs ordering this and that, the stone-faced officer on duty, the vigilant questions, the general militaristic smell of the place. But he disguised his prejudices, gave a pleasant smile to the cop at the desk, and asked to see one of the officers who had responded to the theft of Nina's Bronco.

After turning his ID this way and that, as if to make better sense of it from a different angle, the cop said, looking closely at Paul, "Officer Scholl's on duty," buzzing the inner sanctum. Officer Scholl came out and asked him to walk her over to her car. She was going off duty now, and was dressed in a red turtleneck sweater over slacks and ankle boots, civilian clothing that flattered her stocky body.

They walked out together into the damp mountain world, where breezes whispered softly, and plump, new, green acorns on a huckleberry oak shrub made the ugliness of human behavior in a place like this so much more difficult to stomach than in any given urban slum.

"There's nothing to report," Scholl told him with a frown after he explained his mission.

"Any progress on the missing files?"

"Nope."

The speed in her step made him rush to keep up. "Things have been happening in these cases that suggest—a possibility that someone is using information from the files."

She stopped, turned to face him, and put her hands on her hips. "What things?"

"Sorry. I can't discuss the specifics."

"Huh. You people." She took off again. They reached her car, a midsized family sedan. She pushed a button on a keyring remote to click the lock open. "Doesn't matter that we can't do our job, doesn't matter if people may get hurt, must keep the lying client's secrets."

Frustration overrode all other feelings. "Officer, we need those files back."

"You're a real one-note samba."

"I know you don't have the best opinion of Nina Reilly. But she appreciates your getting her vehicle back, and says you've been very professional in your dealings with her."

"My personal feelings don't interfere with my job."

"Exactly what I'm saying. I'm glad you were able to put your differences aside and find her Bronco."

"You have new information I can use?"

Paul was silent.

"Of course you don't. We got the vehicle back, that saved her a bundle, but now some backseat litter's missing, which no one will describe. Well, that's just tough, isn't it? Tough for us, tough for her." She opened the car door. "Mr. van Wagoner, I'm off duty. I've got better things to do than to listen to you grumble about this problem not getting priority over the dozens of other cases we're handling."

"Listen, I'm aware you have bigger trouble in this town than a defense attorney's missing papers. I was a cop."

"I know," she broke in. Seeing his surprise, she said, "You think in a little town like this when a city type like you comes nosing around we aren't interested? You run an investigative agency in Carmel, which has business when it wants it. You've been coming up here for a couple of years now, working mostly for Nina Reilly and only occasionally for other private clients. You were fired from the SFPD years ago. You went to work for the Monterey Police Department and that didn't work out either. You have a buddy on the force here, Sergeant Fred Cheney. He speaks well of you or I wouldn't be standing here."

"How is he?"

"Working too hard."

"So what you're saying is—"

"Don't give me any more shit about Nina Reilly's petty problems, 'kay? It's my investigation and it's open. I do my job whether I like the vic or not. Anything else?" She got in her car and stomped on the accelerator, swinging out of her parking space with a cop's practiced skill.

Hands in his pockets, Paul watched her drive away. Scholl hadn't liked talking to him but she had done it. Was she looking for the files at all or had she back-burnered them? He couldn't say. He didn't like the way she said Nina's name. He didn't like her tone, civil in the middle and hostile around the edges. He could use police help on this—hell, he could use any help at all on this. He couldn't think of another case where leads had vaporized into smoke so fast.

He walked beyond the courthouse to the city jail. Cody Stinson had not been moved to Placerville as yet, which was convenient. At the jail, Paul submitted to the usual rigmarole before being admitted to a visiting area. Stinson came in shortly after.

"You!" he said. As slight in build as Mario Lopez was built-up, Stinson was spending his time in jail creatively, sculpting a new goatee. "You're the one who tackled me. They ought to arrest you, not me. I wasn't doing anything illegal at that shelter. I even knocked. What in hell was that woman doing with a gun, anyway? I didn't do nothing!"

Paul explained his purpose. "We just want to know who tipped you off about the two women you met at the beach."

"Why should I help you?"

"I'm trying to get to the bottom of all this. If I do, and if you are innocent, that's got to help you, Cody." This was sticky strategy. If Cody was innocent, well, he might jump. If he was guilty he still might jump, because people in jail leap for any old broken rings if they think there might be some advantage. "If we find another bad guy in all this, you'll get out of jail."

Cody thought for a while, scratching his chin with a stubby finger. He had bad skin, which the overhead lights exaggerated. "I got a call."

"From?"

"I don't know. Somebody. Probably a guy, but it sounded like the voice might have been changed. Synthesized or something."

"What did this person say?"

"Told me some names and where these people lived. Told me that these women were running around telling the cops and the D.A. and anybody who would listen that I strangled Phoebe that night. That they saw me at the camp later that night."

"When did the call come? What day of the week?"

"I don't know. Last weekend. Saturday, I think."

"To your house?"

"Yeah."

"You listed?"

"Yeah."

"So you decided to talk to the witnesses, straighten them out."

"That's right. Like I told you, I'm an innocent man. They've got no business running all over town wrecking my good name."

"So how'd you find them?"

"I called around. Called Brandy Taylor's house in Palo Alto. Their machine message gave her cell number out. I called the number a couple of times. When I finally reached her, she asked did I know where Bruce was? So I, uh, played along you might say. Told her he wanted to meet her, that his cell phone was broke so he couldn't call her himself. Can you believe she bought that? People ought to be more careful. She must have been desperate to see the guy."

"You met her at the beach just to talk?"

"That's right. But those two ladies, they're loons. Before I could even introduce myself, they started screaming and jumping around.

I tried to settle them down, and the one got knocked over. Things went from bad to seriously bad. Then, you know, I holed up at the Hilltop in Truckee. Laid low."

"While you waited for some money to come in."

"That's right. Mario tell you that?"

"Yes."

"He has a share coming, if I ever contact that guy that owes us, which doesn't look too likely with me stuck here."

"Mario would be delighted to hear that."

"Yeah, he probably thinks I'm planning to stiff him. Maybe I will. Least I can do for Phoebe."

"You mean because if you didn't kill Phoebe, odds are, he did."

"Yeah. Bastard," Cody said. "How could he do that? You think you know someone. Oh, I'll never get over her. I can't believe she's gone. You ever see a picture of her?"

Paul nodded.

"Then you know she was drop-dead hot. But she was some-body, you know? A real nice person, warm. Homey. She also had this completely lousy singing voice." He sang a few notes in a grind-ing, off-key falsetto. "Like that. Bad enough to bend a spoon. She knew she sounded terrible, but she didn't give a damn, sang all the time anyway, loud." He sighed. "She'd tickle my face with that silky black hair of hers to wake me up.... We were just starting to talk kids when Mario showed up." He shook his head, sounding forlorn. "Jealousy's a mean, unpredictable son of a bitch."

"While you were at the Hilltop, you got another call? I mean, how did you know those two women were staying at the women's shelter?"

"I called Carol—a family friend—and we got to talking. We were guessing where two ladies who wanted to feel safe might hide. She told me about the shelter. Before her divorce she escaped from her former old man there once."

Paul remembered that name. "Carol Ames is the woman who gave you the alibi for that night."

"She wasn't lying. She never even knew I left. She sleeps hard. It was easy to sneak out."

"Who is she?"

"Just Carol. She's always around."

"A girlfriend?"

"No, man, I was with Phoebe and Carol was clear on that. Carol's from way back. After I had the run-in with Phoebe and Mario at the campground, I went over to her apartment. She's a good lady and she opened the door and said I could stay. I was blasted. She could see I didn't want to be alone. I sat down at her kitchen table, thinking about going back. She tried to talk sense into me, but you can't talk sense to a jackass, which is what I am. So we went to bed. She fell asleep but I was tortured, man, thinking about Phoebe. So I snuck out. Look where it landed me."

"What happened at the campground that night, Cody?"

He sat back against his chair. "Mario had just gotten out of prison that day and he came by my place to collect some money I really do owe him. This was in the afternoon. Well, Phoebe was there, hiding in the back room, scared to death he would find out we were now a couple, right? So I wouldn't let him in. I gave him twenty bucks to camp because money was tight temporarily, and I couldn't cover a motel room right that minute with what I had in my pocket. Phoebe was in a crappy mood after he left and she wouldn't even talk to me. Anyway, a while later, she took off without saying where she was going. I figured I'd find her at the campground. I should have just left them alone. But Mario can get rabid when he drinks."

"You thought he might get rough with her?"

"Well, yeah. Now wait a minute. I don't mean I was afraid he'd kill her! I never thought that."

Paul nodded, listening.

"So I went over to see if she was there. She was."

"And what did she say?"

"Not much. He told me they were back together, everything

was simpatico now. We all got to drinking out of nervousness and that's when Mario and I got into it a little. I found it hard to accept that she would just walk out on me like that. So we fought over her. She was in the middle, torn, you know? Mario was her original boyfriend and she felt loyal. But I know she cared about me a lot."

"You folks caused quite a commotion. The ranger got involved, as I understand it."

"Right. He broke it up and sent me on my way."

"But you came back. What did you do, park your bike on the street and walk in?"

He nodded. "The last thing on my mind was to wake up Mario. I just wanted to talk to Phoebe alone, without his influence. I ducked in and woke her up, and believe me, it wasn't easy. She was passed out. When she finally seemed conscious we went outside the tent and I asked her, did she want him or me. That's what it came down to. Him or me. I told her I loved her."

"And she said?"

"She told me to go away and we'd talk in the morning. She kissed me and I still thought I had a chance. I had no reason to kill her, man!"

"And that was the end of it."

Cody's eyes hardened. "That's right. She crawled back into the tent and that's the last time I saw her alive."

"And what time was this?"

"Nighttime, late. How should I know?"

Jack's face when he caught sight of Paul arriving at Bueno Nalo Restaurant in Sacramento that night with Nina: priceless.

Once upon a time, while Nina and Jack were still married and living in San Francisco, that look of raw irritation at being thwarted from some private ambition would have scared her, made her jump to attention and try to alleviate it. She had been deeply involved with Jack then and his disposition prevailed over hers. She would tiptoe around his fits of temperament as if avoiding potent, half-hidden land mincs.

Now the look on his face made her laugh. He looked like a small, spoiled child, face puckered, tantrum brewing. Smiling, saying hello and sitting down, she wondered again what he could possibly want with her aside from a good legal fee.

Paul seemed in a fine humor. Ignoring Jack's mood, he left to wash his hands as soon as the margaritas had been ordered.

"I expected to meet you alone," Jack said.

"But that was not to be." The drinks arrived and Nina slouched a little and had a short sip. "Oh, sorry," she went on. "A toast. To—to Saturday nights."

Jack, unbending, said, "I'd like you to send Paul on his way."

"Why?"

"Because I need to speak frankly with you. About your situation. Talk law with you. We're putting Paul in a spot. The conversation's not privileged if he's here."

"He'll never tell. Besides, he's our investigator. It's work-product."

"Okay, the truth. I want to have dinner with you, just you. Get a little undivided attention." He rubbed some salt off the glass and had a taste of it. Grimacing, he took his napkin and wiped all around the rim, saying, "Could you just tell him we have to talk alone? Please?"

"Why don't you tell him?" All this was so familiar. Jack's power play, her automatic resistance.

"That's a laugh. He'd never leave."

Nina looked down. "I want him here, Jack. Please don't make a big deal about it. Back to business, remember?"

"Well, I'm disappointed."

"Why? Why should we be alone?"

"Because we have a lot to say to each other."

"Not anymore."

"I've been thinking some more since our phone call. I want you to see how I've changed since we were together."

"For Pete's sake," Nina said, exasperated. "One thing sure hasn't changed. You're the king of chutzpah. Paul and I are together. He's in the bathroom right now, unaware that his good buddy is trying to undercut him. And what is it you want? An ego boost? I don't believe you're pining for me. I can't."

Jack said, "Whoa. Please, Nina. Don't turn into a lawyer on me. Don't use words to hurt me. I've been hurt a lot recently."

"I'm s—"

Fortunately for Nina, Paul slid in beside her before she could break down and apologize to Jack's large, sorrowful eyes. "Ah," Paul said. "I see you started without me." His sharp eyes took in the situation. "What's up, buddy?" he asked Jack.

"I wept on Nina's icy shoulder. But to return to our earthly concerns, Nina, report."

"Well, on the way here, I delivered two checks to Fresno, one to Kao Vang and one to Mrs. Vang, for a hundred and five thousand dollars apiece minus legal fees and costs. Mrs. Vang cried, then thanked me and put a white scarf around my neck and gave me a blessing."

"And Kao Vang?"

"He muttered in Hmong. Dr. Mai didn't even try to translate. The tenor of Kao's remarks was that he wuz robbed. I think he put a juju on me, or the Hmong equivalent."

"Any chance he'd go after his wife for her share?" Paul said.

"I think she can handle herself. I doubt Kao is a violent person, Paul. We're always so paranoid."

"Call it cautious until proven paranoid."

Jack set down his drink hard. "It's out of your hands now. You made the payout. Case closed."

"I still don't have the file with my intake notes," Nina said. "And the other robber, the arsonist, is still out there."

"Loose ends," Paul said. "How I hate loose ends. Especially when it's possible they connect. Maybe the second robber in this insurance case took your files. He knows about the money now, and he makes a move on one or both of the Vangs. Case maybe not closed is my feeling."

"I talked with both of them about that," Nina said. "They are aware that they need to be careful. I even took Mrs. Vang to the bank and helped her deposit the check. But I know what you mean, Paul. I'm still concerned."

"Part of it has to do with the events of the other two cases," Paul said. They ordered the specials and a pitcher of margaritas this time. Now halfway through his drink, Jack seemed to be settling down, but Nina had an uneasy feeling that the three of them should not have sat down together tonight.

"Okay, status report on the other two cases," Jack said.

"Warning flags," Paul told him, "described in brief. In the Cruz case, the girlfriend, Ali Peck, insists the subpoena originated with Riesner."

"So we still don't know if Riesner knew about her all the time and saved that little surprise for the last day of the hearing, or if the thief called him and told him, or if Riesner stole my Bronco, or Lisa stole it, or Scholl—" The waitress brought fresh salsa and chips, and salads of greens, orange slices, and jicama. Both Jack and Paul watched her saunter away.

"I think the first he heard of Ali Peck was the night the Bronco was stolen," Paul went on. "Cody Stinson told me he got a call. No reason for him to lie. So I think we do have somebody out there with the files and a phone. Could be Riesner got a call, too, just like he said. If he knows anything more that's useful about this supposed phone call, we have to know it." He attacked his salad. "We need to ask him."

"What, and expect a straight answer?" Nina asked. "He lies just because he can. And, Paul, you can't go to him. He'll call out reinforcements the minute he sees your face."

"Let me guess why," Jack said, taking a tortilla chip from the bowl and loading on the salsa. "Paul's famous composure."

"This from a man who prides himself on drawing blood in a courtroom without the benefit of a weapon," Paul said. "Need I say

more? And while we're at it, shall we discuss your cool with
Riesner, Nina? That little pepper-spray episode?"

"Maybe a third party could convince him that it wouldn't hurt
him to help for once," Jack said. "Like me."

Paul and Nina looked at each other.

"You?" they said.

"I could explain that I represent you in the matter of the lost
files. I'd make him see how he doesn't want us thinking he had
something to do with it."

"Scholl had the best opportunity," Nina said. "She found the
Bronco. Maybe she stole the Bronco, discovered the files in there,
did some damage, then took her time to let me know she had found
my truck. And Lisa Cruz, well, she has a grudge against me, which
was resurrected when Kevin hired me. I wouldn't put anything past
her. Wish I knew more about these people."

"They're on my To Do list, Nina," Paul said. "Along with
Riesner."

"How far do you need to take this investigation?" Jack asked.
"Maybe it's a waste of time at this point. The cats are debagged and
running wild already."

"Know your enemy, Jack," Paul said. "Nina's got one, and I
think she ought to know who it is. This might be the skirmish before the battle. She's got to be prepared."

"Sandy called a friend of hers at Riesner's office to hear what she
could hear," Nina said. "She found out that the same night the files
disappeared, Jeff Riesner hosted a family reunion at his house. At
least seven relatives stayed over. His house was bursting at the seams.
His secretary went over there and spent the evening serving hors
d'oeuvres. I know, I know, that is by no means an airtight alibi. But
for him to sneak away in the middle of the night with so many people around him—it just doesn't sound right. Besides—auto theft?"

"Then why don't I just ask him again?" Jack said. "It may be the
only chance we have to find out who outed the girl, right?"

Paul said, "You don't know this dude, Jack."

"You're the only one allowed to help Nina, is that it?" Jack asked.

Another shift in the weather, both Paul and Jack glowering.

"Give it a shot," Nina said, worn out with her peacekeeping efforts. "I'll have Sandy call you with the number."

But the swift changes of atmosphere of the last few minutes seemed to have billowed up into a major storm.

"Jack, get over it." Paul put his hand on Nina's knee this time. "Deal with reality, meaning me, or get off the case. She doesn't need you anyway. According to your own view, there is no case anyway. The clients are muddling through without their files. Maybe you should just head home while you can still drive under the DUI limit."

Jack took a big slug of his second margarita. "Some friend," he said. "Some freakin' friend you are."

"You left her! Have you forgotten?"

Nina waved her hand. "Hey, guys, remember me? The one who pays you both? How about we finish our talk, have a nice dinner with lots of ice water, and all of us hit the road. We're tired and hungry and as a result we're not at our best. So, how about we pack up our troubles and enjoy the meal?" Big hot plates of flautas and enchiladas and chiles rellenos had materialized in front of them. The aroma quickly softened their glares. They picked up their forks and dug in.

Nina took a bite, then put her fork down. She had lost her appetite. "Let's start over. I think the issue here is, what about these loose ends? Am I out of the woods yet? Jack says I am. Paul seems less certain. And I, well, I'm going to chew my fingernails, not just because there are some details we don't know, but because I got my clients and myself into this situation in the first place."

"Don't blame yourself," Paul said.

She waved that away. Of course she blamed herself.

She forged on, "Paul, thanks to you, we have something new to work on. We know that Cody Stinson says he got an anonymous phone call telling him about Brandy. If he did get that call, it was from someone motivated and cruel enough to place those two women in a potentially life-threatening situation. So who might that be? Mario didn't steal the files. He was in jail. Cody didn't steal the files, because at that time he had no idea the girls were witnesses."

"Maybe he did," Jack said.

"But—"

"Maybe he noticed the girls that night at the campground and decided he better check them out. Maybe he followed one of them to your office. Maybe he followed you home that night, seeing you put your briefcase in the truck. He's about to snag the files and he thinks, let's dirty the waters, I'll take the truck, too."

Nina popped a slice of orange into her mouth and considered this. "Maybe," she said. "Paul, can you find out if Stinson has ever been arrested for auto theft or theft in general?"

"Sure will," Paul said. "Then what?"

"Maybe we return to our normal impossible caseloads and pardon Nina for her terrible misdeeds for the time being?" Nina said. "The leads peter out at that point. The police aren't going anywhere. Maybe nothing further will happen."

"Cody claims he didn't kill Phoebe," Paul said. "Do we care if he's telling the truth?"

"Trust me, they all say that," Jack said.

"I'm not a rube, Jack. I'm telling you both, he left some real questions in my mind."

"What do you recommend?" Nina said.

"I'll pass on my concerns to Fred Cheney at the police department. Beyond that, Cody has his own lawyer. I'll keep tabs. That's about it."

"Okay."

"What about the sisters?" Jack said. "They had a bad scare. They could still file a complaint against you."

"And Brandy's fiancé, Bruce Ford, was accosted by Stinson," Nina said. "He's a lawyer. It's my fault Stinson did that. He was angry."

"You know, I have a different feeling about lawyers since they became my sole clients," Jack said. "They are deeply conservative. They want to avoid personal trouble. Ford didn't get hurt. Would he waste a lot of his valuable time filing a complaint against you?"

"What about all those lawyers that flood the courts by filing trivial legal cases?" Paul asked. "You hear a lot about them."

"We already know you have a low opinion of lawyers," Jack said. "Maybe if you'd gone on to law school yourself you wouldn't have that attitude. I told Nina where that jaundiced attitude comes from."

Paul said, "You did, eh?" He fixed Jack with a stare. Nina looked back and forth.

"About time she knew, buddy."

"Don't call me buddy right now, McIntyre. I'm wishing you had never horned in. You're useless. Are you gonna charge her six hundred bucks for this dinner?"

"You'd love it if she gave it up. Admit it."

Paul said, "I sleep with one, I work for them, and I still talk to you, though I'm starting to wonder why. I have no chip. I got lucky and didn't get in. It's a lousy profession. It's a guaranteed heart attack by age fifty. So I will be blunt and I will say that if Nina gets drummed out of the corps, she may end up happier and healthier." He wiped tomato sauce off his lips with his napkin, not looking at Nina.

"You don't care if I get disbarred?" Nina said, floored. "Don't you know how much I love—" She choked up. "Don't you understand that it's everything to me?"

"Anyway, this is the last supper. You're terminated, McIntyre." Paul still wouldn't look at her.

"My job is never over until every single person involved in the file theft is dead of old age," Jack said, "whereas you ought to hit the road, head home to your dying business, and give Nina a break from all this. I'm advising Nina of that. Nina, I want you to go home, take in a movie or something. Rest, babe. I think you squeaked through."

"Thanks," Nina said. She smiled and Jack smiled back at her.

"The next time I take you to dinner we won't even talk law," he said.

"No reason for a next time, then," Paul said.

Nina paid the bill, the only decision that evening Paul and Jack didn't dispute.

19

PAUL KISSED NINA GOOD-BYE and gave Jack the finger as he climbed back into his Mustang for the long drive back to Carmel. He drove fast to the highway, started to take a right at the exit to go west, then changed his mind and swerved into the left lane, making a left instead.

He headed east, driving all the way back to South Lake Tahoe thinking he might catch a glimpse of Nina's Bronco, but he never did. The night was beautiful, and the drive up and down the mountains into the wavery blue, black, silvery town stirred him, as it always did. In Meyers, he cut through on the Trail to avoid traffic, then booked himself back into a room at Caesars with the flirt at the front desk, who had no rooms unreserved for the weekend but found one anyway.

He didn't call Nina. He had work to do the next morning, and he didn't want any discussion or argument about how he would do it. He wanted to know who stole her files. Someone was after her, and he wanted to know who. He wanted to know whatever there was to know.

Sunday morning, showered, shaved, and fed, Paul hit the Yellow Pages. Lisa Cruz was listed, which he took as a good sign. Pioneer Trail led straight behind the casinos a mile or so to Woodbine Road.

He took a right, checked out the street, then pulled back onto the Trail and parked out of sight around the corner. Pulling a clipboard with a pencil tied to it from the floor, he got out of the car and locked it.

Lisa Cruz lived a few houses down from Pioneer Trail in a neat cabin with a porch trimmed in blue. He knocked on the door of the house next to her cabin, then on the door beyond her cabin, then up and down the block, talking with her neighbors. He saw no sign of Lisa or her kids.

"I'm from the city," he said, waving his clipboard officiously and making meaningless check marks when a friendly door opened here and there. "We're going to be doing some road work on Pioneer Trail next week and just wanted to let you folks know in advance so you won't be too inconvenienced." Actually, this might not even be a lie. Road work on the Trail happened during the dry weather in preparation for winter every year. He was probably doing them all a favor, reminding them. "Work on the potholes and drainage. You should be getting a notice in the mail about this. 'Course, you know how the city is about this stuff. Schedules change, so don't bet the ranch on it." He scratched his head and shared a laugh. Then he squeezed out any gossip worth squeezing.

After speaking with four people on that block who seemed to know what they were talking about, and two with strong feelings in the various matters, he walked around the corner to Lisa's mother's street to encourage further tattle.

Before hitting the police station, he called ahead to make sure he could chat with his buddy, Sergeant Cheney. Cheney answered the phone.

"You again?" Cheney asked.

"Did you get my message?" Paul asked.

"Yeah. I got that guy's record for you, and now you gotta quit compromising my integrity. No more favors."

"How about a burger at Heidi's? My treat."

"Now you mention it," Cheney said, "I'm hungry and you owe me."

They arranged to meet at the restaurant at one o'clock. Paul arrived early, picked a corner booth, and sipped coffee, enjoying the spirited racket of the happy weekend crowd. Cheney arrived late by fifteen minutes.

"You're skinnier every time I see you," Paul said, standing to greet him.

"Don't try to butter me up," the sergeant said, pleased.

He really did look better as time went on. His smooth caramel skin glowed with health. Cheney, somewhere in his fifties, had a much younger wife he worked hard to keep happy. "Don't tell my wife but I switched to a diet where you drink these disgusting drinks instead of eating real food."

"Sounds hard," Paul said.

Cheney picked up his menu. "Nah. Much easier not to eat than eat the crap she wants me to eat."

They ordered. While they waited for their food, Cheney filled Paul in on Cody Stinson's record.

Their order arrived, Paul's a thick sandwich, Cheney's a salad. Cheney proceeded to eat most of Paul's sandwich.

"Man, there's nothing like a little bacon fat to get my mouth drooling and my insides moving."

"Good. When you're finished, I'd sure like help figuring out Officer Jean Scholl and Jeffrey Riesner."

Cheney crumpled his napkin and set it on the table. "I knew this was going to cost me." He licked a blob of mayonnaise off his finger. "I guess this means you've heard the rumbles."

"Yeah," Paul lied. "What I want to know is, what's your take on all this?"

Sunday went well, mainly because Nina and Bob spent most of the day at Matt's house helping him to put some new asphalt shingles on the roof before the winter weather arrived in full. She was doing what she could to make something up to Matt. After the incident at the women's shelter, Matt had called her. The idea of his pregnant wife with her rifle fired up and ready to take out a dangerous criminal type had brought back all his fears about Nina's law practice. He asked her again to keep his family away from her clients.

Matt would be pleased if she left the law. She hadn't paid much attention to these attitudes of Paul's and Matt's in the past, but the lost files had spotlighted just how difficult the past few years had been. During her first homicide case up here, she had been shot; she tried not to think about that, but she carried the scar. She had been threatened and so had Bob. The man she loved more than she loved herself, her husband of only a few weeks, had been killed by someone she had trusted.

She had landed in a challenging town, doing criminal-defense work. And she had wanted the challenge. Now she had the reputation and the respect she sought, but at such a cost.

So when they stopped at four and Matt and Bob sat down to rest and watch TV in the living room, Nina took Andrea out back. She respected Andrea as the most well-balanced person she knew, and the wisest.

"I wonder if I'm relieving suffering, or causing it. I'm confused, Andrea."

"You do good work, Nina," Andrea said. "You help people in trouble and you don't get much support. I'm proud of you. Don't forget that."

Nina kicked at a stone that had fallen off Matt's rock wall. Squirrels ran along the top, chittering. "It's all I ever wanted to be. I don't have any other identity."

"Now, there you're wrong. You're a mother, a householder, a person full of promise, and you're young yet. What are you, thirty-four? Five? If you had to change jobs, you could go back to college."

"And study what?"

"Well, psychology for instance. You could be a counselor. Or a teacher."

"I am a counselor. I counsel people, I plan their lives, I defend them when they're attacked, I help them order their business affairs,

I speak for them, I take care of their problems. This work is so broad in scope—I never get bored, that's for sure."

"I know it's hard. The responsibility is killing," Andrea said. "I just want to say that I admire you. Now don't turn away. Let it sink in. Accept it. I admire you. A lot of people admire you. Are you listening?"

But she wanted to know what to do with her life. She felt so troubled by what was happening, she had lost her touchstones. "That wasn't what I was getting at."

Andrea laughed. "But that's what you got."

"We're bummed that it's come to this," Brandy said, frowning, hands in her silk trouser pockets.

"We're very unhappy," Angel agreed, even her hair subdued. She looked like Annie Lennox. Sweet dreams were not made of this, however.

"What has it come to?" Nina asked, knowing she did not want to hear the answer. Monday morning often went haywire as the weekend's buildup piled in. Sandy tapped in the next room. Messages sat in sorted piles on the desk. Forty-seven other cases called to her from the file cabinet. Meanwhile Brandy and Angel blocked the doorway to the inner office.

"Ladies, take a seat," Nina said. "What's on your mind this morning?"

They came in and sat down. "It wasn't my idea," Brandy said. "And Angel's husband, Sam, thinks it stinks, too. We want you to know that."

"No question. It stinks," Angel agreed.

A knock on the door interrupted them. Nina got up to answer and found Sandy there.

"Nina, Paul's on the phone. Will you take the call?"

Nina apologized to the two women, closed the door halfway behind her, stepped into the reception area, and picked up the phone.

"I'm sorry to butt in like this. I understand you're busy."

"It's a bad time," she said. "Something's up with Angel and Brandy. I'm in the middle of it."

He hesitated. "I can call back."

"No. Tell me, what's going on?" she asked. Sandy licked an envelope slowly. Then her hands took their stations, hovering over the keyboard, unwilling to break into the conversation.

"Listen, Nina, I've got several things to tell you but since you're busy, we'll discuss those later. But I want to say—things went frosty at that dinner. I shouldn't have said what I said about you practicing law."

"It's okay. I'm taking a poll, actually."

"The condo in Carmel is always waiting for you." He paused. "You are so dear to me."

Nina glanced back through the crack in the door into her office, where the two women were engaged in a frantic, whispered debate. "Paul, I'm sorry. I can't think about that right now. I can't even talk anymore."

"No problem," he said. "I'll check in later."

"Okay." She put the phone down.

Sandy's fingers resumed their customary tapping. Nina walked back inside her office.

"We've been beating around the bush," Angel said, taking charge, "but now, here goes."

Brandy stood up suddenly and went over to the window. She put a hand on the ledge but never once looked outside. She looked at Angel, at the desk, at the file cabinets, at the framed documents on the wall. She looked everywhere except at Nina. "I told Bruce the whole story, beginning to end, about what happened at the campground, about seeing Cody Stinson, about meeting him in the woods and Angel getting knocked over and me getting grabbed—"

"He was upset," Angel added unnecessarily. "First off, he hated that she was here without him, and second, Cody Stinson went to see him and scared him good."

"I really don't want you to get the wrong idea about us," Brandy said. "We're not vindictive or vengeful people."

"Not at all," Angel said. "None of us are."

"So when Bruce showed up at Angel's on Sunday with this letter, we were surprised."

"Shocked, you mean."

Nina got the drift, and drifted away. She looked out the window at Mount Tallac, crowned with white. Then she turned her attention to the lake, the ancient, sacred lake. She considered the hill of beans that was her life, insignificant beside those two regal natural features, and felt a stab of sorrow, because petty or not, it was her hill, her life, and she had loved everything about it. Now along came a letter from a lawyer and it would explode and she could do nothing to stop it. Subterranean terror. Fractures in her beautiful geography.

Maybe the women had some inkling of the full effect of their revelation, and maybe not, but at last Brandy managed to say what they had come to say.

"Bruce wrote a complaint to the California State Bar about you. And I signed it," Brandy said, standing up.

"So did I," Angel admitted, also rising.

"We thought it would be really low not to bring it to you personally and say that—"

"We're awfully sorry."

Nina couldn't trust herself to speak, so she didn't speak. She kept her back to them, trying to control a quiver that had started up around her shoulders and threatened to take over her body.

"Sorry," they said again in unison, and left.

No sooner had the two women wandered out than the phone rang.

"I am in conference," Nina said to Sandy. Closing the door, she leaned against it, hyperventilating. Only two things in the world could inspire this level of dread. The other was an IRS audit. The audit was definitely a remote second to a complaint to the state bar.

Eyes closed, she took the blow. When she started to feel like she couldn't stand it, she leaned over and let her arms hang and made herself breathe. She had had a panic attack once before and she was afraid it might happen again. Be cool, be cool, she told herself.

Call Jack, call Paul, call—

A knock. "Phone," Sandy said. "They said it's important."

"Not now."

"Urgent."

"Who is it?"

"Heritage Life. The adjuster in the Vang case, Marilyn Rose. She says she has to talk to you. Something about the check."

Like a ninety-year-old in ill health, Nina leaned on the desk as she went around it and sank into her chair. She rubbed her face and somehow put Bruce Ford aside.

"Hi, Marilyn," she said. "How are you?"

"Hoping you didn't send that check to the Vangs yet."

"Why not?"

"Well, did you?"

"Over the weekend."

"Well, then we're both in deep shit," Marilyn said rapidly. "Now I'm definitely going to get canned, and I owe it all to you. I trusted you. I liked you. You're going to get a letter and by God you'd better have an explanation or my ass will be out on the street, and I've got a mortgage and a sick husband and two kids and if that sounds like I'm scared shitless, well, Counselor, I am in fact scared shitless. It hurts me, it does, the way you used me, and it amazes me that I could misjudge another human being the way I misjudged you. My supervisor is sitting in her office right now writing up a report to three vice presidents in our company, and I'll be spending all evening groveling on their carpets. I'll be applying for employment opportunities at Hooters with this job market. But by God, Nina, you're going down with me. You are. I'm not going down alone. I can't believe a fellow woman would do this to me—"

Nina held the phone away from her ear and rubbed her temples, where the headache drummed. Sandy watched from the door. "Get on the other line," she mouthed.

She listened again. Marilyn said, "I'm so horribly disappointed," and burst into tears.

"Marilyn?"

"I just had to call you myself because I thought—I thought we were friends."

"We are friends. Marilyn, listen to me. No, listen. Please. I have no idea why you are so angry."

"Don't play any more games with me or try to finagle your way out of this."

"Please tell me what you think I have done."

"You can't hide the truth anymore. Your file was mailed to us."

"What file?"

"You know what file. Your file on Kao Vang. The convenience-store arson."

So astounded was Nina that all she could think was, did they read my confidential file? "You read it?"

"The mail clerk read it. My secretary read it, then my assistant. Then I read it. Now the entire upper echelon of Heritage Insurance Company Incorporated has read the file or knows what it says and we have an office in Irian Jaya, so that is a lot of people. Nobody knew what it was at first. It came in an envelope and it looked like one of ours. So, yeah, it got read, that's right, and there's nothing you can do about it."

Nina's thoughts ran in circles. "But what—there's nothing in that file but my intake notes." Her mind scurried through what she could remember and could find nothing that would generate such heat from an insurance company.

"How could you?"

"Oh, Marilyn, I'm so sorry I've hurt you somehow. But I don't know how! Marilyn, who mailed you the file?"

"No return address."

"Damn!"

"A concerned citizen," Marilyn said, and laughed a hysterical laugh. "I'll never forget my assistant coming in and handing me that thing. Turning point of my professional life. Done in by a con."

"But all that file had were my notes! And I'm very concerned that my client's attorney-client privilege——"

"That's the least of your problems. It's not going to protect you. You're finished, and you finished me along the way. I just wanted you to know how much you have hurt me. You may not have even thought about me. I'm just a faceless bureaucrat who you scammed. I'm going now. You'll hear plenty more, but not from me. You ruined my life."

"Don't go! There's been a misunderstanding. I haven't done a thing wrong, except maybe allow confidential files to fall out of my care. Look, Marilyn, pretend for just one second that I don't know what you're talking about. Tell me what I did. Please. Please, Marilyn."

"This is ridiculous. As if you don't know. Well, now we do. We know you knew all about who set that liquor store on fire—your client, Kao Vang. He set it on fire himself to collect the insurance. You knew it when you called me about the claim, you knew it when you put together that big package of fraud and deceit you brought me. You knew it this whole time and you deliberately acted as his accessory. It says so right there in your file."

"Marilyn," Nina said from a throat that felt ashen and weak, so cold had she become, "my file says nothing of the sort."

"In your own handwriting. There's no wiggling out of this one. At least you should be honest with me, honor our relationship, and admit it between you and me——"

A colder wind blew through Nina and she thought, they're taping this, or someone else is listening. "I didn't try to defraud the company or hurt you, Marilyn. If there's something in that file that purports——"

"Purports—ha!"

"...purports to be my handwriting, saying that Kao Vang set

that fire, then it's a forgery. A forgery, all right? A forgery!" But she was talking to dead air.

Sandy came in a few moments later. Nina stood at the window, eyes open, blind. "Here," Sandy said, holding out two ibuprofen and a shot glass of the Courvoisier a client had given the office the previous Christmas. "Come on, drink it down. You look like the phlebotomist just drained all your blood out. Sit down. Come on."

"It's a forgery."

"I called Paul and Jack. I canceled your meeting at the health department. You're going home."

"Someone. Is out to get me. What Paul said, cautious until proven paranoid. No need to be cautious. Too late for that."

"Did Vang really torch his own store?" Sandy had heard enough of the phone call.

"No! I mean, not that I know!"

"So she's all mixed up. Maybe there's something you wrote in there that she misunderstood?"

"I certainly didn't write anything like that in my notes. That's the point, Sandy. If there is a note in the file now, I didn't put it there. Someone else did. Someone stole the files to get me."

"It always was a possibility."

"Someone evil. It's evil. People hurt besides me. Collateral damage."

Sandy pulled her into the reception area, closing Nina's office door behind her. "You don't look well. I'm gonna drive you home."

"That's just what they want. To destroy my livelihood. Make me close the office. Take control out of my hands. Make all my decisions for me."

"Here's your jacket. Put it on." She held the jacket open and Nina stepped into it. "Let's go." Locking the door carefully behind them, she led the way into the parking lot, Nina following behind. Sandy put her in the brown car and drove her home to Kulow

Street. Marching up to the front door, Sandy found Nina's keys, opened the door, and pushed her inside. "Now go lie down. I called Andrea. She's gonna bring you some lunch. Sleep it off. You never get enough sleep. Go on, upstairs. Do I have to tuck you in?"

"I have to figure this out. I have to."

"Not right this second you don't."

"Someone is out there."

"Are you afraid?" Sandy said.

"Yes."

"Do you want me to stay down here until Andrea comes?"

"It's not that kind of fear." Nina went upstairs automatically, welcoming the relief of numbing shock. She pulled the curtains shut on the sun. Zombielike, she dropped her jacket, blouse, and skirt on the floor. Then she got down under the covers and held her hand across her mouth. But there were no sobs, no tears. She had reached a place where tears couldn't reach.

A good long stretch of vacancy passed during which she inhabited her body and her mind, but they glided along without her, her body under the covers: warm. When she came out of her suspended animation, rose and threw water on her face, she smelled soup and heard Andrea banging pans around the kitchen.

Downstairs she greeted her sister-in-law, and made her sit down. Nina poured the soup into bowls, found crackers, sat down and made small talk, deflecting any questions about why she had returned home at ten in the morning to be put to bed like an invalid. Andrea refused to leave until Nina told her what had happened, so Nina did, without going into detail about the cases.

Hand on her slightly swelling stomach, Andrea said, "You seem almost nonchalant."

"I'm not. Someone is trying to hurt me. Has hurt me."

"What's next?"

Nina hadn't thought that far. "I don't know."

"Maybe the worst has already happened."

"There were three files. We've only heard from two."

Andrea grasped her hand. "You'll get through this. You always do. Whatever happens, you have me, and Bob and Matt and your dad. Nina, you have us. You'll always be okay."

Comforted by what sounded like a blessing, Nina fought off tears. So, she could feel again. Progress.

She sent Andrea home. Upstairs, she brushed her hair carefully, put on lipstick, got a fresh suit jacket, and put on her work heels.

Then she called a cab and went back to work.

Sandy looked startled to see her. "You okay?"

"Fine," she said. "Let me have a look at my calendar for this afternoon."

"Three appointments I was just about to cancel, one court appearance. Last but not least, a meeting with Kevin Cruz."

"We better get busy, then," she said, closing the door to her office and on Sandy's expression, which showed a newly active fault line in the center of her forehead. Of course, there had to be a meeting with Kevin. That would complete this disastrous day.

"Paul's on the line."

"Later."

"Says he won't wait."

She picked up.

"Nina," Paul said. "I've got to tell you a few things I found out this weekend from Sergeant Cheney. I had lunch with him at Heidi's on Sunday."

She felt disoriented. "You're here?"

"No. I'm home. I drove back to Carmel on Sunday night."

"You didn't let me know you were in town?"

"No point, unless I found something out."

"You did, didn't you?"

"He looked into Cody Stinson's record. Stinson was in fact charged with auto theft once, at the age of eighteen, although he pled down to a lesser charge. Now he's twenty-six. I think he's discovered drug trading is more lucrative and easier to hide. They caught him for that just once."

"He might have stolen my car, then," Nina said. "He knows how."

"That's right. If he was caught once, you can bet he did it more than once."

"You think he did it?"

"I just don't know," Paul said. "And I talked with Lisa Cruz's neighbors. Turns out, she got in trouble with one of the neighbors. He cut a tree down that blocked his sun. She claimed the tree was on her property. She sued him. When she lost, his house mysteriously caught fire. Nothing ever proved, but he bought himself a Rottweiler and hasn't had any more trouble."

"She tried to burn him out?"

"He was away at the time. All the neighbors knew he spent Christmas with his aunt in Montana. Another time, the windshield on a neighboring teenager's car was broken. His family's trash ended up decorating the street. Lisa didn't like the noise he made coming home late. Everyone incriminates Lisa, although no one says it to her face. Since her father died, she's had a pretty tenuous hold on sanity, sounds like. She's not popular in the neighborhood. Does a lot of screaming. They worry about her."

"Great," Nina said. "I'll pass that on to Kevin's new lawyer."

"When her father died, she accused you to all and sundry of being responsible for causing his death. Couldn't stop talking about how ruthless you were in ruining his business. How careless you were about what effect your client's lawsuit would have on a sick man. When she found out Kevin hired you to represent him, she went apeshit, according to her neighbors."

"Oh, Paul."

"I'd call her a viable suspect."

"Where was she the night the Bronco was stolen?"

"At home. Well, we all know how close to home she sticks when she's got her track shoes on. And she doesn't live far from you."

"Okay."

"You don't sound right."

"Just keep going, Paul."

"Then there's Officer Scholl, the self-made woman. She's a go-getter from a poor family in rural North Carolina. First in her family to go to college, male or female. You know she went to Duke?"

"No."

"Smart lady. Unfortunately, she had to drop out due to lack of funds. She moved to Tahoe when her parents had both passed away, looking for a new life, I guess. She was one of the first females hired in the department. This part you already know: She's wanted to move up from Patrol to the Detective Unit for years. When she thought she finally had it locked in, you came along to ruin it. Plus, there's something about a T-Bird, some kid's car was trashed or stolen by one of your clients."

"I know the case."

"Did you know he was paralyzed in a car crash a few weeks after you got your client off?"

"No. How awful."

"She blames you."

"What?"

"She got to know the kid really well, became close to the family. They kind of adopted her. She felt like an older sister to the boy. When your client wrecked his car, he cadged lifts with friends to get to and from his job. One of them drove drunk."

"I never even heard about it."

"Why would you? Nothing to do with you. Unless we're dealing in the old philosophical idea: Anytime you walk across the street you ripple the air and change the weather off the China coast. There's that, if you're dying to blame yourself."

"I like to think I'm doing some good," Nina said. "According to them, I'm just a one-woman wrecking ball!"

"You are doing good," Paul said. "On the whole. Unfortunately, everyone's talking about Scholl, her vendetta against you."

"Just another day in court for me, and a life-changing experience for her."

"Getting a lot of attention on the road lately?"

"Three speeding tickets in the last month. Can that really be what you mean?"

"My advice: slow down. Scholl's calling in chits. Sorry to tell you, she hates your guts. She tells everyone she's waiting for her big chance to get back at you. Ring any bells?"

Nina didn't know what to say, as the bells tintinnabulated.

"Know what else I think? I think Scholl's jealous."

"No."

"Yep. Envious of your success. Thinks you grew up with a silver spoon."

"Ha."

"Yeah, funny. But she doesn't know that. You're the success she wants to be. Respected in the community. Getting lots of positive press."

"Yes, they love me. Until they hate me."

"So we come to Jeffrey Riesner."

"No, we don't." She had heard enough. She knew every case rattled the status quo, affecting many lives. She did her small bit, nothing more, serving a society that kept its peace by agreeing to abide by rules. But human order was so thinly imposed over disorder.

What good am I doing? she thought.

"We need to talk about ol' Jeffy," he insisted. "Let's start with a little personal history. You know anything about his family?"

"No."

"Turns out Riesner's mom is the old-fashioned salt of the earth. Stayed home with her kids, gave them stability, loved them to death, built up their egos. His father's an alpha male who fought his way to the top of one of the biggest firms in San Francisco. When Riesner got married to the girl next door, he went to work for Pops and was riding high. Mom was happy. Everyone was happy. Then his wife decided she had to live in the mountains so she could pursue her dream to become an Olympic skier. With his parents' encouragement, he said no. But she's not loyal like Mom. She left him, and he followed her up here."

Nina remembered his blond wife, glimpsed once on a boat, model-pretty.

"Must've given him quite the headache. Mom's disappointed, not having her darling son in town to spoil. Pops is disappointed he's such a loser he'd give in to a woman. So he needed to show them. His goal became becoming the biggest fish. Impress the folks in the way they really understood, by making money and being a huge success. That worked for a while. He made partner, got lots of press, won a few biggies that even got reported in San Francisco. Something for the folks to brag about. Convinced his wife to give up her ridiculous hopes and start working on a family. By then he didn't want to leave. And the spotlight was back where it belonged, on him."

"And then I come along—"

"You waltz in, fresh from San Francisco, cute as a button, getting all the attention, dancing your way into all the best cases. He's floundering lately. Everyone cites your last coup as the reason why."

"My last coup?"

"The gambling interests he used to represent lost faith in him. Some negotiation strategy you pulled?"

She remembered.

"Apparently you hustled him out of a fee. Worse, you called him 'asshole' in front of some very important men."

"That was naughty of me."

"Anyway, a couple of weeks ago, he got into a shouting match outside the courtroom with his partner Michael Stamp and a few things were said—let's just say his partners are grumpy about a loss of income. There's more going on behind closed doors there, and I worked on finding out what this morning, but the people at his law firm are trained well. They don't talk to strangers, except to sing Jeffy's praises."

So, it was as she had suspected when Stamp cornered her that morning at court. Riesner's firm had finally been kicked into taking the competition—her—seriously. How unsettling for Riesner. Still. "Paul, Riesner's a professional in a tough business. He's had years of success up here. He wins plenty. He's got friends, contacts, a wife he seems to care about who's willing to play the game his way. So why does he hate me?"

He paused, then said, "It's instinctive. You're a woman; he's an alpha male."

"So what?" she said, frustrated.

"He wants you to be beta."

She met with two new clients, hosted a deposition, and appeared in court on a hit-and-run case that was held over, going through all her activities with the competence of years of practice. She thought clearly, spoke articulately, operated at her keenest level of thinking, and kept her mind on her tasks.

She supposed people whose family members had wasting diseases went through something similar every day. Each day, they got up, leaving behind someone, maybe a lover, maybe a parent, in the bedroom, maybe crying, maybe screaming. They straightened a tie or stocking, and walked out the door into life moving on. The mountain grew cold and accepted the snow; the lake roughened under the wind.

At four-thirty, Kevin Cruz did not appear. Instead, a courier delivered a letter, or rather, the copy of a letter.

Addressed to the California State Bar.

To Whom It May Concern,

I feel that I must inform the state bar of a serious breach of ethical duty by my attorney, Nina Reilly, Esquire, of South Lake Tahoe. While representing me in a custody case she engaged in a sexual relationship with me.

As a result, it's my feeling that her representation of me was compromised because of personal feelings and entanglements that made her objectivity impossible. I lost temporary custody of my children, and will probably lose permanent custody as a result of her immoral behavior, which made it hard for me to concentrate on how my case should be properly handled. I also believe that, for her own personal reasons having to do with maintaining a long-term serious relationship with me, she didn't want me to get custody at all.

As an attorney practicing in California, she has a duty to uphold the highest standards of ethics and legal behavior, and in those two arenas, she has failed. I respectfully request that the state bar open an inquiry into her legal practice, which I think will result in the exposure of further illegal or immoral activities.

I am available for any questions and look forward to your response.

Sincerely,

Kevin Cruz

Attached to the letter was another letter, this one an original, from Kevin Cruz, firing her as his attorney of record.

Without a word, she handed the letters to Sandy.

Sandy read the first letter, fixing on every word, while Nina struggled to keep control. What she wanted to do was laugh, laugh loudly, uproariously—

"Sure hope at least he was hot in the sack," Sandy said.

That did it. Nina started to chuckle, and that grew into laughing, and she went to the window, tearing up from her laughter, and said, her back turned to her secretary, "Sandy—ha, ha, ha— what a staggering day of heartbreaking shit. Sandy, I'm so screwed."

Silence. Then, "I find that objectionable," Sandy said calmly.

Nina stopped laughing, although she had to work hard to do it. "I'm—I'm sorry if I offended you," she managed to say.

"It's not offensive enough," Sandy said. "Change it to you're fucked, and I'm with you."

Their laughter boiled up and overflowed. Sandy had a weird laugh, a sort of hupping laugh, hilarious really. "You want—hup, hup—some more cognac?"

"That's a good one—ha, ha, a new tradition—I'll pass—"

"Save it for—the—hup, hup—boyfriend—good idea," Sandy said. "Hoo, boy. Ah." She dug a tissue out of a box on Nina's desk and wiped her eyes. "Girl," she said, "life is cold."

Nina sobered. "You've got that right." She sat down heavily. "Kevin. Kevin. Why?"

"I never liked that guy."

"I did, at first."

"How's he think he's going to get away with this? Don't you have to be able to prove what you say?"

Nina said, "I'll bet he's got proof."

"Of what? That very bad scene you told me about?"

Nina nodded. "Photos or a video, carefully cut. Two scenes. One outside the restaurant across the street. A clinch. The other, at his condo. Heavy petting. Carefully edited. Heck, he's probably got love letters. Like my new Vang intake notes that I didn't write."

"Why would he do this to you?"

"I lost the hearing. That's enough reason, if you're unbalanced and obsessed. But wait, the files were taken the day before we lost. He lost because the files were taken. So—he didn't take the files. This is—could this be separate?"

"Can any of this help him get his kids back?"

"I don't see how. From a judge's point of view, it makes him look worse."

"He's a cop. He would know how to steal a car. Maybe he's got some gripe against you about some old case."

"Could be."

"He's your enemy."

"No question, but, Sandy, today's pattern is no coincidence. Three files, three disasters all at once, as if timed for maximum impact. Kevin's just one of the three. Maybe he has been set up, too."

"You know that powwow Joe and I organized? Someone told a

story there about a big bird that lived at Lake Tahoe that ate the people. An old man was carried up to its nest and found himself lying next to a corpse. He took a piece of obsidian he had with him and stuck it inside the corpse. Then he watched the bird finish off the corpse and listened to the bird howling when he felt the pain of that sharp rock inside. When the bird died, he cut off its wing and used that to get back down to the lake. He told the people the bird was dead and they celebrated. Now they were safe."

"I'm not sure why you're telling me this story, Sandy."

"Put some rocks in your pocket. Don't be afraid to play dirty."

"I have to call Jack." Nina went into her office. The California State Bar would be calling soon. She needed to get ready.

BOOK THREE

MARCH

She walked to the podium, warm under the spotlights. In front of her on a high dais sat three justices of the First District Court of Appeals, San Francisco Division, three wise old men in solemn black robes.

Today was her first day in court.

They watched her, maybe a little curious because they had never seen her before. She set her notes in front of her, the tabbed background material, the appellate briefs. Behind her and to the side she felt the eyes of the deputy attorney general opposing her on the appeal and the many other lawyers here today to argue their cases. Her mouth felt full of cotton and her head felt— empty.

She had so much to fear, and so much at stake, and yet this wasn't even her case. She was a substitute for another lawyer who was in the hospital.

For one whole week she had immersed herself in the issues, driven down to Soledad Prison to talk with the client, studied every case in the briefs, reviewed the evidence. The voice in her head that always stood in the way got louder every day, saying, you can't do this. You're not good enough. You haven't had enough time handling this case. You'll be tongue-tied and the whole court will laugh at you.

You will lose.

But other times, as she sat at her desk in the lamplight long after closing hours, searching for just the right words to persuade the justices that her client deserved another trial, a new feeling would well up in her: a determination to win. She couldn't fail him. She had to act as a conduit, expressing the principles that would result in justice for him.

She dealt with the seesaw between fear and determination by working harder and longer. The night before the argument, at 4:00 A.M., Bobby woke her up, crying. She gave him some water and led him to the bathroom, then helped him back into his little bed.

I have a child, she thought to herself before going back to sleep, I have this child and have kept him alive. What could be harder or more important than that?

The morning scheduled for arguments in her case dawned in the traditional San Francisco way: foggy, cool, mysterious. She dressed in her black suit and wore her mother's watch. At the courthouse downtown, standing outside the doors, Nina experienced one more moment of savage fright. A man's liberty was at stake. His defense was entrusted to her, and who was she? Just a young woman without much self-confidence, not brilliant, not impressive, not experienced—who was she against the state of California?

Her case was called. She walked to the podium, under the lights. She laid down her papers and set her mind on her client, Klaus, her mother, all the people who had supported her over the long, lonely years and brought her to this place.

She opened her mouth and began to speak.

EXHIBIT ONE

OFFICE OF TRIAL COUNSEL
STATE BAR OF CALIFORNIA
Gayle Nolan, NO. 101447
Attorney at Law
555B Franklin Street
San Francisco, CA 94102
555/698-4947

THE STATE BAR COURT
THE STATE BAR OF CALIFORNIA
HEARING DEPARTMENT—SAN FRANCISCO

In the Matter of
Nina F. Reilly, No. 379168
<u>A Member of the State Bar</u>

TO: NINA FOX REILLY, Respondent herein:

IF YOU FAIL TO FILE AN ANSWER TO THIS
NOTICE WITHIN THE TIME ALLOWED BY
STATE BAR RULES, INCLUDING EXTENSIONS,
YOU MAY BE ENROLLED AS AN
INVOLUNTARY INACTIVE MEMBER OF THE
STATE BAR AND WILL NOT BE PERMITTED
TO PRACTICE LAW UNTIL AN ANSWER IS
FILED.

You were admitted to the practice of law in the state of
California on January 12, 1994. Pursuant to Rule 510,
Rules of Procedure of the State Bar of California, reasonable cause has been found to conduct a formal disciplinary
hearing, commencing at a time and place to be fixed by the
state bar court (NOTICE OF THE TIME AND PLACE
OF HEARING WILL BE MAILED TO YOU BY THE
STATE BAR COURT CLERK'S OFFICE), by reason of
the following:

COUNT ONE

1. In 2001, you were a sole practitioner in the law firm of Law Offices of Nina F. Reilly, Attorney at Law, 2489 South Lake Tahoe Boulevard, South Lake Tahoe, California.

2. While acting in your duties as an attorney, you occupied a position of trust for many clients. For our purposes here, one client group, consisting of Brandy Ann Taylor, Bruce R. Ford, and Angel Guillaume, is represented in this count.

3. Beginning on September 6, while serving in a lawyer-client relationship, and with a primary obligation to preserve the confidences and secrets of your clients, for the separate parties as referenced above, you failed to protect client information as required under California Business and Professions Code section 6068 (e) by leaving client files in an unlocked vehicle, which was subsequently stolen from you. You failed to implement the proper safeguards to ensure that client information remained confidential, a violation of your duty to perform competently.

4. Disclosure of the contents of those files has caused harm to your clients. After the loss of your client files, these three individuals were threatened and attacked by a man, Cody Stinson, whom they revealed in private conversations with you, their attorney, they had witnessed fleeing the scene of a murder.

COUNT TWO

1. While acting in your duties as an attorney, you knowingly assisted in the commission of a fraud against the Heritage Life Insurance Company Incorporated, by Kao Vang, former owner of Blue Star Market located in South Lake Tahoe, California.

2. Representing Kao Vang in an insurance claim

against Heritage Life, you knew that arson had been committed by your client for the fraudulent purposes of obtaining an insurance settlement. The gross amount of that settlement, since paid in equal portions to Kao Vang and his wife, See Vang, was $210,000.

3. As a result of your personal, speedy delivery of funds to Kao Vang, he left the country before the fraud was apparent, making recovery of the fraudulently obtained funds difficult or impossible. The funds delivered to See Vang have been attached awaiting disposition of this count.

3. Your collection of any portion of that settlement constitutes a separate fraud.

COUNT THREE

1. While representing your client, Kevin Cruz, in a custody case, you engaged in a sexual relationship with him.

2. You employed undue influence in entering into the relationship, and implied that this level of intimacy was required in order for you to continue representation.

3. In violation of Rule 3–110 of the Rules of Professional Conduct of the State Bar of California, you continued to represent this client, even though the relationship damaged and prejudiced the client's case, and resulted in the loss of temporary custody of his two minor children.

By committing the acts described above, you willfully violated your oath and duties as an attorney. In particular, you violated California Business and Professions Code section 6068 (e); and Rule 3–110 of the Rules of Professional Conduct.

20

"IN THE MATTER OF REILLY," Judge Hugo Brock said in a soft voice. He had climbed the stairs to his seat with grave eyes downcast, without a word to his clerk. Decorum above all, Nina thought. He's the type who worries about losing control in the courtroom. How will he handle Jack?

More to the point, how will Jack handle Judge Hugo Brock? She had asked Jack this very question. His answer was, "Don't worry. Hugo beats the alternatives."

The huge digital clock on the judge's dais ticked off the seconds before the momentous switch to 9:30 A.M. In this moment before the hearing began, close together in the tense, windowless room, they all sat at attention, ignoring one another. The judge's clerk, a girlish-looking woman with festive auburn hair and a midcalf-length blue skirt slit demurely up to her knees, paid no attention to anyone. Black headphones covering her ears, she stared at her computer, with them corporeally only. She might even be working on some other matter, transcribing the words of some other poor practitioner who had suffered in this very chair the previous week.

So defendants felt like this! Nina glanced at Gayle Nolan, the chief trial counsel. Jack called her Pit Bull Nolan, more or less an admission that he considered her competent. In navy wool, glasses low on her nose, her hair in a gray pageboy, she had a haggard expression. Retirement could not be far away, assuming that the state bar still gave its staff retirement benefits. The big money no longer rolled in from California's attorneys, but the criticism of the whole disciplinary system got louder every year.

Now, from the hot seat, Nina began to see why. Salaried employees of the not-very-large entity, Gayle Nolan and Hugo Brock were coworkers. Their motivations should be radically different, exemplifying the enormous gap between judicial and enforcement branches, but in the end these two both represented the goals of the California State Bar.

And what were those goals? The president of the state bar had said in a speech Nina attended, "At the state bar, public protection is our number-one priority."

This seemed a perversion to many California lawyers, who thought the state bar dues they paid each year should go to an organization with the number-one priority of supporting and encouraging them. When had the focus become weeding out the bad apples in the profession? Whatever happened to stabilizing the wobbly apples and protecting the ripe apples? How could the judge and the prosecutor work out of the same small, half-crippled system and not walk in lockstep?

As Nina whizzed through these thoughts, Gayle Nolan glanced back at her through designer glasses so enormous, so thick, so encrusted with decoration that the face behind them blurred. A blessing.

Her own eyes were bothering her, so she put on her horn-rims. With surgical fussiness, Jack wiped his glasses on his handkerchief, allowing not one mote of fuzz. Every single person in that courtroom was viewing the world through a layer of polymer or glass.

She looked down and discovered she was wringing her hands. She made an effort to sit still and betray nothing. Whatever she did, look scared or look calm, she felt that she looked guilty. Such are the thoughts of a defendant.

"Let's start by, uh, clarifying the order of proof. I understand we have a change in the usual presentation, Counsel," Judge Brock said.

Gayle Nolan stood up. "Yes, we do, Your Honor. As you know, this is a bifurcated hearing, with the first part presenting the culpability portion and the second part, mitigation. Right now we are just dealing with culpability. We have three sets of complaints here in three matters. Mr. McIntyre and I have agreed to put on each of the matters separately. I will put on the prosecution witnesses for Count One and Mr. McIntyre will cross-examine each witness and we will complete all the proof for that count before moving on to Count Two. If that is all right with the court."

"So we will look at the Brandy Taylor matter first?"

"Right."

"Actually," Jack said, moving in to make his first impression, "we agreed to start with Officer Scholl, the officer who took the police report involving the stolen files. Her testimony relates to all the cases."

"I was getting to that," Nolan said. "That's right, we will begin with Officer Scholl." She clamped down on the words, as determined as a basketball player getting the ball back for her team.

"Sorry," Jack said. "Didn't mean to step on your toes within the first two minutes." He smiled, but the judge and the prosecutor stuck to their poker faces.

"Fine," Judge Brock said. "Are we ready, then?"

"Ready," Nolan said.

"Ready, Your Honor." Jack patted Nina's hand.

"Call Officer Jean Scholl." Officer Scholl hustled in. "Raise your right hand." She swore to be truthful, then launched into a minor complaint about having to take the whole day off to be in San Francisco for this hearing. The uniform accentuated her strong build and handsome unadorned face. Setting her clipboard in her lap, she gave Nolan, who was standing, her full attention.

"Good morning. I'm Gayle Nolan, I represent the State Bar of California."

"Good morning," Scholl said.

Over the previous several months, Paul had uncovered some

more interesting details about Officer Scholl. Early in her career, she had worked with Kevin Cruz. On one occasion, Scholl had been along for the ride when Kevin Cruz busted a group of three young men for cocaine possession with intent to sell. The bust netted Kevin his first and only promotion, but rumors flew.

The three young men were honors students from UC Davis up for a weekend of skiing. None had ever been arrested for drugs before. One was in the middle of writing a senior thesis on the effects of illegal drugs on brain function. One had already inherited more family money than an oil baron, and therefore had little to gain and a lot to lose from selling drugs. Nevertheless, they had all been convicted, thanks to the testimony of Cruz and Scholl.

Scholl was as biased as they come, and maybe more. Nina leaned forward and tried to catch her mood, which was all too easy.

"You are a patrol officer with the South Lake Tahoe Police Department?"

"For the last eight years I've worked with the Patrol Watch Unit. Lately, I've also been working in conjunction with the Detective Unit, assisting on burglaries and robberies and undertaking some traffic-case investigations. It's a small department so I get involved in several types of police work."

"On or about September seventh of last year, were you called to the scene of a reported auto theft?"

The officer consulted her clipboard. "The call came in at seven-fifty A.M. Officer Dave Matthias and I responded and arrived at 96 Kulow Street, a single-family residence in the Pioneer Tract, at eight-twenty-four A.M."

"And were you met at the scene by anyone?"

"By the defendant there. Ms. Reilly."

"You already knew Ms. Reilly?"

"She's an attorney who does—did—a lot of criminal-defense work. Trying to get her clients out of things. I had her in traffic court several times."

"You testify regularly in the South Lake Tahoe court, where the defendant practices law?"

"Just about every week. She's only been around a couple of years, but she picked up quite a few defendants. She started showing up as defense counsel in some of the big felonies up at the lake, which surprised and upset some of the local attorneys, I can tell you. She pushed hard for the high-profile cases, getting her name in the paper to promote her business. Quite a few of my colleagues came into contact with her."

All of a sudden, the humdrum opening questions and answers had flown into unfamiliar realms. Police officers always tried for at least a semblance of objectivity. She had never heard Scholl get opinionated like this. Jack wasn't moving, so she shifted in her chair. He had warned her not to expect the usual rules of court.

"You had several chances to observe the defendant at work?"

"Right."

"How would you describe her work?" Jack sat like a fleck of lint. They should be talking about the Bronco, not about how this cop liked being cross-examined by Nina in court!

She nudged him. Jack leaned over. "They can't do this," she said. He held up a hand to shush her and turned his attention back to Scholl.

"Well, I felt that she wasn't—I guess you would say, systematic. She rushed in at the last minute. She showed up late once or twice, as a matter of fact. She would try anything to get her clients off. Tricks. She had a reputation."

"Jack!"

He gave Nina a nod, nothing more.

"A reputation in the police department?"

"Yes."

"And can you describe that reputation?"

"Everyone said she would do just about anything to get her clients off. She attacked the officers in court, gave us a hard time and made us go over each and every detail hoping to find something wrong. She was—well, fly-by-night, always looking for some jazzy way to slip by the facts."

"Can you give the court any specific example of this irresponsibility?"

"Objection," Jack said, finally jumping up like his nimble name-sake. About time. None of this would have been admissible in the courts Nina knew. Jack had entered the game late, but he would put a stop to this ridiculous character-bashing.

"Counsel should rephrase that," was all Jack said, and sat down. Nina gave him an incredulous stare.

"I'll decide that," Judge Brock said. To Nolan, he said, "The word 'irresponsibility' calls for a conclusion. So I'll sustain that objection."

"Thank you, Your Honor," Nolan kowtowed. "Did you observe how Ms. Reilly related to her clients?" Boggled as a kid in a toy store by the myriad possibilities for character assassination that appeared available to her, Nolan seemed to have forgotten her question about the specific acts of irresponsibility she'd been trying to learn about a second earlier.

"You bet I did," Officer Scholl said. "She was much more friendly with them than the other attorneys, I thought. She's a toucher. There were physical intimacies. She would hug them, set a hand on their shoulders right in the middle of the hearing. I saw her put an arm around one of her clients. She acted more like a friend than a person in a business relationship."

Nina's mouth dropped open. Now she knew exactly what Scholl had been thinking during those long days in court when she picked at Scholl's police reports, looking for ways out for her clients. Now she understood the broader picture. She had won against Officer Scholl, and Officer Scholl did not forgive or forget. Nina no longer harbored doubts about whether Scholl had it in her to frame Nina and run her out of town. Scholl detested her.

Nolan cleared her throat. "So the defendant called you to her home. What did she tell you?"

"That her vehicle, a Ford Bronco, had been stolen during the night."

"Could you summarize her statement to you?"

"She said she drove home from her office in the rain the night before about six P.M. and ran inside. She had not been able to locate her key earlier in the day, so she used a spare one. Later that night she remembered that she had some important files out in her car but she was sleepy so she went to bed instead of going out to retrieve them. Around seven the next morning she discovered the vehicle and its contents were gone."

"Okay, let me back up a little. She said she lost her key?"

"Yes."

"And that whole evening she knew that she had left it somewhere. Meanwhile, the vehicle sat outside unguarded and unprotected—"

"We're leading just a little bit here," Jack said.

"I withdraw that question. What exactly did the defendant say about what she did for the time period between six P.M. and seven A.M. with regard to locking her truck or removing the key from the ignition?"

"She claimed she locked the truck with her spare key. Is that what you mean? She said she knew the truck was out there and her key was gone and her files were in the back in the briefcase but she basically couldn't be bothered."

"She knew the main key was missing by then? In the hands of absolutely anyone?"

Officer Scholl had the character at least to glance down at her report on that one. "Well, she claimed she didn't think about that."

"All right. Now, she mentioned some important files had been left in the Bronco."

"Yes. She was very insistent about us finding the files. They were in a burgundy leather briefcase, she said. She cared more about the files than the stolen vehicle."

"And what did she tell you about these files?"

"She described them as client files, which had labels and names. She said the files held confidential information. Different information in each file. And what she called client-intake forms."

"And did she give you the names of the clients?"

"No, she wouldn't give us the names. She stated that the names were confidential. She wouldn't say what the cases were about or if there was anything in the cases that might make somebody want to get at the files. I warned her that that would hinder our investigation but she wouldn't budge."

"And was the failure of the defendant to provide information about the files a hindrance to your work?"

"I asked right away, could the thief be after the files? She said she didn't see how. I said, how can we find out if you won't give us any details? I had to leave it at that."

"What else did she tell you?"

"That her son had an ongoing friendship with an individual named Nicole Zack, who stayed at the house now and then. Nicole Zack is known to local law enforcement. She has had several arrests as a juvenile and a conviction for shoplifting. She was arrested for murder last year, which is how the defendant got to know her. She got her off."

"The defendant in this instance had a close relationship with her client?"

"Obviously. Close enough that they hang out together at night at her house."

The comment didn't make a point, it slashed like a machete. Fussy adherence to petty concerns, reckless disregard for issues of serious import, and suggestive interactions with notorious lowlifes— Nina had done it all. The prosecution's entire case relied on nothing more substantial than the imaginative slanders of this officer who hardly knew her.

"Do something!" Nina whispered to Jack. He shook his head sharply, warning her to stay out of it. As the questioning went on, Nina's hands shook with frustration.

"The son had no car? He had to ride around on a bicycle?"

"He's underage for a license."

"And Nicole Zack?"

"She doesn't have one yet. Not that that would stop her."

"Did the defendant tell you anything else?"

Officer Scholl examined her report again. "Not until later. She called and gave us the names of three files. She said she had checked with the clients and they had allowed her to do that."

"And what were those names?"

"Angel Guillaume and Brandy Taylor. Kao and See Vang. Kevin Cruz. But she claimed it was all confidential. She wouldn't tell us anything about the contents of the files."

"Now, Officer Scholl, were you also assigned the investigation of this theft?"

"I was. I located the vehicle several days later at the Heavenly parking lot. It looked like somebody had a long joyride and dumped the vehicle there. The defendant couldn't identify any damage. I had it examined for forensic evidence and fingerprints. There were a number of prints of the defendant and her son. Dog hairs all over. Trash in the backseat, half-empty Gatorade and water bottles, a coffee cup that had been there awhile."

Oh, great. Now she bad-mouthed Nina's domestic inadequacies.

"Nothing that would help identify the perpetrator," Scholl added.

"What about the missing key?"

"Left on the seat. Wiped clean of prints."

"Were the files found in the vehicle?"

"No. The files were missing, and so was the briefcase."

"Were the files ever located to your knowledge?"

"Not to my knowledge. I did interview Nicole Zack and the boy. I put out an APB on the truck. I did what I could, but without the defendant's full cooperation, I couldn't mount a full-scale investigation. I just had to wait until the truck got dumped. The auto-theft case is still open."

"Let me ask you something now, Officer. Do you have any independent knowledge that these files were ever in the defendant's stolen vehicle?"

"No."

"The defendant could have accidentally left her briefcase in a supermarket or lost them in some other, even more egregious fashion?"

Officer Scholl looked thoughtful. "For all I know."

"And used the auto theft as an excuse to claim she wasn't totally responsible for the loss?"

"I never saw any files. I don't know if there were in fact any files in a briefcase in that vehicle."

"And has the perpetrator of the theft been identified at this time?"

"Not at this time. As I say, I'm still in charge of an open investigation."

"Thank you. Nothing further."

"We will take the midmorning break," said Judge Brock. Nolan left. The clock stopped. The clerk took off her headphones and disappeared.

Jack nodded at the door.

"I'll stay here for a minute," Nina said, "and try to remember how hardworking and innocent I looked to myself only yesterday."

"I warned you. They trowel on the accusations. Hearsay, opinion evidence, all sorts of character-battering is an integral part of the proceedings. You'll get a better crack at showing a balanced picture of your career, who you are, how well you've done in your work, during the next phase, the mitigation hearing. This is a different kind of court."

"Yeah, it's a quasi-court practicing quasi-law with quasi-rules of procedure. And quasi-protection for the defendant."

Jack said, "You're right. Welcome to the Bizarro universe of law."

"I read the rules, but I can't believe the way they play out in practice. This is not supposed to be a criminal action, but it sure feels like one."

"If only it were a criminal matter," Jack said. "Then you might have the statutory presumption of innocence. You don't get that here. You already know that the technical rules of evidence in criminal cases aren't applicable. The case doesn't even have to be proven beyond a reasonable doubt. It's unclear how much hearsay evidence can come in, and Hugo likes to hear it all."

"Then why do I need an attorney?" Nina said rather rashly. "You don't object. You can't keep the worst slimeballing out. You can't do anything but sit there."

"I haven't cross-examined yet."

"Is that when you start defending me?"

"Look, we got off to a rough start this morning. I'll take some of the blame."

"I hate sitting there unable to open my mouth and defend myself. I feel like a crash-test dummy." She helped herself to some of the bottled water.

"Back at my office, I have a quote from Kafka taped inside my drawer. Funny guy, in his bitter European way. *The Trial* speaks to some of your ordeal. You remember, this clerk, K, keeps getting hauled off to this court in this crummy run-down warehouse, and he can't find out what the charges are. At first he scoffs, but he finally starts believing in the whole strange system. At that point he's doomed."

"Then he and I have nothing in common," Nina said. "I refuse to let this sorry system ruin my life."

"All they can do is lift your license."

He said it lightly, but she heard the worry behind his words. Jack was being kind. They both knew this could go beyond the California bar court into a criminal investigation of fraud. "That can't happen," she said. "We won't let it."

"If it happens, it won't be the end of the world."

"Nobody is running me out of this career that I worked so damn hard to achieve."

Silence while he digested this. "Good, because you're exactly the kind of lawyer we need out there, dirty-kneed, trudging through the trenches." He lifted her chin to look at her. "Ah, Nina. How life changes."

"I've never feared change, Jack. I see it as an opportunity." She got up. "I'm out of here. When does the kangaroo court resume?"

Jack looked at his watch. "Nine minutes. Nina—"

"What?"

"Relax a little with the constant pen and paper, okay? It makes the judge nervous. And you might want to slap a little lipstick on or powder your nose or something. Look like a winner. You look too worried."

Wanting to fume in private, Nina went down a floor, an old trick of hers when she wanted to be alone, and paced around in that hallway. Nine minutes passed, then they returned to their tables in the ice-cold court.

Judge Brock entered and they all stood and sat down again in a clumsy shared motion. The clerk detached, plugging her headphones into some distant place like Mars, her eyes looking somewhere into the middle distance of the room where there was nothing but dead air to view. Officer Scholl was advised that she was still under oath.

"Good morning, Officer," Jack said, receiving a curt nod in return.

"So you already knew Ms. Reilly from traffic court?"

"Yes."

"You hand out the traffic citations, she fights them?"

"That's about it."

"How many times have you come up against Ms. Reilly?"

"Oh, five or six."

"And every single time, she beat your ticket, didn't she?"

"Objection," said Nolan.

"Goes to bias."

"Overruled."

"She beat you, didn't she?" Jack said with a little smile.

"I can't remember every case."

"Do you need me to refresh your recollection by having you go through this stack of records here and then putting in evidence each of the instances?"

"She got her client off on the tickets each time."

"You say she resorted to trickery. What tricks did she pull?"

"She took advantage of the situation. She attacked the calibration of the radar gun. She continued cases until I or the other officers had a conflict and couldn't make it to the court appearance, and got a dismissal that way. She knew we couldn't remember every detail of a traffic stop from months before. She made one little inconsistency look like we were lying."

" 'We were lying'? Wasn't it just you up there?"

"She made it look like I was lying, which I wasn't."

"So you were humiliated by her tactics?"

Scholl flushed. "I take personal pride in my work."

"She blighted your otherwise good record?"

"My record is otherwise very good."

"Did the issue of your frequent losses in court on cases against defendants of Ms. Reilly come up during discussions with your superior officer about an upcoming promotion to the Detective Unit?"

Scholl paused and thought before she spoke. "Yes."

"Did you get the promotion?"

"No."

"Do you attribute your failure to be promoted to Ms. Reilly?"

"I can only say the citations were good, and I was accused of lying on the stand, and the judge dismissed the citations. And this was a factor."

"Did she ever get sanctioned by a court for her tactics?"

"I wouldn't know about that."

"Did she ever get found in contempt?"

"I have no way of knowing."

"So she attacked the prosecution's case and got her clients off on the tickets," Jack mused as if to himself. "Guess that didn't make her too popular with law enforcement up at Tahoe."

"Exactly. She could not be trusted."

"It sure didn't make her very popular with you, did it?"

"I—I didn't like her tactics."

"You didn't like her success, you mean. How do you like criminal-defense attorneys in general, from your viewpoint in law enforcement?"

"They are a necessary ev—they are part of the system."

Smiling, Jack said, "They could all get shipped off to Timbuktu and you wouldn't miss 'em, would you?"

"Not really."

"I appreciate your forthrightness," Jack said. He had a rhythm going, Nina thought. He wasn't half bad. A small relief released some of the built-up pressure in her chest.

"Now, you mentioned that it didn't help your investigation that Ms. Reilly wouldn't tell you her clients' names."

"I felt she was not cooperating with the investigation."

"Ever heard of Rule 1.6 (a)?"

"I'm not a lawyer."

"Indeed you aren't. Let me put it this way. Did you know that there is a rule of practice for attorneys that prohibits them from revealing any information relating to the representation of a client unless the client consents after consultation?"

"Not even the name?"

"Not even the name."

"No. I didn't know that."

"And Ms. Reilly did give you the names as soon as she had talked to her clients?"

"Yes, but without knowing more about what was in the files we couldn't tell if the theft might be related to one of the clients."

"What about the attorney-client privilege? Ever heard of that?"

"Yes, but I'm not a lawyer. Like I said."

"But it caused you trouble, Ms. Reilly fulfilling her duties as a lawyer?"

"I'm just saying—"

"Did she do anything besides protect the confidentiality of the files that caused you a problem?"

Officer Scholl thought that through. "I felt she was defensive about her relationship with Nicole Zack. I felt that individual was a suspect."

"Didn't you tell her Ms. Zack was bad news, in so many words?"

"It's the truth."

"And she defended Ms. Zack to you?"

"She wouldn't hear a word against her."

"Let me ask you this. Did you at any time in your investigation develop a shred of evidence, a scintilla of evidence, that Ms. Zack had anything to do with this theft?"

"No. But I still—"

"Now then. You testified that Ms. Reilly is a touchy-feely type who has gone so far as to hug a client in your presence?"

"That's correct."

"In what circumstances did she do this?"

"Well, the jury came in."

"With a verdict?"

"Yes."

"An acquittal?"

"Yes."

"And they hugged each other?"

"That's right."

"Do you believe that hugging a client after an acquittal leads to moral turpitude, oh, for example, sleeping with her male clients?"

"Objection! There's so much wrong with that question I don't know where to start," Nolan said, on her feet.

"Why, Counsel, isn't that exactly what you were trying to imply?" Jack said innocently.

"Rephrase it, Counsel," Judge Brock said, amusement twitching the corners of his mouth.

"Well, you know that Ms. Reilly is accused of sleeping with one of South Lake Tahoe's finest, don't you?"

"Yes."

"Do you think she gets too intimate with her clients?"

"She befriends them. She hugs them."

"Shocking, isn't it."

"Counsel, let's move on," Brock said.

"Just one last thing. When you found Ms. Reilly's vehicle, it was full of papers and used coffee cups?"

"It was pretty trashed."

"Do you attribute that to Ms. Reilly's generally being a trashy person?"

"What kind of question is that?" Nolan said. "I object. Counsel is making fun of the witness."

"She's calling my client trashy, Your Honor."

"Move on."

"Was the truck locked when it was found?"

"No."

"Anyone could have had a few Gatorades and left them in the back. The thief could have gotten thirsty while riding around in the stolen vehicle, isn't that correct?"

"Correct or incorrect, it's irrelevant and it's frivolous," Nolan said.

"Anyone could have left that trash," Jack said. "I feel it's a relevant point."

"Objection sustained," the judge said.

"Did you have the Gatorade bottles tested for DNA? Trashy people drink out of the bottle, you know."

"We don't have the resources to go that far for a simple auto theft."

"How about the coffee cup?"

"It looked like it had been there a long time."

"You assumed it was Ms. Reilly's cup?"

"Well, it seemed to be."

"So let's see if I can summarize your testimony up to this point," Jack said. "You took the report, you can't stand Ms. Reilly or criminal-defense lawyers in general, you did a half-assed investigation and got lucky and finally stumbled across the truck, and you think Ms. Reilly must have slept with Kevin Cruz because you saw her hug a female client after an acquittal by a jury?"

"Objection!"

"Sustained."

"Ever see Ms. Reilly and Officer Cruz together, Officer Scholl?"

"No," Officer Scholl said flatly.

"You're darn right you haven't. I have nothing further, Your Honor."

"Jack," Nina whispered after he sat down. "What about the fact that she hates me for making her look like an idiot on the stand? What about the fact that she may have cooked up this whole malicious plot?"

"Let me ask you a question. Should we rock Brock to sleep with harebrained theories about what happened, or should we try to win this case?"

21

GAYLE NOLAN WALKED to the courtroom door and opened it. Stepping inside, she called her next witness. Bruce Ford entered, moving quickly to the stand. His date of birth put him in his late twenties, although he seemed older to Nina. Bristly hair fringed his face, and dark curls were cut tight to his head. Like almost all lawyers, he had to correct his eyes with specs, but these were a hip green-tinted pair. He appeared well ironed into an expensive suit, but not happy to be here.

She had heard Nolan had twisted his arm to come. He didn't want to come out publicly against a fellow attorney, although mean-spirited letter-writing was apparently acceptable practice. She shifted in her seat as Ford described his tax practice and educational background.

Gayle Nolan remained seated as she asked questions, the black notebooks on each side of the table framing her like big guns. Here was the chief trial counsel's place of power, Nina thought, behind these windowless walls, in this aridity, fighting what she probably considered the good fight, sinking incompetent attorneys.

Attorneys like *her*.

"Mr. Ford, please tell us the circumstances that brought you here today."

Bruce Ford took his glasses off and wiped them with a handkerchief, then placed them carefully back on his nose. "My fiancée, Brandy, hired Ms. Reilly as her attorney. She and her sister, Angel

Guillaume, were present at South Lake Tahoe's Campground by the
Lake the night that Phoebe Palladino was killed. They had seen
something that night, somebody running away from the tent Phoebe
was in, so they went to ask Ms. Reilly for advice. They needed to
talk to the police but were afraid about what would happen if they
did. Turns out they were right to worry about that, only they
should have been worrying just as much about who they chose to
hire."

"Shouldn't you object?" Nina whispered. "He wasn't even my
client and he's stating opinions."

"We want the judge to see we respect his intelligence. He knows
opinions differ from fact."

"So Ms. Reilly was not specifically your attorney?" Nolan asked
Bruce Ford.

"She was representing my fiancée."

"What happened to you after your fiancée consulted Ms.
Reilly?"

"I was in my office one day. A guy bullied his way through my
receptionist and into my office. He introduced himself as Cody
Stinson, but at the time that meant nothing to me. I didn't know the
name. Well, I see a lot of different types. First, I assumed he was a
potential client who was just worked up about something. I get a lot
of that. Then he started talking about strangling someone, and I suddenly realized he wasn't there to consult me about anything."

"In your opinion, Mr. Ford, why had he come there?"

"He was there to threaten and intimidate me."

"What was the intimidation designed to accomplish?"

"He wanted my fiancée to quit talking to anyone about what
happened at the campground. He was perfectly clear on that point.
He swore she'd be sorry if she didn't 'shut her mouth'—only his language was much cruder than mine is here today. He threatened me,
said he'd get me if I didn't do something about her."

"Then what happened?"

"I don't know how I did it. Years of handling my alcoholic dad,
I think. Anyway, I threw him out."

"Did he go peaceably?"

"He broke a porcelain lamp that was on the secretary's desk."

"How did he do that?"

"Knocked it down. He was yelling. Very angry."

"After he left, what did you do?"

"Moved in with a friend."

"Why?"

"As he was leaving, Stinson taunted me. Said he knew where I lived."

"You were frightened?"

"Very."

"Did you tell anyone where you were?"

"Not for a couple of days."

"You didn't call your fiancée?"

He stretched his neck uncomfortably. "We were—having a hard time, but I tried to reach her. Didn't have much luck."

"After a few days, you made contact?"

"She found me. I knew she could if she wanted to badly enough."

"What effect did this incident have on your business?"

"I couldn't work. I didn't take calls. It cost me money and made it hard for me to complete the work I had at hand. It had a distinctly negative effect on my business."

"And on you personally?"

"I suffered tremendous emotional distress. I had to see a doctor. It exacerbated the problems with my fiancée."

Jack, taking a different tack, stood when he talked to Ford, although he stood behind the table. He moved his weight from one side to the other, his compact body swaying like a tree in a wild wind as he thought on his feet. "Mr. Ford, why didn't you know about Cody Stinson in the first place?"

"I hadn't talked to my fiancée, Brandy Taylor, for a couple of days."

"And why was that?"

"She was out of town."

"But you were on speaking terms."

"Of course." But the eyes behind the green tint blinked.

"Did she later tell you that she had been instructed by her attorney to contact you?"

"I don't remember that."

"Did she say she tried to reach you before Cody Stinson ever came to your office to tell you what was going on?"

Ford had a toothache, judging from the tortured crook to his mouth. "Yes."

"Why couldn't she reach you to warn you?"

"My cell phone was out."

"Why couldn't she find you at the office?"

"She left some messages," he admitted. "I was upset. I didn't call her back. Believe me, I regret that very much now. I was wrong."

"Mr. Ford, isn't it true that you moved in with your friend several days before Cody Stinson showed up at your office?"

He was silent.

Busted, Nina thought. Jack hadn't told her about that.

"You were having some problems in your relationship and moved out. You weren't taking calls from your fiancée at home or at the office, isn't that so, Mr. Ford?"

The tongue went back to work the bad molar again. "I'm not proud of how I behaved. I hate fighting with her. I guess the timing of the whole thing got confused in my mind," he said.

"I guess it did, Mr. Ford. So any harm to your business, aside from a lamp that may have been broken accidentally, is really due to the problems you were having in your relationship, isn't it?"

"Listen, that guy scared me. He threw me off my stride. He threatened my fiancée! He had no business doing that. She was scared to death. I felt so horrible when I found out."

Ford didn't come off too badly, just as a protective boyfriend, but his indignation no longer carried the heft of righteousness. The judge lost interest. He turned toward the clerk and said something. The clerk nodded, then focused harder on the mysteries unfolding on her computer.

"How did you know about that?" Nina whispered to Jack.

"I read it in his eyes."

"You did?"

He took pity on her bewilderment. He whispered, "Paul just found out. He called me late last night. Just when you write him off as useless, he comes up with something."

The next witness, Brandy Taylor, brought a breeze through the door with her, rushed up to the witness stand, and said "Sorry" when she almost tipped over the bottle of water on Nolan's table.

Brandy wore a red jacket over a flowing chiffon skirt. Judge Brock gave her his full attention.

She gave her vital statistics, then began her story, her attitude apologetic. "I didn't want to complain, but my boyfriend was so upset. He's a lawyer and he said that it was like a civic duty, that what Ms. Reilly did to us was harmful. We could have died. You know, the truth is, we were all scared."

Pushing her gaudy rims up tight to her eyes, Nolan straightened her padded shoulders and brightened all around. She laid on the sympathy lightly, as if knowing a heavy hand might twist things the wrong way. She didn't say outright, "Poor you," but a warmth under her questions carried the implication with every sentence. "Tell us, in your own words, Ms. Taylor, what happened."

Brandy told the court at great length about their trip to the campground, angling around her troubles with her boyfriend, emphasizing the fun of a visit with her sister, Angel. She said the arguments at the tent next door escalated after Cody Stinson arrived, and she described the arrival of the park ranger and how relieved they felt. Then, she said, they couldn't sleep anyway. "We got up in the middle of the night to use the—uh—bathroom."

"You and your sister both?"

"We both went, yeah."

"Tell us what happened then."

"Well, it was super late at night and really dark. Even though the campground's lit and you can see the lights reflecting on the lake through the trees, it's not like daytime. On the other hand, it's not so dark you can't see. It was also quiet. When we got to the bathroom we waited a minute for this other woman to finish, then we were quick. It was on the way back that I saw Cody Stinson leaving Phoebe's tent."

"Which caused you to consult with Nina Reilly?"

"That's right. We were frightened and didn't know what to do."

Brandy wasn't enjoying this. In spite of Jack's admonition, Nina scribbled on her notepad, the mindless doodles she hoped looked like serious note-taking to anyone who happened to notice. The doodling helped her think, as if the stick figures and their little randomly generated activities freed up her mind for more logical paths.

She doodled an outhouse with a half-moon cut in the door, a woman walking away, two shadowy figures waiting.

Hmm, she thought, the woman in the washroom, out and about in the middle of the night. Brandy and Angel had mentioned her on their first visit to Nina. Could that mean anything? The campground had been crowded.

Could be anyone.

Could be someone?

When Brandy got to Cody's attack, she became teary. Gayle Nolan, entirely pleased with the girl's performance, egged her on, but Brandy wiped her eyes quickly, saying it was months ago now, and nothing had happened since Stinson was put in jail. She even put a plug in for Paul's role in Stinson's capture, which Nina appreciated, even though Jack seemed unmoved.

Nolan didn't let Brandy go before detailing the injury to Brandy and her sister. They had been menaced, attacked even, by this man who should never have had the information he had, which came straight out of Nina's confidential client file.

When Jack's turn came to question Brandy, she uncrossed her

legs and pushed her back against the chair, as if recoiling from what she expected to be an unpleasant scene. Instead, he gently prodded her about the things Nina had done to prevent any harm the information in the file might have caused.

"She hired an investigator, who followed you even though you didn't request protection. He was there when Cody Stinson confronted you at the beach, correct?"

"That's right. She didn't have to do that. I like Ms. Reilly, don't get me wrong. I know she didn't mean for us to get hurt."

"Would you mind going into a little more detail about what happened when Cody Stinson 'jumped out' at you?"

"Certainly. We were just walking along, and there he was. I recognized him right away and I started screaming and kicking him, because Angel and I have two brothers, and I think it was just a reaction to the situation, you know? Because I recognized him right away. Angel kind of leaped onto his back."

"And got knocked down."

"Right."

"What exactly did Cody Stinson do?"

"Well, he was shouting," she said dubiously. "What do you mean, what did he do?"

"Did he pull a knife?"

"I didn't see one. Doesn't mean he didn't have one, though."

"What was he saying?"

She shook her head in disbelief. "I wasn't listening, to tell you the truth. I was scared out of my brains."

"Is it possible Cody Stinson just wanted to talk?"

"He knocked Angel down," she said slowly. "So, no. I wouldn't say so."

"After she jumped on his back."

"He jumped us," she said firmly.

"After you screamed and kicked him."

"What was I supposed to do! He's a murderer and he shows up in the woods by the beach where I'm supposed to be meeting my fiancé! I'm damn proud we fought back!"

Jack calmed her down, praising her quick thinking, all the while making his points for the judge. When they got to the event at the women's shelter, he tried for similar points. Why did Stinson knock? Hadn't he said he just wanted to talk to them that night, too? Wasn't it possible the broken window was just a result of his frustration about not getting their attention? He established that the Taylor-Ford home and Ford's office were listed, as were Angel's address and workplace, "accessible to anyone that can read."

When he finished, his usually cool forehead had a sheen of moisture. "Brandy's got the judge diving for his hanky," Jack whispered to Nina. "Did you have to pick a client who's so damn adorable and sympathetic?"

Cody Stinson's jail jumpsuit hung on him. Escorted into the court by a guard, he took the stand nervously, stroking his goatee while Nolan shuffled through her notebooks for a minute. Then Nolan introduced herself and established that he was at present incarcerated and awaiting a trial in a murder case.

"You know why you're here today?" Nolan asked.

He pulled his mouth into a pucker. "I guess to say bad things about that attorney over there, Nina Reilly."

"Do you know Ms. Reilly?"

"Not personally, no."

"You have nothing personal against her."

"No."

"And no reason to say bad things."

"Right."

"You are accused of murdering Phoebe Palladino at Campground by the Lake in South Lake Tahoe in the early-morning hours of September the first, last year?"

"I didn't do it."

"You've spoken to your attorney regarding your testimony here today?"

"I've waived my right to be silent and take the Fifth Amendment in writing. I want to talk about this. If I don't say anything, I'll never get out. You know, they let Mario Lopez go because of those bozo women. That's just so lame."

"We're not here to determine your innocence or guilt, Mr. Stinson. What we'd like you to tell the court is how you received information about a confidential file on your case. How did you hear that Brandy Taylor and Angel Guillaume had some information of interest to the police regarding you in that case?"

"That's easy. Somebody called me and told me."

"Somebody?"

"Just a voice on the phone."

"What did this person say exactly?"

"He—or she, whatever it was, said that these two women were running all over town telling everybody that they saw me kill Phoebe, which was a lie!"

"Up until that point, the police were looking at another suspect, isn't that so?"

"Mario. Mario Lopez, that's right."

"In fact, you had established an alibi, which the police seemed to believe."

"That broke down when those women said they saw me at the campground."

"Made you mad, didn't it?"

"Well, let's face it. I knew I didn't hurt Phoebe. I was just trying to save everybody the trouble of getting confused about what happened. I knew it would look bad, me being at the campground that night later. If I could, I would have kept my alibi."

"Not only did it make you mad, it attracted the police's attention."

"Right. It looked like, up to that point, they didn't think I was involved."

"In fact, you were arrested as a result of the information Brandy Taylor and Angel Guillaume gave to the district attorney's office. You must have seen that coming. You must have been upset."

"Your Honor," Jack said, "asked and answered."

"Let's not belabor the point," said Brock. "Continue."

"What specific information did that person who called give you regarding the identity, whereabouts, and intentions of these witnesses?"

"He gave me their addresses, including one for a beauty salon where one of them worked, and the Ford guy's office. Told me they were planning to go to the D.A. to say things about me."

"When you received this information, what was your reaction?"

"I wanted to talk to them."

"You wanted to talk," Nolan repeated, eyes rolling slightly. "Mr. Stinson"—Nolan waved a stapled pile of papers at him—"isn't it true that you stalked and assaulted these two women on at least two separate occasions with the intention of scaring them so completely they would never testify against you?"

"That's sheer bullsh—they jumped me!"

"And, Mr. Stinson, in between surprising the two women on the beach and again at the women's shelter at Tahoe, where you broke a window, frightening and disturbing the residents, you took the time to drive to Palo Alto and use these terrifying tactics, verbally abusing and attempting to assault Brandy's fiancé, Bruce Ford?"

"What is this? I thought this was about how bad she was, not how bad I am! I didn't attack nobody, not Phoebe, not those women, not that wuss Ford. I just wanted to straighten things out with them."

"By straightening, do you mean you wanted them to leave town and not testify against you?"

He folded his arms. "That would suit me, yeah. Because they were lying."

"Uh huh," said Nolan. "If you had not received that anonymous phone call, would you have known about the potential witnesses?"

"Probably not. No."

"You would not have gone after them?"

"To talk to them! No."

"That's all."

Jack stood while Nolan sank back into her chair.

"Mr. Stinson, tell us more about what happened at the beach that day that you came upon Brandy Taylor and Angel Guillaume. What was your intention on that day?"

"I went there to talk to them, I swear. How many times do I have to tell you people?"

"Did you take a knife along?"

"No!"

"A gun?"

"No."

"A weapon of any kind?"

"I didn't take a weapon. These were women. I didn't go looking for trouble."

"Yet you ended up in a fight, didn't you?"

"Like I said before, they jumped me first. Of course I'm not going to just take that. I pushed 'em off."

"And at the women's shelter?"

"Christ, I even knocked! Next thing I know, there's a lady I never saw before waving a rifle at me."

"When you went to Bruce Ford's—"

"Okay, I was a little drunk. I said a few things. He's a man, supposedly. I didn't expect him to give in easy. I was just trying to be forceful, but I never laid a hand on him."

Jack shifted gears. "Mr. Stinson, were there many people camping nearby the night that Phoebe Palladino died?"

"The place was packed."

"Isn't it possible someone else at the campground saw something that night, even saw Brandy and Angel leaving their tent, and you leaving Phoebe's tent?"

"Sure. Anything's possible. Who would have thought those two would happen to need to pee just the very second I was leaving the tent, huh?"

"Are you hard to find?"

"What?"

"Are you listed in the local directory?"

"Yes."

"So anyone, anyone at the camp that night, might have called you?"

"Anyone can call me."

"So an attorney's missing files aren't the only way someone might come to know about you or your return to the campground later that night?"

"You're good, man," Cody Stinson said. "That's right except for one thing. How would anyone know my name?"

"Did the ranger take your name?"

"Well, yeah, but—"

"Who was there when he took down your name?"

"We had quite an audience, yeah, we did. You're right! Maybe it was the old guy from Cambria at the campsite on the other side who kept hollering at us to shut up who saw and heard everything. Maybe he called me."

"Thank you. That'll be all," Jack said.

On the way out of court, Nina walked over to Cody Stinson, who was sitting at the small round table in the reception area leafing through a magazine. "Thank you for your testimony," she said. "I think you tried to be very honest," which was a way of flattering him without saying he was honest, since she didn't know.

He put his magazine down. "You're the first to say so."

"I've been wondering about the woman who alibied you," she said. "My investigator tells me her name is Carol Ames."

"She doesn't know anything. Anyway, she's out of the picture now."

"You haven't spoken with her lately?"

"No. Why?"

Nina smiled. "I don't know why I thought about her. I guess I wondered if she was a girlfriend or something."

"Not that it's your business," he said, "but I loved Phoebe.

Everyone forgets I lived with her for nearly a year before Mario got out."

"Oh, well. It's probably nothing—"

"What?"

"Forget it," she said. "I just—you don't know where she is?"

"Not at the moment. But I could find her easy enough if I wanted to."

"Hmm. Well, thanks anyway."

She walked away, feeling his eyes on her back, a thought forming in her mind. She felt like a girl plucking daisies to determine her lover's deepest feelings, impractical, but she couldn't sit back and do nothing.

22

"THANKS FOR PICKING ME UP," Nina told Paul. "I can't believe we're doing this. I couldn't face a two-hundred-mile drive all the way back to Tahoe tonight, and anyway, I left my car there. Wish dropped me here this morning. He said he wanted to play in the city, but I know he just wanted to help."

They walked side by side through the evening crowd toward a nearby parking lot to retrieve his Mustang. "We'll be efficient," Paul said, "make this a nonstop run if you like. But why are you going back tonight? You're going to have to leave very early in the morning to get back here in time for court."

"I have to get back to Bob. I spoke with Matt at lunch. He's spending the night at the hospital with Andrea, and his kids are staying with friends. I couldn't manage to organize anything else for Bob on such short notice."

"Is Andrea okay?"

"Fine, I'm told, except her blood pressure's up. She needs some bed rest. It's tough when you've got two kids already and you're nearly nine months along."

"What are you going to do about Bob?"

"Well, after tonight, he could stay with Matt, although it's a bad time for them." She fretted. "Maybe I'll just pack him and his books up and bring him back here. He could stay at the hotel with me or at Jack's until we're through."

"Good plan."

"Paul, today at court—Brandy mentioned some woman in the campground bathroom at about the same time Cody Stinson returned to the tent. And then Stinson testified and mentioned this woman, Carol Ames. What do you know about her?"

"You mean Cody Stinson's alibi?"

"Right."

"I told you I checked into their history. She's an old flame. They broke up when he took up with Phoebe, nearly a year before Phoebe was killed. She's been dating other guys since then, although I'm told there's nothing serious. She's some kind of freelancer. Works out of her house doing medical billing, I believe."

He opened the door for Nina, which she appreciated. She reached down and took off her shoes and loosened her belt. "I don't like being a defendant."

"Hang in there."

"Jack seems to know what he's doing."

"Seems to."

"Anyway, about Carol Ames. Wonder what she saw in Cody. She sounds almost respectable."

Paul got in and buckled up. He looked left, then right, then turned right on Howard and began to zigzag up and down short blocks, apparently hoping to blaze an unknown route to the Bay Bridge that no one else in San Francisco had discovered. "She loved that drug-dealin', motorcycle-lovin' Cody Stinson," he said, "for whatever reason. But then, all couples are hard to picture." The car lurched across an intersection on a red light. "Look at you and me."

"Oh, no, let's not." She planted a kiss on his cheek. "I just want to hop on the back of your Mustang and ride off into the sunset, or toward the sunrise, in this case."

"We don't spend enough time together, Nina. You're with Jack all the time."

"I spend more time with him now than I did when we were married, isn't that odd? I like him better this way, doing his job, be-

ing a pro, standing by me like he never did when we were married."
She smiled. "He's redeemed himself."

Paul said, watching the road, "He's seeing someone."

"Good," Nina said. She hesitated. She didn't want to know
about it. "Were you worried that Jack and I might—"

"Not a bit," Paul said. "I'm the better man and you're smart
enough to know it."

"You weren't a little bit—jealous?"

Paul snorted.

"You were," Nina said.

"I'll be glad when this inquisition is over and we can both get on
with our lives. Then let's resume where we left off in Carmel last
summer, Nina. Could we do that?"

"Paul, why did you take the LSAT?"

"Why did you?" He didn't sound happy.

"Did you really want to be a lawyer?"

"I would have been a terrible lawyer. I'm not a desk type. And
lawyers work too many hours. I like what I do now."

She didn't quite believe him. Was that why Paul seemed so cav-
alier about the risk of her disbarment, because of some disappointment in his past? She thought about that, but couldn't reach any
conclusions, so she turned her attention to the erratic behavior of
their fellow rush-hour motorists and the way Paul skidded through
intersections on reds. Beginning to adjust her belt lower on her hips,
she stopped and thought, well, if I die, at least I won't have to come
back here tomorrow morning to face the hangman.

They reached the bridge. Traffic suddenly moved right along.
Paul sped up.

"Maybe Carol Ames liked excitement. She got that with Cody. I
keep thinking about her," Nina said. "About the campground.
About what happened that night. About how Brandy and Angel saw
a woman leaving the bathroom. It could have been any female
camper, of course. It probably was. But I just keep thinking about
Cody's friend, Carol. How she loved him. How he came to her that

night for the first time in a long time. Don't you think she'd notice if he left? I would."

Paul said, "There's no special reason to put the two women together, Ames and the woman in the bathroom. But it's a thought. Ames moved out of her place a while ago. You want me to locate her? I know who could help. John Kelly could."

"Who's that?"

"Stinson's best friend. An old friend of Carol's, too. I ran into his name a couple of months ago when I was looking at the drug connection. He did a little business with Mario and Cody a long time ago."

"Do you think this is too far-fetched?"

"For me it's just another evening like so many evenings before, without my love in my arms. I might as well eat poorly and hunt down another guy's old girlfriend. Oh, Nina, I miss you."

Inspired by this comment and further comments on the topic, they didn't make it all the way to Tahoe nonstop. At eight-thirty she called Bob from her mobile phone explaining that she would be a little later than expected. She and Paul registered at a historic hotel on the main street in Placerville, stripped, and jumped together into the fresh, starchy sheets. For an hour they kissed, murmured, and touched each other's skin. For Nina, the release felt fantastic, her passion intensified by her inner turmoil.

Later, eating shrimp salad on the balcony overlooking the main street while Paul had a nap, Nina realized that she wasn't thinking at all about the hearing. Paul was the subject on her mind.

She loved Paul. She didn't know what she would do about it, but she felt a decision was imminent, forming somehow out of her situation.

She woke him up a few minutes later. They got to Tahoe by ten. Kissing her warmly, he dropped her at the house on Kulow, declining to come inside. "I love you," he said.

She kissed him again, not able to say the words.

· · ·

"Bob?" she said, unlocking the door to their cabin. Strange that Hitchcock did not seem to be anywhere around. She dropped her small suitcase and briefcase right inside the entryway and dragged the house, calling for Bob and for Hitchcock. She checked Bob's room, finding the door closed, lights off, and blinds shut. Hitchcock was definitely not at home, and neither, it seemed, was Bob.

In the kitchen, she pulled out some old wheat bread, spread peanut butter and jelly on it, and called Matt at the hospital. "How's it going?"

"Andrea's doing well. Should go home in the morning."

"Matt, have you seen any sign of the boy?"

"Your boy? Why, no," he said. "How'd it go at the hearing?"

"I'll tell you later." She asked some more after Andrea, but the questions were *pro forma* and he knew it, so they kept the conversation short. Pouring herself a drink from a pitcher of iced tea she found in the refrigerator, she called Taylor Nordholm's house and got stuck in a diatribe his mother launched about the high school. "Have you seen Bob?" she finally asked.

"No."

So, where could he be? Where was he now, her wandering boy, the boy of her tender care, the boy who was her joy and light, child of her love and prayer—then she realized where Bob must be. Resisting the impulse to stick her head out into the backyard and scream bloody murder, she ran upstairs to change into jeans and a sweater. She ran outside and fired up the Bronco.

She drove the couple of miles to the Bijou, parked across from the dilapidated cabin, and got out. Straightening her shoulders, she thought, well, I'm a Mom, I spell M-O-M. Mom.

She knocked on the door.

"Nina!" Daria Zack, eyes wide, her blouse open almost to her navel, answered the door, Hitchcock drooling beside her like a huge, black witch's familiar. "Wow, did I not expect you."

"Bob here?" Nina asked.

"Um. I don't know," Daria said. "Maybe."

Well, Nikki had always described her mother, Nina's former client, as a flake. Nina now knew what extremes of flakiness were possible, as she walked inside the sparse living room and greeted a man in his twenties, half dressed, sprawled across a few pillows near the fireplace.

"Hi," he said feebly. Holding one hand across the fig-leaf area, he put his other hand over the smoldering joint in the fifties ashtray, as if he could hide these things behind six-inch hand spans.

Politely greeting him, Nina thought, Bob better not be here. At least Hitchcock remembered his manners. Since her arrival, he had stuck close to her heels.

"You could check her room," said Daria, some small recognition of the seriousness of the situation dawning.

"Okay," Nina said, heading toward one of the two bedrooms.

She tried the door and found it locked, so she knocked. There was no answer.

"Maybe they left," Daria offered from a few feet behind, buttoning up the middle button on her blouse.

Nina knocked again. The door opened. Nikki, entirely too relaxed-looking, stood in front of her. "Oh, hello, Nina." Behind her, Bob loomed, a worried look plastered across his mug.

"Ms. Reilly to you," she told Nikki. She grabbed Bob's arm and propelled him through the living room, out the front door, and into the car. Hitchcock jumped into the backseat.

"What's your problem!" Bob asked as she pulled away.

"Why aren't you home?"

"You said you'd be late. We wanted to practice—"

"Do not, please, do not give me that. She was high. I could see it in her eyes."

Silence, then, "It was just really dark in the room. She doesn't get high, far as I know."

Really dark in the room. Reassuring words. "Are you?"

"What? Mom, I'm not even fourteen!"

"Are you," she repeated, her voice steely, her hand on the wheel curled rigid as pipe, "high?"

"No."

"Bob, we've talked about this."

"About what?"

"Drugs."

"I don't do that stuff. I have zero interest. I told you!"

"Daria's boyfriend was smoking pot in that house while you were there. That's not only unacceptable, it's illegal."

"She told him to quit it and so he put it out. She's not pushing a drug agenda, Mom."

"Would you have taken anything if she was? Because my impression is that these people have a hold on you."

"Nobody's got a hold on me," he protested.

Unfortunately, that included her. She decided to use Paul's frequently stated solution: Nail his feet to the floor. She told him there would be no further practice of any kind, music or otherwise, with Nikki. Bob folded his arms, stared straight ahead, and no doubt hated her all the way home.

After Paul dropped Nina at her cabin, he called Wish, who needed to tell him all about the terrific spinning restaurant he had found at the Hyatt Regency in San Francisco before agreeing to meet him in half an hour.

"Hey," Paul said, pulling up next to him in the parking lot of the Starlake Building.

"Hey." Wish climbed in beside him. "Where to?"

"Ever heard of this outfit?" He handed Wish a piece of paper Nina had written for him.

"Big Lake Sport Fishing," he read. "Sure. They've got an office at the Keys."

Turning right onto Lake Tahoe Boulevard, Paul glanced over at him. "You look sleek."

"I do?" Wish wore a brown leather jacket over his jeans.

"So you had lunch in the city."

"Yeah, after walking up to Chinatown and playing around for a couple of hours. I found a couple of Japanese animes I've been looking for."

"Didn't you drop Nina off this morning at nine? Strikes me as funny, you being in the same vicinity several hours later. So I surmise a special reason for hanging around. Hmm." He tapped his chin. "Whatever could it be?"

Wish grunted.

"Lunch with a lady."

"You caught me red-handed, Copper."

"How was the food?"

"Good, like I told you already."

"Brandy after?"

"Huh?" said Wish.

"A joke. You had lunch with Brandy Taylor, didn't you?"

"She asked me."

Paul turned toward the Keys.

"She just needs a friend."

Paul turned the radio on.

"Aren't you going to ask me what we talked about?"

"No."

"She told me something."

"She did?"

"Yeah," Wish said, unaware of the sensation he had caused. "You remember the sex-problem thing with Bruce? She told me what was going on. I guess she told her sister, too, and her mom, and maybe other people, but she just can't bring herself to tell Bruce."

Paul sighed and put the car back where it belonged on the road. "Okay, so what did she tell you?"

"It's a secret. I do have a question, Paul. If you know something about a guy, and if you told him you could maybe help mend a relationship, but it means you'll ace yourself right out of the love picture, plus it isn't the kind of thing you ever want to talk to another guy about, especially not a stranger, what do you do?"

"Hmm."

"Plus there's this added issue, which is, um, I, um. Aack. I have the same problem."

Johnny quick draw? Johnny no comeback? Johnny shoot blanks? What in the world had Wish in such a tizzy?

"I like her, but I'd have to love her a whole lot," Wish went on glumly. "A whole, whole lot."

"Do the noble thing." She wanted Bruce, not Wish, that much Paul knew. Poor Wish.

"Is that like, your personal wisdom, how you live your life?"

"What have I ever done to make you think a thing like that?"

Up ahead, lights illuminated the white-lettered sign for the sports-fishing business. They parked and walked up some outside stairs toward a second-story office that overlooked the marina. Paul had been told John Kelly often worked a late shift, doing paperwork and accounts in the office. Sure enough, the windows shone with lamplight. Wish raised his hand to knock.

Paul pulled it back. "Shh." He looked around the side of the building into the window. "He's in there, all right." He led Wish back to the car. "Now we wait."

Wish settled back against the car seat. "Who is this guy?"

"Cody Stinson's best friend."

"And we're following him, why?"

"I checked with a guy I know at the Tahoe jail. Late this afternoon, Cody gave his old pal John Kelly a call. Nina was hoping he just might lead us straight to Carol Ames, and I think it's a definite possibility."

"Cody's alibi? Why would he lead us to her?"

"Nina thought Cody might call on him to track Carol down tonight. John Kelly knows Carol and Cody both. He used to pal around with them back in the days when they were together."

"Sounds like a stretch."

"Well, maybe it is. But you know, Wish, in this business we feed on unsubstantiated rumors, innuendo, and gossip. Why not plain old hope now and then?"

A few minutes later, Kelly came out, locked the door behind him, and hopped on a motorcycle.

"Well, look at that."

Paul followed at a discreet distance as Kelly wound his way around the parking lot and back out to the boulevard. He rode on for a little more than two miles to Ski Run, turned left again, toward the lake, and parked in a lot by the marina.

Kelly walked out toward one of the docks, stopped at the locked gate, and let himself in. A dozen boats floated in the black water, creaking as they bobbed on the crests. Kelly walked past several large cabin cruisers and stopped at a sailboat on the right side. He looked from side to side. Presumably satisfied no one else was taking an interest, he stepped aboard.

"Is she there?"

"Let's find out," Paul said. Moving quietly, they tried the gate, which Kelly had kindly left open, and walked up the dock toward the sailboat. A cold March wind winnowed its way inside Paul's light windbreaker, and the marina lights danced like fairies over the water under a pale yellow moon.

A window cracked in the sailboat cabin made the two voices intimately accessible to Paul and Wish, who were crouched, as if that position might make them less visible.

"How'd you find me, John?" a woman asked, her voice nervous, but warm and mellow on the cold air.

Kelly said, "I called the apartment all day. Your roommate told me you weren't expected, but I remembered your dad's boat. Carol, Cody's concerned."

"You talked to him?"

"He called me from San Francisco today. He's at that hearing about the attorney who's caused so much trouble. What's strange is, your name keeps popping up."

"You shouldn't have come."

"Don't tell me you're scared of me, Carol. That would hurt my feelings. I just want to pass along the word. Cody wants you to stay hidden, in fact, he's gonna insist."

"I have work, you know—"

"I know all about that. Take it with you. This is just for a couple of days, 'til things die down. He's worried they'll try to call you and ask you about that night at the campground."

"He was with me that night! Those girls were wrong, saying they saw him there."

"Yeah, sure. So I heard. So everybody heard. But at this hearing today, he admitted he was there that night. He now says you were asleep and didn't hear him go."

"You're kidding!"

"You've been out of the loop."

"He told me to lay low and not to contact him. Oh, he's such an idiot. Shit. We had him covered. If he had just stuck to that we could have gotten him off!"

"Oh, well. At least the police believe that you sleep heavy and had no idea what he was up to that night. Cody's not so sure about these lawyers. He says they're thinking too hard, digging too deep."

"Tell me Cody didn't admit to killing Phoebe."

"No. He's an idiot but even he's not that stupid."

"Why'd he cave in like that? Those women can identify him in court. He could go to jail for life, John! He had a good alibi. If he had just kept his mouth shut—now these silly girls are going to get up in court and get him put away—"

"Look, that can't be fixed. But we can prevent them from dragging you into this any further. Now, since it was so easy for me to find your dad's boat, maybe we can come up with someplace a little harder, at least until this hearing is over. I thought, maybe my sister's place."

"I'm fine here."

John Kelly convinced her otherwise, and since his persuasion involved no physical urging, Paul let him. When Paul and Wish understood the two would be leaving the boat soon, they slipped back up the dock to the car and got in. After a few minutes, Kelly climbed on his bike and Carol Ames, small, dark-haired, and skinny, took the wheel of a Saturn. Kelly followed her as she pulled out, and Paul followed him. Ten minutes later, the bike and the Saturn pulled up to a house off the Kingsbury Grade. Kelly escorted Carol to the door, rang the bell, and saw her inside. After a few more minutes, he left.

"Well, now we know where she is. What are we going to do about it?" Wish asked.

"Wait," Paul said.

Wish closed his eyes and leaned his head back on the Mustang's headrest, where a dent that fit perfectly was forming.

By midnight, most of the lights in the houses on the street were dimmed. Even the crickets seemed to be sleeping.

"It's quiet," Wish said, startling awake. "Too quiet."

"Very funny," Paul said.

Moments later, the door to the house opened. Out came Carol Ames, dressed all in black, thin as a fork. She unlocked her car door quietly, got inside, and released the parking brake, rolling down the street in neutral until she was well past the house.

"Did you know she would leave again?" Wish said. "Who are you really, Mr. Psychic Hotline?"

"I didn't know." Paul started up his car and flipped it into gear. "I just didn't know how we were going to get her alone. I thought we might have to wait until she left for somewhere in the morning." They drove down the hill, well behind the blue Saturn. "This is good. I like the darkness."

"Now you're really scaring me," Wish said. "Okay, I give up. Where is she going in the middle of the night? Only place I can think of is the casinos, but here we are going the other way, west."

"I have an idea," Paul said. He didn't like the idea, but it was borne out soon enough, when the blue Saturn parked a few doors down from the Guillaume residence.

"Isn't that where Angel lives?" Wish asked. "But I don't understand. If she's going to see Angel and Brandy, she better hit the road for San Francisco, because I happen to know they stayed there tonight."

She got out of the car and unlocked the trunk, pulling something heavy out. She approached Angel's house, unscrewing the lid of what appeared to be a fairly large can. At the edge of the house she stopped and listened, then moved closer and peered quite methodically through windows. All windows dark. No car in the carport. Quiet fir trees, a dark Tahoe night. Stopping at the back corner of the house, she wadded a piece of paper around a rock and hurled it through a kitchen windowpane. Then she tipped the can.

Paul and Wish grabbed her. For a small person, she fought big. After landing a light punch to Paul's sternum, forcing him to stop breathing momentarily, she dropped the can on the ground. Wish sneaked up behind and pinned her while she scrambled for it.

"Out of gas?" Paul asked. "Let us help you with that." He swooped down and wrenched the can from her grasp. "That's strange. It's full."

"Who the hell are you?" she asked, keeping her voice to a guilty whisper. "I'll scream for the cops! You can't do this to me!"

Paul showed her his identification and introduced Wish. He explained who they were. "Want me to make that call for you?" he asked.

She hung her head.

"Seems to me, you owe us an explanation. What was your plan here?" Paul asked. "I have to say, it doesn't look well conceived."

"I wasn't going to burn the house down. I just wanted to show them I meant business. I was only going to burn a little."

"Well, take your pick," Paul said. "The police or us for company." He explained who they were and that they were working for Nina Reilly in a hearing only distantly related to Cody's case.

"Don't call the cops, please. It was just insurance," she said. "Something serious to scare them off so they wouldn't want to testify in Cody's case when it comes up!"

"You ought to be ashamed," Wish said.

"There was nobody home."

Paul sent Wish through the window to retrieve the rock. "Reach inside to unlock it. It should be easy to open now."

Wish came out complaining, sucking on a tiny cut on his finger. He handed the uncrumpled note to Paul, and the rock, which Paul stuck into a paper bag under the seat of his car.

"Testify in the Stinson case and you'll see some real damage done," the printed note said.

"What is your relationship with Cody Stinson?" Paul asked, pocketing the note.

"Old friends."

"Nothing more?"

Silence.

"I understand you two were close once but he left you for Phoebe. That must have been a shock."

Carol said slowly, "Yeah. It was."

"You've been a good friend to him, Carol, considering he dumped you. Giving him that fake alibi."

"I wish I hadn't." She pushed back some loose hair, and Paul saw water forming in her eyes. "Aw, shit! This has been the worst nightmare!"

Paul didn't ask her any more. Nina had a plan, and he would stick with it, and that involved getting Carol Ames to the California State Bar hearing tomorrow.

So Paul blackmailed her into joining him for the long haul all the way back to San Francisco. No police, just a long midnight ramble.

The night passed in a blur of black trees, moonlight, and splashed puddles. After dropping Wish at home so that he could get to his classes the next day and allowing Carol Ames to pick up her bag from Kelly's sister's house, they hit Highway 50 and started the long descent to the flats.

Carol, who asked to be called Carol and "not Ms. Freaking Ames," asked Paul some questions: Would Cody be there, who else might be there. He told her Cody would be there but Brandy and Angel would not, lies. As for what she would be expected to do, well, Paul told her, she would tell what happened that night. Now that everyone knew Cody had been at the campground and she couldn't provide her old friend a real alibi, she had to tell that to the court to back him up, further nonsense, but he was tired and couldn't come up with a better story.

Fortunately, she too was tired, apparently too tired to dispute his illogic, and of course she really didn't want him talking to the police or anyone else about her little excursion through the trees with a gas can in the night. In spite of it being the middle of the night, she couldn't shut up. "Oh, hell," she said at intervals, and "Oh, God. I can't believe this is happening after all these months. I can't take it."

In Placerville she finally fell asleep, mouth open, taking breaths in soft little gasps. She awoke frequently, jarred loose by any jump of the car or noise on the road. By the time they hit the Oakland Bay Bridge, dawn was at the Mustang's hoofs.

Paul turned the radio to KQED, counting on news to keep him awake and correctly positioned in the middle lane. When that didn't work and he almost took out a black Jaguar, he tuned in to AM radio where the blaring ads did the job. They also woke Carol again, who rummaged in her bag for a brush and asked for an immediate pit stop. In the city, they located a diner on Mission with spacious accommodations. She emerged from the rest room briskly, wearing a ton of eyeliner, not that it helped.

He was very tired, and that made him mean. She looked haggard and her peculiar hairdo didn't help. "You look nice," he said to counteract his thoughts, thinking, in fact, she looked more like how he felt, as if ragged fingernails were scratching at his pupils. She smiled at the compliment, which made him feel even more degenerate. But he wanted her to feel good. He bought a *Chronicle,* which they split, and eggs, which they ate in relative peace.

When the time came, they walked the few blocks over to Howard Street and rode up the elevator to the sixth floor.

Nina had not wanted him to confront Carol in any way. She had asked him to bring her to the court and conduct a simple test: Escort Carol into the presence of Angel and Brandy without Carol knowing Brandy and Angel would be there.

"Why not just show Brandy and Angel a photograph of her?" Paul had asked.

"It's too late for that, even if I had one. If she was there that night, I want her to tell the bar court what she saw, what she knows. If she can back up Cody Stinson's story that he's innocent, which I suspect she can, we can prove to the court that he had no reason to attack Brandy, Angel, or Bruce, and that the loss of my file was not damaging in that case. And because of all this, Mario's out of jail. Maybe they need to arrest him again before he disappears."

He liked her theory, which fit into his philosophy of successful investigation, demanding equal sprinkles of wishful thinking and genuine possibility. He was only sorry she had not put him on to it during the past six dry-as-dust months.

After they passed through the metal detector and into the reception area, Paul looked around. In the left adjacent, windowed room, the chief trial counsel's witnesses waited. In the right room, Paul caught a glimpse of Nina and Jack.

He took Carol by the arm and led her into the left room, throwing the door open wide. They entered.

Gayle Nolan, seated at a table, stood. "Who—?"

Brandy set a cup down and stood, too. "Why, what are you doing here?" she said.

"You know this woman?" Paul asked, holding tight to Carol's arm.

"No. I mean—" Befuddlement blew across Brandy's face and settled into confusion. "She was in the bathroom at the campground the night Phoebe died. Wasn't she, Angel?"

Angel, remaining seated, stared. "You," she said. "I noticed your haircut that night. Update on the old Vidal Sassoon," she said. "You're the one who tossed her cookies, right? That was such a mega-bad night."

By now, Nolan had stepped behind Paul and was motioning the guard at the door for help.

Paul pulled Carol out of the room. "Sorry," he said to Nolan. "My mistake."

Nolan shut the door firmly behind them.

Paul touched Carol's arm but she pushed him off, but not before he had a chance to realize how shocked she was. Her whole body was trembling, and the shadowy sockets of her eyes receded until her eyes were dark holes burnt into charcoal. "You set me up," she cried.

At this point, they were joined by Nina and Jack, who had taken note of the commotion. Jack motioned them all back into the other witness waiting room.

"You lied to me!" Carol said, looking wildly around. "Where's Cody?"

"He couldn't make it after all," Paul said.

Nina took over. "Look, as you've probably figured out from that little scene in there, we know everything."

"Everything?" Carol asked.

"Everything," Nina lied. "Now you go into that courtroom when they call your name, and you tell the truth. Tell them Cody didn't do it, and how you know all about that. He didn't, did he?"

"No." Carol looked at her, looked at Paul, looked down at the floor. "I have to think," she said. "Why don't you all just leave me alone?"

The clock on the wall ticked and nobody breathed. Tears smeared through Carol Ames's eyeliner and trickled like glue down her face.

Opening the door to the courtroom, the clerk announced that the judge was ready. Nina and Jack went in, Nina touching Paul on the sleeve as she passed him.

"It won't take long," Paul said. "They're asking the judge to take you out of order. You won't even have to wait."

"Do I have to do this?" Carol seemed to be asking herself more than Paul, although he felt he should answer. Saving Paul from evaluating whether the truth would serve or a lie would get him into trouble, the clerk poked her head into the door again.

"Carol Ames?" she said. "Please follow me." Jack wasn't giving Carol time to think, Paul realized, assembling the last of his own little gray cells. Bravo, smart move, old buddy, now get Nina off and get the hell out of her life, willya? He handed Carol a tissue, and when she didn't seem to know what to do with it, he wiped her face.

"I'm afraid."

"Just tell the truth, Carol. Tell the truth about Cody."

She hung her head again and followed the clerk into the courtroom. Paul put his head on the table and fell asleep.

Nina watched the young woman slump up to the stand to be sworn and waited impatiently through preliminaries that established her age, her place of residence, and everything else.

"You followed Cody Stinson to the campground the night Phoebe Palladino died, didn't you?" Jack asked the young woman.

"Yes."

Nina thought she looked awful, as though a tractor had run over her face.

"Why did you do that?"

"Love," she said.

Nina felt Jack startle by her side, although his face revealed nothing. "You were in love with Mr. Stinson."

"I never stopped loving him."

Jack's manner grew more elaborately casual, always a bad sign for the witness, Nina thought.

He consulted notes. He cleared his throat. He smiled a sympathetic smile. "You thought that night that he had come back to you, for good this time."

Carol Ames lowered her head. "Yes. He told me he and Phoebe were history."

"So when he left in the middle of the night—"

"I didn't know what to think. I got in my car and I followed him. He parked his bike on Rufus Allen and walked into the camp-ground, so I did, too." Tears had started down. "He got her out of the tent and they sat down by the fire. He begged her to leave and take off with him, told her how much he loved her—I was out of my mind. Just an hour before that, he made love to me. He said he'd move in again in the morning. But he never stopped thinking about her. Phoebe."

"You were upset, so—" Jack said.

"I ran to the bathroom. I threw up. I was feeling crazy. Those girls came in while I was cleaning up. I didn't say a word to them, just went back and stood in the trees. Cody was just leaving.

"I waited. I went to the tent and pulled the flap open. After a couple of minutes, I took a look. The big guy was out cold, and she was, too. So I—I went inside. And I strangled her."

23

"Pandefuckingmonium," said Jack with satisfaction. He had recovered from the shock of Carol Ames's testimony during the break
called by Judge Brock after Carol was taken into custody by the bailiff.
Nina watched as Paul uttered words of comfort and kept her steady.

She took Jack aside. "I'm having a hard time analyzing the impact of this," she said. "I'm having a hard time thinking at all. I never
imagined she would confess. She must have been working up to it,
feeling guilty all these months. I know it's a huge break for us, but a
girl is dead—"

"An actual courtroom confession and we didn't even know it
was coming. Moments like this are why we practice law, Nina. Of
course, it helps that we're the side that benefits."

"Paul came through," Nina said, "as usual. He found her and
brought her here and saved the day."

"Don't worry, I'll clap him on the back just as soon as the marshal unleashes her." The federal marshal had just arrived. Pinpoint
eyes fixed on Carol Ames, he consulted with the judge. Paul, who
had slipped into the courtroom when he heard the ruckus moments
before, patted her hand. The marshal went over to them and quietly
began telling Carol her rights. He took her by the arm and as she
was led away, she cast one last glance back at Paul. Paul gave her a
thumbs-up and a reassuring nod.

"I hope you didn't promise to correspond with her from

prison," Jack said as Paul came over. "You know those relationships never work out."

"I'll make sure she gets good legal counsel," Paul said. "We owe her that. In a way we tricked her into incriminating herself."

"Whatever brings out the truth," Jack said. They moved out into the reception area and huddled at the far end.

"Okay, ramifications," Jack said. "Strategy adjustment. This girl killed the woman at the campsite. Ergo, Cody Stinson didn't do it. Ergo, Stinson's story that he was just trying to talk to these nervous Nellies is true. No attempted murder. No intent to assault. No intent to harm the clients. That's the bottom line. The loss of the file, the fingering of Stinson as the killer by Brandy—she was wrong anyway."

"But Cody Stinson says he did get a phone call from the thief," Nina said. "And he scared these people as a result."

"Only because they mistakenly thought he was a killer and made some wrong assumptions based on their fears and on the way he looks," Jack said. "I think we've dodged this bullet. I sure as hell am going to argue that at the close of the hearing. I think we're home free on this count, babe." He grinned at Nina. "Your insurance company is going to be happy about this. They reserved half a million dollars in payouts to Bruce and Brandy and Angel, figuring they'd sue you for malpractice in civil court next."

"When I think of all those sleepless nights feeling so guilty because I thought I sicced a murderer on Brandy and her family, I—I can't believe it," Nina said.

"Enjoy the moment," Jack said. He checked his Rolex. "Okay, time's up. Now we go back in and we argue 'ergo' to Hugo."

Nina hung back with Paul. "Thank you," she said.

"Hey, it was your idea."

"Half-brained and dimwitted. Desperate and you know it. But you were willing to take it all the way. I'm always thanking you. You work it and work it until finally you crack it."

This time Gayle Nolan came over to Jack and Nina's table as

soon as they sat down. "Is that confession for real? Is that gonna stand up?" she asked Jack.

"It'll stand up. You going to let the South Lake Tahoe D.A.'s office know they've got an innocent man locked up?" Jack asked.

"I just put in a call. What they do about Stinson is up to them. You knew she was gonna confess?"

"We didn't have a clue."

"You sandbagged me," Nolan said, but she didn't show much conviction. She had seen the shock on all their faces.

"You're buried up to your neck, but it's your own fault. You brought the charges against this lady," Jack said with unmistakable triumph in his voice.

"Get this, Jack," Nolan said. "Maybe the first count goes away, but there are two more. Don't get cocky." She continued to ignore Nina.

"Ms. Nolan," Nina said.

"What?"

"The judge has just come in."

"What? Oh." She skittered back to her chair. Judge Brock took his place. Various "X" expressions followed one another across his face. Vexed. Flummoxed. Perplexed.

"We're back on the record and I'd like to know, what now?" he said in his mild voice. "I don't like uproar in my courtroom. Are you planning any more shocks like this one, Counsel?"

"We were as astonished as the court," Jack said, rising. "Astonished and gratified. It's obvious Mr. Stinson was telling the truth when he testified that he was only trying to tell these people that he was innocent of the—"

"No more surprises, is that clear? If you have something like this, I want to know it's coming."

"Of course, Judge."

"All right. This isn't the time for argument. The court notes for the record that based on her purported confession to a murder, the previous witness, Carol Ames, has been taken into custody. Now let's move forward with this. It's eleven-thirty. We have half an hour. It's still your turn, Counsel. You have a couple more witnesses on Count One listed."

Jack said, "Well, we excused them, Your Honor. We are ready to move on to Count Two."

"You're resting for the defense on Count One?"

"Yes."

"All righty then. Ms. Nolan, are you ready to go on Count Two?"

"Yes. The witness from Heritage Insurance is waiting outside."

"Let's move on, then. Count Two. Call your witness."

"Marilyn Ann Rose."

Marilyn Rose walked up to the box and was sworn. A heavyset woman with a pleasant, open face, she wore a demure, dove-gray pantsuit. Nina knew that Marilyn's husband had died three months earlier, leaving her two children to support on her own. After the Vang fiasco she had left the company and moved out of state.

Her company had hired a lawyer who had managed to prevent Jack from deposing her. However, they knew what she would say about the Vang case. The actual document about to be introduced as evidence, Nina's original intake notes, was the problem on this count.

The prosecution's forensic writing examiner, Harvey Pell, came next on the problem list. Nina tried to yank herself mentally into the new universe of problems Count Two represented.

"Good morning, Ms. Rose. My name is Gayle Nolan and I represent the State Bar of California."

"Good morning." Nolan took Marilyn through a recitation of her job duties as a claims adjuster and brought her to the Vang case.

"I'm now showing you Exhibit 15, which has been previously admitted into evidence by stipulation. So Ms. Reilly presented you with this claim on or about August twenty-eighth of last year?"

"That's correct." The claim letter with its attachments was about four inches thick. Marilyn stared at it. They all stared at it.

"The claim was for how much for the losses due to the convenience-store fire?"

"They asked for two hundred fifty thousand dollars. The policy limit."

"And the claim contained a copy of the police report concluding that the fire was caused by a criminal agency?"

"Yes."

"And was the arsonist identified by the South Lake Tahoe police, at the time the report was written or at any later time up to the time that you adjusted the claim and sent out the check?"

"Not to my knowledge."

"Was there any evidence in this claim letter or otherwise, up to the moment you sent out that check, that the store owner, Kao Vang, might have carried out the arson himself?"

"No. Of course our own investigator had done independent work on the fire, but he was unable to identify the arsonist and advised that he had no evidence that the claim was anything but legitimate."

"Now, the defendant represented to you that she was Mr. and Mrs. Vang's attorney?"

"That's right."

"You talked with her on numerous occasions throughout the adjusting process?"

"Yes. On the phone. Not in person."

"Did she give you her version of the facts of the fire?"

"She said all she knew came from the police report, that her clients had suffered a lot. Told me about two previous violent incidents at the market. It all jibed with the theory she pushed on me, that the arson was a revenge act after Mr. Vang shot a robber during his second attempt to rob the store. She kept saying we had to have a heart for these people and even though the supporting inventories and receipts were in pretty bad shape, she practically begged me to give her clients the benefit of the doubt on the settlement."

"And what was your response to her request that your company settle this matter for a generous amount?"

"I stuck my neck out and eventually offered two hundred ten thousand. That's about right for a store of that type and size. To be honest, I suspected there was some padding in the inventories, and I suspected that if I had every scrap of paper translated and scrutinized it wouldn't add up to that much. But these people weren't your average store owners. They obviously didn't use a standard system of accounting and were obviously new to American business systems. I took a chance and gave them as generous a settlement as I could."

"You mailed out the check to Ms. Reilly?"

"Actually, she came and picked it up. The whole thing was a big rush for some reason I didn't understand."

Yes, and if she hadn't heeded Jack's advice and rushed those checks to the Vangs out—Nina stopped herself. She had already revisited that decision during more than one midnight.

"Looking back," Marilyn Rose continued, "I have to assume that the time pressure was something Ms. Reilly invented as a strategy."

"Objection. Speculation. Move to strike that last sentence."

"She's in the best position to understand why these events occurred," said Nolan, but she wasn't really fighting it; the point was made.

"Sustained."

"Then what happened?"

Nina tensed. Now they moved to the meat.

"I received a manila file folder in my regular mail delivery with some papers in it." Nolan went to her cart and pulled out the familiar file folder. Nina and Jack had had an opportunity to examine it, along with the notes inside, and to have it copied. As with the Bronco, there had been no prints and no lucky hairs or other forensic evidence.

"You kept the envelope it arrived in?"

"I had my secretary go back and retrieve it from the trash, yes."

Nolan pulled out Exhibit 17, the full-size standard brown envelope. Marilyn Rose's name and address were printed in capitals. After Marilyn identified it the envelope was received into evidence.

"Now. Do you know who sent this file, Exhibit 16, to you?"

"To this day I still have no idea. The police came out a week or so later to run some tests on it, but our legal counsel ensured that the file never left the company's possession."

"All right. You received the envelope, took out the file inside. Did you read the contents on that occasion?"

"Of course. I was quite curious. I didn't realize it was her legal file."

Jack shuffled his papers and got ready.

"And what was in the file?" Nolan asked.

"Objection," Jack said. "The contents of that file contain attorney work-product and are privileged. The files did not lose their confidential aspect when they were stolen and inadvertently read by a third party. I have briefed this point thoroughly for the pretrial conference and ask that the court reconsider its ruling at that time."

"The exhibit has already been admitted into evidence per my pretrial order," Judge Brock said. "We have already gone over this several times."

"For the record, Your Honor. These files were stolen. The clients haven't waived the privilege. I understand that the state bar feels it can delve into confidential client files whenever it wants to. But my client and I, as practicing attorneys in the state of California, have to raise this objection again. And for the record we will appeal that pretrial ruling."

Nolan, ready for this, spoke up. "The state bar has the right to discover the work-product of an attorney against whom disciplinary charges are pending when relevant to issues of the attorney's breach of duty. I cite Code of Civil Procedure Section 2018 sub e and also Witkin, Cal Evidence third, Volume 2, Section 1145. This court has already issued a protective order limiting the testimony in some respects today. The evidence is relevant and crucial to showing that the defendant defrauded this insurance company."

"You've said all that in the previous court conferences," Jack said. "And I know there has been a ruling. Nevertheless, I can't stand here and let this testimony come in without protesting. It's a violation of the whole legal system that you are opening this confidential file in this hearing against the wishes of the client. It's—"

"Your ongoing, undying objection is noted," said Brock, making a small foray toward personality. "Now let's move it."

Jack's face darkened. "This state bar court is requiring the violation of the Code of Professional Conduct required of attorneys and also the Business and Professions Code. Neither Ms. Reilly nor her client has attempted to waive the privilege of confidentiality."

"Your objection is overruled."

"This state bar court is without jurisdiction to flout the most sacred principles of the legal profession," Jack said. "Any ruling based on this violation will be void."

"Siddown, Counsel. Shout to the State Bar Journal after the case is over, not that you'll get any attention from them. But don't grandstand in my court. I won't have it."

Jack sat down.

"You didn't have a chance, but thanks for trying," Nina whispered.

"I did it for myself, too. I took the same oath when I was admitted."

"What was in the file, Ms. Rose? You may answer," Nolan asked, picking up the questioning without hesitation.

"A form that was headed Client Intake Interview."

"Now, showing you Exhibit 18, a three-page document previously introduced into evidence after objection and argument. Is this the form?"

Marilyn took the sheets gingerly. She flipped to the last sheet and nodded her head. "This is it."

Nolan took Marilyn through the next minutes after receipt of the envelope: She had read Nina's intake notes several times, spoken with her superiors, then returned to her office and called Nina. As Marilyn described the telephone confrontation and Nina's denials, Nina vividly recalled the unnerving call that had sent her home to bury her head under the covers.

"And what exactly about this document caused you to call Ms. Reilly?"

"The last sentence on the third page."

"Read that sentence to us, please."

"It says, 'Client breaks down, says he set fire himself!' There's an exclamation point. Then it goes on, kind of scribbled, 'Advised him don't say any more, don't want to hear this.'"

Judge Brock followed along on his copy. Nina read hers. Still it tore at her. She hadn't written those words. Kao had not confessed. There was no evidence Kao had set fire to his own store, except for this damning, damnable forgery. For six months they had been trying to figure out who would go this far, and they simply couldn't figure it out.

Only now, in this airtight room, did she see in great detail the hundred holes in her defense, the big, unresolved questions. On the other hand, every case she ever defended arrived in court too soon. There were always unanswered questions. That kept things alive and ever hopeful. She still had hope, as her clients must, watching the red digital clock change, minute by minute, that the tides would turn again. She would prevail against all odds. Jack would work a miracle or Paul would. The judge would somehow forgive her for that one moment of carelessness weighed against a lifetime of diligence and duty.

"And Ms. Reilly said that within two days of picking up the check she personally delivered it to her clients?"

"Yes."

"In your experience, is that the usual turnaround time for clients to receive their settlements from law offices?"

"I've been doing this work for thirty years and I don't remember ever seeing a check go into a trust account and out to a client that fast."

"And have you ever received any explanation as to why this check was turned over so fast?"

"Just what I said. She claimed there was some mysterious danger to them."

"Now, then. What did you do after speaking to Ms. Reilly about this file you received?"

"I went straight to my boss and told him the whole story. I was distraught. He had me write up a quick summary, and I packaged it with the claim file and a copy of the check. It was turned over to our legal counsel. A month later, I took my early retirement and left the company. I had gotten sloppy over the years. I had let her talk me into paying out too much money, even aside from the file. You get old and you lose your edge. You get lazy. I was finished. Then I—I lost my husband. It was time to go home to Kansas City."

"Did this matter have any impact on you personally?"

Marilyn blinked back tears. "It made my husband's last months—hard."

"I have nothing further," Nolan told the judge.

Jack cross-examined. The answers were more of the same. Marilyn's mood did not improve and neither did her testimony's impact on their case. He kept the cross short. When Jack finished, the red numbers showed in five-inch-tall characters five minutes past twelve.

"We'll recess until one-thirty," the judge said. "We have the writing examiner ready, is that correct?"

"He'll be here," Nolan said.

"Court is adjourned."

They all trooped out. Nina headed for the bathroom. As she washed her hands, Marilyn came out of one of the stalls.

"I'm very sorry you had to go through this, Marilyn," Nina said. "But I didn't lie to you. Somebody forged that document."

"Don't even try," Marilyn said.

"Someday I hope you'll—"

"I have a flight to catch. Pardon me if I don't wish you luck." She brushed coldly past.

24

NINA WAS SWORN and took the stand. She and Jack had hashed this out and the pretrial struggles with Gayle Nolan had been fierce, but they had won many concessions: The scope of her testimony would be limited solely to the Vang case and notes.

From the witness box Jack looked far away, and she felt the Promethean presence of Judge Brock just to her right. Lines of tension pulled all around her. The judge seemed troubled to have a member of the bar seated in the box, though he must be used to it; she turned her head slightly to acknowledge him, but he looked away, shunning her.

Marilyn had wounded her. She wanted to protest, to defend herself, but the witness box was like a cage. She understood finally why even the most obstreperous witness answered respectfully and fell into the formality of the court ritual. She felt chastened already, and the questioning hadn't even begun.

Nolan said from her table, "Ms. Reilly, you are a member of the State Bar of California and the defendant in this action?"

"Yes."

"On or about August eighth, you were practicing law in your office in South Lake Tahoe, California?"

"Yes."

"Did you meet with a person named Kao Vang for the first time on that day?"

Jack sat upright in his chair, waiting for Nolan to make a false move, but with the rules of evidence as loose as they were, he would not be able to do much.

"Yes."

"In what regard?"

"To discuss whether I would represent him in an insurance matter."

"A claim against Heritage Insurance?"

"Yes."

"And did you agree to that representation?"

"Yes." She watched Jack. He nodded encouragingly. They had agreed that she would go that far.

"What did you agree to do for Mr. Vang?"

"I would respectfully like to state that I am only answering this entire line of questions because I have been ordered to do so by this court after making written objection through my attorney. Otherwise I would not answer these questions."

Nolan smiled at that. Tapping her chin, she said, "Well, I don't know why not, since at least thirty or forty people have seen the contents of the file by now, but let's go ahead. You submitted a claim for Mr. Vang based on an alleged arson that destroyed his business, am I correct?"

"Yes." The business was co-owned by Mrs. Vang, Nina wanted to say, but she and Jack had decided that she would volunteer nothing.

Nolan got up and went around to the front of her table, placing her at front and center. She folded her arms. "And during the course of that first meeting with Mr. Vang, was anyone else present?"

"Just Mr. and Mrs. Vang and their translator, Dr. Mai."

"Did you or anyone tape record that initial conversation or videotape any part of it?"

"No."

"Did you take any handwritten notes?"

"Yes."

"Is this your usual procedure when first meeting with a client?"

"Yes. I have a form called Client Intake Interview. I fill in basic information about the client. Then I take notes of the discussion."

"As the conversation is taking place?"

"Yes, although I might add something after the meeting is over that I want to remember."

"And what is the purpose of this note-taking?"

"Well, to remind me of the information."

"Who else sees this form?"

"No one, except my secretary, who might see it while she is affixing it to the file or—that's about it."

"And she might read it?"

"I have never told my secretary not to read it. She is free to read it. She needs to know what the case is about in order to perform her duties."

"Does the client see this form?"

"Never."

"If I asked you as your client to give me a copy, why wouldn't you give me one?"

Nina said, "Because I may place my personal reactions and judgments into those notes. Not just the information stated. These are my personal confidential notes."

"Are they entered into a computer at any point?"

"Never."

"Where are those intake forms kept?"

"In a locked file behind my secretary's desk."

"All the time?" Nolan had begun walking back and forth as she warmed up.

Nina watched her like a cobra hypnotized by a flute-playing swami.

"From time to time I take files home that contain client-intake notes." She glanced at Jack, who hid his embarrassment on her behalf well from the court and poorly from her. Oh, why in hell had she done that!

"And why would you take files home?"

"To work on them." Do not volunteer, she reminded herself. Nolan was leading her toward the precipice.

"Did you, on September sixth of last year, take the client file of Mr. and Mrs. Vang to your home? The file that contained your in-take interview?"

"Yes." Nolan took her through the truck sequence, the evening, the storm, her fatigue, the lost key, the next morning, and the real-ization that the files had been in the truck. Nina kept her voice low and pleasant. She looked at the judge, as she had so often counseled her clients to do, but he turned his eyes to something on Nolan's table and did not notice. She felt again, acutely, how she had let the three sets of clients down, but right alongside that feeling ran a defi-ance she simply could not quash.

"When was the next time you saw the Vang file?" Nolan asked, pacing in front of her, not looking at her either. Nolan was trying to keep her train of thought, keep the rhythm going, get the points out bang-bang-bang. Aware of Nolan's thinking and Jack's thinking as well as her own, Nina felt psychologically jerked around, as though she were playing all the roles in an enigmatic drama.

"I didn't see it until my attorney and I went to your office. You called my attorney and said that the file had been recovered from Marilyn Rose, the previous witness."

"And at that time did you come to my office with Mr. McIntyre?"

"Yes."

Nolan dug out Exhibit 16. Nina tensed. "Is this the file you saw at my office?"

Nina took the exhibit and saw the familiar blue label, "Kao Vang." "I'd have to look inside." Nolan nodded and Nina opened it. The only contents were the three sheets of scribbled notes she had taken. The claim and its supporting documents had been kept in an-other file. She turned to the last page and saw the last sentences, the damning ones she hadn't written.

Nolan said very carefully, "And is that the file you saw in my of-fice, with the same contents?"

"Yes, it's the one I saw in your office."

"With the three-page form inside?"

"Yes, but this is not the three-page form in my original file. This form has been altered." At last we come down to it, Nina thought.

The judge seemed to sigh and deflate a little. He looked down upon her at last, and she nervously decided she preferred his detachment after all.

"So," Nolan said. "It's the same manila folder?"

"Yes."

"It's the first page of notes you wrote at the time of the interview?"

"As far as I can tell, yes."

"Same second page?"

"As far as I can tell, yes."

"Same third page?"

"No. There are additional words. The last sentences. I didn't write them."

"These words? 'Client breaks down, says he set fire himself! Advised him don't say any more, don't want to hear this'?"

"Yes."

"Ms. Reilly, please close that exhibit. Now, I want you to tell me the first full sentence on the second page."

"Objection!" Jack said. "Irrelevant. Just because she can't recite the whole thing by memory doesn't prove that she can't recognize words she never wrote."

"She says she doesn't remember writing these words," Nolan said. "Let's see what words she does remember."

"That's not a fair test, Judge. She knows what she was thinking at the time, what information she had heard at the time. That's one reason she knows she didn't write the words, because of the fact that the information was never given to her."

"I think you're getting ahead of yourself, Counsel," Judge Brock said. "I will allow some limited testing of the witness's memory as to the file contents."

"The first full sentence on the second page, Ms. Reilly," Nolan said, coming closer. "What does it say?"

"I have no idea," Nina answered. "However, I know that what I wrote in that first sentence was based on something the client told me. So I know I wrote it. I also know that the last sentences on the third page are forged because they reflect information my client never gave me."

"But you testified earlier that the notes often contain observations and judgments that are your own thoughts, did you not?"

"Yes, but the forged statements were not observations or judgments of mine at the time of the interview."

"You also testified that you sometimes add things in later, after the client has left."

"I didn't add those final nineteen words. They were forged."

"So you say. Is that your handwriting in those final sentences?"

"It looks like my handwriting. I might not even know it wasn't my handwriting, except I know I never wrote those last words. That's a forgery."

"You'll admit it looks like your handwriting?"

"It's a decent forgery, I guess."

"You insist that it's a forgery. So who forged it?"

"I have no idea."

"Why would anyone do that?"

"I can only speculate."

"But do you have any personal knowledge? Can you enlighten us in some verifiable fashion as to who, why, when, where, anything at all?"

"Not of my own personal knowledge. However, I feel this is part of a pattern. In all three of the files there was some sort of interference prejudicial to the client. In the Vang case, these sentences were forged. In the Brandy Taylor matter, Cody Stinson received an anonymous call. In the Cruz matter, Ali Peck was called anonymously. Mr. Cruz has also now filed a blatantly false charge against me."

"You may feel all sorts of things. But do you have any proof that there is someone out there trying to harm your clients?"

"The whole train of events. The theft of my files in the first place."

"But that could just as easily have been a car thief who inadvertently rode off with your files, am I correct? For all you know?"

"But then the file contents were read and used. That's more than a car theft."

"Do you have any personal knowledge that the person who, as you put it, interfered in each case is the same person each time?"

"Makes sense to me," Nina said. "Person or persons."

"Okay, let's look more closely at your theory that this is all part of a pattern. Now in the Brandy Taylor matter, Ms. Taylor told you, and you noted in the file, that she had evidence that Mr. Stinson had committed a murder. And I will remind you that Mr. Stinson testified that there was then a call to him stating exactly this damaging information."

"Correct."

"And in the Cruz matter, Mr. Cruz told you, and you noted in the file, that a witness named Ali Peck had information harmful to his custody case. And then let me represent to you and to the court that attorney Jeffrey Riesner will testify that he received a phone call informing him precisely about this harmful witness."

"Yes." Nina knew where Nolan was going, and that Jack couldn't stop her. Helpless, she clenched her fists tight, holding on to her anger.

"So the file contents were read and reported to others, as you say."

"Yes."

"And isn't it true that exactly the same thing happened in the third case? That your client Mr. Vang told you a secret, just as Ms. Taylor and Mr. Cruz did. You wrote it down. And just as in those two cases, Heritage was contacted, and the company was told the damaging information. Isn't that the pattern?"

"No," Nina said, continuing the struggle to keep her feelings off her face and out of her voice.

"This third party, whom none of us has identified, if this third party did all this, it would seem that his M.O. was to reveal secrets, not to make them up, wouldn't it?"

"The Vang case was different. There was no secret in that case."

"Mr. Vang didn't break down and tell you that he had burned down his own store?"

"Absolutely not!"

"Mrs. Vang never said that?"

"No!"

"You didn't learn that from someone and add it to your own notes?"

"No!"

"Who did burn down that store, then?"

"The police haven't arrested anyone."

"So Mr. Vang hasn't been cleared?"

"He was never arrested. There's no evidence that he burned his store down!"

"Oh, yes there is. There's his confession in your file. And the little matter of his flight to Laos."

Nina drew a long breath. "Even if he confessed to me, which he didn't, it would be privileged information, inadmissible in any real court."

"Strange to hear you say that, when it was your carelessness that allowed it to fall into the public eye, isn't it?"

"Objection," Jack said. "Argumentative."

"Sustained. Let's move on, Counsel."

"Isn't it true that there is no other suspect in connection with that fire and that Mr. Vang admitted to you he caused the fire?"

"Compound," Jack said.

"Rephrase the question." It was dizzying. Nolan was cross-examining Nina on direct examination. Nina struggled to get her bearings. She couldn't anticipate what Nolan would ask next. The suspense in this box made strategic thinking impossible. Every moment, she felt the guillotine blade trembling above.

"Did Mr. Vang admit he caused the fire at the time of the interview?"

"No. No."

"Did he deny it?"

"In so many words, yes."

"Isn't it true that you conspired with the Vangs to put in a fraudulent claim for them, knowing the arson was caused by Mr. Vang?"

"No, that is not true. Why would I put my career in jeopardy by doing something so unethical and criminal?"

"You're a sole practitioner?"

"Yes."

"Your income varies sometimes substantially from month to month?"

"Yes."

"How much did you charge Mr. Vang for this work you did for him?" Nolan held up the exhibit that contained her billing to the Vangs.

"Two thousand four hundred dollars."

"For writing a letter to the insurance company?"

"The case involved an extensive set of exhibits. I put in numerous hours helping the Vangs collate their receipts."

"Couldn't your secretary have done that? Collate receipts?"

"I preferred to do it."

"Let me see, you were charging forty dollars an hour to collate receipts, so that would be—oh, here it is. Sixty hours. Sixty hours you put in to write this letter?"

"To meet with the clients, to help them assemble their claim, to negotiate, to write the claim letter, to follow up—yes. Sixty hours. In the end, the negotiated claim was for more than two hundred thousand dollars."

"Isn't it true that the price for your honor and integrity was two thousand four hundred dollars? That you were willing to commit a fraud for that amount, assuming you could hide behind the attorney-client privilege and no one would ever know your client had told you he did the arson?"

"Objection! Argumentative, compound, misstates the testimony, calls for a conclusion," Jack said.

"It's totally untrue," Nina answered before the judge could rule, but her voice was choked. She could not disregard the cavalcade of feelings coursing through her, no matter how determined she felt. Such a pathetic amount of money it was they figured for the price of her soul. "I'm proud of my profession! I would never . . . !"

Judge Brock cut her off. "I will sustain the objection. Rephrase, Counsel."

"That's all right, Your Honor. I am finished with this witness."

"Mr. McIntyre?"

"Ms. Reilly," Jack said. "I just want this to be very clear for the record. Are you positive you never wrote those last nineteen words?"

"Positive."

"You had no intent to defraud the insurance company, and so far as you know, Mr. Vang did not commit any arson?"

"That's right."

"You spent sixty hours working on this claim and obtained a settlement of two hundred and ten thousand dollars for your clients?"

"Yes."

"Let the record reflect that Ms. Reilly's fee amounted to one point one percent of the recovery," Jack said. "I have nothing further of this witness."

"We will adjourn. Court will resume at three."

Freed, Nina got out of the box and walked tall back to Jack's table. Gathering up documents from the other table, Nolan gave her a cynical smile. Jack took Nina by the arm. "Out we go," he said.

The elevator arrived, jammed with people. Jack pushed forward and stuffed her into an invisible gap.

"How did I do?" she asked Jack as they ate sandwiches across the street.

"You sounded tremulous, but Brock will make allowances for that," Jack said.

"I didn't feel scared, Jack, if that's what you're thinking. My anger shook me. I had no idea how difficult it would be testifying. I wanted to leap off the stand and land a good one-two on Nolan's nose. I kept seeing those dumb glasses under my high heels, broken on the floor. I bet her eyes look weak without them."

"You okay now?"

"Yeah."

"Chin up."

After the break, Nolan called Sandy to the stand. She sat down in the box, arranging herself calmly. Dignified and impeccable, she wore her standards, a denim blue skirt and a white blouse, and had spiked her upswept black hair with a turquoise stick. Nina knew she had never testified in court before but wasn't worried about Sandy. She could take Nolan down with a sneeze.

"So you took the new file that was handed to you and affixed the Client Intake Interview form to the back of the file?" Nolan asked.

"Yes. Like I always do."

"Did you read the notes?" Judge Brock leaned in closer, wanting to hear the answer to this one.

"Might have," Sandy said.

"What's she doing!" Nina whispered. Jack shook his head slightly. They were both astounded. Sandy had told them several times that she had read the notes.

"Might have? Did you or did you not?"

"I might have."

"You mean you have forgotten whether you read them?"

"Don't put words in my mouth," Sandy said. "I'm the only one that does that."

"Well, what do you mean, 'might have'?"

"Maybe I did," Sandy said. "I often did."

"It was your practice to read the intake notes?"

"I often did."

Clearly unnerved by Sandy's attitude, Nolan handed Sandy the exhibit and had her read the notes. "Did you read these before or not?" she demanded. "You must answer to the best of your recollection."

"I may well have," Sandy said, nodding her head at the file. "I usually did."

"Your Honor, I request that this witness be compelled to answer the question."

"I think she's doing the best she can," Brock said. "Ms. Whitefeather, did you have any knowledge from that file or otherwise that Ms. Reilly knew her client had committed an arson?"

"No, sir. If I read these notes at the time, and it was my practice to do that, these last two sentences weren't there. I do know that. Because I would have talked to her about it if they were. And she never would have filed the claim. Never. She's one of the honest ones."

"Request that whole statement be stricken," Nolan said, glowering.

"She's honest," Sandy said again. "Unlike some I have known."

"Maybe I shouldn't have asked the question," Judge Brock said. "Sorry, Counsel. But her answer stands."

25

AT LAST, a break.

Nina got into the elevator for the sixth floor with Jack with her head high and her self-confidence at an all-time low. Her entire life had been served up on a plate to prejudiced critics who made their livings feeding off the failures of their colleagues. Gayle Nolan didn't hide her intolerance or feign objectivity. She hadn't been acting; she felt disdain for Nina. Contempt, even! Nina's colleague, who didn't respect her, who even wanted to see her on her knees!

Although Judge Brock was less overt, she had a definite impression that her very presence in his courtroom embarrassed him, as if, in his view, only the worst lawyers fell this far down the system. He lumped her in with the dregs.

And Jack, standing beside her, humming a little tune? What did she want from him at this low point? Reassurance that she was a good person, this was what she wanted. But Jack gave her what she herself gave her clients: objectivity, strategy, a push forward. He assessed her like he assessed steak in the market. He had other worries besides her emotional well-being.

She felt like running right out those doors onto Howard Street, getting into her truck, and driving—where? She would never again look at a stricken client's face without remembering this day.

Assuming she ever had a client again.

· · · ·

Their turn had come. With Kao Vang unavailable in the hills of Laos, they had only two witnesses for the defense on the Vang count, Mrs. Vang, who wouldn't be arriving until later, and the handwriting expert, Lyuba Gleb, who was waiting for them as they came out of the elevator.

"Hello, there," she said, shaking hands with Jack. "How is it going?"

"Just fine," Jack said.

"You look so nice today, Jack," Mrs. Gleb said. "I had no idea." A chic woman of a certain age, she wore a neatly fitted Chanel suit. The flaring, emphatic eyebrows gave her the look of character she wore so gracefully. Her Roman nose and lips were accentuated by a faint mustache, and it all added up to a formidable, smiling, relaxed lady.

"You look ready for anything they can throw at you," Jack said.

"What is to throw?" Mrs. Gleb said. "I can only tell the truth. Although, of course, it is a truth about art. They have their own expert all ready to refute what I say, isn't that right?"

"Yes, Dr. Harvey Pell. I don't see him around."

"Look for a bright spot in any room. He seeks the limelight. You should see his signature, two lines under it like he is Napoleon. So they have brought him all the way from Chicago. He is competent, so I was surprised to read his opinion." She turned to Nina. "Don't worry, darling, I am right and I will make the judge see this."

"Mrs. Gleb. You are a questioned-document examiner?" Jack asked.

"Yes. My specialties are handwriting identification, disputed handwriting, anonymous letters, and graffiti. I perform infrared photo work of all sorts. I am an expert on ink identification and on nineteenth-century paper. I have performed this work since 1972."

"What is your educational background?"

"I received my baccalaureate in chemistry from the Sorbonne in 1970. I was employed by the Sureté in Paris to assist in certain analyses of papers in a war-crimes case. That is where I received my on-the-job training. I was sent to the U.S. to take part in several seminars on handwriting identification during the seventies. I continued working at the Sureté and became head of the department investigating questioned documents in 1978."

"Please describe your experience."

"I served as head of the department from 1978 to 1984. During this time I often testified in the French court system. I began consulting for Interpol in the area of check forgeries. In 1985 I accepted a position as chief document examiner with the Bank of America and oversaw all of its forensic documents cases for the following ten years. I then went into independent consulting and most especially assisting police departments all over the country in questioned-documents cases."

"In which courts have you previously qualified as an expert witness in this area?"

"I have qualified and testified as a questioned-document examiner in various courts in Douglas County and Washoe County, Nevada; in Queens and Manhattan counties, New York; in San Francisco, San Mateo, and Marin counties in California during the past five years."

"Have you—"

"I am a member of the American Academy of Forensic Sciences, the International Association for Identification, and I am a member of and certified by the American Society of Questioned Document Examiners."

"And are you—"

"In addition to my consulting work, I have taught numerous seminars for bank and insurance examiners all over the country."

"Request that this witness be qualified as an expert in the area of examination of questioned documents," Jack said.

Nolan barely looked up. "No objection."

Jack picked up his legal pad. "During November of last year, were you requested by me to examine a certain original document and to provide your expert opinion as to whether the last two sentences of that document were written by the same person who authored the rest of the document?"

"Yes, you retained me for that purpose."

"Directing your attention to Exhibit 18, is this the document I gave you to examine?"

Mrs. Gleb took the exhibit. From a pocket she pulled out a small box and from the box she took a small magnifying eyepiece, which she appeared to screw into her eye. She bent to the document, and suddenly, all her animation froze on the task. Even her breathing halted. She wasn't kidding around.

She lifted her head and rejoined them in court. "Yes, this appears to be the original document. I recognize the writing. I know it as well as my own at this moment."

"All right. And did you examine the document during the month of December and thereafter?"

"Yes. It was obtained for me by you, and I examined it at my lab. I returned it to you in early March."

"And what did you understand to be the purpose of your examination?"

"Well, as you said earlier, to find out if this attorney, Ms. Reilly, who did write all of the document up to the last two sentences, also wrote the final nineteen words."

"Please describe the steps you took in examining the document."

"First, I examined the ink content. I had it analyzed by a lab that I have used for years, Allied Laboratories. Their report came back in January."

"And their conclusion?" Jack had the report and Nolan had stipulated that it could come into evidence.

Mrs. Gleb raised an eyebrow. "The ink in the final nineteen words was identical to the ink in the previous sentences."

"What did that mean to you?"

"That the same pen had been used. I called you and questioned you further."

That the pen used in the forgery belonged to her had distressed Nina for a full day. Only late that evening did she figure it all out and call Jack.

"You asked about the circumstances of the theft of the document, correct?" Jack asked.

"Yes. And you advised me that Ms. Reilly's briefcase had been stolen. And inside was her Waterman pen. I had the ink reanalyzed, and all the ink used on this document was the standard ink used in Waterman ballpoint-pen cartridges."

Nolan took notes, unperturbed. She knew all this already.

"Were you able to make any sort of examination as to the paper?"

"Just on the off chance that the entire third sheet might have been substituted, I performed my own analysis of the sheet. The third sheet was from the same standard type of yellow legal tablet as the others. I could not determine from the paper anything else. I did examine the entire document microscopically for overwriting, underwriting, any evidence of alteration. I found no sign of alterations."

"What other examination did you undertake?"

"In my primary examination, I compared the last sentences, which are the ones in question, with the writing in the rest of the document. I used glass alignment plates to check the angle of writing, the height, the spacing. I used a comparison microscope as to one word that was repeated, the word *don't*. I examined all the writing on the third page using magnifications from ten to fifty times in an attempt to ascertain whether there were signs of forgery."

"And what would be some of the signs you might look for?"

"For example, signs of tracing. Signs of hesitation in the writing, wavering. Difference in pen pressure. Difference in slant and shape of letters. As to the writing itself, differences in, as I've said, height, angle, spacing."

"Were you able to come to any conclusion regarding the question you were asked to address?"

"Yes, I did."

"And what was your conclusion?"

"I determined the writing in the last two sentences was a forgery. By a forger of limited skill and mediocre talent, I must add."

"And on what specifically did you base this conclusion?"

At Mrs. Gleb's signal, the bailiff brought up a slide on a screen to her right. Nina couldn't see it very well.

"Lights," Brock said.

The last words floated up there in the darkness.

"No immediate sign of hesitation. The writing flows," Mrs. Gleb said. "However, there is an alteration in the pace of the writing, the flow, here. Look at the two dots above the *i*'s. They are directly above although the rest of the writing rushes forward, like Ms. Reilly's writing. These *i*'s were dotted too carefully, later. Compare this with Ms. Reilly's enthusiastic, optimistic *i* on page two of her notes."

The *i*'s appearing in the phrase *liquor-store killings* in the part of the document Nina had written had dots that were far to the right of the letter. Nina looked at her *i*'s. They did seem to hurry toward the right margin of the paper.

But there was more to come. "Now the ends of the words," Mrs. Gleb said. "Examine the final nineteen words again." Magnified several times, they achieved the monumental abstract forms of a Motherwell painting, which was fitting, considering the monumental effect of these nineteen words on her life. To Nina, the last sentences looked like they arose out of the same hand as all the others—hers.

"Now look at this sentence from page one," Mrs. Gleb went on. "I have put the two sentences side by side for comparison." Nina saw no difference. "Note the terminals on the final letters of each word. The final letters in the last sentence have very small tails on them, you see? This writer wanted to put on even longer tails but restrained himself or herself. The writer of the last sentence wanted the final strokes to go upward, the sign of an extrovert, a gregarious person. You know how the song goes, 'people who need people'?

Our forger probably enjoys parties and loads up his or her spare time with all kinds of frivolous social events.

"Now, in contrast, study the final letters on the words Ms. Reilly admits she has written. No tails. The letters finish and by golly they are finished. Abruptly. Look here. The final stroke on the small *d* comes down below the basic line. This is a primitive stroke and denotes that the writer is opinionated and perhaps unreasonable at times. Ms. Reilly is perhaps a stubborn personality who casts off unnecessary details. She is not gregarious. She is not extroverted.

"Third point of difference. The breaks between letters. Look at the word *advised* from the last sentence. Note the breaks after the letters *a* and *d*. Under the microscope—where is that slide—thank you—very faint connecting lines can be seen. The forger is again acting contrary to his or her real personality in placing breaks between the strokes. The forger wants to connect these letters to the rest of the word, because he or she is a logical person, wary of intuition.

"All forgers are devious by nature, able to subsume the real personality. This forger is able to duplicate Ms. Reilly's handwriting in a workmanlike manner, with only small, crass hints of form that reveal a covert crudeness in the character. He or she has some limited talent as a craftsman, with these limitations exposed by the roughness of this effort. It is Ms. Reilly, with her tricky breaks between letters— look here, she is practically printing—who is the creative person, the artist. I must say I cannot understand what she is doing in the law."

As this unfortunate sentence came out of the garrulous expert's mouth, Nina tried to suppress a nervous giggle. She hoped the judge wouldn't agree with Mrs. Gleb.

"Anything else?" Jack said quickly.

"Point four. The loops that extend downward from the *y* and the *f.* Look at the lower loops of the nineteen words in question. The forger extends the stroke downward and there is just the minutest angle as he swoops into a big loop like Ms. Reilly's. He doesn't really want to make that big loop, he just wants a long line down. He is faking it." Nina stared at the letters. The lower loops looked enormous. The bottoms of some of the loops didn't look smooth, as though someone had done just what Mrs. Gleb was saying. She pictured the forger in a workshop lit by candlelight, crafting away like Geppetto.

"This forger is a practical type, perhaps interested in money. A controlling personality. Not a natural looper. In contrast, Ms. Reilly makes almost exaggerated lower loops, expressing the earthy demands made upon her by her own nature. Her loops indicate that her nature is sensuous. Her instinctive physical drives are strong."

Mrs. Gleb paused while Nina died of embarrassment. She hadn't sat in on Jack's previous discussions with Mrs. Gleb.

"Anything else you based your decision on?"

"A strong feeling, my own intuition based on many years of experience," Mrs. Gleb said. "However, I would have disregarded that if I did not find the other external evidence I have discussed."

"And your conclusion, once again, based on your years of training and experience?"

"The final nineteen words were not written by the same person who wrote the rest of the document."

"Thank you very much. No further questions."

Gayle Nolan got up, every line in her face arched and incredulous. "Mrs. Gleb, what are the names of the last two books you have published?"

"Let me see. I have published ten. The last book was titled *Graphology in Everyday Life.*"

"And the one before that?"

"*The Psychology of the Hand.*"

"That is also supposed to be a book about graphology?"

"Yes. Graphology is my current area of interest."

"What exactly is graphology?"

"It is a type of psychology, a method of determining personality by examining handwriting."

"And you used graphology in making these observations about

the last sentences and the preceding sentences in Exhibit 18, didn't you?"

"Over the years I have developed greater insight into traditional methods of examining questioned documents using the methods of graphologists, and I took advantage of my insight in this case, yes."

"Now, you testified that you examined the ink on the two samples and found them to be identical, right?"

"Yes. From the same pen, the lab concluded."

"And you assume that the forger used Ms. Reilly's pen, which was found when the briefcase was stolen?"

"That's what I understood."

"But in fact you have no personal knowledge that the pen was in the briefcase, right?"

Mrs. Gleb, unflappable, said, "None of us was there at that time. However, I saw the contents of the briefcase as listed in the police report Ms. Reilly gave on the day after the theft, and she mentioned her Waterman pen."

Nice comeback, Nina thought.

"Let's assume that we don't know what happened to the pen," Nolan said. "And all you had to go on was that the ink was identical. What would be your conclusion then? Based on that one fact alone?"

Jack stood up and said, "I think we're running into trouble with this hypothetical. I object, lack of foundation. It's not a fair question, Judge. No handwriting examiner ever looked at just one thing."

"I understand the point, Counsel," Judge Brock told Nolan. "We'll go on."

"All right, Your Honor. Now, Mrs. Gleb, the paper didn't help you either, did it, since the questionable sentences were written on the same paper?"

"That is true."

"So you were quite handicapped in terms of doing any sort of chemical analysis?"

"Yes."

"Did you look for fingerprints?"

"Yes. Allied Laboratories did that. They discovered many

smudged fingerprints. Apparently the papers passed from hand to hand at the insurance company. None were identifiable."

"So you had no hard evidence of any forgery, isn't that right?"

"Objection," Jack said. "What's hard evidence?"

"Let's rephrase," Brock said.

"The point is, all you had was the handwriting itself, is that correct?" Nolan asked.

"It was quite sufficient."

"Okay, you said that you examined the angle of the writing, the slant, the spacing. You couldn't conclude anything from that, right?"

"Not from that."

"Did you find any evidence of tracing?"

"I would say, no."

"Differences in pen pressure?"

"Nothing obvious."

"Wavering? Hesitation?"

"No. This was a confident person."

"So you based your conclusion on four factors, you testified."

"That, and my overall experience. Many, many years of experience."

"Right. The first factor you mentioned was the dot above the *i*."

"Mm-hmm."

"Now, exactly how many *i*'s were you able to observe in these disputed final phrases?"

"Six."

"And in every case, was the dot directly above the short line of the letter?"

"As I testified, only two of the six *i*'s had dots directly above the line. But these distinct variations from all the other *i*'s in the document are quite dispositive in my opinion. These two dots were damning, as they show a deliberation and care that does not come from a person taking notes, but only from a person forging a document."

"The two damning dots were above, rather than to the right, as in the other *i*'s on the other pages?"

"Yes."

"What was the difference?"

"I don't know what you mean, the difference."

"Between the dots? What you called the forged dots and the nonforged dots. How much out of alignment were the nonforged dots from their roots or slashes, whatever you call the rest of the *i*?"

"Well, the difference would be in millimeters."

"Couldn't Ms. Reilly have made a couple of dots just a millimeter closer to the main letter because she had something on her mind that was affecting her writing a little? Something that maybe made her feel a little less headlong than usual? Like finding out her client was a crook and deciding right then, as she was writing, that she would go along with it?"

"It's true the sample was small. Only the two letters. However, people don't usually vary much in the same piece of writing written at the same time."

"But she'd just had a big piece of news there at the end."

"Even so."

"Okay, let's move on to your second factor. What you call the terminals on the final letters of the words. You say there is evidence that in the questioned passage this extroverted forger wanted to curve up the terminals?"

"Yes. There was a tendency."

"Let's see that side-by-side slide again. A tendency, you say. Does that have anything to do with something we can observe?"

"Slide 12, please," Mrs. Gleb said. A giant swooping geometrical design appeared. "That is the terminal *s* on the final word, *this*, found in the last sentence," Mrs. Gleb said. "Note the slight movement upward."

"It's slight, all right. In fact, it's microscopic, this tendency, isn't it?"

"Most crucial details in this work are only observable under a microscope."

"Hmm. Your third factor. The breaks between the letters. Looks to me like this so-called forger did put breaks between the letters."

"Under the microscope I saw faint connecting lines."

"Show us the slides then."

"The slides did not pick up these slight lines."

"Ah! Because they were only tendencies, too?"

"I saw them, but there are limits to photography. There was an almost imperceptible attempt to connect the letters in several instances."

"Which you cannot show us in court today?"

"I can only testify they were seen by me."

"And from these imperceptible tendencies, by the way, you adduced quite a lot about our so-called forger. He or she is a logician, a craftsman who will never be a Rembrandt. Unlike Ms. Reilly, who could dazzle the art world?"

"These are my observations."

"These are your fantasies."

"Objection!"

"Let's move on." Judge Brock obviously didn't like to rule on things because inaction cut down on points to appeal.

"And now we move on to your fourth and final factor. Put that slide up, please. Okay, we have a little angularity on two of the letters, on the lower loops, right before they start to loop upward."

"Where the forger wanted to stop."

"You certainly are deep into the mind of this mythical forger, aren't—"

"Objection!"

"Move on."

"I'd like a ruling."

"Sustained." That's more like it, Nina thought. At least a tiny semblance of real law practice endured.

"So the forger wanted to stop? To just make a straight line instead of a lower loop?"

"Correct. That is demonstrated by this stoppage, this angle here, for example."

Nolan smiled. "It was hard for this speculative person to duplicate the evidence of Ms. Reilly's huge appetite for life, her sexual vigor?"

"Objection!" Jack roared.

"She's the one reading palms," Nolan said.

"Counsel, restrain yourself," Judge Brock said, his voice as affectless as ever, still attempting to demonstrate that he was a mere shell of a man, a nonpartisan vehicle for justice, in contrast to Nolan, who now openly flaunted the instincts of a starving she-wolf.

"That's what you testified, isn't it? The so-called forger is practical and money-oriented, not much of a lover, I take it. He was faking it, right? But according to you no one could ever accuse Ms. Reilly of faking it."

"Your Honor, Counsel's sarcasm isn't getting us anywhere and is squandering the court's valuable time," Jack said. Nina bristled at his mildness. In good old Judge Milne's court back at Lake Tahoe, the bailiff would be carting Nolan off to the tank, high heels kicking, on a contempt citation. Not only was Nolan assassinating Nina's character, she was indulging in jokes at her expense, trivializing the whole proceeding as unworthy of serious attention. She wanted Nina clapped quickly into the stocks so the outraged townspeople could hurl rotten eggs at her.

"How much of your conclusion is based on court-approved techniques of questioned-documents analysis, versus graphology, Mrs. Gleb?"

"It is all relevant and important."

"You can't separate the two?"

"There is no separation. Let me say to you, Madam Attorney, that any examiner who tells you he isn't using his intuition in the examination isn't doing his job."

"Right, intuition. I have nothing further for this witness."

"You may step down."

Mrs. Gleb left in a cloud of expensive perfume.

Jack had told Nina he tried out two other examiners before trying Mrs. Gleb, who had seemed so—so unperfumed back then. After examining the document, these alternative experts both admitted the likelihood of forgery, but had refused to stake their reputations on it.

Nina looked at the gigantic, swooping strokes of her handwriting, naked and eager on the screen. She looked down at her legal pad, at the notes she had been taking this morning with their huge lower loops everywhere. She turned the page hastily.

"We will take a final short break. You have one more witness on the Vang matter, is that right?" Judge Brock asked Jack.

"Yes. Mrs. See Vang," Jack said.

"All right. We'll take her then."

Outside in the general waiting area, Mrs. Gleb cornered them before they could escape. "Know one thing," she said. "I am right in what I say. You must ignore the mean-spirited sarcasm, as I'm sure the judge will do."

"Thanks for coming, Mrs. Gleb," Jack said. "We appreciate it."

"Right is on your side, darlings, and what's more practical, I'm there, too. Call me if there's anything more I can do for you. I'm at the Marriott until the weekend."

26

THE BREAK ALLOWED just enough time for mutual recrimina-
tions.

"Why couldn't you control her better?" Nina said to Jack as
soon as they were on the next floor down and out of earshot. "She
had some important points to make that had nothing to do with my
voracious sexual appetite! I'm sure she signs her name with giant
capitals, the better to express her inflated ego."

"I talked to her at least three times on the phone. I saw a summary of what she would testify. She never mentioned those lower
loops. Sometimes they do get carried away up there on the stand, as
you well know."

"You should have seen it coming. She's flamboyant. I could see
that right away. An expert should be conservative."

"Hey, we owe her. Remember, we couldn't get any other expert, and the truth is, she has a fantastic reputation in spite of Nolan's
vivisection, and she didn't come off as badly as you make out. The
forger used the same ink as you, the same paper, and wrote just a few
words. There was no signature, and the fact is, nobody else had the
guts and confidence to stick his neck out."

"Graphology," Nina said. "Sorta like astrology, right? I'm sure
Judge Brock is having a private yuk in his chambers right now over
that testimony. So how are we doing, Jack? Are we burying me
alive? Because that's how it feels."

"Put aside your insecurity. Zip that lip and sit tight. We attack this thing point by point. Commit that to memory. Let's go back in."

Nina didn't want to return to court and be a good girl. She was sick of Jack telling her what to do and irritated to trigger-finger sensitivity by her perpetual state of fury. She had abuse heaped up in her throat, backlogged. Jack deserved further tongue-lashing if she was to deliver him the conventional and complete client reflex.

She breathed four deep breaths, her mother's advice from childhood for fending off tension and anger, and went back into the chamber of horrors, where the formidable Dr. Pell waited at the door.

The former FBI man, with his dark hair and devilish air, bore a remarkable resemblance to the actor Andy Garcia. He kept his testimony earnest, succinct, and, well, Nina had to admit it, fair. To keep the issues straight and so that he could get back to work in Quantico, they had taken him out of order.

Gayle Nolan held the floor. Pell had brought his own set of slides, but he didn't talk about loops. He testified merely that nobody could tell if the last sentences were forged or not, as the forensic evidence was insufficient and the sample too short for an examination of the phrasing. "There are no smoking guns," he said. "No misspellings, no obvious variances from the preceding writing."

"So the writing is consistent with the writing in the rest of the document?" Nolan asked.

"Yes, it's consistent. But—"

"There is therefore no evid—"

"Objection," Jack said. "Let the witness finish. He was stopped before he could complete his answer."

"Did you wish to add to your answer?" Judge Brock said.

Ignoring Nolan, who clearly did not want him to continue, Dr. Pell said, "Yes. I have to add that while it is consistent, that does not mean that I can conclude that this sample is indeed the handwriting of the defendant. It's consistent, but then a passable forgery will be consistent. I simply don't have enough to go on. I can only say that there is insufficient evidence to conclude these nineteen words were forged."

"There is no evidence that this is a forgery, Dr. Pell," Nolan said. "None. Is that correct?"

"That is correct."

Jack cross-examined Dr. Pell, making sure he reiterated his inability to draw a conclusion either way. So far, Pell had not injured them fatally and Jack kept it that way, sticking to his own agenda, making his points without allowing any wiggle room. Apparently Nolan had had the same trouble they had finding an unequivocal opinion.

Dr. Pell stepped down, leaving them all understanding that there was no way expert testimony would prove whether or not Nina had written the final words.

What they had in the Vang case at this point were two conflicting pieces of evidence: the writing itself, apparently made in the usual course of business and therefore legally presumed to be what it purported to be, and Nina's testimony along with Sandy's addition, bless her heart.

The only other witness they had would be Mrs. Vang, who had arrived and was waiting outside with the omnipresent Dr. Mai. She would testify that Kao Vang had spent the evening and night with her and therefore could not have set the fire.

During the preceding six months, much had happened in the Vang family. Kao Vang had left town and by all accounts was back in his home village in the middle hills of Laos, but he didn't answer his letters. Mrs. Vang had divorced him and was now studying computer science at Fresno State. The children had stayed with her.

Nina had continued to learn about the Hmong in America and by now realized what tremendous steps away from tradition Mrs. Vang had taken in obtaining a divorce, in living alone, and even in keeping the children, who ordinarily would have stayed with the

father's family. The Vangs had suffered in the U.S. but they had sur-
vived, each in separate ways.

Kao Vang had taken his share of the money ahead of the insurance company's lawyers and was a rich man now in his home country, pretty much untouchable by Heritage. But Mrs. Vang's share of
the settlement check had been placed in an escrow account pending
the outcome of a civil lawsuit alleging fraud, which Heritage had
filed against the Vangs.

And against Nina, as a coconspirator. She had been sued by
Heritage, but the proceedings were on hold while this proceeding
went forward. The fight over Mrs. Vang's share of the settlement
money, of course, meant that today, in this court, Mrs. Vang had a
credibility problem, which Nina knew would be exploited to the
fullest extent by Gayle Nolan.

Small and unassuming, Mrs. Vang came in, was sworn, and took
the stand.

When a witness first sits down, an instant occurs in the box during which the rest of the courtroom takes a long look and forms impressions. Nina's first reaction was personal. Mrs. Vang looked better
than Nina had ever seen her. Her posture was erect and the exhausted expression from the days of collecting receipts and making
the claim was gone. She wore a modest pantsuit and held a stylish
purse in her lap. She did not look like a liar.

Nina's second reaction was professional. Mrs. Vang might make
an impressive witness. They should get everything they could from
her. Jack watched her, too, squinting in his concentration, no doubt
forming a similar opinion.

The only problem was that Mrs. Vang's answers would have to
be translated. She spoke only limited English. Nolan had agreed
without comment that, in the absence of a local certified Hmong-
language translator, Dr. Mai could interpret. Sitting in a chair directly in front of Mrs. Vang, between Nolan and the witness box,
Dr. Mai wore the same old shirt and pants. He made no eye contact
with Nina or Jack.

Judge Brock looked tired. Naptime. Not good. He consulted with his clerk in whispers.

"Good afternoon, Mrs. Vang."

Dr. Mai spoke briefly and she answered softly in English, "Good afternoon."

Jack took her through the litany of misfortune that had befallen the family, first in Laos, then in the U.S. He came to the second robbery, in which Kao Vang had been armed and shot and killed the robber at the Blue Star Market.

"And you were present when all this occurred?"

"I was in the back room looking out through the curtain, very frightened. Mr. Vang, he pulled out the gun from under the cash register and he shot this man, Song Thoj." Dr. Mai translated her words carefully, without emotion.

"What about the other man?"

Mrs. Vang looked troubled. She obviously didn't want to talk about the other robber. She looked at Dr. Mai, who frowned.

"There was another person at the store that night, wasn't there?" Jack said. "Mrs. Vang, you have sworn to tell the truth."

She spoke. Dr. Mai's frown deepened. He hesitated. A long moment passed before he translated her answer. "How did you know that?"

"Just answer the question," Judge Brock told her.

Jack was already satisfied. He had established his new arson suspect but he forayed further, just as Nina would have done.

"Yes, there were two of them," Mrs. Vang said quietly.

"And what happened after Mr. Vang shot one of them? What did the second person do?"

"Ran away."

"And, to your knowledge, was this person ever arrested in connection with the robbery or arson?"

Struggling with herself, she shook her head. She did not want to say anything but did not want to commit perjury either.

"Speak up," Brock said again, and she answered, "No."

"So to your knowledge, this second robber saw his partner shot by Mr. Vang and he got away."

"Yes."

"Then your store burned to the ground some two months later?"

"Yes. Completely destroyed."

"During the night of July fourth and into the following morning?"

"Yes. Independence Day it started burning. The fire went on for many hours."

She spoke without rancor but Nina could hear the emotion camouflaged by her impassivity.

"And you were where during that entire night?" Jack asked.

"I worked at the store until five. Mr. Vang worked until twelve and then closed up. He came home by twelve-fifteen A.M. I was awake. We went to bed. About four A.M. the fire department called us to say the store was on fire. We went there right away without even taking the time to get dressed. Our Blue Star Market had already collapsed. Everything gone."

Jack said, "Now, Mrs. Vang, was Mr. Vang with you that whole night between the time he got home and the time the fire department called?"

"Yes. We were in bed."

"And you were present in Ms. Reilly's office during the time of the first consultation with her?"

"Yes."

"Did you or your husband ever tell Ms. Reilly that he started the fire himself?"

"No. We never said anything like that."

"Thank you. Nothing further."

Jack sat down, smiling.

Nina whispered, "You should have asked—"

"I got what we needed. Shh," Jack said.

Nolan started in on Mrs. Vang. "So let's see. Mrs. Vang, you're telling us that your, um, ex-husband had nothing to do with this fire. Right?"

"Yes."

"And you collected, or tried to collect, between the two of you, two hundred ten thousand dollars as a result of this fire."

"I have collected nothing. The company took the money from me."

"Ex-actly. And the company's suing you, right?"

"Yes."

"And you of course deny that your husband had anything to do with it? And he's conveniently absented himself from court process so he doesn't have to speak up?"

"Objection! What's this 'of course'? These editorial comments are improper, Judge."

"Let's move on," Brock said. Nina was sick of the judge's now stock response, which evaded so many issues.

"So you have all that money at stake, though?"

"Objection!"

"The point is taken, Ms. Nolan. Move on."

Nolan took a breath, then pointed her finger at Mrs. Vang. "Did Ms. Reilly help you cook up this story about there being two robbers?"

"Objection!"

"Rephrase that, Counsel."

"That testimony you just gave, that you saw a second robber, that's untrue, isn't it?"

"No."

"You still claim a second person was present?"

"Yes."

"Then, Mrs. Vang, why oh why didn't you mention it in the police report? Why did you and your husband in fact tell the police that only one man, the man your husband killed, came to the store that night?" Nolan asked. She pushed her pointing finger closer to Mrs. Vang as she spoke, triumphant.

Mrs. Vang looked down. She spoke in a low voice. "I am ashamed to say we lied."

"You lied then? Or you're lying now?"

"No, there were two men."

"Come on, Mrs. Vang. What reason could you possibly have to lie to the police when you had just gone through such a terrible event? Why would you lie to the police?"

Mrs. Vang began to weep. Dr. Mai looked distressed.

"Well, Mrs. Vang?" said Nolan.

In a voice punctuated by weeping, Mrs. Vang spoke, drawing out a large cotton handkerchief to hold to her eyes. "I can't say," she said.

"Can't? Or won't?"

"I can only admit, there was another man. Because it is true."

Nolan shook her head in disgust. "I have nothing further from this witness."

"You may be excused," Judge Brock said, but Jack was already saying "I just have a few questions on redirect."

"Remain seated," Brock told Mrs. Vang.

Jack bent his head toward Nina. "Well? Do we do this to her?"

"She won't lie," Nina said. "And the details are important, why the second man was motivated to commit arson. Ask her—ask her if she knew him."

"Mrs. Vang," Jack said, "had you ever seen this second man before?"

"I can't say." Jack glanced at Nina and she nodded.

"You knew this man, didn't you? Mrs. Vang, you are in a court of law and you have sworn to tell the truth."

"Yes. This is the land of the free," Mrs. Vang said.

"You must speak the truth."

"I am ashamed." She wept.

Jack gave her a second. "You knew this man?"

"Yes."

"Who is he?"

"Moua Thoj."

"Same last name as the man your husband shot in his store?"

"Yes. Song Thoj's brother."

"Tell us about it, Mrs. Vang," Jack said kindly.

Mrs. Vang spoke at some length this time, haltingly, in Hmong. Eventually Dr. Mai held up his hand to stop her. Nolan sat at her table, disdainful but also taking furious notes.

"She says—excuse me. Moua and his brother, Song, belonged to a gang in Fresno together. We told our daughter she cannot ever see Song, but our daughter lied to us and she saw him one day after school. We found out later. He was angry that we would not consider him to be our daughter's husband. He and his brother, Moua, they came to the store and robbed it and shot my husband."

"Why didn't you tell the police who did this?"

"Because my husband said no. In our country a girl who lied to her parents and saw a boy alone is considered not a good person for a marriage. She dishonored our family. My husband almost died because of this dishonor. Better to try to handle it ourselves. So we made our daughter stay home from school, and my husband wanted to take her back to Laos."

"But then there was a second robbery."

"I believe the brothers came back to the store again to kill Mr. Vang, not to rob. Because still he would not allow the marriage. Their family—they had lost face. They came in and I was watching. And Song said, 'You fool!' to my husband. He had a gun. And Kao Vang reached under the counter and shot Song and killed him. Moua ran away."

She spoke with the despair of a person telling the truth.

Judge Brock had awakened and pricked his ears. Nolan had stopped writing and gripped the side of the table as though she wanted to jump up.

"Then came the fire," Jack said.

"My husband and I were having great trouble. He was very bitter that our daughter had brought all this harm to us. He insisted that she go back to Laos. I couldn't let that happen. It is no good for women in Laos. She would have a terrible life. I thought, we must take our chances here. And so, after the fire, I left my husband and I took my daughter and son. I could not have done that at home. But in this country, women are free."

"Are we just going to let this witness rattle on forever with her stories?" Nolan said.

Judge Brock said, "I want to hear this."

"And did you ever see this Moua after your husband shot his brother?"

"We were still working at the store. He came in and threatened us again. He said Kao owed him revenge money because Kao killed his brother. I told him I would call the police. He ran away again. But the next night—then the fire. All was lost."

"Mrs. Vang," Jack said, "why didn't you tell the police this time about Moua?"

"What is the use? What could they prove? My husband said, we are trying to get a settlement for losing our store and then we are going back to Laos right away and away from this country. I helped him. But I was unhappy and frightened. I will never go back to Laos. My daughter and son will be citizens. I left my husband and took my children. I am staying here."

"Do you know where Moua is now?" Jack said.

"I hear his family moved to New York when an investigator showed up asking many questions one day some months ago. He won't come back. He is afraid of the police coming now."

So Paul had scared Moua Thoj away by asking all those questions back in September, Nina thought, and made things safer for the Vangs, a ramble in the dark that resulted in inadvertent good.

"And your daughter is where?"

"She is with me. She works at the same store as me."

Jack gave Nina a look that said, anything else?

"We have suffered," Mrs. Vang said. "But here there is hope."

"I have nothing further," Jack said.

Recess for the day. They marched out. Mrs. Vang and Dr. Mai came over to shake hands.

"We'll get you your money," Jack told her. "We're going to win."

"Good luck," Nina said. "To you and your children."

• • •

Bashing all around. Jack bashed Paul, Paul bashed Jack, and Bob had a birthday bash.

He was fourteen tonight, and since they were stuck in San Francisco, Paul had suggested the spinning Equinox restaurant for the celebration, based on Wish's rave review. The view, spectacular at sunset, had turned foggy and now swirled romantic and ambiguous in gray, black, and white. Of course, the place lacked kidpizzazz. Bob was the only person under thirty here, Nina thought, unless you counted how childish Jack and Paul were acting. They had traded bad jokes from the moment they met at the entrance to the restaurant. For men who collided as often as they did, they sure had fun together.

Fortunately, Bob seemed not to mind the company of adults or his recent exile. Since Nina had dragged him back with her to San Francisco to sleep in the Galleria Park Hotel on Sutter Street, he had amused himself exploring the city. Incapable of hanging around a hotel room doing schoolwork, so far he had spent his birthday riding around on the cable cars by himself for hours at a time while Nina sat in the court. He planned to take the ferry to Sausalito the next day. As a result, his face rubbed red by the wind, flush with health and fresh local lore, he couldn't stop talking.

Although Jack had offered to put him up, Nina knew stranding him in Bernal Heights would just cause trouble. Downtown he could find so many things to do, and now that he was six feet tall, she didn't worry as much about him in this city he knew well. Also, although she considered it, she couldn't make herself go back to Jack's condo, not with her memories of what had gone on in the past between her and Jack, and her fantasies of what had come after. That phase of her life had ended.

A waiter came by to take their orders, shutting Bob up while he pored over the menu. First, they chose drinks all around, with Bob deciding on root beer while the others dived into the harder choices. Paul and Jack engaged in a hot contest over dinner wine, then settled for one red and one white. The men picked food quickly, Paul ordering prime rib, Jack the pork tenderloin. Bob vacillated lengthily between penne pasta and salmon, driving the waiter to erase two orders before the pasta scored the winning vote. Nina went with the evocatively named lemongrass-skewered sea scallops.

The Bay Bridge tiptoed nearer, inching toward them like a virtual property tour as the floor spun, making a full revolution every forty minutes. Bob, gulping his root beer, stared out the window, fascinated by the misty scene. Rain began drizzling down the window and fought the fog.

"You going back to Carmel tonight?" Jack asked Paul.

"What? And miss the ongoing human drama happening right down there on Howard Street?" After a brief foray into the events of the day, they declared a moratorium on court talk. They all felt hopeful; they all felt like they needed to forget it all for an hour or two. Then Bob started talking about his favorite piece in a recent *MAD* magazine, an article about phrases you really don't want to read in news articles about yourself.

"*Helpless bystander,*" Paul said.

"*Hail of bullets,*" Jack contributed.

"*Horrified onlookers,*" Nina said.

"*Identified by dental records,*" Bob said, winning the competition for the biggest laugh.

Tiring of that game, they small-talked about the big view outside. Nina tried to point out landmarks, but Bob knew them all and in the end, he proved to have the superior knowledge.

This was Bob's fourteenth birthday and Nina wanted to celebrate him, his life, his importance to her. She raised a toast to him, recounting the story of his birth, which she always tried to do on his birthday. Bob listened happily. Paul and Jack made messy, funny follow-up toasts, harking back to themselves at fourteen, promising Nina Bob would not behave at all like they had behaved at his age, not to worry, while Bob assured her he planned to do exactly that.

While she smiled at the horsing around, she found her mind drifting away, in spite of her resolution, from Bob to tomorrow's testimony on the Kevin Cruz count. What could motivate him to file that gigantic lie of a complaint? What would it take to get him to abandon it? Listening to the chat with half an ear, she pondered these questions until she noticed Bob watching her. She ruffled his hair, ashamed of herself. She was missing yet another milestone moment.

Still, she had an idea, and the idea turned in her mind like a windmill.

When the food came, the men attacked theirs. Bob twiddled his fork in the pasta and ate a few bites, and Nina tasted the shellfish and decided she was very hungry. The waiter brought cupcakes with candles, as she had arranged, and they all sang "Happy Birthday," Jack hoarsely, Paul self-consciously, and Nina too loud, to make up for their small number. Afterward, Bob opened presents. Jack gave him a scrimshaw-handled penknife he had bought in the Caribbean. "Carved by a pirate," he said with a wink. Paul gave him a certificate for karate lessons.

A knife and an education in how to fight, Nina thought, adding to the pile her own gift, the newest video-game system, a true gift of guilt. Now he could fight for real and for fake. All violent bases were officially covered.

His eyes opened very wide. "Mom, I can't believe this!"

Neither could Paul or Jack, who had listened to her rail against video and computer games for years, but for once they must have agreed. Neither said a word as Bob opened two more boxes, with games that had names that made Nina cringe and Bob glow.

A few other small gifts from family and friends and a major contribution to his college fund from his grandpa rounded off the collection. Last, he opened his present from his father.

"How weird," he said. "A Swedish dictionary."

Everyone found the gift very mysterious, and the note accompanying the present even more suggestive: "Did you know the North Sea is warm enough to swim in?"

"I thought Kurt lived in Germany," Jack said.

"He does. I'm just as mystified as you are," Nina said. They bagged up the presents in a green garbage bag and left the restaurant.

Paul and Jack indulged in a final jousting match over who could drive her and Bob back to the hotel, which Paul won, asking Nina to join him for a nightcap in the bar downstairs. She promised to meet him in a few minutes.

Back in their room, Bob flopped on the bed. "This is the best birthday. This is the best city in the entire universe. Mom, thank you so much."

She hugged him.

"Is it okay if I call my dad to thank him for the dictionary?" Bob yelled through the door as she washed her hands in the bathroom.

"Isn't it the middle of the night for him?"

"He says call anytime. He says he doesn't like to sleep much anyway."

"Okay, then."

When she came back into the room, Bob was deep in conversation. He waved her out, so she went downstairs to meet Paul.

Paul had switched to tonic water, but Nina had another glass of wine. "One more can't possibly make a difference."

"Drink water with it, then, like the Italians do. We don't want the judge to get the wrong impression of our upright young do-gooder tomorrow morning, rolling her bloodshot eyes at him."

"I think Bob loved his birthday party. Thanks for coming. The guest list would have been awfully sparse otherwise. It probably isn't your favorite kind of thing."

"I had a great time. Bob's a good kid. It was nice to relax and remember there is life outside the courtroom, and it's a pretty good life." He paused. "Isn't it, Nina?"

But she was distracted. "I keep thinking I've handled things badly. I didn't push you to investigate more over the last six months—even though you nagged me about that more than once."

"I do not nag."

"I wanted to believe things would magically resolve."

"Entirely natural. You didn't want to face trouble, so you ignored it. Everybody does that."

"Don't defend me," she said. "I get enough of that in court from Jack."

They laughed together.

She took a breath. "Paul, it's been hard. I've had doubts. . . ."

"Big surprise."

"No, hear me out. Almost everyone in my life tells me this job is destructive. But I've thought it through. Law's part of me. It isn't everything, but I believe, when it all shakes down, I've helped these people, in spite of it all. I stood up for them."

"Yes, you have," he said.

"But here's what I'm facing right now. These people I tried to help are trying to ruin me. It's demoralizing."

Paul took her hand. "Get up." He got the waiter to come over. "Save the table? We'll be back in five," he said, slipping him a bill. The waiter nodded and left.

He put a finger to his lips, took her by the arm, and led her straight out of the hotel and onto Sutter Street.

Neon shivered in the puddles. A man in a torn sweatshirt staggered by, hit Paul up for a buck, and moved on. A taxi careened around the corner, loaded with laughing passengers. Way up the hill, a cable car clanged, beginning its precarious descent through a riot of traffic.

"Yikes," Nina said. "Kind of a contrast to the piano bar."

"Yeah, isn't it great?" Paul said.

"It's so clear after rain here. You can even see the stars."

"Orion," Paul said, pointing. "The one constellation I'm sure about." He pulled her tight to keep her warm. "See what's happening? Mad dashing to and fro. Chaos on the street. Stars exploding."

"Guys peeing," Nina said, watching one. "Ugh."

Paul laughed. "You want life neat. It isn't."

"They're saying I'm unfit to do my job."

"You're so much more than your job."

They stood for a long time on the street. When they went back inside, Nina felt recharged, plugged into a power source. They warmed up again at their table. "I hate having the state bar after me. They're my colleagues."

"The bar court only operates based on the information it's given—in this case, complaints that look perfectly legit. There's a hidden agenda here, but it isn't the California State Bar's."

"Yes," she said. "We come back to that. My enemy." She tinkled a spoon against her glass, took a sip, and tinkled it again. "Oh, Paul! Here's an idea I had while we were celebrating with Bob."

"Oh?"

"It's about Mrs. Gleb. You know, after she testified she practically begged us to find something else for her to do."

"What are you thinking?"

"I don't want Jack to know about this, okay? I don't want him to get into trouble."

"Then I'm your man."

She hesitated for a moment. "It involves Mrs. Gleb, and it involves you, and it involves some pretty shady stuff."

"I'm liking this."

She explained what she had in mind. Paul took out a pocket notebook. They took turns writing in it, erasing, and adding for several minutes.

Nina said, "I believe Kevin wouldn't have lied about our relationship on his own. He had nothing to gain. It's my theory he is being manipulated by someone smarter and more powerful. Lately I've been thinking maybe he and Lisa are in cahoots."

"What a wild thought," Paul said. "So she put him up to hiring you and then accusing you of the harassment for some kind of sick revenge? Boy, that's damned nefarious. She didn't strike me as that smart. I can see her better taking a bat to your car."

"Maybe she offered him a better deal on the custody?"

"I guess that would be her bargaining chip," Paul said.

"Anyway, for the moment, Lisa's out of the picture because she's in Tahoe. But Kevin's here."

"So we put Officer Scholl and Jeffrey Riesner on the short list," Paul said.

Nina nodded. "Now, Scholl was Kevin Cruz's associate in the past. She worked closely with him on the case that got him his first promotion. She hates me. Maybe she's blackmailing Cruz into doing this. Maybe she knows something about that drug seizure that would get him kicked off the force."

"He planted the drugs on those college students?"

"Could be. Everyone said it was a strange bust."

"Hey, how come he isn't fired already, considering Ali, the under-aged wood chopper?"

"I hear he got himself a good attorney for a change," Nina said with a straight face.

They cracked up.

"Okay, let's move on to the subject of Jeffrey Riesner," Paul said.

"Okay. He loathes me. He knows that Sandy and I know about past activities regarding a will that was rewritten in his favor that could cost him his job. Even though we've kept our mouths shut, he has to be worried."

"Then there are the clients you stole."

"And the way I mortified him in front of the big gaming guys. Oh," she said. "Those were *good* times."

"But we have to consider what his connection is to Kevin," Paul said.

"Right. Well, the only thing that connects them is the custody fight. Riesner represents Kevin's wife. This presents a real problem. What in the world could Jeffrey Riesner do to benefit Kevin in any way?"

"How about—he promised to throw Lisa to the dogs. Maybe he told Kevin he knew something that would definitely assure that Kevin would win his kids in the permanent-custody hearing."

Nina shook her head. "No. Riesner would never intentionally

lose a case. Ten angels couldn't persuade him to do that. Maybe a million bucks would, but Kevin doesn't have a million bucks."

"Has the permanent-custody hearing come up yet?"

"I believe it's set in two weeks. There have been some delays," Nina said.

"Because of Riesner?"

"Why, yes, now that you mention it. Paul, I think you might be on to something. Maybe I'm just collateral damage in a fierce divorce fight. Kevin cares more about his children than he cares about me. He sacrifices my reputation to get his kids. Kevin is a fool if that's it, because Riesner won't come through with his end of the deal." She thought hard about that. "He's got the timing worked out so that Kevin's final custody hearing comes up after this hearing. He can get me, then double-cross Kevin later."

"Kevin's a cop. He's not that stupid."

"He is stupid, Paul. Stupid with desperation. I think he'd consider suicide if he lost permanent custody. I think he might fall for it."

"You're actually saying that Jeffrey Riesner stole your truck?"

"Seems incredible, but—Riesner could have picked up my key that Thursday at court. I just don't know. On the whole, I'd say Jean Scholl is the better suspect. It's nothing for her to rip off a car and take the files at her leisure. And she makes sure there's no forensic evidence to discuss. And she knows forgers, if it comes down to that."

"I always thought that was a squirrelly investigation she ran. So tonight we arrange for further information about the clandestine activities of one unscrupulous manipulator," Paul said, putting the pencil to paper. "Who's the big, bad wolf? Kevin Cruz, Officer Scholl, or Jeffrey Riesner?"

"Or if it's not them, we'll learn that, too. We'll try to use Kevin to flush out the wolf."

"Keep thinking about Lisa Cruz, even if she isn't around at the moment."

They wrote for a long time, drafting and redrafting.

"I won't be forced out," she announced when they were satisfied with their work. She drank an entire glass of water, set it down, and stood up. "I'll run up to tell Bob we'll be a few more minutes and pick up some samples we can give Mrs. Gleb. You wait here."

"Okay, boss."

They took a cab to the Marriott and located Mrs. Gleb on the fifth floor.

Mrs. Gleb answered in a red silk robe. Pink silk mules with delicate heels flopped on her feet as she moved to invite them inside. They sat down in two chairs next to a table stacked with books. Mrs. Gleb perched on the bed, tucking her legs comfortably beneath her.

"I expected you," she said after Nina introduced Paul.

"You did?" Nina asked. "Why?"

" 'Truth is on the march and nothing can stop it.' "

Nina shook her head. "Sorry. I don't know that expression."

"I am reading Zola tonight. You have the same passion for life, struggle, and intensity. You refuse to lose, isn't that so?"

"In this case, that's so."

"And you need me," she said smugly.

"Mrs. Gleb," Paul said. "You know all about forgery, right?"

"Correct."

"Ever tried your hand at it?"

"Darling, I'm very, very good. You saw me on the stand. I tell the truth."

"It's not exactly truth we've got in mind here," Paul said. "In fact, the opposite."

" 'Noble lies to persuade the city,' " said Mrs. Gleb.

"Ignoble, noble, whatever," Nina said. "Let's get cracking."

First thing, back at the Galleria Park, after a long good-bye at the door with Paul, Nina hit the bathroom, drank some more water, and gargled. Then she asked Bob how things went with his dad.

"Mystery solved," he said. "Say, Mom, what do you think about me taking a little trip this summer?"

"To visit Kurt?" To keep her voice calm, she turned away from him. Couldn't she get through tonight without another challenge? She had organized a last-minute party. She had bought Bob presents he loved that she hated. She rummaged in her suitcase for pajamas and a robe. How she would love a bath. She checked her watch. Not too late yet. Maybe Bob would give this up, give her until morning when she would be fresh—

"He misses me. And I never get to see him." While Bob pressured her, he also watched the muted television.

"Of course you miss each other," she said automatically. There were so many times, now, raising his son, when Kurt was recalled by a bend in Bob's earlobe or a certain quality in his changing voice. He played a peculiar role in their lives, dipping in like a seagull to snatch fish now and then, otherwise flying around far away. She was not ready to deal with Kurt's sudden interference or yet another need of Bob's. She needed to sleep and gather up vibes that would give her strength for tomorrow. "I don't know."

"Mom, he needs me, too. I told you that."

She tended to her clothes, folding some dirty ones into a zipper pocket, throwing others on her bed for the next morning. "Let me think about it, okay?"

"I hate when you say that. You might as well just say no."

"I don't mean no."

"You do. *Think about it* is a euphemism for *no way*."

"I am not saying that. I'm saying it's probably all right, okay?"

"So the answer is going to be yes?"

"Just let me have a day or two to sit on the idea."

"Don't bother. I have my answer." He turned the sound up on the television. "You have to tell Dad, though. I'm not going to break his heart."

"Bob, I'm saying the answer is probably yes, not no! Nobody's heart needs to be broken here! I just need time to be sure. I need to check some things."

He brightened instantly, jumped up, and hugged her. "I'll call him and tell him tomorrow night, okay? We've got a lot of things to talk about. And that'll give you some time."

"I haven't promised you anything. Remember that," she said, knowing it was useless. There was no going back. He had heard his power word, *yes,* and now he would never let her forget it. She sighed. "So what was all that stuff about Sweden and the North Sea?"

"He's teaching at the Stockholm Music Institute this summer. Says there's a great program up there for me that he'll pay for. He'll arrange everything. Mom, I can learn Swedish!"

Well, she thought a few minutes later, drawing a bath so hot it would burn her skin red, why the heck not? Swedish made as much sense as anything.

27

"DID YOU SEE THE WAY he looked at me?" Nina said the next morning to Jack as they walked through the metal detector and into the reception area. Jeffrey Riesner sat in one of the small upholstered chairs in front of the circular table, lounging like a man who was relaxed and rich and on top of the world. Nina, on the other hand, had suffered another of the long, dark nights of the soul with Bob sleeping in the next bed over. She wasn't far from rolling her bloodshot eyes at the judge after all, although eyedrops borrowed from the clerk at the hotel had helped.

"Ignore him," Jack said.

"I knew this would be a tough day."

"All days here are tough, Nina," Jack said, holding open the door to the witness waiting room on the right for her. They walked in and shut the door behind them. "Now forget about him. We've got to get to this Cruz guy."

"Jack, he's gloating! I can't help believing he's behind this, and it's driving me nuts, not knowing. Him or Scholl or Lisa or Kevin. Scholl or Lisa and Kevin together—"

"Drink your coffee," Jack ordered. "All of it. And concentrate on what we can do right now. I'm thinking Riesner's testimony will last until the lunch break. Then I want you to do something, Nina."

If Riesner had his letter, and Scholl had hers, she would be too busy to do anything for Jack. If all had gone right, the three players had received letters at their hotels late last night that would occupy at least two of them during this upcoming lunchtime. Thank goodness all the witnesses had agreed to stay in town for the duration of the hearing in case they were needed. "What?"

"I want you to talk to Kevin."

"No, Jack." That couldn't help now, and if her and Paul's plan worked, it would not be necessary anyway. They would know who had set her up, and could proceed accordingly. Jack got his dark look, so she justified her refusal. "I tried to talk with him several times over the past several months, right after I got that letter from him and two other times. He doesn't want to talk to me. Anyway, now we're in the middle of this."

Although she thought of it frequently, she had never confronted Jack with the fact that if he hadn't insisted on her rushing the insurance check to the Vangs over that fateful weekend, she might have averted that particular catastrophe by waiting until Monday, when Marilyn Rose had called, hoping she hadn't yet sent the check. She didn't blame Jack for pushing her to send it before she was ready. That wouldn't be right. Still, she wished he could acknowledge the error. If he had noticed, he apparently didn't see it as his mistake at all.

"Kevin Cruz's case isn't a criminal matter," Jack said. "He doesn't have a lawyer representing him on this. You have as much right to talk to him as anyone."

"What exactly could you expect me to say at this point? 'Thanks for the nonexistent roll in the hay? Hope it was good for you 'cause it wasn't for me'?"

"According to us, you never slept with this guy, never got involved sexually, were set up. It's always hard to prove a negative. Look, I know it's a long shot, but use your feminine powers of persuasion. Shut him the fuck up before he kills us."

"Jack, I have no leverage with this guy."

"You afraid?"

"Don't be idiotic."

"Then do it."

They had squared off. She had her arms folded. He had his folded. Jack, master of all he surveyed, she remembered him well. She couldn't help laughing at the two of them, on the same side but acting like enemies, adversarial as they always had been and always would be, wishing to control each other, wishing the best for each other. He wanted her to do what he wanted her to do. She wanted different.

"Whatever you say," she said, because she used to say that when he made unreasonable demands and it always placated him long enough to get him off her back. She rubbed his arm to show she was friendly. She wasn't willing to fight that way, using feminine wiles or legal wiles either; she was going to fight dirty. Jack would approve of their alternate plan when he heard all about it later if it paid off, because when it came down to it, Jack loved to win, however it happened.

Before they went into court, she planted a light kiss on his cheek. She wanted him to remember her sweetness.

After Judge Brock took his seat and the digital clock erupted into life, the attorneys spent the first few minutes going over some technicalities, then Nolan called Jeffrey Riesner.

This morning, the state bar attorney wore a slightly less rigorous uniform, a blue suit so light it verged on pastel. Nina herself had slicked her hair into a relatively tame position, tied it in a band at the back of her neck, and wore her best suit, in forest green, with a gold abstract pin her mother had left her stuck prominently upon her left lapel. If they were going to bring her down, she would go down looking like the woman of substance she was, not as a victim.

Riesner swore to tell the truth and sat down, a subdued and normal-appearing form of the devil Nina knew to be hiding up there in plain view.

Gayle Nolan introduced herself, then went through his credentials at great length, while Riesner, acting the consummate professional, casually gestured with his Stanford ring. He was wearing a blue pinstriped suit Nina could swear was identical to the one he had worn the first time she met him. Well, he knew what worked. He looked sleek and vulpine as always. His bright, white canines twinkled as he flashed his teeth.

"He's an attorney in good standing with the bar," Nina whispered to Jack. "We get that already!"

Jack shushed her.

Nolan finally got to the questions. She asked Riesner to summarize his custody case and representation of Lisa Cruz in that matter, then said, "You received a phone call on Friday, September seventh of last year regarding Ms. Reilly's client in that custody case, Kevin Cruz, is that correct?"

"That's correct."

This was so Riesner, to parrot her formality when a simple yes would do. Nina couldn't help it, she bristled over every word he spoke, every hand gesture, every slight movement of his cheek. Here it was, the moment in this hearing she had so dreaded. The colleague she disliked most in the world was here not only to witness her public vilification, but also to add to it. At last, it appeared, Jeffrey Riesner might win one big case against her, the biggest.

"Please tell the court the content of that call."

He cleared his throat, a sound that made Nina want to gag. "Very early, I would say about six A.M. on Friday, September seventh, I received a telephone call at my residence. I had a particularly busy day—too many clients to count needed my personal attention, so I was already working, preparing for court. I answered the phone myself. I can't tell you if the voice belonged to a man or a woman. It's my considered opinion this person was using some kind of a sound-altering device.

"The voice said that Kevin Cruz had a lover, an underage teenaged girl named Alexandra Peck. The voice also offered me her phone number, which I wrote down. I checked a cross-directory listing to get an address to match that number. I called, and spoke with one of her parents, verifying that she did indeed know Kevin Cruz and had been in contact with him almost daily through a cadet program. Her mother described them as former colleagues and friends. I then woke a few people up to arrange a subpoena demanding that Miss Peck appear in court at a custody hearing scheduled for that very day."

"And you notified Ms. Reilly of this new witness when?"

"That same morning, via fax."

"And what was her reaction to the news that her case was about to burst wide open?"

"Oh, she did the best she could do to discredit my motives and professionalism to the judge. That's pretty much her defense style, resorting to personal attacks."

He stopped short of sticking his tongue out at her.

"And what did the judge decide?"

"To allow Ali Peck to testify, of course. Everything I did was perfectly legitimate. I did what I could to provide opposing counsel with prompt notification. Naturally, the judge wants all the information possible before determining a custody case. He didn't want to decide based on false or limited information, when there was someone sitting right there in court with pertinent testimony, ready to come forward."

"And what was Ali Peck's testimony?"

At this point, Nina tuned out. She knew what had happened in court that day and she did not care to hear his version. She scribbled on her notepad and tried to drum up a tune to hum mentally. His voice settled like yellow smog over the court.

Of course he presented himself in the best possible light and Nina in the worst as he gave lengthy answers to Nolan's questions. They finally got to the heart of the matter. Yes, Riesner said, he believed that he had won temporary custody for his client based on Alexandra Peck's testimony against Kevin Cruz. Yes, the leak of what had been in Nina's confidential file was probably the strongest determining factor in that win.

Once Nolan had finished, making sure the points were made and triple-made, Jack stood up.

"Today in court, you say you received an anonymous phone call informing you about Ali Peck, is that right?"

"Yes."

"Yet that's not what you told Ms. Reilly, is it?"

"I told my opposing counsel exactly what she needed to know, no more than that."

"You suggested that Ali Peck had contacted you, didn't you?"

"You know how it is sometimes, when someone is just after you and after you about something—you toss them a bone because you don't want to be engaged in exhaustive argument or confrontation. It's not something I'm proud of, but you know, I wasn't under oath when I was talking with her, unlike today."

"You lied to her, didn't you?"

"I wouldn't characterize my comments that way at all. I may have allowed her to believe something that was incorrect. It's the way things work in law. Sometimes you allow misunderstandings to float if they will serve your client."

"Help us out here. I don't think this is very clear. In what way does having an anonymous phone call versus a direct phone call serve your client?"

"It was my judgment that Ali Peck's evidence would seem more credible to opposing counsel if she jumped to the conclusion that the information came directly from the girl, and was willingly offered. It was just a way to push opposing counsel a little off-balance, make an appearance of more strength than we had, a tried-and-true method I'm sure you've used in your day," Riesner said.

"It's your judgment that it's okay to lie if it suits your purposes."

"I did not lie. I said clearly that I did not know who made the call—" And he stirred up a frothy brew of obfuscation and confusion, trying to keep his actions palatable to the California State Bar. The testimony went on like that for a long time. Jack continued to beat away at him and Riesner continued to parry until Jack finally sat down again. He hadn't scored, and he knew it.

"You don't make points with this guy," he whispered to Nina. "You make war."

"Now you know."

28

STANDING IN THE HALLWAY outside the courtroom area and past the elevator banks, Nina decided they had a few minutes before they had to leave, and Paul had disappeared into the rest room. She called Sandy to check in. To her surprise, Wish answered the phone. "Where's Sandy?"

"Oh, uh—" He sounded distracted. "Sorry, there are two people who've been waiting in here for half an hour. What should I do with them?"

"Who are they?"

"I think they need legal representation." His hand went down over the phone and she heard some muffled conversation. "Yep, that's what it is."

"Take their names and numbers. Tell them we'll call them to arrange an appointment later on today or tomorrow morning. Then send them home."

"Okay."

She waited while he achieved this feat.

Sounding relieved, he came back on the phone. "They were waiting at the door when I got here. Mom left in such a rush she didn't tell me what to do about them."

"Where is she?"

"Remember that thing where the president came to Tahoe a few years ago and put some money into Indian projects and returned some land?"

"Yes," Nina said.

"She headed a committee about that. She has also been on the Washoe Tribal Council and is real active in pressuring the government to return tribal homelands in the Tahoe Basin to the Washoe. Plus she and Dad have been doing a lot of work organizing the tribe, helping with zoning problems, helping people to figure out what to do with tribal lands, that type of thing. And of course, you knew she was a member of the Leviathan Land Council when they were persuading the feds to designate an abandoned sulfur mine a Superfund site?"

"Uh. I guess I heard something about that." But not from Sandy. Anything she had heard, she had read in the papers.

"So she got a call yesterday. Some big shot is in town and wanted to talk to her."

"What about?"

"A job. They've been after her for a while about it."

"What? She never said a word to me."

"They want her to work with the Bureau of Indian Affairs this summer on some huge report the government is doing about, uh, Indian affairs, I guess. Supposed to take months, but you know how those things go on for years."

Holy—Sandy could leave her? Before she had time to absorb the blow, Wish spoke again.

"Don't worry, Nina. Don't get the wrong idea. She would never leave you high and dry. She just went to tell them no. Oh, and she left a note—something she wanted me to tell you." He shuffled papers. "Here it is. 'I talked to that graphologist lady after court when I was up there.'"

"That's all it says?"

"Uh oh. There seems to be a second part missing. I tossed a bunch of these tiny sticky yellow slips a few minutes ago. Hang on and I'll look."

"Wish, I'm sorry. I don't have time to wait right now. Tell you what. You call me if you find it, okay?"

"Mom won't like this. She said it was real important." He shuffled a few more papers. "But I guess it'll have to wait. Nina?"

"Yes?"

"Is Brandy around?"

"Not today, Wish."

The phone on the other side went down with a clunk. When
Wish picked it up, he sounded congested. "I've got a major problem."

"Brandy?"

"I can't stop thinking about her. There's no future for us because
she loves that guy. Maybe someone else will come along like her,
someone that—"

"Wish, she's going to marry Bruce—"

"I've been thinking about generosity. Courage. All that stuff.
How good people do the right thing even if it costs them. And don't
complain or even blow their own horns about it after, you know,
except maybe Peter Pan. He was an awful braggart."

"Is there something I can help you with, Wish?" She didn't have
time, but he sounded so woeful.

"Let me talk to Paul, okay? I'll call back when I find that paper
Mom wrote."

Paul had reappeared at her side. She handed the phone to him
and went to get her things from the witness waiting room.

"I took your advice," Wish told Paul. "I told Bruce Ford to get
circumcised."

"You—what?"

"Just think, a girl caring so much that her fiancé wasn't circumcised that she couldn't marry him, but was still too chicken to tell
him how he could fix things. She'd leave him first!"

Paul put a hand to his mouth to keep it shut.

"What's funny is, once she broke down and told her sister,
she told everybody who would listen. So why not tell him, is
what I asked her. But she just couldn't do it. So I did. I gotta tell
you, Bruce Ford's her kind of man, completely. He'd do anything to please her, turns out. They definitely belong together. No

way would I go through that, not even for someone as foxy as Brandy."

"It was the right thing to do."

Wish made an inarticulate sound.

"Wish, I'm sorry. I have to go." Nina was standing over in front of the metal detector, pointing to her watch. "Nina says thanks for taking care of the office."

On the way out, they almost collided with Kevin, who was coming out of the state bar's witness waiting room and into the hallway, hustling like a man with a plan.

Nina grabbed Paul's arm, waved good-bye to a surprised Jack, and led him to the stairs. "Let's go. Kevin already caught an elevator."

They made their way down to the first floor and into the narrow, T-shaped plaza beside the building in record time and scanned for a place to hide. Paul led Nina to a spot behind the fountain, where they had a clear view all the way to a burnished steel sculpture by entry gates that opened onto Spear Street.

"Are you sure it's a good idea to stay so close? What if they see us?" Nina fretted.

"We need to be close in case they leave, Nina. We need to watch them." Paul adjusted a small earpiece that led to a wire directly into his shirt pocket.

"I never saw a white man's face so red. I'm thinking, I'm hoping he's mad enough that he gives someone a piece of his mind and we hear every word. But even if we do, Paul, it's illegal, listening in like this. We can't use anything we hear in court."

"We want to know what's going on," Paul said. "The rest will follow."

"Oh, no," she worried as lunchtime pedestrians whizzed past. "I hope he's not too mad."

"All we said was that there's a change of plans, meet me, essentially." Paul peered around the fountain. "Kevin's there sitting on one of those concrete benches, puffing on a cigarette," he said, holding his finger to his ear. "And it's quiet. Reception's good." Invisible construction efforts involving orange cones had most of the traffic on Spear Street at a dead halt. "I can hear him thinking."

"If it's Riesner, he's thinking Riesner's going to screw him. If it's Scholl, she's going to turn him in. Did you get your gun back from security when we left court?"

"I did."

"Because I don't want you to use it."

"Of course you don't."

Litter flew in the wind in misty whirlpools. Nina pulled her jacket tighter. "Too much fog. I can hardly see the spot."

"It could be worse," Paul said. "It could be raining."

"No sign of anyone," Nina said. "Oh, God, Paul. What if nobody comes?"

Paul stood beside her, eyes narrowed, head turning from side to side. "Don't these thousands of people have anything better to do on a March afternoon than wander the town? We should have chosen a spot with fewer than seven thousand people at a time."

"They would want to meet in a public place. Somewhere close to the court." The letters had been short and to the point. To recipients Scholl and Riesner, Mrs. Gleb had happily, chuckling and drinking tea all the while, forged two separate notes that said, "I changed my mind. I won't testify. I'll meet you down in the plaza right outside the state bar building at the Spear Street entrance at twelve-fifteen today if you want to know why." The signature at the bottom, KC, had all the small crabbed character of Kevin's real signature, which Nina had brought her.

To Kevin, she had sent another note: "You won't be testifying. Meet me at twelve-fifteen where the plaza outside the state bar building opens onto Spear Street." She hadn't signed it.

If there was no conspiracy, there was no reason for anyone to show up, including Kevin. They would all be mystified, and would continue with the process of bringing Nina to her knees.

"Nina, look." Paul thrashed back and ducked down, pushing her down beside him.

"Ow. I don't see anyone." She poked her head around the fountain. Leading with his finger, he pointed the way.

"What?"

"Can't you see? It's Jean Scholl, right by that wall, keeping out of sight."

So it *was* Scholl. She had responded to their forged note. Scholl was behind the whole thing. Nina's thoughts made her shiver. All this because she had crossed the wrong cop in the ordinary course of her business. It seemed incredible, impossible, but here was the living proof.

Simply doing her job was dangerous. Her brother, Matt, had said that more than once.

"See her now?"

"No."

"Her back is to us, but I'd recognize that rear end anywhere."

"But, Paul, why is she hiding? Isn't she supposed to be meeting Kevin?"

"Don't know," he said shortly. She noticed his hand.

"There'll be no shooting here!" she said. "There are too many people! Someone could get hurt!"

"Nina. Nobody gets hurt if they behave. That goes double for you. Now what have we here?"

Kevin Cruz came walking up and looked around. He put his hands in his pockets.

"What's Scholl doing?" Nina asked, rubbing her ankle with her hand.

"Watching. Waiting."

Kevin checked his watch.

"He came, Paul. That means he expects to meet her. So why is she hanging back?"

Paul started to laugh. He laughed so hard for so long, Nina got worried. "What's the matter with you?" she said.

"It's Scholl," he finally gasped out. "She's—she's—"

"She's what?"

Suddenly, Kevin shifted his body so that he was facing toward the street, away from them. He tensed with anticipation.

"Someone else is coming," Nina said.

Jeffrey Riesner strolled into view. Kevin stood up to meet him.

"I don't understand," Nina said, pulling back. "I thought we were going to pin down who's who in this. They all came. Are they in this together? I'm confused. What do we do now?"

"Nina, take a good long look at Scholl. Look at how she's hiding. Check out the piece she's holding."

"It's weird all right. She's watching."

"Nina, she's investigating! She's being a cop!"

"What?"

"She got a suspicious message and decided to check it out. Thatta girl."

Nina's attention dodged toward the two men, who were engaged in heated debate. She scooched in close to Paul. He took the tiny receiver out of his ear, and they both listened.

"You told me you had that judge in the bag!" they heard Kevin say, his voice rising clearly above the dull background roar of the city. "You said you could get me the kids!"

Riesner's voice was lower, but in intermittent pieces they caught the gist. He wanted to know what the hell Kevin thought he was pulling, switching allegiance at the last minute. "I promise you won't see your kids again until you're drooling and senile, asshole."

So Riesner was behind it all after all, Nina thought. He was the poison, the thin red snake slithering behind all of them, but the realization gave her no relief, no pleasure.

Apparently, Scholl had heard enough. Stepping out from behind the doorway on Spear Street where she had been hiding, she tucked her gun into a pocket and, holding it out of sight, faced the two men.

"She'll arrest them," Nina said. "My God, Paul. It's finally over."

"Maybe."

"Hello, boys," Officer Scholl said to Riesner and Cruz. She stood directly in front of them, looking at ease in the middle of a seething crowd of city folk.

"You?" Jeffrey Riesner said. "What brings you here?"

"Curiosity," she said. "Then I couldn't help overhearing," Scholl said. "Excuse me for crashing your party, but you two have sure been cooking, and whew, does it smell."

A hole opened around the three where they stood next to the sculpture. They looked like everyone else, but they were not. They were connected, a unit, and the air around them seemed particularly charged. Those passing drifted uneasily around their fringes.

"I've worked out this much." Holding her hand very near her body she exposed her gun to Riesner, who reacted with a jump back. "You," she said to him, "got him"—she pointed at Cruz—"to lie, with the ultimate goal of pulverizing our favorite lady lawyer in return for the custody of his kids. I also have a gnawing suspicion that you stole yourself a key one fine day in court and made immediate use of it. And—" She thought, then put a finger to her chin. "The forgery. Your case last fall—the counterfeiter you defended. I'll bet he could tell me a few things about how he paid a hotshot like you. Tinkering with Reilly's paperwork? Or did he just show you a few tricks of the trade?"

Kevin Cruz stared at Riesner. "You did all that?"

Riesner said, "Why don't you run on back home to Tahoe and write a few tickets, investigate a couple of nasty fender benders. Try to salvage something before you make a complete fool of yourself, Scholl. You have nothing on me. I've got a position in that town and powerful friends. Don't do anything you'll regret later."

"And you, Kevin," Scholl said, ignoring him. "What a shame. I'm deeply disappointed in you. He has an excuse. He's a lawyer. It's his business to lie and cheat to get what he wants. But you're an officer of the law. Didn't you tell me after that last time you'd walk a straight line? Didn't you promise me that?"

"Welcome to real life, Jeanie," Kevin Cruz said.

"What did he tell you? That Judge Milne was an old golf buddy who just needed a little whisper from his pal to give you what you want? Because that's a laugh, let me tell you. Milne's straight."

"Why did you come here? What is this?" Riesner asked. "Some kind of lame shakedown?"

"Not exactly," Scholl said.

"What do you want?"

"Right this minute, to get out of here. I don't think it's a very good idea, us sharing our feelings like this in such a public forum. We need to talk privately. You up for that? A little talk in a private place, and a lot less trouble all around?"

A smile played around Riesner's thin lips. Talk? He was an expert. Sure, he would talk.

Tipping her sunglasses so that she could see better through the fog, Scholl's eyes darted around, suddenly narrower. "Tell me something. You got letters?" she asked the two men.

"Yes."

"Hmm." She frowned. This time, she scanned the street and then the plaza very deliberately, looking straight toward the fountain. Nina and Paul ducked back. Too late? What had she seen? Scholl whispered something to the two men, and they took off at a fast clip, heading left up Spear Street toward Market.

Paul tucked his earpiece into his pocket. "We still don't know the whole story," he said. They walked quickly to the silver sculpture. Paul took just a second to retrieve the bug he had placed there earlier.

"Let's follow them," Nina decided, taking the lead.

"Okay." Paul quickly overtook and passed Nina, using his elbows when necessary to make his way through the energetic street crowd.

In the sunless afternoon, the San Francisco streets were filled with Hopperesque scenes of lit stools and loiterers. Three people stepped in front of them to panhandle. Paul took Nina's arm and sidestepped them.

"Where are they going?" Nina asked, huffing, clutching her bag to prevent it from hitting people. "I thought we'd have a chance to confront them back there. Scholl really threw me off."

"When I saw her there, I could have sworn she was about to arrest them. I wonder what she plans to do now."

"What do we do? Just run up to them and tell them what we know?"

"No," Paul said. "We're outnumbered, and Officer Scholl has her weapon. Change of plans. Let's not be stupid, but let's not let them get away. We follow, then get the cops."

The trio up ahead hit a red light at Mission, so they crossed over Spear to the Rincon Center and crossed again to pass Lightning Foods. Nina and Paul stayed on the opposite side of the street behind them, dodging the new concrete berms that lined the sidewalk, protecting the Federal Reserve Bank on the corner of Market Street.

"They're going for the Hyatt," Nina guessed. "That's so strange. This is where we celebrated Bob's birthday."

A cable car sat in front of the hotel, a smattering of passengers perched on its wooden benches. The conductor let loose a clang, sang, "He-e-ere we go!" and it took off up the hill. Nobody stopped to watch. Riesner entered the hotel first from a side exit on Market Street, catching hold of an opening door and holding it for Scholl and Cruz.

Nina and Paul ducked past the valets in the parking area and into the automatic revolving door. They took escalators up to the main hotel level.

One of the world's signature hotels, the San Francisco Hyatt was remarkable for a huge interior courtyard framed by balcony corridors that angled up from the lobby level almost to the full height of the tower. Skylights at the top cast natural light down on the busy restaurants and services that lined the courtyard, and a huge, tubular gold sculpture formed a centerpiece. Water below the sculpture gurgled in a square black pool and spilled in unreal sheets to another level, shivering like a stretch of Saran Wrap.

On one side of the courtyard, glassed-in elevators shaped like funicular mailing tubes sailed up to the hotel rooms lining the open corridors. The effect was very *Blade Runner,* a glimpse into a fantastic world where architecture substituted for, and sometimes outdid, nature.

Nina and Paul skulked between pillars and behind the sculpture while their three quarries repaired to the 13 Views, the main courtyard restaurant.

"They're talking," Nina said. "Now what?"

"Wait," said Paul.

After a few moments, Riesner got up.

"She's letting him go?" Nina asked, amazed.

He walked toward the rest rooms and disappeared inside. Scholl watched him go in. A minute passed. Although she continued to watch for Riesner, she and Kevin began to talk again.

A moment's distraction was all it took.

With the swooping, invisible speed of a short-track ice skater, Riesner skidded out, ducked around behind Scholl, and headed for the elevators. Nina and Paul, trying to stay out of sight, followed as quickly as they could.

By the time they got to the nearest elevator, the doors were already closing. The elevator ascended, Riesner clearly visible through the glass. Then it stopped. Then it started up again. Nina and Paul tipped their heads back, observing it.

"The fifth floor," she said. "He got off. Let's go." She pressed the elevator button.

"No, Nina. You stay down here and watch these two. And call the police. Wait for them. Direct them up to the fifth floor. I'll hold him until they get here."

She experienced a fear so intense in her belly she thought she would fall down with the pain. "I don't want you to go."

"Look, Nina, he's a white-collar coward, not a mobster," he said. "I'm tougher than him, and I hope you know that much. And then, I've got a gun, remember?" He touched the back of her neck with his finger. "You okay?"

"I'll be fine as long as you are."

"Got your pepper spray?"

She patted her bag.

"Keep it handy."

He hurried down to the end of the long courtyard and took the stairs up.

Leaning against a wall near the restaurant, Nina took out her mobile phone and tried to make a call to 911. Busy. She tried again, got through, and waited on hold. Was this legal, no one answering an emergency call instantly? While she held on with growing dread, watching Scholl and Cruz with one eye, her call-waiting buzzed. She took the call.

"Hello?"

"It's me. Wish."

"I can't talk."

"Wait, Nina, this is important! I found the rest of the note from my mom. It says, 'Received transcript of Gleb testimony. Forger is extrovert, likes money, craftsman.'"

"I'm sorry, Wish, I have to go."

"And I forgot to tell you, she left a paper bag with something in it—wait a sec—" Paper rattled through the phone line and then Wish said in a puzzled voice, "Huh. It's this wooden lazy Susan my dad uses out in the garage. She brought it home from her old office one Christmas."

An image came to Nina of a man in a dark basement, carving for hours to make a perfect tiny puppet replica of Nina that he jerked around in private. "That's your mom's way of warning me it's Riesner," she said.

"We cracked it!"

"We sure did," she said, clicking him off. What a trial that boy must be to his mother.

"911," a woman's voice said suddenly.

Okay, elapsed waiting time not long at all. "Yes, I'm—" A sharp poke to her back stopped her.

"I'll take that." A hand reached out and snapped her phone shut.

"Hello, Counselor," Jeffrey Riesner's voice said. "I spotted you and your knucklehead friend back there quite a while ago. Nice of him to leave you alone for me. Makes things much easier." He yanked her bag away and tossed it on the ground, and dumped the phone after it. "Now I think we take a little walk. This way."

He steered her along the low rectangular pond, back toward the elevators. She swallowed, trying to find her voice. "You don't want to do this!" she said.

"Shut the hell up and get in there." He shoved her into a waiting elevator and pushed a button. Once inside, she faced his moist face. She faced his gleaming gun.

"You won't shoot me. You're not a killer," she said. "You're a lawyer."

"You don't get it, do you? You will never again embarrass me in front of my colleagues. You will never win again."

"Wait. We can make a deal, Jeff."

The floor numbers lit up as they passed. There was no thirteenth floor, which made the fourteenth floor her unlucky alternative. The elevator stopped there. He pushed her out. "Walk."

She walked down a long hallway, echoes of laughter and music emanating from the gaping open space beyond the balcony's edge. She thought of screaming. But he would shoot her. He held her in a grip like iron.

"There will be no deals," he said. "There will be a sad death, your death, because, by God, I will not let you get away from me. If I can't see you ruined I will see you dead. Suicide, out of disgrace. Too bad it's such a crude solution."

"Kevin Cruz won't be a party to this! And what about Scholl?"

"Cruz? He's in my pocket too deep to peep. And Scholl's an id-iot." Riesner imitated Scholl's deliberate voice. " 'Thing is, you stole the Bronco. That makes you my problem and I'm takin' you in.' All she could think about was your broken-down truck! I'll find a way to keep her quiet and happy."

"What's this about? Why do you—hate me?"

His hand on her tightened. "Because your smelly perfume and your messy hair make me sick. Because you steal my clients. Because you despise me. But most of all because you are ruining me. They want to fire me."

"They can't! You're a partner! Besides, you can always get another job!"

"They want to fire me and hire you to take my place."

"What? No! But I would never take it!"

"Ever since you fucked me so completely in that casino case, ever since then, they've been riding me. I lost our biggest client that day. The casinos want me gone and you in. It's been Reilly this and Reilly that. So brilliant. Such a star in the legal firmament." The words sputtered out of him like spit. "I won't be humiliated by a woman. By you."

Nina struggled to say something soothing, something to save her life, but she couldn't do it. She just couldn't do it. She hated him at this moment almost too much to try to save herself. He watched her try.

"It's—just—business," she managed finally, thickly.

"I am my business."

Seeing they were coming to the end of the long hall, she stopped, turned, and faced him. "You don't have to kill me. You're good enough to get out of this."

"For years now I've watched you," Riesner said. "Clicking down the halls of the court. I detest the sound of your officious, vain little shoes."

"Jeff—I saved your life once."

"Your mistake." His stony expression scared her more than anything. She had always been able to goad him before, always been able to arouse some kind of reaction. This time, the granite cold of his eyes told her everything. He meant to kill her.

He moved in closer and put a hand on her rear, pinching her buttock. "Get up there. Hmm. You'll need a life—" He caught her around the waist with his free hand.

She jerked away from him. Knocking back against the balcony's wall, she felt for her suit pocket.

He grabbed her, lifted her up to the shoulder-high railing while she struggled, and pushed. The balcony wall did not end with the usual narrow railing. Extending beyond it only a couple of inches below the edge of the balcony railing was a flat metal grid at least two feet wide, exactly like a ladder on its side, designed to prevent nasty accidents. Now, out of balance on that grid, fighting for her life, she rummaged in her pocket, turned toward Riesner, pulled out the pepper spray canister she had stuck in there on Paul's reminder, and sprayed directly at his face.

Nothing came out. The canister was empty. She had forgotten to get a new one after using it on Riesner once before!

Unable to get her loose from his position on the floor, he threw a leg up and joined her on the grid.

"Paul!" she yelled. "Help!"

Trying to get her off-balance, Riesner hit her in the face.

Her eyesight blurred on his face. She leaned back, then smashed the canister straight into his eye as hard as she could.

His hands flew up and he tumbled on top of her. She wriggled away and by some miracle did not fall. Jumping off the metal grid, she threw herself back to the safe floor of the corridor.

The empty can dropped into the void beyond the railing. When she hit him, Riesner had slipped close to the edge, and as he squirmed around, his body suddenly went over. He managed to grab for, and catch, the edge. Both hands held on. His eye bled.

Without climbing back onto the grid, Nina could not reach him. She lifted a leg up over the balcony wall, heaved herself up, wedged her legs in the gaps between the bars, and grabbed for his wrist, trying to pull him back up. Impossible. He was too large, and she too small. Calling out for help, and seeing no one nearby, she strained to hold on, she sweated, she pulled, and all the while he shouted at her, terrified words of pleading, of fear, of wrath.

Way down in the restaurant below, faces turned up toward them, pulled invisibly by the gravity of the situation. Once the people saw the dangling man, they shouted and cried out, chairs creaking, footsteps running. Down the hall from them a door opened. A hefty man, one towel around his waist, another rubbing his sopping hair, looked out and then toward Nina.

Nina cried out.

The man dropped his hand towel and ran toward her, his bare feet slapping along the rug.

He was too far away! She could feel every tendon, muscle, and bone in her arms stretched to the breaking point; through her pain she could feel them snapping, separating, and through her fingers she felt the rapid-fire beating of Jeffrey Riesner's heart in his wrist. She looked into his face, the open mouth saying things she could no longer hear, the eyes stained red. A moment passed between them.

He forgave nothing.

Suddenly from behind her, a hand thrust forward, grabbing for the wrist Nina was holding with both hands. Paul! His fully extended arm could barely reach to the edge of the safety grid. She let go and jumped off the grid and back to the floor as he climbed up over the wall toward Riesner, listening to his labored breathing as he lay down on the grid, pulling with one hand, both hands, and all his strength.

The barefoot man arrived behind Nina, wet hair dribbling down his neck, panting with fear. "What's going on?" he asked, frantic. "Can I help?"

But he could not reach Riesner, who was dangling too far away, hanging by one arm now, held aloft by Paul and nothing else. Too busy straining the muscles in his arms, his mouth stretched into a grimace of effort, Paul said nothing.

Nina shook her head. "Stay back," she told the barefoot man.

Slowly, methodically, rhythmic as a man bringing up a bucket from a well, hand over hand, Paul pulled him up. Riesner's foot scrabbled against the rails. One time, two times, three times he lifted his slick leather shoe, trying to find a toehold. Suddenly, his foot stopped on the thin metal edge. Then, more scraping while a second foot looked for and found its place.

Paul helped him up. Suddenly, shockingly safe, Riesner looked through the safety grid into the vast open space of the atrium. A hush cloaked them all in woolen quiet, a hush filled with breathless anticipation as a hundred people watched what was happening above them. Riesner looked at the people below, their frightened faces, watching his shame.

Horrified onlookers.

He looked at Paul and Nina.

Paul broke the silence, his voice holding a fury Nina had never heard before. "I should have smacked you harder in that bathroom a couple years ago. Maybe it would have wised you up."

"So it was you," Riesner sputtered. A fleck of foam coagulated on the side of his mouth. He wiped blood out of his eyes. "You son of a bitch!"

Paul whispered to him, "You're history, punk."

Riesner moved suddenly, striking like a snake. In a last desperate motion, he grabbed Paul by the neck and tried to take him along into the abyss. He managed to get him over the ledge. They toppled onto the grid together, Riesner twisting Paul around so that he lost his balance. Paul's foot slipped and he began to go over.

"Paul!" screamed Nina. She flung her entire body over the railing and grabbed his jacket, slowing his momentum just slightly.

Paul looked up at Nina and smiled. In a long moment, an eternal moment that hovered somewhere between life and death, he said, "Love you."

"No! Paul! Don't leave me, please don't. I love you!" Nina screamed.

And slowly, imperceptibly, Paul stopped falling. His fingers tightened on the metal edge. His arms whitened as he began to straighten himself up with brute strength, even with Riesner still clutching him in a crude headlock, even with both his legs hanging into space. Riesner's right hand clutched at Paul's throat, grasping for his windpipe, clawing at him.

Nina saw a strange change come over Paul's countenance—strong, certain, terrifying.

Once he made it back up on the ladder platform, Paul's hand

shot out. He took Riesner's hand into his and began to squeeze, increasing the pressure until Riesner began to scream. The bones in his fingers began to pop, then his hand, and then with one violent twist, Paul shattered Riesner's arm and dumped him back on the corridor walkway in a heap. The lawyer shrieked in pain.

"Loser," Paul said, breathing hard.

Riesner rolled over, cradling his useless arm, faceup, contorted. Nina and Paul stood over him, looking down.

Tears started up and rolled down Riesner's face. He stood up slowly, brushing himself off with his good hand. Casting one quick glance into the eyes of his conquerors, he examined the faces of the onlookers below. How they ogled.

Nina had no trouble reading his face. His humiliation was complete. No one would ever respect him again.

Whirling around, fast as a gust of wind, he jumped over the balcony rail and hurled himself headlong into space.

Screaming all the way, he fell sixteen stories, down past the pretty green plants and white linen tabletops gleaming with glassware to the pretty concentric circular patterns on the atrium floor.

They heard him land.

EPILOGUE

AFTER THE CALIFORNIA STATE BAR CASE against Nina fizzled, Nina left Tahoe and moved to Carmel to be with Paul.

But that did not mean her tangled life tied up neatly with a big red bow.

Three days after Jeffrey Riesner's death, the hearing before the California State Bar Court on Howard Street resumed. Officer Scholl testified about Riesner's campaign to ruin Nina, which he had outlined in extensive, vituperative diaries, obtained from his home with a search warrant. No carvings of Nina were mentioned, however, although she would always wonder. Scholl explained in full, honest detail her mistake in letting Riesner out of her sight. In spite of her embarrassment, she was steady and firm in her testimony, blaming no one but herself.

She outlined the plot to bring Nina down. "He'd been looking for an opening for months, then one rainy day, he saw her car key lying on the table in court. That was the start. He said he went to her house late that night just because he wanted to see what he might find. It was his luck that she left her files in there." He was good enough with his hands to carry off a crude forgery, then he had blackmailed Kevin Cruz into charging Nina with harassment.

The California State Bar withdrew all charges against Nina Reilly.

Two weeks later, amid public fanfare, Officer Jean Scholl won her promotion to the Detective Unit and the congratulations of the mayor.

Nina had thanked her privately.

"I was just doing my job. Finding the person who stole your vehicle," she told Nina from behind her mirrored shades.

Lisa Cruz, who agreed to start a new therapy program, got permanent physical custody of the children. The D.A. hadn't yet decided what charges to file against Kevin. Within a few weeks of his return, the South Lake Tahoe police force kicked him out.

Cody Stinson got out of jail free. Heritage Insurance released Mrs. Vang's share of the money, and Marilyn Rose called Nina.

Bruce Ford had a minor surgical procedure, no complications.

Andrea had given birth to a beautiful baby girl in March. She named her June.

After the dust settled, at the end of May, Nina closed up her office in the Starlake Building.

She offered Sandy a generous severance package, which Sandy rejected. "Severance? That sounds like broken, and we're not." She had groused and dragged her feet about the changes until she realized Nina was happy, then cheered right up. On her last day at the office, Sandy appeared in brand-new tennis shoes, ready to start a round of paid consultation with the Bureau of Indian Affairs. "Don't think you're getting rid of me," Sandy had said. "I'm not through with you yet."

Bob went to Sweden.

Nina put him on a plane, breathing a sigh of relief that she had taken care of the Nikki problem. The day after he arrived in Stockholm, he called to check in. Voices laughed and roughhoused in the background, low hums, high giggles.

"Who's that?" Nina had asked.

"Oh, Mom, in the rush and everything did I forget to tell you? That Swedish hard-core crust band Nikki's been working with on the Web site—well, they invited her here for a month, and here she is." Something jostled the phone, and he came back on a moment later. "They're all here right now. Kurt's letting them practice in the rehearsal room at the symphony today. Awesome acoustics!"

Paul hired Wish to summer in Carmel as a paid intern, to run his office and help oversee some of the subcontractors that he hired for routine security jobs. Wish arranged for college credit for his work and was learning to surf. At the moment, he was renting a room in the house Nina had inherited from her aunt Helen in Pacific Grove, sharing with two other students who needed a roommate and were renting from her.

Leaving Tahoe turned out to be as hard as she had expected.

Closing up the office, farming out her cases, painful good-byes Nina could not escape because the small legal community knew everything that had happened, all these acts came hard. The concern and good wishes almost overwhelmed her decision to leave. Almost.

"Will you be back?" they all asked. "What will you do?" they said.

So she told them the truth. She would never quit law. She had thought over the past months and realized Brandy was set to get happily married. Mrs. Vang had begun a new life in a new country. Kevin's children had a devoted parent, not him, but then, he didn't deserve them.

Once again, she had reached down into the insane disorder of human relations, twisted, pried, and fought for a fair outcome. She had done more good than harm. That was all she could ever hope for. Like a California condor overcoming a brush with extinction, soaring on the wind, she had proven she could survive on her own. She also knew she didn't have to anymore. She would never give up law. But now, with her heart clamoring for attention, she decided to listen to it.

Leaving the house could have been terrible, but Paul and Matt and Jack had her packed and out in a jiffy, laughing and teasing, music loud, dust flying, boxes accumulating as high as Mount Tallac. Andrea would be using Nina's cabin to house a mother and her four children for a few months because the shelter couldn't accommodate so many comfortably. After that—

"You'll come back, Nina, won't you?"

Nina parked in a lot across from the bookstore cafe on Lighthouse Boulevard in Pacific Grove, went inside, and ordered two coffees. Where was Paul? He should be here by now. Outside, wispy fog flowed down the street. Now an ocean, not an ancient lake, bounded her town.

Drinking the milky brew, she felt a moment's dislocation. She had returned to her old town, down the hill from Pacific Grove Elementary, where she had gone to school. So much had happened in the years in between.

From behind her magazine, she watched a mother dump sugar into her daughter's cup of milk at the end of the counter, the little girl smiling and begging for more until the mother finally called a halt to the sugar feast, promising more, all the sugar she wanted in the next cup. Nina walked to the front and looked out the window. Night had fallen and the silver lights decorating the cafe windows blinked on.

Where was he? When she didn't see him on the street, she returned to the counter to wait, her heart at ease for the first time in a long time. He would come, and they would take a long walk through the town, stop at the Pier One, maybe go to the movies, then go over the hill to Carmel, home.

She could count on him.

Waiting, happy, she swung on her stool, back and forth. The delighted little girl a few stools away observed her, then spun, too, but in circles, her legs kicking out and in, long after Nina had stopped.

Watching the girl turning, hands gripping the spinning seat, ten or twelve or twenty times, Nina felt dizzy with possibility and hope. She knew now she could not control the life that flowed like the Pacific Ocean through her, its cold tides, its heavy weather, its clement, sunny days.

She wondered what the future would bring.

She swung around all the way around, just once. Simple thoughts swung through her head:

My name is Nina and I live down the street.

I am me.

ACKNOWLEDGMENTS

WE WOULD LIKE TO OFFER OUR SPECIAL THANKS to Peter von Mertens and Lynn Snedecor for reading the manuscript and making many helpful comments, Ann Walker for Tahoe leads, Bill Dawson for his intense interest in the issues that plague legal practitioners, and Deputy Sheriff Tom Hill of the South Lake Tahoe Police Department for answering questions about procedure.

Our brother, Patrick O'Shaughnessy, contributed the usual spice to our characters and plot, and continues to be the best worker's comp attorney in California, in our opinion.

Brad Snedecor was, as always, an indispensable creative accomplice.

Thanks to the California State Bar court personnel for their consideration.

The *California Bar Journal* was a source for information about bar court proceedings. We consulted a number of informative Web sites and books about the Hmong people for the story of the Vang family, including www.geocities.com/CapitolHill/Congress/8725/unip2001.htm and *I Begin My Life All Over: The Hmong and the American Immigrant Experience* by Ghia Xiong (contributor), Lillian Faderman. For Mrs. Gleb's testimony, we wish especially to acknowledge *The Psychology of Handwriting: Secrets of Handwriting Analysis* by Nadya Olyanova, ©1960, Sterling Publishing Company.

Our greatest respect and admiration go to our terrific agent,

Nancy Yost, and to our perceptive editor, Danielle Perez. Many thanks to Irwyn Applebaum for his patient and benevolent style, and to everyone else at the Bantam Dell Publishing Group for all their hard work on our behalf—what good people.

And finally, an escapist lift of the coffee cup to the fine and clever company in the back booth at the Plantation Cafe: Bill Cheney, Ruth and Bill Dawson, Laura Ferrari, Jim Nicholas, Pat Spindt, and Sylvia Walker.

All mistakes are our own.

PREFACE

Proven reserves in the North Sea equal over seventy percent of the proven reserves of the United States.[1] World wide, offshore reserves are estimated to contain as much as 2.3 trillion barrels of oil—more than estimated land reserves.[2] Advancing technology and high oil prices have made the exploitation of offshore oil off every continent and at ever increasing depths both technically feasible and commercially attractive. At the same time, continued growth in world oil demand and the political nature of the world oil market have made the discovery and development of new reserves of oil urgent for both oil-consuming nations and multinational oil companies.

If the exploitation of offshore petroleum resources is to take place along rational lines, then law must keep pace with these developments. The delimitation of zones of jurisdiction (national or international) is only a small first step. To be sure, without a stable framework of international law governing at least jurisdictional matters, offshore development is unlikely to take place at all. Oil companies typically are unwilling to undertake enormously expensive offshore exploration and production operations at the risk of losing their rights to oil with a change in the legal status quo. But merely defining jurisdictions is hardly sufficient. Considerably more complex is the drafting of detailed laws and regulations providing for the apportionment of offshore mineral rights, the taxation of offshore production, the safety of offshore workers, the orderliness of onshore development, the protection of the marine environment, and so on. Legal rights must be linked to legal responsibilities if development is to take place along lines satisfactory to the affected coastal states and to the international community. What is necessary, then, is the establishment of a continental shelf regime of considerable sophistication.

The legal arrangements governing offshore resources pertaining to the North Sea states, particularly Norway and the United Kingdom, are among the most advanced now in existence. Large-scale offshore development will soon be taking place in a variety of other regions. Indeed, offshore oil reserves, which at present provide seventeen percent of world consumption, are widely expected to provide fifty percent or more by the mid-1980s.[3] Thus, an examination of the evolution of North Sea law offers an insight into challenges soon to be faced in offshore areas around the world.

This book is based primarily on research and interviews conducted by the author in northwest Europe. Its Purpose is to document the relevant national and international law, and, further, to identify the political and economic interest for which that law was conceived. It is hoped that this analysis will facilitate realistic generalization from the North Sea experience to other offshore regions where patterns of interest may be somewhat different.

The first three chapters, therefore, examine the economic and political context for the evolution of North Sea law. Chapter 1 offers what seems essential background for the discussion—an examination of the European oil market over the past quarter century. Drawing from this account, Chapter 2 provides a history of the development of new petroleum supplies in the North Sea as one aspect of the European oil market. Chapter 3 seeks to describe the patterns of interest associated with North Sea petroleum development that are dominant at various levels of political authority. It is an important argument of this book, developed in Chapter 3, that those interests that are dominant at the national level have been almost exclusively determinative of the legal arrangements now governing offshore development, at the expense of interests at the regional and local levels. Chapter 4 discusses the international legal basis for this priority of national interests by examining the legal origins of national jurisdiction over the North Sea shelf. Chapter 5 provides a detailed discussion of the substantive continental shelf law of the United Kingdom and Norway.

As with all scholarly undertakings of this scope, this book is the product of the thought and effort of many people in addition to the author. Funding for the research done in northwest Europe was provided by the Neil A. McConnell Foundation, to which I wish first to express my gratitude. A complete listing or satisfactory acknowledgment of the contributions of all who assisted me in this book is not possible, but certain people must be given explicit recognition, for without their help it could not have been written. David Keany of the Senate Foreign Relations Committee Staff interested me in this subject. Dr. George Springsteen of the U. S. Department of State and Clifton Brown of Riggs National Bank, Washington, D. C. were most helpful in providing contacts abroad and assuring me access to needed information. I am, of course, indebted to those in Europe who gave generously of their time to discuss with me this intricate and politically sensitive topic. I would be remiss if I failed to acknowledge the invaluable assistance of Tamasin Foote and Dorothy Bedford in the preparation of the manuscript. Special thanks are given to Dr. Richard A. Falk and to Dr. Lynn T. White of Princeton University for their constructive review of the manuscript and the many helpful suggestions for its improvement. I take, nevertheless, full responsibility for this work's inevitable shortcomings.

NOTES

1. Oil and Gas Journal, December 27, 1976, pp. 104-5.
2. Offshore, March 1977, p. 42.

CONTENTS

x

LIST OF FIGURES

Oil and Gas Fields in the North Sea.

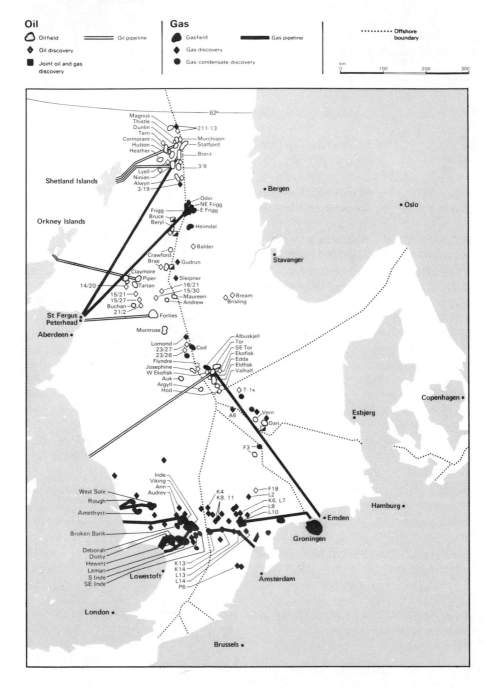

Source: Shell Briefing Service, Royal Dutch/Shell.

1

THE EUROPEAN OIL MARKET
AND THE EVOLUTION OF
NATIONAL OIL POLICIES

Three aspects of the European oil market have been of particular significance to the pattern of development of North Sea petroleum: movements in the price of oil, the assumption by oil of the dominant position in European energy-use patterns, and the growing influence of politics and government policy upon the oil market. These three phenomena are, of course, closely related. For example, the competitiveness in price of petroleum products with all other forms of energy in Europe was largely responsible for the growing role of oil in European energy consumption patterns. Likewise, the growing importance of oil in the European economies stimulated governments to institute more extensive controls over the oil market, including controls over prices.

The development of new and politically secure sources of oil in the North Sea was shaped by these phenomena and their interaction. In particular, the legal arrangements now governing offshore resources reflect strongly the increased role that European governments are seeking to play in the oil sectors of their economies.

OIL AND EUROPEAN RECONSTRUCTION

European industrialization was founded on huge indigenous supplies of coal. Unlike the United States, where a shift to petroleum began in the late nineteenth century, Europe remained almost wholly reliant on coal through the beginning of World War II. In 1925, coal supplied 96 percent of the total energy consumed in Western Europe, compared with 74 percent for the United States. In 1938, coal still supplied 91 percent of the total energy consumed in Western Europe,

1

while the proportion had dropped to 54 percent for the United States. [1] Petroleum, at the outset of World War II, supplied only 8 percent of the energy consumed in Western Europe, compared with 32 percent for the United States and 21 percent for the world as a whole. [2] This 8 percent constituted all of Europe's energy imports at that time.

World War II, in so many ways a watershed for Western Europe, led to a permanent alteration in the pattern of energy use in European society. Coal mining facilities, transportation networks, and coal-based industries were devastated throughout continental Europe. Indeed, much of Europe's industrial base was destroyed. During the subsequent reconstruction, European industry and society were particularly sensitive to prevailing forces and trends in energy economics; the industry and society that ultimately emerged bear the imprint of the postwar energy market. Just as Europe's original industrialization was founded on plentiful indigenous supplies of coal, Europe's reindustrialization following the war was founded on plentiful imported supplies of oil. The United States supervised directly the rebuilding of parts of Germany during the occupation and was extensively involved in the rebuilding of the rest of Western Europe through the Marshall Plan. The prodigious domestic oil supplies of the United States provided a means to see Europe through the energy crisis created by the destruction of Europe's energy infrastructure. Thus, the new generation of European industry was weaned on petroleum-based energy.

In the years immediately following 1945, imports consisted mainly of refined oil products from the United States. However, European governments became increasingly concerned about the drain of dollars from Europe to American refiners and in the late 1940s and early 1950s they took steps to bring about an expansion of domestic refinery capacity. The governments encouraged the oil companies in this regard by offering low-interest loans for refinery construction and by making known that prohibitive duties would be placed on refined oil products once a sufficient domestic capacity had been built. Moreover, the development of larger and more economical tankers reduced substantially the cost of bulk crude oil transport. [3] European refinery capacity grew 6700 percent between 1946 and 1955. [4] Accompanying this growth was a complementary growth in European oil distribution networks.

While Europe was developing an infrastructure to support a high level of oil consumption, several major oil companies were beginning to exploit on a large scale vast oil finds made in the Middle East during the preceding two decades. (Saudi Arabian crude was first produced in 1939.) The cost of producing a barrel of Middle Eastern crude oil is extremely low. It was estimated to be approximately 12 cents a barrel in 1968 (including a 20 percent return on investment). [5] Oil has always sold for many times this figure because of oligopolistic practices within the world petroleum industry and because of heavy taxation by governments in both consuming and producing countries. Nevertheless, throughout the 1950s and 1960s oil was competitive with every other energy source available in Europe. The low price of oil and the greater convenience of using liquid (as opposed to solid) fuel allowed oil to erode the market for coal and inhibit the development of alternative energy sources. By 1960, oil supplied nearly one third of the energy consumed in Europe. [6]

The exact price of a barrel of crude oil during this period, is difficult to obtain. By the early 1950s the major international oil companies, * which at that time controlled nearly all of the Middle Eastern concessions, had already become vertically integrated, encompassing every phase of the production, processing, and distribution of oil from the well head to the gas pump. Since crude oil merely passed from one subsidiary to another within the same company, the transfer price was notional. The prices used by the oil companies in the internal accounting would have revealed much about the economics of oil and the profit margins being enjoyed by the companies. They, therefore, remained a closely held secret. Full public information on the price of Middle Eastern crude oil during the 1950s and 1960s is not available to this day. Nevertheless, an idea of the movement of the price of Middle Eastern crude is important to this study since these prices have determined the feasibility and, more recently, the urgency of offshore petroleum development. On the basis of information on oil product prices, refinery costs, and oil tanker rates, M. A. Adelman estimates that the price of Middle Eastern crude oil (f. o. b., Arabian Light marker crude, 34°, loaded at Ras Tanura) was $2.22 a barrel in 1947. [7] The price apparently slipped to $1.75 a barrel in 1949 where it held until 1953. In 1953, prices were hiked by all the major companies to $1.93 a barrel. Prices again began to settle until 1956 (and the Suez crisis), when prices were raised to $2.08. Under increasingly competitive market conditions this price was impossible to maintain. A downward trend in oil prices began in 1957 and continued through 1970.

---

*The so-called majors are Exxon (still known as Esso in much of Europe), Shell, BP, Gulf, Texaco, Mobil, and Socal (or Chevron). In the Middle East and Europe they are joined by an eighth sister of comparable size and influence: Compagnie Francaise de Petrole. The French government formed this company in 1924 and still owns a 35 percent share of it.

The source of this new competition is not difficult to discern. In 1957, the major oil companies were paying $.88 a barrel in taxes to the Saudi Arabian government (taxes varied between $.80 and $.95 in the other Middle Eastern countries).[8] Operating costs, including a 20 percent return on investment, may be presumed to fall in the $.10 to $.20 range. Given the 1957 price of $2.08, the profit on a barrel of Middle Eastern oil clearly was enormous. This highly favorable market attracted the interest of a number of so-called independent oil companies—companies that while often large by corporate standards (Phillips Petroleum, Atlantic-Richfield, Amoco), were nevertheless smaller than the oil majors and not characterized by total vertical integration. A number of these independents obtained concessions in the Middle East during the 1950s, and by the late 1950s were producing crude oil at significant rates.

For the most part, this oil could not be marketed in the United States. With the support of the Texas Railroad Commission, those oil companies that controlled the American distribution network effectively restricted oil imports (quotas finally became law in 1959 when the companies could no longer stem the tide of cheap foreign oil and Congress officially limited imports to 13 percent of oil consumption).[9] Coordination of this kind was not possible in Europe. Europe was the only other major industrial market for oil and it was toward Europe that the independents directed their strongest efforts. Their principal weapon was price competition and as a greater and greater number of companies sought to sell their oil in the European market prices began plummeting. By 1960 the price of oil had reached $1.50, and it was to fall farther in the next decade.

THE 1960s

Early in the 1960s, exploratory work in the North Sea was begun, though commercially significant quantities of oil were not found until 1969. During the decade from 1960 to 1970 the petroleum market was characterized by surplus and steadily slipping prices. Major new finds made in Libya in the late 1950s were developed rapidly. Not only were tanker rates and the risks of transport lower with Libya (because of its location on the European side of the Suez Canal) but the Libyan regime seemed, in the early 1960s, politically more stable than those of the troubled Middle East. These new supplies sent oil prices even lower. They had fallen to $1.17 a barrel by 1965 and remained below $1.25 through 1969.[10]

Cheap oil continued to erode the European market for coal, but now at an accelerated rate. This process was not looked on with indifference by the European governments. It was clear that domestic

coal could not compete with foreign oil and that the coal industry
would rapidly be eliminated if no action was taken. Government action
seemed warranted for at least two reasons. First, it appeared un-
wise to allow Europe to become totally dependent on foreign oil producers and allow domestic energy production to lapse. Second, the
coal industry was a considerable political force. Miners, like fisher-
men, cannot easily adapt to new forms of work; their work is nothing
less than a way of life. Consequently, coal production was subsidized
throughout most of Europe and the use of oil was taxed. Import restrictions were imposed. Taxes on heavy fuel oil rose in West Germany from 4.2 percent in 1960 to 68.8 percent in 1970. Similar taxes
rose in the Netherlands from 5.3 percent to 36.5 percent, and in
France from 11.7 percent to 18.0 percent. Taxes on domestic and
consumer uses of petroleum—for example, as gasoline—were far
higher. The high price of European gasoline, which so shocked
American tourists, reflected enormous European taxes of well over
100 percent rather than high imported crude oil prices. At the same
time, subsidies to coal production in 1970 rose to 9.5 percent of the
pithead price in West Germany, 14.9 percent in the Netherlands, and
31.5 percent in France. [11]

Despite these measures, oil, by 1970, substantially underpriced
coal throughout Western Europe. In West Germany, coal for industrial
use rose in price from $2.97 per barrel of oil equivalent in 1957, to
$4.80, in 1970. At the same time, heavy fuel oil for industrial use
fell in price from $5.17 per barrel to $3.02. In the Netherlands, coal
rose from $3.95 to $4.17, while fuel oil dropped from $4.27 to $2.30.
In France, coal rose from $4.02 to $4.97, while fuel oil dropped from
$4.09 to $2.11. [12] These prices are prices to industrial consumers
and include the various taxes and subsidies in effect in each country.
The hard economics of the energy market proved impossible for government policy to resist. By 1966, oil, virtually all of it imported,
had overtaken coal as Europe's principle energy source.

Trends in other energy sources during this period may be
noted briefly. Natural gas is difficult to transport except by pipeline
and until indigenous natural gas supplies were discovered in Europe,
consumption of this fuel was minimal. The most significant natural
gas finds were made, beginning in 1959, in northern Holland and,
beginning in 1965, in the southern portion of the North Sea. Smaller
finds were made in Italy and elsewhere, and imports were obtained
from the Soviet Union. Between 1960 and 1970, annual gas consumption grew in Western Europe about 550 percent, from 12.3 billion
cubic meters to 80.6 billion cubic meters. Gas, in 1970, supplied 8
percent of the energy consumed in Western Europe. Annual consumption of primary electricity produced by hydroelectric and nuclear installations grew more modestly, from 229.5 billion kilowatt hours to

337. 3 billion kilowatt hours (about 50 percent). Hydroelectric and nuclear power, in 1970, supplied 3 percent of the energy consumed in Europe.

By 1970, imported oil satisfied 60 percent of Europe's energy needs. Oil consumption had grown 1200 percent from its level in 1950 while overall energy consumption had grown 225 percent. By 1973, these figures were 1700 percent and 275 percent. [13] There seems little reason to suppose that the proportion of oil use would not have continued to grow if politics, rather than economics, had not become the primary force in the world oil market.

THE 1970s

The vast supplies of oil in the Middle East could have accommodated rising European oil demand for some time. However, by 1970 the supply no longer outstripped demand to such an extent that concerted political action by the producer governments was impossible. European requirements were expanding. In addition, U. S. imports of petroleum suddenly began growing rapidly in 1970, as American demand soared above leveling indigenous production. Between 1970 and 1974 U. S. imports of petroleum—mostly from the Middle East—grew at an average annual rate of 27 percent compared with 2. 5 percent for the period from 1960 to 1970. At the same time Japanese demand for imported petroleum was exploding, reaching in 1974 over one third the total Western European demand and over 40 percent of demand within the EEC. [14]

The oil surplus was over. The dependence on Middle Eastern supplies that the oil-consuming nations—particularly European nations and Japan—had developed while prices were low now placed these nations in a condition of serious economic vulnerability.

Libya, which by 1969 was supplying one quarter of Europe's oil, [15] was the first producer nation to take advantage of this vulnerability. In 1970 Libya negotiated with Occidental Petroleum a $. 30 rise in the posted price of oil (that is, the price used by the government to calculate taxes and royalties). This was not difficult since Occidental's only oil supplies were in Libya and Libya was threatening them with nationalization. More difficult was singling out each of the major oil companies and achieving a similar renegotiation. But the oil market had shifted from a buyer's to a seller's market. The oil companies needed what oil supplies they had and could no longer threaten convincingly to pick up and go elsewhere. Libya obtained its price increase with all the companies operating on Libyan territory.

The improvement in terms that Libya achieved seems trivial in light of the price increases soon to be imposed by the Organization of

Petroleum Exporting Countries (OPEC). But the OPEC cartel acted
on the basis of the political leverage that Libya demonstrated. It is
worth noting that 1970 also was the year that Phillips Petroleum,
another U. S. independent, announced the discovery of the first commercial oil field in the North Sea—the giant Ekofisk complex in the
southern portion of the Norwegian zone. The Libyan example was no
more lost on the North Sea producing nations than it was on the Arab
producers.

The years 1971 through 1973 were years in which prices and
terms for Middle Eastern oil production were negotiated and renegotiated. A general agreement reached in Teheran and Tripoli in 1971
was followed by a new escalation of prices agreed upon in Geneva in
1972, which was followed by a further escalation of prices agreed
upon in Teheran in 1973. At the same time, the Arab countries demanded the opportunity to participate commercially in the operations
of the oil companies. Complex arrangements were made whereby the
Arab governments could become commercial partners in oil operations, paying their way largely with options on future production.
These arrangements were unquestionably to the financial disadvantage
of the companies and further increased government revenues. They
also provided the governments with a higher degree of control over
operations within their borders. It is interesting to note in this connection that Norway had made substantial government participation
a prerequisite for offshore licenses issued in the late 1960s. Great
Britain began requiring government participation in new licenses in
1975.

In October of 1973, the Yom Kippur War broke out. The Arab
nations embargoed the supporters of Israel, using the integrated
transportation and distribution mechanisms of the major oil companies
to implement a selective oil cutoff. In the resulting oil shortage they
were able to impose a price increase that dwarfed all previous price
increases. Posted prices were quadrupled, with Arabian light crude
reaching $11.51 a barrel. This was fully nine times the apparent
going price of Arabian light crude in early 1970. The posted price
was raised again in December 1976 to $12.98. Arabian light crude
was being sold at $13.30 a barrel in January 1978.[16] As a result of
these price increases and participation arrangements, government
revenues for Arabian light crude increased from between $ .80 and
$ .90 a barrel in the late 1960s, to $1.52 in early 1973, to $10.65 in
1976.[17]

The immediate effect of the sudden price increases on the
energy-importing economies of Western Europe was to cause a slight
slump in oil demand in 1974 (about 2 percent for the EEC Nine) and
1975 (about 5 percent). Demand growth rebounded in 1976 at an
estimated annual rate of 7.5 percent.[18] Much greater effects were

felt in the European balance of payments. A small surplus of $500 million in 1973 toppled into a deficit of $12.25 billion in 1974.[19] Several countries recovered rapidly—notably Germany and the Netherlands—and the EEC showed a modest balance of payments surplus in 1975. A slow recovery in industrial activity, the resumption of internal demand growth, a further hike in the price of oil in late 1975, and dwindling exports to the hard-hit developing countries, sent the EEC back into a balance of payments deficit in 1976 of $7.8 billion. This deficit was reduced in 1977 to an estimated $250 million.[20]

The immediate effect of the OPEC price increases might be viewed as that of an excise tax on petroleum. Consumers are receiving less petroleum for more money. This does take into account trade effects; these extra expenditures are creating a higher demand for European exports in the Middle East. But the demand for exports is not keeping pace with increased OPEC revenues. In fact, the OPEC current accounts surplus, which in 1972 stood at $2 billion and in 1973 at $9 billion, leapt to $61.8 billion in 1974. The OPEC surplus was $31.8 billion in 1975, $42.3 billion in 1976, and $40.0 billion in 1977.[21] OPEC is not likely to reach balance of payments equilibrium—that is, purchase as much in imports as it receives for its oil exports—until the early 1980's.

The net result of the "excise tax" on oil and of the drain on the European economies caused by deficits is slower rates of economic growth. Such slower growth rates can already be observed. The average rate of growth of the EEC economies period from 1960 to 1973 was 5.0 percent. In 1974, the aggregate GNP of the EEC grew only 1.9 percent and, in 1975, it fell 2.2 percent. A modest recovery was experienced in 1976 with GNP growth at 4.7 percent. However, growth settled to 2.3 percent in 1977.[22] Recent OECD projections forecast that economic growth in the EEC will stabilize at around 3.4 percent per year by 1980 and at 4.0 percent thereafter to 1985.[23] This and other projections will be examined more closely further on in this discussion.

EUROPEAN NATIONAL ENERGY POLITICS

A number of European countries are being plagued by dual economic evils, inflation and recession, in large part because of oil price increases. Political pressures are strong on the governments in power to alleviate future economic hardships as best they can. Moreover, there is widespread concern regarding the security of oil supplies on which Europe has become so dependent. A number of policy approaches to the energy problem have been undertaken, most of which involve granting the governments greater authority over the energy market, and particularly over indigenous energy resources.

One index of these trends is recent German energy policies. Germany, of course, has a strong tradition of laissez faire and minimal government intervention in the national economy. In the energy field this has meant that, until recently, government efforts to influence the energy market have been restricted to fiscal measures—taxes, subsidies, and duties. The government permitted a predominant portion of the domestic oil market to be controlled by foreign companies. In 1973 only 6 percent of German refining capacity was in the hands of German-owned companies. [24] However, with the security of future oil supplies coming increasingly into question, the German government has taken more direct steps to alter the structure of the domestic market. In the late 1960s it encouraged seven German energy companies to merge into a single large oil corporation, now called Deminex. Between 1970 and 1974 the government provided the new corporation with $205 million in venture capital and grants. [25] The purpose of Deminex is to secure supplies of oil for the German market through exploration, the purchase of oil concessions, and the conclusion of long-term agreements with foreign oil companies. Deminex is now actively participating in North Sea development activities. In 1973 the government began efforts to create a still larger corporation by encouraging two major German energy companies, Gelsenberg and Veba, to merge. The government secured a 51 percent interest in Gelsenberg and a 43 percent interest in Veba. The merger plan was approved in late 1974 after the government agreed to invest $67 million. [26] The new corporation, which has the appearances of a national company, now controls 20 percent of German refining capacity—more than the largest multinationals in Germany—and a substantial portion of the retail market. These activities on the part of the traditionally noninterventionist German government suggest the considerable significance of trends in Europe toward a greater public role in the energy economy.

In France, tight public control over the oil industry has a long history. The French government formed CFP (Compagnie Française de Pétrole) in 1924 to compete with the major American oil companies. Since that time the government has created a number of semipublic companies to participate in the domestic energy industry and exert influence over it. Of particular significance to North Sea development is the state-owned company Elf, created, after the loss of France's Algerian possessions, as an exploration company seeking new and secure supplies of oil in all parts of the world for France. Elf is now developing the second largest known gass field in the North Sea.

In addition to participating in major corporations the French government has conferred upon itself direct powers over the petroleum industry. In 1963, for example, it allocated market shares among the major refiners. The government also regulates investment, including plant expansions, and petroleum trade. Petroleum may be imported only under license, and in the fall of 1974 the government announced a ceiling on oil imports of $10.1 billion for 1975, a cut of 10 percent from 1974. [27]

The Dutch government, for a number. of years, pursued a curious mixture of policies involving substantial government participation in oil and gas production, yet a more laissez faire attitude toward the energy market as a whole than characterized most European countries. Unlike its EEC partners, the government, for example, allowed the Dutch coal mining industry to expire (all mines had been shut down by 1975) with only limited intervention to prevent an abrupt collapse of the industry. The Dutch government allowed a compensating large expansion of the domestic gas industry based on onshore and offshore reserves. Nearly 64 percent of the commercial energy consumed in the Netherlands was supplied by gas in 1974. [28] In that year, domestic consumption accounted for about half of the Netherlands' total gas production, with the remainder being exported. Recently, however, the government has become concerned that Dutch gas reserves may become depleted too rapidly and consequently has resorted to more active intervention in the market. Strict limitations have been placed on foreign orders for future gas exports and the government is undertaking measures to reduce the proportion of gas consumption in total energy consumption. [29]

Such examples, drawn from northwestern European nations bordering on the North Sea, should be sufficient at least, to suggest the growing role of the state in European energy economics. Perhaps the most dramatic examples of all have occurred in the United Kingdom and Norway with regard to petroleum production activities in the North Sea. Not without reason are the Norwegians referred to within the oil industry as blue-eyed Arabs. However, since the offshore energy policies of these two countries will be a dominant concern of subsequent chapters, we will forego a discussion of them here.

EUROPEAN REGIONAL ENERGY POLITICS

The growing politicization of the oil market in the major European countries has come into conflict with efforts by the EEC to achieve supranational control over the European energy market. These efforts, including recent claims of authority over North Sea oil, have consistently met with major opposition and have been largely unsuccessful. To date the EEC Commission has not been granted powers to determine national policies as it has in fields such as agriculture. European governments have deemed energy policy to be of such substantial national concern that divergences in European national interests with respect to energy have been sufficient to prevent unity in policy formation. Probably the most basic differences have resulted from inequalities in the distribution of indigenous energy resources. Since the EEC grew out of the European Coal and Steel Community it inherited significant problems and responsibilities with respect to coal. Countries with domestic coal industries sought to provide those industries with varying degrees of protection and special treatment. Those without coal industries were unwilling to support Community efforts on behalf of these industries. The discovery of larger hydrocarbon reserves in the British and Dutch offshore has created a similar line of cleavage. The North Sea producers have not been willing to surrender national sovereignty over the disposition of their offshore resources to supranational authorities. Norway, in fact, declined membership in the EEC in 1972 largely because voters felt that membership would ultimately entail some degree of community control over the Norwegian offshore.

Yet another line of cleavage has arisen between those countries that are home for major multinational oil companies—Britain and the Netherlands—and those that are not. The British and Dutch have been more willing than their European neighbors to give their multinationals, and indeed all seven of the majors, a more or less free rein in their domestic petroleum consumption market (offshore production is a different matter).

Finally, differing national economic ideologies should be noted. Although a modest convergence in policy is apparent as nations under pressure of dwindling energy supplies have opted for greater degrees of state control, differences in overall economic approach are traditional and remain basic to the European nations. Recent German government intrusions into the national energy economy stand out as exceptions to a broad policy—still enunciated vigorously at top levels—of laissez faire and government nonintervention. France stands at the opposite pole in the European context with its longstanding efforts to determine through policy the shape of the national economy.

The EEC Commission has sought from member states various powers with respect to energy, but has received almost none. In 1969, free trade within the Community was instituted as all quantitative restrictions on trade among EEC members were ordered eliminated. Agreement could not be reached, however, to include the energy sector and this sector has since stood out as an exception. The Commission sought in particular to make British and Dutch oil and gas production available to all EEC members on an equal basis for purchase. Great Britain and the Netherlands have vetoed these efforts (unanimous approval for such proposals is necessary in the Council of Ministers). The Commission sought in 1970 to equalize fiscal policies with regard to energy within the Community. This proposal was also soundly rejected. To date, Community powers relating to energy remain few. The Commission has gained limited access to national and private data on energy trade and investment. Agreement has been reached on stockpiling emergency petroleum reserves. The Commission prepares reports and forecasts on Community energy needs and has published guidelines for national policies. Nevertheless, it has no enforcement powers.

The most successful initiative to date in obtaining regional energy cooperation in Europe is that undertaken by the United States at the Washington Energy Conference to establish an International Energy Agency (IEA). The agreement among 14 European nations, Japan, and the United States creating the IEA was signed in Brussels in September 1974. The IEA action of greatest concern to North Sea development was taken in early 1976. The IEA agreed to institute a floor price on oil of $7 a barrel to protect investment in alternative sources of energy—including, of course, costly operations in the North Sea. [30] Nevertheless, the IEA has failed to achieve the principal objective of its major architect, Henry Kissinger—that is, a greater unity among oil-consuming nations, particularly with regard to relationships with OPEC.

Efforts to achieve a greater coherence in European energy policies have thus been largely unsuccessful. While a high degree of cooperation and integration has been achieved in Europe in other areas, energy matters have appeared so crucial to preserving national well-being and national power that governments have been unwilling to surrender any significant authority over them. This concern for maintaining sovereign prerogatives in energy matters appears to be most intense in connection with indigenous supplies of energy. Throughout the postwar period, coal has been the subject of major governmental concern in those nations with large coal reserves. In contrast, imported oil received consistently less government attention even as the oil crisis brewed during the late 1960s and early 1970s. With the discovery of indigenous hydrocarbon reserves, however, these attitudes have shifted. Both governments and important elements of their constituencies have come to perceive a need for greater centralization of political authority over energy matters and, thus, the expansion of the role of the state. The nationalism of North Sea politics has found expression in North Sea law.

THE FUTURE OF THE EUROPEAN OIL MARKET

Before the oil crisis, projections of future oil production and consumption patterns abounded. [31] Nearly all predicted accelerating world demand for energy in the 1970s and early 1980s. In particular, the consumption of oil by the industrial nations was expected to grow faster in the 1970s than it had even in the 1960s. There was a sense in a number of the forecasts that appeared shortly before the crisis of the growing political instability of the international petroleum market. But few were so prescient as to anticipate the swiftness with which the producing nations would seize control.

Since the crisis, projections have been scarce and provisional. The market was thrown into disarray and the trends on which previous forecasts had been based were broken. A recent study published by the OECD in early 1977 is probably the most authoritative and current now available. [32]

The OECD does not project a significant change in the proportion of oil use in Europe's overall energy consumption pattern through 1985. This is due to pessimism regarding the ability of the European nations to make substitutions for or conserve oil to any substantial degree—pessimism based on dismal experience in these areas since the oil crisis. Among the EEC countries, where oil now constitutes about 54 percent of consumption, the percentage is projected to drop to 51 percent by 1980 and remain at 51 percent through 1985. The OECD also calculated an Accelerated Policy Case, under which governments were assumed to take the most vigorous feasible measures to lessen dependence on foreign energy imports. In this scenario, OECD Europe's consumption of oil is projected to drop to 44 percent of total consumption by 1985. [33]

These gloomy prospects were only moderately brightened by prospects for secure internal supplies of oil in the 1980s (primarily North Sea oil, but between 11 and 14 percent from other European regions). In 1976, indigenous oil production amounted to roughly 2 percent of oil consumption in the EEC. By 1980, this percentage was expected to rise to 12 percent, and to 13 percent by 1985. For OECD Europe as a whole (now including Norwegian oil) the figures were roughly the same. Indigenous oil reserves would allow the EEC to reduce its dependence on non-European sources of oil to 44 percent of total energy consumption by 1980 and 42 percent by 1985. The figures for OECD Europe, again, are roughly the same. In the accelerated policy scenario it was projected that OECD Europe could conceivably reduce its dependence to 34 percent of energy consumption by 1985. An acceleration of North Sea production was not considered feasible and was not a part of this scenario. Savings on imported oil were to be brought about by other means. [34] Thus, according to OECD, North Sea oil, though significant, is not likely to alter in any fundamental way the energy prospects for the European region even if a high level of cooperation in energy policies is achieved.

Trends toward a greater admixture of politics in oil economics are likely to continue. As the OECD projections indicate, oil is unlikely to become significantly less important to the industrialized economies in the near future. Assertions of greater government control in the energy market are, therefore, almost certain. In justifying the institution of government participation in the British North Sea in 1975, Eric Varley, minister of energy, said, "No other government outside the United States has thought it wise to be completely dependent on the oil companies."[35]

Where petroleum resources are indigenous, the arguments for a major government role have been more compelling. It had become customary in international law as well as the popular mind to view mineral resources as national rather than private resources.[36] In defending the vigorous terms Norway imposed on oil companies operating in the Norwegian North Sea, the Norwegian minister of industry in 1974, Ingvald Ulveseth, put his country's position in these terms:

It is simply that we don't see any reason why the private oil companies should get more than their fair share on the work they are doing. After all, while their efforts found the oil they didn't create it; the oil belongs to the Norwegian people.[37]

Those in the oil business resent this growing government encroachment. But they are buyers in a seller's market and generally have little choice but to live with it. The chairman of Shell Chemicals UK, W. C. Thomson, complained:

What is new is the extent to which governments are now intervening in all aspects of industrial life, often for political or social reasons that have little to do with economic realities. The rules of the game have a somewhat Alice-in-Wonderland quality—that is, the rules today are what governments say they are, and they may be changed tomorrow.[38]

The major oil companies have always given the impression of tremendous political power, which at one time appeared virtually unchallengeable. This appearance was shattered by the events of 1970 through 1974 both in the Middle East and, as we shall see, in the North Sea. Companies such as Exxon have confronted countries such as Norway (with a GNP that is roughly half of Exxon's gross sales revenue) and found themselves playing very much of a subsidary role in the achievement of national interests. Clearly it is possible to exaggerate the importance of these trends and Norway is something of an extreme case. Yet countries in the North Sea and elsewhere are now learning the true extent of their bargaining power and it is unlikely that present trends will be reversed.

NOTES

1. Joel Daimstadter, Energy in the World Economy (Baltimore: Johns Hopkins Press, 1971), p. 89.

2. Ibid., p. 91.

3. Peter Odell, Oil and World Power (New York: Taplinger, 1970), pp. 96-97.

4. M. A. Adelman, The World Petroleum Market (Baltimore: Johns Hopkins University Press, 1972), p. 377.

5. M. A. Adelman, statement in U. S. Congress, Senate, Committee on the Judiciary, Subcommittee on Antitrust and Monopoly, Hearings, The Petroleum Industry, March 11, 1968, p. 8.

6. Daimstadter, op. cit., p. 89.

7. Adelman, World Petroleum Market, op. cit., p. 340.

8. Sam Schurr and Paul T. Homan, Middle Eastern Oil and the Western World (New York: American Elsevier, 1971), p. 122.

9. Adelman, statement in U. S. Congress, op. cit., note 4, pp. 150-54.

10. Ibid., pp. 190-91.

11. Wayne H. Ferris et al., Energy Policies in the European Community, study prepared for U. S. Energy Research and Development Administration (Springfield, Va.: National Technical Information Service, 1975), p. 214.

12. Ibid., p. 205.

13. All energy consumption statistics drawn from United Nations, World Energy Supplies 1950-1974, U. N. Statistical Papers, Series J, No. 19 (New York: United Nations, 1976).

14. Ibid.

15. Anthony Sampson, The Seven Sisters (New York: The Viking Press, 1975), p. 246.

16. International Financial Statistics, May 1978, p. 331.

17. Petroleum Economist, January 1977, p. 2.

18. Petroleum Economist, November 1976, p. 416.

19. The OECD Observer, November-December 1975, pp. 9, 10.

20. OECD Economic Outlook, No. 22, December 1977, p. 65.

21. OECD Economic Outlook, No. 20, December 1976, p. 67; OECD Economic Outlook, No. 22, December 1977, p. 67.

22. OECD Economic Outlook, No. 20, December 1976, p. 15; OECD Economic Outlook, No. 22, December 1977, p. 15.

23. World Energy Outlook, a report by the OECD Secretary General (Paris: Organization for Economic Cooperation and Development, 1977), p. 25.

24. Oil and Gas Journal, December 31, 1973, p. 90.

25. Ferris et al., op. cit., p. 18.

26. Ibid.

27. Ibid., p. 16.

28. World Energy Supplies, op. cit., pp. 99, 557.

29. American Embassy to the Netherlands, Industrial Outlook Report—Petroleum, staff report, September 10, 1976, p. 2 (mimeographed).

30. Petroleum Economist, March 1976, p. 104.

31. The EEC has periodically issued projections. See for example, The Community Oil Sector, Medium Term Forecasts and Guidelines (Brussels: Commission of the European Communities, 1972). OECD has also been active in energy forecasting. The most complete statement issued before the crisis was Oil; the Present Situation and Future Prospects (Paris: Organization for Economic Cooperation and Development, 1973). Perhaps the best-known precrisis scholarly study is Adelman, World Petroleum Market, op. cit. See also Schurr and Homan, op. cit.

32. World Energy Outlook, op. cit.

33. Ibid., pp. 54, 55.

34. Ibid., pp. 45-46.

35. Sampson, op. cit., p. 333.

36. See, for example, "General Assembly Resolution of 1962 on Permanent Sovereignty over Natural Resources," UN General Assembly Resolution 1803 (XVII). Article I, section 1 declares "The right of peoples and nations to permanent sovereignty over their natural wealth and resources must be exercized in the interest of their national development and the well-being of the people of the State concerned."

37. J. Ross-Skinner, "Norwegian Oil: Interviews," Duns Review, August 1974, p. 64.

38. Petroleum Times, July 9, 1976, p. 3.

2

THE DEVELOPMENT OF
NORTH SEA PETROLEUM

The North Sea is a semienclosed expanse of water bordered on the west by Great Britain and the Shetlands and on the east by Belgium, the Netherlands, Germany, Denmark, and Norway. It is roughly 375 miles wide and 600 miles from north to south, covering 200,000 square miles. Commercially, the North Sea is often viewed more broadly and North Sea development taken to include, to the west of Great Britain, the Western Approaches, the Celtic and Irish Seas, and areas to the west of Scotland; and, to the north of Great Britain, the continental shelf of Norway up to the Barents Sea. Operations in these areas are generally extensions of activities in the North Sea. For the most part, however, development to date has focused on the North Sea proper up to a latitude of 62° N., above which an official delimitation of the seabed has not yet been negotiated.

THE GEOLOGICAL SETTING

The North Sea covers two large sedimentary basins. One, in the southern North Sea, stretches from the Netherlands to middle portions of Great Britain. The other, in the northern North Sea, extends from southern Norway to Scotland and the Shetland Islands. It also extends in a northerly direction up the Norwegian coast well beyond the present development limit of 62° N.

Sedimentary rocks, because they are porous, occasionally serve as reservoirs for hydrocarbons. A basin formation suggests an ancient sea in which organic matter may have collected and, in stagnant, anoxic conditions, become the basis for the formation of hydrocarbons. Such a process, it is now known, took place in the

17

Southern and Northern North Sea Basins. Extensive exploration has determined the Southern Basin to be a region in which, for complex geological reasons, hydrocarbons appear mostly in the form of natural gas. The Northern Basin, (see Figure 2.1), has proven to be primarily an oil province. Other sedimentary basins exist in the Western Approaches region, the Celtic and Irish Seas, areas to the west of the Hebrides and the Shetlands, and off the coast of Norway northwards into the Barents Sea. Considerably less is known about these basins. However, geologists believe there to be a strong chance that petroleum (a term that encompasses hydrocarbons in gaseous and liquid form) is present in significant quantities.

The seabed of the North Sea is the continental shelf of Europe. Throughout virtually the entire region water depths do not exceed 200 meters, or approximately 650 feet. In the portion of the North Sea south of 57° N. depths are generally less than 90 meters, or 300 feet. One major exception to these geological generalizations, with substantial implications for North Sea development, is the Norwegian Trench. The trench lies close to and parallels the southern Norwegian coast, reaching a maximum depth of over 1,000 feet. It separates Norway from that portion of the North Sea shelf over which Norway exercises jurisdiction, making it difficult to lay pipelines from offshore fields to the coast. The trench has potential legal implications as well. Under present international law, an important rationale for the exercise of national sovereignty by the coastal state over continental shelf resources is the geographical notion that the shelf is the natural extension of the continental land mass. Certain international legal scholars have maintained that presence of the trench vitiates Norway's claim to a portion of the North Sea continental shelf. This debate, effectively decided in Norway's favor in 1965, will be reconsidered in Chapter 4, which discusses the international legal basis for claims to the North Sea.

OFFSHORE TECHNOLOGY

The rapid evolution of offshore technology has made possible the exploitation of hydrocarbon resources in this region. Offshore technology was originally developed in the United States and deployed in the Gulf of Mexico and off the coast of California. The first offshore oil platform to operate out of sight of land was emplaced in a few feet of water off the Louisiana coast in 1947.[1] By 1950, the oil industry had developed a water depth capability of about 50 feet in the quiet waters of the Gulf.[2] By 1965, the depth limit for exploratory drilling (not oil production) had been extended to 600 feet. In 1976, exploratory drilling took place at over 3,000 feet.[3] Production—that

FIGURE 2.1

North Sea and Associated Sedimentary Basins

Source: Martin Lovegrove, Our Island's Oil (London: Witherby, 1975), p. 11. Reprinted with permission.

19

is, the extraction of oil or gas in commercial quantities—has lagged behind exploration in terms of depth capabilities but never by more than a few years. The greatest depth for which an offshore production platform has been constructed is 1,025 feet. [4] Designs exist for platforms that could operate in up to 1,500 feet of water, though the costs of such a platform would be close to prohibitive. [5] Currently, several companies are perfecting "subsea" completion systems—that is, oil production facilities that sit directly on the seabed rather than being elevated above sea level on a platform. One system developed by Lockheed particularly for use in the North Sea region has a depth capability of 1,200 feet. [6] Subsea completion systems will in the near future be operable at any depth, under ice or in crowded maritime traffic zones, extending capabilities of the offshore industry to virtually any marine environment.

More challenging than designing platforms for use in water of North Sea depth has been designing platforms to withstand North Sea weather. Prudence and government guidelines[7] recommend that rigs and platforms be able to withstand at least a 50-year storm—that is, the most severe storm that might be expected to occur in the average half-century. In the comparatively sheltered southern North Sea the estimated 50-year storm is characterized by wave heights of 50 feet sustained for 12 hours and hourly mean wind velocities of 70 miles an hour. In the northern North Sea, the 50-year storm is characterized by wave heights of 100 feet sustained for 12 hours and hourly mean wind velocities of 80 miles an hour. [8]

Most companies operating in the North Sea view the 50-year storm as defining a minimum standard. Current designs typically are intended to cope with 100-year storm conditions, which may include wind blasts of up to 170 miles an hour. [9] An additional problem is that the North Sea is seldom calm. In the northern portions in winter, high winds and seas may prevail 25 percent of the time. Structural problems associated with the continual stress on installations are thus of particular concern in the North Sea.

As North Sea exploration was beginning in the mid-1960s, weather data on the region were sparse. Estimates were, unfortunately, conservative and it was noted that so-called 100-year storms were occurring every other year. Several rigs were lost because of designs that were not adequate to withstand actual weather conditions. Disasters of this magnitude are far less likely now because of efforts by industry and governments to ensure that installations used in the North Sea are designed to meet actual conditions. Nevertheless, bad weather remains the primary cause of inconvenience, delay, and accident in the North Sea.

Despite these technical problems the North Sea has been developed rapidly. It is easy to make too much of the physical and technological obstacles that have been overcome in the North Sea and lose sight of the inherent attractiveness of the region to oil companies as a potential area for petroleum exploitation. Indeed, oil companies seem particularly prone to emphasize the technological difficulties in order to underscore the value of their services and enhance their bargaining positions vis-a-vis governments. However, the interest shown by companies in the North Sea suggests a perception of strong positive factors, some of which were identified by Jens Evensen in 1973 when he was head of the legal department of the Norwegian Ministry of Foreign Affairs.

> In many ways the North Sea is a tempting area of operation. The waters are reasonably shallow. Although the climate is rough, the North Sea is never frozen in winter. Furthermore, it is situated in the midst of one of the most densely populated and heavily industrialized regions of the world, making Western Europe the most important customer of petroleum next to the United States. Thus, the methods of transportation of possible oil finds to the markets are the shortest and cheapest in the world, with the possible exception of the United States domestic production. And due to the shallow depths of the North Sea the laying of pipelines does not offer insurmountable obstacles. This is especially important where gas finds are concerned. This, together with proximity to the markets, makes gas finds as valuable as oil finds, contrary to what is the case in remote-lying areas of the world where gas is often considered a nuisance to be got rid of as cheaply as possible. . . .
> The political and economic stability of Western Europe must likewise be an attractive element when considered by the oil companies. [10]

THE OPENING OF THE CONTINENTAL SHELF

Interest in the North Sea as a potential oil province has been traced back as far as the Suez Canal crisis of 1956-57. [11] The blockage of the canal served as an early warning of the vulnerability of European oil consumers to political events in the Middle East. In 1959, Nederlandse Aardolie Maatschappij (NAM), a Dutch company owned jointly by Esso and Shell, discovered an enormous natural gas field onshore in the Groningen province of northern Holland. Although minor oil and gas finds had been made throughout much of Europe, the Groningen field, because of its size, altered petroleum geologists' perception of northern Europe. It is the second largest of the world's known gas fields.

The sedimentary basin in which the Groningen field occurred was known to extend westward toward Great Britain. Consequently, a number of companies initiated exploration programs in the Southern Basin to determine the nature of this formation and the prospect for offshore petroleum. The early exploration programs were not intensive, however, for three principal reasons. First, as will be recalled, this was an era of rapidly expanding Middle Eastern supplies and falling oil prices. Concerns about political instability in the Middle East were unquestionably present but were qualified, in part by large discoveries of oil in northern Africa, which was at this time perceived to be politically secure. Second, governments were generally more concerned about support for the declining coal industry than about speculative efforts to locate oil offshore. [12] Third, and in partial consequence, a legal framework did not exist defining rights and responsibilities with respect to continental shelf resources.

Oil companies, with a few exceptions, limited their exploration effort to "passive" methods not involving penetration of the seabed (primarily seisomographic, magnetic, and gravimetric surveys). Such passive methods are adequate only to detect structures that might contain petroleum. Companies did not, for the most part, engage in exploratory drilling, which is necessary to detect the actual presence of petroleum. This self-imposed restraint was due in part to the fact that the cost of exploratory drilling exceeds that of passive methods by several orders of magnitude. In the absence of an accepted framework of law, companies were hardly willing to risk large investments in exploratory drilling when they might be divested of their rights to discoveries by the institution of an unanticipated legal regime.

The limitation of early exploration efforts to passive surveys was due also to the fact that drilling was, and still is, perceived politically as more provocative than surveys where rights to a seabed region are unsettled. In the early 1960s, passive surveys conducted by ships and airplanes were apparently tolerated by the North Sea littoral states as exercises of high seas freedoms. Such surveys are not now permitted in any region of the North Sea without permission from the government having jurisdiction.

By 1963, there was a growing consensus within the industry that the North Sea, at least in the Southern Basin, probably contained significant quantities of petroleum. Pressure on governments increased to arrive at agreements and promulgate laws necessary to allow exploration efforts, including drilling, to go forward in a stable legal environment. The first steps in this direction were taken as each of the North Sea governments proclaimed sovereignty over the

resources of the continental shelf adjacent to its coast. Denmark
and Great Britain accomplished this through ratification of the 1958
Geneva Convention on the Continental Shelf, which asserted the right
of nations to declare sovereignty over shelf resources. Germany,
the Netherlands, and Norway did not ratify the convention before
proclaiming sovereignty over shelf resources unilaterally. The
Netherlands and Norway have since become parties to the Convention; Germany remains a nonparty.

THE DEVELOPMENT OF THE SOUTHERN BASIN

The United Kingdom

In 1964, the United Kingdom adopted the Continental Shelf Act.
Provisions of this act were influential for the policies of both the
Netherlands and Norway. The legislation of these three most active
North Sea nations has evolved along essentially similar lines. Though
international boundaries in the North Sea had not yet been laid out,
Parliament authorized the Ministry of Power to allocate drilling
licenses to private companies at its discretion and with such condi-
tions attached as the Ministry deemed appropriate.

The "discretionary system" of license allocation, used by Norway and the Netherlands as well as the United Kingdom, enables government to attach conditions to licenses that, among other things,
facillitate active government involvement in offshore activities. While
under the American system of tender bidding for offshore leases
companies compete with one another in terms of the size of the money
bid offered the government, under the European system the basic
license fee is fixed and companies are encouraged to compete in
terms of a variety of concessions offered the government. Of course,
many of these concessions have substantial financial consequences
for both the companies and the government. While the European system has been criticized as economically inefficient,[13] it unquestionably gives government far greater power, direct and indirect, to
control the pattern of offshore development than is possible under the
American system. As it has developed in Europe, the discretionary
system has allowed governments to utilize the competitiveness of
private companies seeking scarce offshore rights as a lever to encourage acceptance of what might otherwise be considered onerous
financial terms and regulatory constraints.

In accordance with procedures drawn up by the Ministry, licenses were to be issued for blocks of the United Kingdom continental
shelf measuring roughly 100 square miles. A total of 960 such blocks
were offered in 1964—that is, roughly one-third of the area that was

generally believed appurtenant to the United Kingdom. Blocks in the immediate vicinity of prospective boundary lines were not offered.

The British government was particularly concerned to ensure that licensees not leave their blocks unexplored but rather explore them as rapidly as was feasible. Candidates for licenses were therefore required to submit a proposed program for exploratory work. Companies vying for choice licenses were encouraged to compete in formulating these programs. The authorities were also careful to allow a number of small companies without major Middle Eastern holdings onto the shelf to spur exploration activities. In the first round of British licensing, a total of 394 blocks out of the 960 offered were actually applied for and 348 allocated among 51 companies. [14] Because of government encouragement and early discoveries, exploration on the British continental shelf proceeded swiftly.

Agreement on boundaries was reached with the Netherlands and Norway in 1965 and a second round of licensing was held in November. Included among the 122 blocks allocated in this round were blocks immediately adjacent to the new boundary lines.

Within a month after this second round, British Petroleum made the first commercially exploitable discovery of hydrocarbons in the North Sea. British Petroleum's first North Sea exploratory well struck a large gas field, 48 miles off the British east coast in the North Sea's Southern Basin. Named West Sole, this discovery ensured sustained enthusiasm during the early phases of exploration. A second large gas field 40 miles off Norfolk was discovered four months after West Sole. Named Leman, the field is now believed to be the world's largest offshore gas field.

Further gas finds followed in quick succession. Indefatigible was discovered two months later, followed by Hewett in October 1966. Dottie was discovered in 1967, Rough and Deborah in 1968, Viking and Ann in 1969. (The chronology of North Sea development is illustrated in Figures 2.2 to 2.5.) All these fields are clustered within 100 miles of one another and within 60 miles of the English coastline. The shallowness of the water (West Sole was drilled in 80 feet of water) and the proximity of the fields to the coast allowed the installation of production facilities and the laying of pipelines to shore to proceed without major difficulty. By 1968, several fields were ready to begin production.

As frequently has proven the case in the North Sea, however, the resolution of technical problems was not the definition of commercial success. Political difficulties confronted the companies as clauses in the Continental Shelf Act (Section 9) left the companies no acceptable choice but to sell their gas to the Gas Council, Great Britain's nationalized gas distributor. Negotiations over the price to be paid were begun in 1966. The Gas Council insisted that the price

FIGURE 2.2

North Sea Development to December 31, 1964

Source: Shell Briefing Service, Royal Dutch/Shell with modifications by the author.

FIGURE 2.3

North Sea Development from January 1, 1965
to December 31, 1965

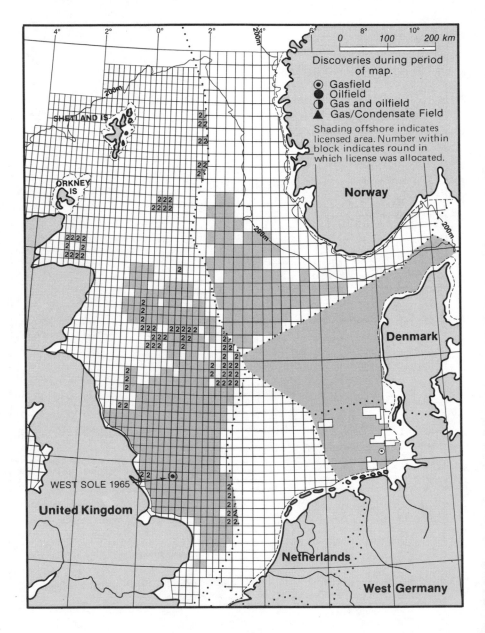

FIGURE 2.4

North Sea Development from January 1, 1966
to December 31, 1969

Source: Shell Briefing Service, Royal Dutch/Shell with modifications by the author.

FIGURE 2.5

North Sea Development from January 1, 1970
to August 7, 1972*

*For current map, see frontispiece.
Source: Shell Briefing Service, Royal Dutch/Shell with modifications by the author.

for gas be determined on a cost-plus basis, giving the companies a negotiated fixed margin of profit. The companies, on the other hand, demanded that the market price be paid. These differences were exacerbated by an inability to agree even on definitions. For example, what would constitute the cost-plus price? Were exploration expenses to be part of the price, including the cost of previous dry wells? Similarly, what would be the market price for gas in Great Britain? The gas industry was monopolized. In the negotiations the Gas Council offered 1.8 pence a therm (100,000 British Termal Units) while the companies asked 4 to 5 pence. [15] The economic arguments advanced by each side ultimately made less difference than the relative bargaining power of the parties. The Phillips Group, which had developed the Hewett field, finally agreed to a price of 2.87 pence in 1968. Other companies had little choice but to follow on similar terms.

By 1970, exploratory activity in the British sector of the Southern Basin seemed to have played itself out. Exploration of the region had been comparatively thorough. Moreover, in 1969, oil was discovered in the Northern Basin. The apparently sharp disappointment experienced by the oil companies in connection with the price o of gas landed in Britain encouraged them to invest their high-risk exploration funds in the oil province to the north. Between 1969 and 1971 the total number of exploration wells drilled in the British sector of the Southern Basin dropped from an annual rate of 34 to 7. [16]

The Netherlands

Intensive exploration of the Dutch portion of the Southern Basin did not begin until 1968. The first Dutch law on offshore activities, the Mining Law for the Continental Shelf, was passed in 1965. However, the royal decrees necessary to implement the law and permit a round of licensing were not promulgated until 1967. Arrangements for licensing were similar in their basic format to those implemented by the United Kingdom. The first licenses were allocated in 1968. Between 1968 and 1973, 80 exploration wells were commenced or drilled. [17] More than 20 gas fields as well as two small oil fields have been discovered although many of these are not commercial or are only marginally so. As of late 1977, the Netherlands possessed about 15 percent of proven North Sea gas reserves. The comparable figures are 54 percent for the United Kingdom, 29 percent for Norway, 16 percent for Denmark, and 0.4 percent for Germany. [18] Two gas pipelines have been constructed linking the most important offshore gas fields in the Dutch sector with the Dutch coast.

Dutch onshore gas production, particularly from the Groningen field, continues to overshadow offshore production. However, in a memorandum accompanying the 1978 budget, the Economic Affairs Ministry announced that inexpensive onshore gas reserves would be conserved as a strategic resource and more costly offshore gas and imported oil would be required to play a greater role in the Dutch energy economy in the near term. These objectives are to be implemented primarily through tax policies. [19]

Despite this new policy, offshore hydrocarbons will probably never play the dominant role in the Dutch energy economy that they will in the British and Norwegian energy economies. At most, offshore gas reserves will help stave off the inevitable decline of total Dutch reserves and production. Possibly as a consequence, the development of the Dutch shelf has proceeded more steadily and with less fanfare or controversy than has development on either the British or the Norwegian shelves.

West Germany

Development of the German portion of the Southern Basin began in 1964 when Germany granted a concession of its entire shelf area to a single group, the German North Sea Consortium, for a renewable three year period. Comparatively little exploration occurred and what did was disappointing in result. By 1972, only three percent of all exploration wells drilled in the North Sea had been drilled within the German sector. [20] It is now widely felt that the sort of licensing arrangements implemented by Germany—that is, the concession of its entire shelf acreage to a single entity—does not foster the sort of competition necessary to encourage rapid and intensive exploration. Great Britain, Norway, and the Netherlands have all made provision in their licensing schemes for competition among rival companies seeking access to the shelf. (The actual arrangements of Great Britain and Norway will be discussed in Chapter 5.)

In 1967, upon the failure of negotiations to complete the delimitation of the German shelf, Germany, Denmark, and the Netherlands agreed to submit their dispute to the International Court of Justice (see Chapter 4, The Third U.N. Conference on the Law of the Sea and Future Continental Shelf Law). The outcome of the Court's adjudication, when implemented through subsequent negotiations among the parties, gave Germany jurisdiction over several thousand more square miles of shelf than would have appertained to it had boundaries followed equidistance lines (compare Figures 2.4 and 2.5). However, despite the increase in the size of the German zone and despite the admission of several "newcomers" onto the German shelf, to date discoveries have been sparse and not of commercial size.

THE DEVELOPMENT OF THE NORTHERN BASIN

Norway

The Norwegian government was first approached regarding exploration rights on the Norwegian shelf in 1962 by Phillips Petroleum. However, it was not until 1965 that the government issued a royal decree (April 9, 1965) that set forth the main guidelines for licensing on the continental shelf. Shortly thereafter a round of licensing was held in which 78 blocks were issued. Norwegian blocks are about twice the size of British blocks, or about 200 square miles. Norway in its first round thus allocated something less than half the area initially allocated by Great Britain.

The Norwegian zone, which was separated from the British by a line equidistant from the two coasts (a delimitation treaty was signed in 1965), encompasses portions of the Northern North Sea Basin. During the 1960s, interest in this region was not as intense as interest in the British Southern Basin. The prospects for petroleum were considerably more speculative in the unproved Northern Basin, water depths were greater, and the climate considerably harsher. Nevertheless, the government had decided by the second round of licensing, held in 1968, to harden license terms substantially. The mandatory exploratory work programs were doubled and, more significantly, government participation in licenses was required. This was a major departure in North Sea licensing terms. The Dutch had considered, when they were formulating offshore policy from 1965 to 1967, requiring national participation of up to 50 percent. Pressure from the industry and electoral change, however, ensured that this policy was not instituted. [21]

The Norwegians were more firm in their resolve. Government participation of from 10 percent to 17.5 percent on a net profit basis was required in certain second-round licenses. (Under a net profit arrangement the stated percentage of the field's net profit, above the normal corporate income tax, is paid to the government.) Other licenses included government participation on a carried interest basis ranging from 5 percent to 40 percent. [22] (Under this arrangement the government has the option to become a financial partner in exploiting a field after the field has been declared commercial; the government is "carried" through the risky exploration phase at no cost and pays only its share of development and production costs.) In subsequent license allocations participation on a carried interest basis was required in all licenses. This hardening of terms and generally subdued interest in the Norwegian shelf led to the licensing of only 14 of the 68 blocks originally offered in this second round.

The hardening of Norwegian terms was prescient, however, for in 1970 Phillips Petroleum announced that it had found a "giant oil field" in the southern tip of the Norwegian zone. [23] This field, named Ekofisk, was the first discovery of commercial quantities of oil in the North Sea and the first discovery of major significance in the Northern Basin.

In 1970, North Sea development entered a new phase. The Eko-fisk discovery, like the Groningen discovery, convinced the oil industry that a region with considerable potential for hydrocarbons had been located. Moreover, by that year, national as well as corporate officials were becoming seriously concerned about Middle Eastern oil supplies. In 1970, Libya renegotiated its agreement with its con-cessionaires and oil prices began their swift climb culminating in the 1973-74 oil crisis. The discovery of oil in Europe's backyard in a situation of dwindling world oil supplies and rising prices stimulated a burst of exploration activity in the Northern Basin. Oil companies sought to locate and develop North Sea oil reserves as quickly as was feasible within the restraints imposed by national governments.

Within a short time, several more fields were discovered in the Norwegian sector in the immediate vicinity of Ekofisk, including Tor (1970) and West Ekofisk (1970). To date, ten oil fields have been discovered in this area, making up the Ekofisk Complex. Ekofisk went on stream in 1971, West Ekofisk in 1977, and Tor in 1978. In all, seven fields of this group (Ekofisk, West Ekofisk, Tor, Edde, Eldfisk, Albuskjell, and Valhall) are expected to be in production by 1981. [24] Oil from the complex is being pumped through a 210-mile pipeline to the English coast at Teeside and gas is flowing through a 260-mile pipeline to Emden, West Germany.

In 1971, Frigg, the second largest gas field yet discovered in the North Sea, was located some 250 miles to the north of Ekofisk. The field went into production in 1977, with gas being pumped through a 210-mile pipeline to St. Fergus, Scotland.

The success of exploration on the Norwegian shelf contributed to a growing confidence within the government regarding the value of Norwegian shelf resources and the strength of the country's bar-gaining position vis-a-vis the private oil companies.

A royal decree issued December 8, 1972 instituted new regula-tions for licensing, superseding the original regulations instituted by the Royal Decree of 1965. The new regulations considerably stiffened the financial terms of new licenses, hiking license fees and royalties and shortening the period available to companies for exploration of the licensed area. Also in 1972, the Norwegian parliament (the

Storting) established Den Norske Stats Oljeselskap a. s. (The Norwegian State Oil Company or Statoil) as a joint stock company wholly
owned by the Norwegian government. Statoil's immediate purpose
was to exercise options for government participation in licenses with
participation clauses. Over the long run, however, the government
clearly has aspirations of building Statoil into a major integrated
company. Statoil will have responsibility for the development of much
of the Norwegian shelf including primary responsibility for areas
north of 62° N., the present northern limit for commercial activity.
Statoil's proposed four year budget submitted to the Storting in 1975
included proposed investments of 875 million kroner (10 percent of
the budget) in refineries and distribution systems. [25] The anticipated
scope of the company's activities has created huge capital requirements. Its proposed investments in 1976 of 2. 18 billion kroner exceeded one-third of total investment by Norwegian industry in 1975. [26]
Statoil's capital requirements are being underwritten by both the government and private financial institutions.

The first license to be issued under the 1972 regulations was
for two blocks adjacent to Britain's Brent oil field on Norway's side
of the international boundary. These blocks were allocated outside of
normal licensing round procedures because of concern that the Brent
field might extend across the line and reserves belonging to Norway
(under provisions of the bilateral treaty delimiting the British and
Norwegian sectors of the North Sea[27]) would be depleted by British
development. Statoil was granted a 50 percent share in this license
on a carried interest basis. Mobil was chosen as operator (the company that actually carries out the project) though an interesting license provision required Mobil to train Statoil personnel so that
Statoil may take over as operator, if it chooses, in 1983. [28] Mobil
failed to find an extension of the Brent field but did locate the largest
oil field thus far discovered in the North Sea, the Statfjord field.
Roughly one-half Statoil's huge capital investment in 1976, cited
above, was for its share of the development costs for this field. [29]

In 1973, Norway issued a White Paper announcing a "go-slow"
policy toward oil development. [30] Policy makers were concerned
about the possible detrimental effects on the society of a rapid influx
of oil wealth through the expansion of the petroleum and related industries and increased government expenditures. The Norwegian
economy is small. The population is roughly four million (compared
with roughly 50 million in the United Kingdom). In 1973 unemployment
was under 2 percent and the country's GNP of $20. 3 billion appeared
to be expanding steadily. Hydroelectricity suffices for nearly all of
Norway's primary electricity needs and in 1974 it provided 45 percent of the total energy consumption. [31] The anticipated output of
Norway's offshore oil fields exceeds by several times the country's

small petroleum requirements. Among the policies announced by the government to control the impact of the petroleum boom on Norwegian society was a ceiling on total oil and gas production on the Norwegian shelf of 1. 8 million barrels a day to be maintained through 1990. [32] The principal mechanism to be used to control development was the rate of offshore licensing.

A third Norwegian licensing round was held in 1974. A total of eight blocks were allocated, in which state participation on a carried interest basis varied from 50 percent to 55 percent with provisions requiring an increase to 70 percent or more if certain levels of production were reached. [33] Shortly after the round was held the Ministry of Finance proposed a new excess profits tax of 40 percent to be assessed in addition to the corporation tax and to be applicable to all previously issued licenses. A strong protest was voiced by the oil companies with the backing of at least one prominent Norwegian legal scholar, to the effect that the government was changing essential financial conditions of licenses retroactively and that such an action was in violation of the Norwegian constitution. Nevertheless, a new tax regime was enacted overwhelmingly by the Storting. Under the provision of the act as passed, a special tax of 15 percent was applied after all other taxes and royalties had been assessed. [34] The total government take under the new financial regime has been estimated at between 55 percent and 68 percent of field profits (defined as sales revenues less capital and operating costs). [35] In addition, substantial revenues accrue to the government as a result of the participation of Statoil in many licenses.

Applications for a fourth round of licensing were solicited in 1977 for 15 blocks including several in the neighborhood of Statfjord with good prospects for substantial petroleum reserves. Announcement of the results of the round is expected in late 1978.

Despite the discovery of several new fields since the 1974 licensing round, recent events have cooled expectations regarding Norway's offshore oil wealth and marked something of a reversal in Norway's economic good fortunes. Norway's go-slow policy of restrictive licensing effectively slowed exploration and the growth of discovered reserves. Norway has also slowed the development of discovered reserves through the enforcement of strict safety and antipollution requirements for offshore operations. For example, unlike Great Britain, Norway will not permit a platform to produce oil from any of its wells while drilling is taking place because of the increased hazard associated with this practice. In a similar vein, development of Statfjord was halted in order to bring about compliance with regulations governing offshore housing of workers.

In early 1977, a blowout occurred on one of the production platforms servicing the Ekofisk field. The well was capped after eight days. This event affirmed the resolve of most Norwegian policy makers to continue to set standards well in excess of those the industry would set for itself. Caution appeared particularly warranted in light of the inadequacy of available technology for cleaning up spills under the severe weather conditions characteristic of the northern North Sea.

Stringent government regulations have not been without costs, however. Partly as a result of these regulations and partly as a result of inflation, financing oil development has recently become a problem for Norway that was not anticipated in the early 1970s. The production plan for the Statfjord field, in which Statoil is an equal partner with Mobil, was recently revised because of financial constraints by reducing the planned production capacity of several of the platforms scheduled for emplacement before 1980. As a result, the official estimate of peak production from the field was cut 25 percent in early 1978, to 520,000 barrels a day (to be reached in 1987).

The slow pace of Norwegian development has placed strains on the Norwegian economy. Shipyards have suffered because of an unexpectedly low number of platform orders. Offshore support industries have suffered for similar reasons. Official estimates of future government revenues were cut substantially in 1978 with cuts in estimated production. In 1977, Norway ran a large and unexpected balance of payments deficit, forcing an 8 percent devaluation of the Norwegian kroner in February 1978. These developments have triggered a public debate on the go-slow policy. They have also led to speculation that the government may ease the royalty and tax burdens borne by owners of marginal fields in the Norwegian sector to facilitate the development of these fields and boost Norway's sagging offshore production curve.

Still, Norway's recent economic disappointments must be assessed in light of the extraordinary expectations that began building in the early 1970s. Despite the downgrading of estimates, the Norwegian government expects to receive 52 billion kroner in oil revenues between 1978 and 1981. [36] Continued balance of payments deficits are unlikely. Moreover, Norway has been able to impose on oil companies some of the strictest licensing terms in effect in the world today. Recent events have, in a sense, merely suggested limits to the extent to which Norway can have its cake and eat it too. They have demonstrated that offshore oil production is characterized by risk even in the best of circumstances and that the economics of offshore production are sensitive to government policies even though new sources of crude oil are in high demand. Sentiment apparently remains strong among Norwegians to continue to place substantial government restrictions on North Sea development in the interest of preserving the environment and traditional ways of life, and of conserving resources for the future. [37]

Such concerns are more acute in connection with the development of shelf regions north of the sixty-second parallel, presently the northernmost limit for exploration and development. Substantial reserves of petroleum are believed to exist north of this line. However, extraordinarily harsh weather conditions prevail, coastal ecosystems are more fragile than those further south, and local economies are less developed. As of mid-1976, the commencement of exploratory drilling was planned for 1978. However, the Ekofisk disaster heightened fears that neither the companies nor government authorities had the facilities to cope with a major oil disaster under the harsh conditions of the northern North Sea. The commencement of drilling north of the sixty-second parallel is not now anticipated until 1980 at the earliest.

When exploratory drilling does begin north of 62° N. it will probably be the responsibility of Statoil. A White Paper issued in 1976 mentions the service contract as perhaps the most appropriate arrangement for bringing the technical resources of the private companies into this region. [38] Under this scheme, Statoil would hold a 100 percent interest in licenses issued for blocks north of 62° N. and would contract with private oil companies for services it could not perform itself. As development moves closer to the strategically sensitive Barents Sea—with its proximity to the Soviet Murmansk submarine base—it is unlikely that the Norwegian government will allow any company other than Statoil to carry on development activities.

Great Britain

The development of the British sector of the Northern Basin has proceeded far more rapidly and amid greater public controversy than the development of the Norwegian sector. In general, Britain has been more solicitous of private oil companies than has Norway, and its license terms have been less demanding. This reflects the considerably greater needs of the British economy for both energy and foreign exchange and a consequent national policy favoring rapid shelf development.

The British held a third round of licensing in 1969 and a fourth round in 1971. During these rounds licenses for substantial portions of the Northern Basin were allocated. Licensing procedures generally followed the same pattern as the first two rounds, with one notable exception. In the fourth round, out of a total of 282 blocks allocated, 15 were allocated on an experimental basis, by tender bid.

This was a major departure from standard practice in the North Sea, where, except for this British experiment, licensing has been carried out on a discretionary basis. British officials were somewhat shocked when the auction produced revenues totaling 37 million pounds. For many in Britain, this auction was the beginning of suspicions the British government was not receiving its fair share of offshore wealth—suspicions that ultimately led to a hardening of license terms in 1974.

In 1970, British Petroleum announced the first major oil discovery in the British Northern Basin. Named Forties, the field went into production in 1975. It is sufficiently large that in 1977 it alone supplied the equivalent of over one quarter of Britain's domestic oil consumption (151 million barrels out of 579 million barrels). Further discoveries followed quickly off the Scottish coast in the area of the Shetland Islands. The success ratio in the British Northern Basin—that is, the ratio of discoveries made to wells drilled—has been far higher than the world average of 1:15. In the Northern Basin generally the success ratio has been 1:8. [39] In the area east of the Shetland Islands it has been 1:5.

By mid-1976, there were 14 oil fields in the British sector either on stream, under development, or to be developed, with an estimated total of nearly 8 billion barrels in reserves. Commercial development seemed a strong possibility for 12 more fields. With the sharply higher prices for oil that have been effective since 1975, these discoveries represent an enormously valuable resource. Capital expenditures and operating costs were estimated in 1976 to total $2.27 for each produced barrel for the Forties field (1976) dollars) and $2.47 for the Brent field. These are the two largest fields discovered thus far in the British sector. Total costs for other British fields were estimated to range from as low as $1.89 a barrel to as high as $4.27 a barrel. [40] These figures, set against the then current price of over $12.00 a barrel for Middle Eastern crude, suggest the potential profitability of North Sea development.

In the early 1970s, concern in Great Britain began building that the oil companies would reap huge windfall profits and Britain not receive its full share of oil revenues. This concern grew out of a combination of factors. One was, of course, the rising price of crude oil. Any field considered commercial before the price rise would clearly be enormously profitable following it. A second was the high success rate achieved in the North Sea, which blunted oil company arguments that the companies were entitled to high rates of return because of the exceptional financial risks run during the exploratory phase. On the political plane, the government and public were well aware of the policies of other producing countries—particularly the OPEC group and Norway. The increasing militancy of OPEC not only set a dramatic example for state policy with respect to the private oil companies but deflated arguments that a hard line laid down in Britain might inspire similar policies by OPEC. Plainly OPEC was stiffening its terms with or without British inspiration. It also undermined arguments that a hard line would drive the companies away to more favorable political environments; such environments were now hard to find. Great Britain seemed headed for the dubious distinction of having the least demanding financial terms of any major oil producer. [41]

Domestic political events added fuel to the fire. The prospect of large quantities of recoverable oil off Scotland encouraged Scottish nationalists to push for independence with new vigor. Oil lent reality to the idea of an independent Scotland because it offered a means by which Scotland could achieve economic independence and even prosperity. The growing strength of the Scottish Nationalist Party in Parliament induced British politicians concerned about maintaining the British union to pay heed to Scottish demands that the government exercise greater control over the oil companies to prevent environmental and social damage to Scotland as a result of too hasty development.

The surprising financial success of the auction experiment in 1971 set off a wave of criticism, which exploded into a furor following a report by the House of Commons Public Accounts Committee on North Sea oil and gas issued in 1973. The Committee's most damaging finding was that

> although the major oil companies incurred world-wide tax of thousands of millions of dollars each year . . . hardly any of this money was paid into the U.K. Exchequer. Because of the operation of double taxation relief, liability to the U.K. Corporation Tax was extinquished by credits for tax paid elsewhere. Moreover the size of this relief has led to the accumulation of huge tax losses, of the order of 1,500 million for nine major companies, which could be carried forward indefinitely to be set against future profits. [42]

In other words, the oil companies were writing off taxes paid to the Middle Eastern governments against North Sea profits—a practice that would allow them to pay virtually no corporation taxes for an indefinite period. Since the corporation tax had been counted on as the principal source of government revenue from North Sea oil (the only other major charge on production was a royalty of 12.5 percent) the political effect was a widespread feeling that Great Britain was being robbed of its oil wealth by the oil multinationals.

Oil policy was an important campaign issue in the election held in early 1974 in which the Conservative party was defeated by Labour. Later in the year the Labour government issued a White Paper on future government offshore policy. [43] The White Paper noted that as a result of increased prices oil company profits could total 4 billion pounds by 1980, little of which would be taxed and half of which would be remitted overseas. It proposed that, first, a "ring fence" be set up around North Sea operations for the purpose of accounting. Only losses incurred in the North Sea could be written off against United Kingdom taxes. Second, it proposed that the government obtain majority participation in commercial development on the United Kingdom shelf and that a national oil company be set up to act on behalf of the government in this regard. Government participation would provide an additional source of revenue. It would also provide the government with more information on activities on the United Kingdom shelf and greater control over these activities.

Reform of the British tax system for offshore oil and gas was carried out through the enactment of the Oil Taxation Act of 1975. In addition to setting up the ring fence for allowable deductions, the Act instituted a special tax for oil operations, the Petroleum Revenue Tax (see pages 144 to 146). Under the new tax system (and with the 12.5 percent royalty) the total government take is now estimated to fall between 62 percent and 69 percent of field profits depending on field size. [44]

In 1975, the Labour majority in Parliament created the British National Oil Corporation (BNOC), a wholly owned government corporation to act on behalf of the government in state participation arrangements. The 1974 White Paper had included the commitment to require majority state participation, in some form, in all future licenses. It also contained a commitment to negotiate for state participation in existing licenses, though on a voluntary basis (that is, participation was not legally required). The government made clear, nevertheless, that uncooperative companies could not expect favored treatment in the fifth round of licensing. An applicant in the fifth round, AMOCO, did not come to agreement with the government before the opening of the round in late 1976 and was not considered for licenses. [45] This use of the discretionary system by the British government illustrates something of its flexibility.

These shows of strength were, to a great extent however, intended merely for public consumption. The government could bring the companies to the negotiating table but lacked the bargaining strength to negotiate substantial concessions. For small companies, participation amounted to granting the government bare legal title to a field, entitling it to an option to buy 51 percent of future production at market prices and allowing it some representation on the field's operating board. [46] With larger companies, for example Shell and Esso, the arrangements were even more vacuous. The government option to buy 51 percent of produced oil included a buyback provision allowing the companies to repurchase the oil if any of their downstream refineries encountered supply shortages. It appeared that in these voluntary agreements talk of 51 percent state participation did not have its ordinary legal connotation but rather was intended to allow the Labour government to live up to the letter if not the spirit of its political commitments in the 1974 White Paper.

The fifth round of licensing was held in 1976, with results announced in 1977. Fifth round licenses included as a requirement 51 percent state participation of a more substantive sort than that which the government had been able to negotiate for preexisting licenses, as described above. Under the fifth-round license terms BNOC will furnish 51 percent of the capital necessary to explore as well as exploit allocated blocks (a significant difference from the Norwegian carried interest system) and will be entitled to a proportionate share of total voting rights in field management and eventual oil production. In the sixth round of licensing, the British government is expected to encourage private applicants to bid against each other with respect to terms offered BNOC. Government participation at a level of 51 percent is considered sine qua non. The government is now attempting to find support among prospective applicants for participation on a carried interest basis.

As early as 1979, Britain may achieve net self-sufficiency in oil at 1.9 billion barrels per day total production (at that point exports will begin to exceed imports though it may still be necessary to import particular grades of crude not available from the North Sea). By 1980, British production may exceed that of each of the OPEC producers except Saudi Arabia, Iran, and Iraq.

A White Paper issued in 1978 projected that offshore oil production could add 4.5 billion pounds a year (in 1977 pounds, assuming no change in the price of oil) to the British GNP in 1980, rising to 6 billion a year in 1985. [47] Government revenues are expected to be small to start with because companies will write off the costs of development against profits. However, by 1985 government revenues should reach 4 billion pounds annually. The total benefit to the balance of payments predicted by the government is 5.5 billion pounds in 1980 and 8 to 9 billion pounds by 1985. Offshore development is also providing extra employment. The Ministry of Energy estimated that in 1976 about 100,000 people were employed in the United Kingdom in work related to North Sea oil development, 56,000 to 65,000 in Scotland (where unemployment is particularly acute). [48]

Hope is apparently high in Great Britain that North Sea oil will bring new strength to the declining economy. If revenues are used wisely, as outlined in the 1978 White Paper, to pay off foreign debt, rejuvenate a weak industrial base, and develop alternative forms of energy to take over when the oil runs out, Britain's economy may enjoy a rebirth. More immediately, new oil tax revenues may make possible a lowering of one of the highest personal income taxes in the world (the lowest bracket is 35 percent). Many feel these taxes cripple incentive and are an important factor underlying the low productivity of the British labor force. More pessimistic observers, however, wonder about the competence of the British government to take full advantage of even such good fortune as the discovery of oil in Britain's backyard.

It is interesting to note the modest convergence taking place between the offshore policies of the United Kingdom and those of Norway. While Norway may be forced to relax some of the conditions imposed by certain licenses covering marginal fields in order to permit their development, Great Britain continues to stiffen its license terms. This reflects the fact that Britain is now nearing net self-sufficiency while Norway has fallen behind in its development time schedule and is facing unexpected economic difficulties. However, Great Britain's need for prompt realization of its oil wealth remains far greater than Norway's. A complete convergence between the oil policies of the two nations is not imminent.

Denmark

Denmark has jurisdiction over a small portion of the Northern Basin. In 1963, after being the first North Sea nation to ratify the Geneva Convention, Denmark became the first to allocate rights to its sector of the shelf. A single concession covering the entire sector was granted to the Dansk Undergrunds Consortium (DUC), a group of companies led by the Danish shipbuilder A. P. Moeller. The arrangement resembled that entered into by Germany except that the concession was for an extraordinary 50 years, to be reviewed by the Danish government after 10 years if some form of production was not underway. The DUC passed muster in 1973 and remains the sole operator on the Danish shelf. One moderately sized oil field, Dan, was discovered in 1971. The field went into production in 1972, with oil being stored at the site and loaded onto tankers for shipment to shore. Nine other moderate and marginal oil and gas structures have been discovered as of this writing. The DUC has contemplated the development of several of these fields.

In general, exploration of the Danish shelf has not been rapid or intensive, for reasons similar to those discussed in connection with German licensing procedures. Moreover, much of the Danish shelf is not suitable for hydrocarbon accumulations and is not within either the northern or the southern formations.

Generally, the United Kingdom and Norway have been the nations most affected by North Sea development and have devoted the greatest attention to regulating this development. As we turn to an examination of national and other interests associated with offshore resources it will be useful to focus on these two countries.

NOTES

1. Donald E. Kash, et al., Energy under the Oceans (Norman, Oklahoma: University of Oklahoma Press, 1973), p. 25.
2. Offshore, June 1976, pp. 58-59.
3. Ibid.
4. Offshore, April 1978, p. 90.
5. Petroleum Review, February 1976, pp. 71-76.
6. Ibid., p. 72.
7. For example, United Kingdom, Department of Energy, Guidance on the Design and Construction of Offshore Installations, 1974, section 2: "Environmental considerations," pp. 3-22.
8. A. M. Hutcheson and A. Hogg, eds., Scotland and Oil (Edinburgh: Oliver and Boyd, 1975), p. 17.
9. Ibid., p. 19.
10. Jens Evensen, "Modern Trends in Oil Politics," in North Sea Oil—The Challenge and Implications, Heriot-Watt University Lectures (Edinburgh: Heriot-Watt University, 1973), pp. 47-48.
11. Royal Dutch/Shell Group, Oil and Gas from the North Sea, Shell Briefing Service (The Hague: Royal Dutch/Shell Group, 1974), p. 3.
12. Martin Saeter and Ian Smart, eds., The Political Implications of North Sea Oil and Gas (Oslo: Universitetsforlaget, 1975), p. 93.
13. See Kenneth O. Dam, Oil Resources (Chicago: The University of Chicago Press, 1976).
14. United Kingdom, Parliament, Commons, First Report of the Committee on Public Accounts, 1972-1973: North Sea Oil and Gas (London: Her Majesty's Stationery Office, 1973), p. 45.
15. Dam, op. cit., p. 76.
16. United Kingdom, Department of Energy, Production and Reserves of Oil and Gas in the United Kingdom, (London: Her Majesty's Stationery Office, 1974), p. 21.
17. Dam, op. cit., p. 97.
18. Petroleum Economist, October 1977, p. 395.

19. Petroleum Economist, November 1977, p. 438.

20. P. L. J. Walnesky, "Geology and Exploration," in North Sea Oil: The Challenge and Implications, Heriot-Watt University Lectures (Edinburgh: Heriot-Watt University, 1973), p. 4.

21. Saeter and Smart, op. cit., p. 95.

22. Norway, Ministry of Industry, Operations on the Norwegian Continental Shelf, Report No. 30 to the Norwegian Storting (1973-74), pp. 44-45, 76-78.

23. Clive Callow, Power from the Sea (London: Victor Gollancz, 1973), p. 78.

24. Petroleum Economist, April 1978, pp. 138-39.

25. Norway, Ministry of Industry, Financing of Den Norske Stats Oljeselskap a. s., Storting Proposition No. 143 (1974-75), p. 6.

26. Ibid., p. 7.

27. United Nations, Treaty Series, Treaties and International Agreements Registered or Filed and Reported with the Secretariat of the United Nations, vol. 551, "United Kingdom and Norway: Treaty on the Delimitation of the Continental Shelf between the Two Countries," Article 4, p. 214.

28. Norway, Ministry of Industry, Operations, op. cit., p. 45.

29. Norway, Ministry of Industry, Financing, op. cit., p. 6.

30. Norway, Ministry of Finance, Petroleum Industry in Norwegian Society, Parliamentary Report No. 25. (1973-74).

31. United Nations, World Energy Supplies, 1950-1974, U. N. Statistical Papers, Series J, No. 19, (New York: United Nations, 1976), p. 809.

32. Petroleum Economist, January 1977, p. 23.

33. Norway, Ministry of Industry, Activities on the Norwegian Continental Shelf, Report No. 81 to the Storting (1974-75), p. 22.

34. Dam, op. cit., p. 69.

35. Petroleum Economist, May 1976, p. 121.

36. Petroleum Economist, April 1978, p. 137.

37. A recent poll indicated that 58 percent of Norwegians oppose any acceleration of offshore development. Ibid.

38. Norway, Ministry of Industry, Petroleum Exploration North of 62° N, Report No. 91 to the Norwegian Storting (1975-76).

39. D. I. MacKay and G. A. Mackay, The Political Economy of North Sea Oil (London: Martin Robertson, 1975), p. 63.

40. C. Robinson and V. Morgan, "World Oil Prices and the Profitability of North Sea Oil," Petroleum Review, April 1976, p. 199.

41. United Kingdom, Parliament, Commons First Report, op. cit. xxxii.

42. Ibid., p. xxi.

43. United Kingdom, United Kingdom Offshore Oil and Gas Policy, No. 5696, July 11, 1974.

44. Petroleum Economist, May 1976, p. 121.

45. Offshore, March 1977, p. 48.

46. The agreement with London and Scottish Marine Oil Company, Ltd. and Scottish Canadian Oil and Transportation Company, Ltd. is apparently typical. The Department of Energy informed the company that

> an agreement on participation will provide for BNOC to
> obtain title to 51 percent of your interest in the Ninian
> Field, participating in the operating committee and en-
> joying its proportionate voting rights. In return for your
> remaining responsible for all exploration, development,
> and operating costs. . . , however, you would continue
> to own beneficially all relevent assets and all petroleum
> produced, subject to BNOC having an option . . . to
> purchase 51 percent of the production at market price.

From a letter to the company reprinted in Morgan Grenfel and Co., Ltd., Issues of Oil Production Stock, A Prospectus, London & Scottish Marine Oil Company Ltd. and Scottish Canadien Oil and Transportation Company, Ltd. (1976), p. 39.

47. United Kingdom, The Challenge of North Sea Oil, Command Paper 7143 (London: Her Majesty's Stationery Office, 1978).

48. United Kingdom, Department of Energy, Development of the Oil and Gas Resources of the United Kingdom, 1977 (London: Her Majesty's Stationery Office, 1977).

3

POLITICAL INTERESTS AND
NORTH SEA DEVELOPMENT

This chapter seeks to identify the fundamental interests underlying the evolution of North Sea law that are common among the North
Sea states. Areas of uniformity of interests outweigh areas of divergence and the sources of this uniformity are not difficult to discern.

The nations bordering on the North Sea are highly homogeneous,
both politically and culturally, when considered in a world context.
All are advanced industrial nations in whose economies oil plays a
uniquely important role. As political entities all are organized along
similar lines.

Further, whatever political differences may exist among the
North Sea states, the offshore activities that are the subject of regulation are essentially similar, regardless of the coast off which they
occur. Offshore technology varies little in its application by region.
Only a limited number of companies (the majority of them U. S. companies) are capable, financially or technically, of carrying out large-
scale offshore operations. The prospect of extensive offshore development confronts different nations with potential benefits and harms
that are fundamentally similar. Illustrative of this is the fact that the
Norwegian government commissioned an extensive study of the petroleum laws and regulations of other countries before drafting its
licensing regulations issued in 1972. [1] Not only was a cross section
of nations investigated (including Saudi Arabia, Egypt, Libya, Venezuela, Indonesia, Australia, Portugal, the United Kingdom, and the
United States) but law governing land-based as well as offshore petroleum development was considered relevant, suggesting the homo-
geneity of the petroleum trade in general.

Significant differences, of course, do exist among the North
Sea states and to a certain extent these are reflected in different

approaches to offshore law. Of foremost importance are differences in the scale of the offshore reserves that are within the jurisdiction of each country and the anticipated impact of development of these reserves on the national economy. Also relevant to offshore law is the presence or absence of a major national oil company with international operations (that is, British Petroleum and Shell in the case of the United Kingdom, and Shell in the case of the Netherlands). To a certain extent also, differences in cultural attitudes toward development of any kind and associated environmental degradation have affected the evolution of offshore law within different jurisdictions. However, these and other sources of divergence in offshore law are best assessed against the background provided by an understanding of relevant interests shared by the North Sea states.

A BASIC FRAMEWORK

Political interests may be said to operate at three levels at least: the national, the local, and the supranational.[2] The phrase "political interests," is intended to refer to interests that motivate the relevant authorities and not necessarily to what objectively is in the best interest of the relevant political group.

Political interests operative at the national level have been the primary forces shaping the evolution of North Sea law. This fact is hardly surprising. It reflects a global structure of power, dominated by the nation-state, that has placed the international legal means for asserting control over the continental shelf entirely at the disposal of national governments (see Chapter 4).

The second level at which political interests can occur, and that is of concern in this analysis, is the local level. It is easy (and frequently appropriate) to dismiss this level in examining the origins of law governing national resources lying miles offshore. Nevertheless, authorities representing the interests of local constituencies have, in certain instances, been able to influence the provisions of national legislation and thereby the pattern of resource development. Scottish interests are perhaps the best known examples of this.

A third level at which political interests may have effects is the supranational level. We will focus on regional interests, particularly those represented by EEC authorities. Expanding beyond this level to even broader political or geographic groupings will not be useful. As will be recalled from Chapter 1, the OECD projects that by 1985 North Sea oil could provide only slightly more than 10 percent of the EEC's needs—a significant portion but one that could not change fundamentally Europe's energy outlook. Expanding beyond the regional level would only lead us to political interests relevant to North Sea legal arrangements so dilute as to be of negligible impact.

Mention should be made also of private interests operative at the supranational level—that is, those of the multinational oil companies—as a source of some influence over the shape of the North Sea regime.

NATIONAL INTERESTS

National interests associated with North Sea development may usefully be subdivided into six categories, three involving benefits flowing from offshore development and three involving the minimization of associated harms. These basic interests are:

1. security of domestic oil supply
2. public national revenues
3. private national revenues
4. safety
5. social and economic stability
6. environmental quality

Security of National Oil Supply

Although we are most concerned here with the European situation, it would be a reasonably fair generalization to observe that any nation dependent on foreign governments for a significant portion of its energy supplies would be likely to have a strong interest in developing secure internal energy sources where feasible. In the case of the European nations this interest is particularly strong, for several reasons. First, these nations possess highly developed industrial economies and thus are highly energy intensive. Vast supplies of energy are essential to their continuing economic well-being which, in turn, is often sine qua non for the maintenance of power by those in national office. Second, as discussed in Chapter 1, following the war European industry was built on inexpensive supplies of oil. Not only is oil consumption high, but, as the revised OECD report cited at the end of Chapter 1 indicated, the prospects for substitution and conservation are not bright. Third, before the discovery of the North Sea oil Europe was almost wholly dependent on oil imports from the Middle East. Europe's dependence on the OPEC nations was exceeded among the industrialized economies only by that of Japan. [3] Achieving a higher level of independence in energy is thus a matter of high national priority for those nations capable of making the attempt.

Of the North Sea states in 1973, Great Britain was dependent on imported oil and petroleum products for 55 percent of its total energy supplies, Norway for 48 percent, Denmark for 87 percent, and Germany for 53 percent. The Netherlands, with its supplies of natural gas, was dependent on foreign oil for only 36 percent of its needs. By way of comparison, the United States, in 1973, was dependent on imported oil for approximately 10 percent of its total energy needs. [4]

The strong political interest in obtaining a secure supply of crude oil in these nations has manifested itself in two principle ways in the context of the North Sea. The first has been a drive to secure full national sovereignty over resources with the minimum possible derogation of that sovereignty to authorities at other levels. As the OECD figures reveal, if the North Sea oil were divided equally among the EEC countries, security of energy supply would be achieved by no one. Moreover, Britain and Norway have expressed fears that if the EEC were in command of shelf resources, it would allow production to proceed too quickly and to drain what these countries view as valuable and strategic national reserves to be conserved as long as possible while still meeting national needs.

The second has been a little-talked-about concern for the military security of offshore operations. As Britain and Norway become dependent on offshore oil supplies, oil platforms may become tempting targets to terrorist sabotage or, in the event of war, military attack. As we have seen, the magnitude of North Sea reserves is such that comparatively few platforms can supply a major portion of the energy needs of a nation the size of Great Britain. NATO has become concerned as Soviet intelligence trawlers have visited a number of offshore installations. [5] These problems will be compounded as development moves northwards up the Norwegian coast. Murmansk, which is just beyond the northernmost limit of the Norwegian sector, is the home base for 52 percent of the Soviet submarine fleet, according to estimates made by the International Institute for Strategic Studies. [6] Of apparent concern to the Soviets is the possibility that offshore platforms doubling secretly as subsea listening posts would allow much more accurate tracking by NATO of submarine movements.

Public National Revenues

National political interests in securing maximum public revenues from the North Sea are founded upon two principal bases: need and ideology. The first basis requires little explanation. It is a rare government that does not have difficulty balancing its budget. Additional revenues are a source of additional power both for the nation in general and for those in office in particular. The nature of the second, ideological basis is probably already obvious from the discussion that concluded Chapter 1. Offshore resources are commonly viewed as national resources. The government that does not act decisively to secure for public use, to the greatest extent possible, wealth accruing from the exploitation of these resources will find its political base weakened.

The need in Britain for additional public revenues has already been discussed. Judiciously used, North Sea wealth could transform the battered and declining British economy. However, the ideological basis for securing maximum public revenue has also proven important, as was demonstrated by the uproar surrounding the report by the Committee of Public Accounts. This controversy played a significant part in the fall of the Conservative government. Since 1974, Labour has been at considerable pains at least to make it appear that the government is firmly in control of offshore development and that offshore wealth is flowing into the exchequer to the maximum extent consistent with the continuing financial viability of offshore operations.

Until recently, Norway appeared to be considerably less in need of additional public revenues. Indeed, there was fear that increased government spending caused by higher oil revenues, combined with increased private spending, could cause major dislocations in Norwegian society. These concerns were articulated in a report issued by the Ministry of Finance in 1973.[7] Norwegians can no longer be secure in such predictions of sufficient if not excessive public oil revenues, particularly as the government takes on a greater and greater role in financing offshore and onshore oil developments through Statoil. Moreover, even when it appeared that oil revenues might be destructively high, there was virtually no feeling in the government that the oil companies should be allowed to absorb a greater percentage of North Sea wealth. It is widely felt that the oil belongs to the Norwegian people and that wealth accruing from its extraction, beyond a reasonable return to offshore operators, should enter the public purse. Norway also sends approximately 2.5 percent of its corporation tax to developing countries.

Private National Revenues

The three North Sea states with extensive offshore resources have shown a strong interest in not allowing the return to private corporations on work done in the offshore to exceed certain "reasonable" levels. However, within this constraint, these states have also shown a strong interest in ensuring that national business enterprises, as opposed to foreign enterprises, receive the maximum economic benefit from offshore development activities. The governments of the North Sea states cannot totally exclude foreign companies from their respective national shelves for several reasons. First, their domestic oil industries lack the technical and financial resources to carry on shelf development alone. Second, in the case of Britain and the Netherlands, excessive and blatant discrimination might prompt retaliation elsewhere against the British and Dutch oil multinationals. Third, EEC rules forbid government policies that discriminate against companies from other EEC countries. (EEC rules do, however, permit discrimination against non-EEC countries, such as the U.S. companies make up by far the largest portion of foreign companies operating in the North Sea.) Nevertheless, although foreign companies must be tolerated, a strong interest in maximizing the benefit to the domestic economy is evident in each North Sea state. This interest finds chief expression in the preference shown in licensing to domestic oil companies and in government efforts to assist domestic companies in capturing the greatest possible share of the offshore supply and service markets.

Before the onset of large-scale offshore production the British economy was among the weakest in Europe. National unemployment was nearing the 6 percent level,[8] extraordinary by British norms, and even higher levels in Scotland, where most offshore operations are based. Interest in ensuring that domestic industry benefits fully from offshore activities has, therefore, been particularly strong in Great Britain. This was an important issue taken up by Parliament in the hearing held before the Committee of Public Accounts in 1972-73 (referred to in the previous chapter). The Committee reported in its summary of the hearings:

> Your Committee had questioned the Department [of Energy] about the steps taken by the Department to ensure that British goods and services were readily available [to offshore operations]. We were surprised at the answer that the Department regarded the ability to supply British goods and services as a matter for the industry itself, but were subsequently assured that this did not mean that it had not been a major consideration to get the industry to respond to the opportunities.[9]

That the Committee was "surprised" in the muted language of the report reflects particularly severe questioning regarding the shortcomings of government policy in this area. The government representatives testifying before the Committee acknowledged that greater participation by domestic industry in offshore development was an important national objective. The representatives attempted to excuse past failings on grounds that higher priority interests—particularly obtaining a secure supply of oil—had taken precedence in the early development of the shelf. The Committee summary further stated:

> Your Committee noted that in the granting of licenses one of the criteria was the contribution the licensees had made or were planning to make to the British economy. We were assured that greater emphasis was put on this in each round of licensing. Successive governments had recognised and accepted that the primary objective of rapid exploration made it necessary to call heavily on the expertise and experience of other countries, mainly the U.S.A., and thus to give British industry less time to make itself ready to compete with established sources of specialist suppliers. Nevertheless, administrative pressure had been put on licensees to use British goods and services whenever possible. [10]

Such administrative pressure was formalized in 1975 in a Memorandum of Understanding and an associated Code of Practice that were agreed upon by the government and the United Kingdom Offshore Operators Committee (the trade association of companies operating on the U.K. shelf), the purpose of the Memorandum and Code was to ensure that British industry be given a "full and fair" opportunity to compete for offshore contracts. [11]

Norwegian authorities appear to be motivated by similar interests. The Ministry of Industry reported in 1974 that:

> The Ministry regarded it as a great advantage that Norwegian interests engaged in petroleum exploration and exploitation. This was therefore taken into consideration when production licenses were awarded. In the 1969 round of allocations the percentage of government participation required was reduced for those groups where Norwegian business held interests. When dealing with applications for the assignment of rights in production licenses, one of the conditions imposed was that in addition to government participation there should be participation by Norwegian enterprises. [12]

The use of Norwegian goods and services, where competitive, is an express condition of all production licenses. These requirements are supplemented by further government efforts on behalf of Norwegian industry, indicative of a strong interest in this area. The Ministry of Industry reported:

The Ministry has also found it necessary to adopt more active means in preparing the way for Norwegian suppliers. Particular attention has been given to the importance of public relations activities, on the part of the trade associations and the individual enterprises, to ensure that oil companies do not employ their traditional suppliers simply because they know too little about Norwegian supply facilities. To improve these activities, a liason agency has been organized . . . through which the Ministry is able to give these organizations information concerning activities on the continental shelf . . . to promote Norwegian goods and services. [13]

The government is reportedly seeking to raise the percentage of Norwegian goods and services used in the Norwegian offshore sector to 40 percent of the offshore market. [14]

Safety

The safety of offshore operations is a fourth area in which significant political interests are evident at the national level. A number of serious accidents, including several rig sinkings, marred the initial years of North Sea development, prompting early concern over safety matters.

The national governments' interest in imposing safety regulations should be seen as an interest in imposing standards on the industry higher than those the industry would impose on itself. Each of the North Sea governments has instituted safety regulations, of one sort or another, governing offshore activities. However, safety interests have been subordinated to interests in securing the benefits accruing from production. Offshore work remains hazardous in comparison with work in other industries. [15] It would be possible, through stiff regulations, to bring the risks of offshore work into parity with national norms but it would mean the cessation of most offshore work because of higher costs to the industry. The oil industry seeks to compensate offshore workers for the higher risks run by means of higher wages.

It should be noted that safety interests bear a relationship to interests discussed below, in the quality of the environment and the stability of the coastal social structure. A higher level of safety—at least in terms of structural fitness and the use of proper equipment and procedures—reduces the chance of an environmental disaster. Greater safety also reduces the premium that must be attached to the salaries of offshore workers and thus reduce the disruption off-

shore development causes traditional ways of life in the region supplying labor.

The chief risk in drafting safety regulations is that a particular
requirement will be unrealistic and, in achieving a marginal increase
in safety, will jeopardize the economic viability of entire operations.
Safety regulations governing North Sea operations have, therefore,
been drafted with reference to the regulations of other countries and
in close consultation with the companies affected. Both Great Britain
and Norway also rely on private certification authorities (for example, Lloyds Register of Shipping, American Bureau of Shipping,
and Det Norske Veritas) to inspect and certify the fitness of offshore
installations.

Social and Economic Stability

The social consequences of offshore development include the
impacts of rapid onshore development associated with offshore operations, in what typically are remote regions where traditional styles
of life prevail—for example, Norwegian coastal areas, Scottish coastal areas, and the Shetland Islands. This implies not only extensive
construction (of harbor facilities, platform fabrication yards, refineries, pipeline terminals) and large movements of the labor force,
but also an influx of wealth, which if not handled wisely can create
transient economic boom conditions. High offshore wages can bring
about the collapse of traditional occupations and industries, such as
fishing, because of labor movements. High offshore wages can also
bid up prices, land values, and housing costs. The destruction of
scenic areas and the lowering of the quality of life as a result of ill-
conceived industrial development on the coast and elsewhere must
also be counted among the possible adverse social consequences of
offshore development. All of these effects have been observed, to a
greater or lesser extent, in Scotland over the last several years.[16]
Although onshore development has not reached a similarly advanced
stage in Norway, there are fears that, because of the small size of
the Norwegian economy, the detrimental social effects of offshore
development may be felt nationwide.

Measures taken to minimize the adverse social consequences of
of offshore development generally involve land-use planning. Planning
powers can be used, for example, to prevent the destruction of es-
thetically pleasing areas, to ensure that the level of development
ultimately achieved is consonant with the needs and capacities of a
region, and to ensure a geographic pattern of development that has
the fewest adverse social effects. In some cases, planning implies
the sequestering of oil development in a single small area to localize

impacts, as is the policy in the Shetland Islands. In other cases, such a policy may imply the dispersion of development to ensure that development can be supported by the local environment and economy and to prevent regional inequalities, as is the current policy in Norway.

Environmental Quality

The most significant environmental consequence of offshore development is the risk thereby created of poisoning marine life and fouling beaches and estuarine areas as a result of an offshore accident such as a well blowout or a pipeline rupture. Where oil is loaded onto tankers from offshore installations there is a heightened risk of an oil spill. Pollution is also caused by routine discharges of water containing petroleum from offshore facilities.

Measures taken to minimize the risk of adverse environmental consequences generally fall into three categories: measures to prevent spills, such as the issuance of regulations regarding the design of installations and the use of safety equipment; measures to facilitate the combating of spills through the formulation of emergency procedures and the deployment of specialized equipment; and measures to facilitate the reconstruction of damaged areas, such as the provision of recourse through civil liability laws for damages suffered as a result of pollution.

Oil companies are, essentially, cost-minimizing and profit-maximizing organizations. Concerns about the safety and the social and environmental consequences of offshore development tend to work against the achievement of their basic objectives. But to a greater extent than safety considerations, concerns about the social and environmental consequences of development are external to the financial calculus that determines most corporate decisions. That is to say even in the absence of laws and regulations a rig or platform accident can be extraordinarily expensive in repair costs and production delays. However, the causing of destructive labor movements, the creation of coastal eyesores, and the fouling of beaches generally need not be factors in corporate decisions in the absence of government action to make them so.

In Great Britain, interests in minimizing the adverse social and environmental effects of offshore development have frequently been compromised to the overriding national interest in achieving oil self-sufficiency. A recent American observer of Scottish oil politics noted:

The factor always cited in decisions to go forward with oil facilities in Scotland is the urgent need, perceived by the central British government, to develop North Sea oil as quickly and as massively as possible—at least until the country reaches a position of self-sufficiency in oil. . . . It is a limiting policy for all subsequent decisions, large and small, and it creates great pressure to move ahead with everything from platform-construction site approval to planning permission for refineries. . . . It is clear that the marching orders come primarily from London.[17]

In Norway comparatively more government attention has been focused on the social and environmental consequences of offshore development. Norway's go-slow policy with respect to oil development has placed her in a strong bargaining position vis-a-vis the oil companies by creating stiff competition for access to the rich Norwegian shelf. Norway has consequently been able to impose stringent requirements, by world standards, and generally can count on finding at least one company (and usually more than one) willing to live with them. The extent to which Norway may be forced by economic reverses to compromise the stringent environmental and social policies to which it has thus far been able to adhere remains a question. It may be noted, however, that Norway's economic troubles are at worst, relative. Norway remains one of the most affluent nations in the world. Culturally, Norwegians, in their largely unspoiled country, attach considerable value to environmental quality and to the preservation of traditional ways of life. The sacrifice of any element central to present Norwegian environmental and social policies appears unlikely, although the easing of certain of the requirements most onerous to the companies with only a marginal beneficial effect for the environment or society—such as the prohibition of production on a platform engaged in drilling—may be necessary to ensure that development on the Norwegian shelf remains feasible financially.

LOCAL INTERESTS

Local authorities have tended to be less concerned than national authorities with the first three interests identified above (interests in securing benefits from offshore development) and more concerned with the last three (interests in minimizing associated harms). In conflicts over policy there is, generally, little question about which level of authority will prevail. However, interests dominant at the local level have on occasion been allowed to qualify interests dominant at the national level in substantive matters relating to offshore development.

Scotland provides the strongest examples of this phenomenon, despite the general dominance of national priorities noted in the previous section. The activities of the Scottish Nationalist Party are, in a sense, directed towards transforming Scottish interests from local to national interests; that is, an independent Scotland would be accorded jurisdiction over the resources off its coasts (which include nearly all of the United Kingdom's oil fields) under international law. To preclude this eventuality by preventing the Scottish Nationalists from gaining too large a political base, British government officials and Parliament, to some extent, have been compelled to compromise "national" interests in rapidly securing benefits from the offshore with "local" Scottish interests in minimizing harm. According to one British observer of oil development through the mid-1970s:

> On the whole, London and the oil companies were reasonably united in their belief that the British sector should be exploited fast, but Scottish politics popularized demands that oil found in their waters should be conserved and developed in an orderly fashion. Since oil companies cannot deliver votes capable of swinging an election, British politicians became increasingly cautious about the rate at which the North Sea should be exploited, and extremely sensitive to the environmental impact which the oil industry might have. . . . [18]

Probably the most dramatic example of the vesting of substantial powers over offshore development in a local authority is that of the Shetland Islands. In anticipation of the construction of a major pipeline terminal serving the prolific region east of the Shetlands, the local council, the Zetland County Council, obtained passage of a private act in Parliament entitled the Zetland County Council Act 1974, which conferred upon the Council powers to serve as harbor authority, to construct and operate industrial facilities and to license others to do so, to acquire land through powers of eminent domain, to regulate pipelines as far as three miles from shore, and to levy a small barrelage tax on oil flowing through the terminal. [19] Using these powers, the successor to the Zetland County Council, the Shetlands Islands Council, has restricted oil development to a harbor in the north of the islands and has obtained sufficient representation on the board responsible for the construction and operations of the terminal to give the Council veto power over all decisions other than those that relate to technical aspects of the terminal's operation and will have no significant impact on the islands.

Two observations should be made, however, to set the importance of local interests in North Sea law making in its proper perspective. The first is that these interests have been effective almost exclusively with respect to onshore development. The Shetland Islands Council, which is probably the most powerful and autonomous local authority in the North Sea context, has powers that extend only three miles offshore—the limit to the Council's authority over the routing of the pipelines. Most local authorities have far more limited powers. Yet even powers on the order of those exercised by the Shetland Islands Council are not sufficient to exert any direct influence over operations taking place on the shelf.

The second observation is that in virtually every case, in Norway as well as in Scotland, the powers that local authorities are entitled to wield are delegated by national authorities. While in the case of Scotland local interests have been able to exert political pressure on national authorities, the arena for the compromise of interests and the setting of priorities remains national.

REGIONAL INTERESTS

With respect to North Sea resources, interests dominant at the regional level of authority in Europe—principally in the EEC—also conflict with the most important national interests: achieving security of national oil supplies and maximizing national revenues. Fernand Spaak, Director General of Energy for the EEC, said in 1972:

> It is understandable that the States affected by these new discoveries should wish to obtain the maximum benefit from the development of these resources, but it seems to us that, in view of the contribution which North Sea oil and gas can make to one of our main common objectives—secure supplies—they should give maximum consideration to their value to the Community as a whole. [20]

Article 227 of the Treaty of Rome states the Treaty's applicability to the original member countries (Belgium, Germany, France, Italy, Luxembourg, and Holland). No mention is made of offshore areas in the context either of fishing or of shelf resources. A report published in 1970 by the EEC Commission in Brussels, entitled "The Application of the Rome Treaty to the Continental Shelf,"[21] noted that the Geneva Convention on the Continental Shelf (1958) established the sovereignty of littoral states over offshore resources. The report argued that the exercise of sovereign rights over offshore resources involved economic activities falling under the provisions of the Treaty of Rome and should be governed by that treaty. The Commission's opinion is not binding upon member states, however. A binding inter-

pretation of the Treaty of Rome can be given only by the Court of
Justice of the EEC in Luxembourg. [22]

Strict application of the Treaty of Rome to the continental shelf
would have several effects. Discretionary systems of licensing, which
allow discrimination in favor of national companies, would have to be
altered to conform to the EEC's rules on freedom of establishment. [23]
These rules prohitib discrimination against the commercial interests
of fellow EEC members. Laws restricting where offshore oil or gas
can be landed (such as provisions of the British Continental Shelf
Act 1964, which, in effect, required the sale of U.K. gas to the British Gas Council) would also have to be eliminated. In general, North
Sea oil and gas reserves and business opportunities relating to their
extraction would have to be made available to all members without
preference if the spirit of the Treaty of Rome were fully adhered to.

Clearly such measures would be in fundamental conflict with
the interests now motivating national policy in the North Sea states.
It is unlikely, for reasons discussed at length at the end of Chapter
1, that the EEC has the political influence to gain significant authority
over energy policies in general or North Sea resources in particular
at any time in the near future. Moreover, present trends in the major
North Sea states toward greater government participation in offshore
activities will have the additional effect of putting a greater portion
of North Sea resources off limits to the EEC even if the principle of
EEC control over the shelf is eventually upheld. State property enjoys a de facto privileged status in community affairs—an irregularity
the Commission, of necessity, has learned to live with. France, for
example, has been able to avoid antidiscrimination obligations under
the Treaty of Rome in its heavily controlled petroleum industry
through the use of state-owned oil companies.

Norway is not even a member of the EEC, so that Community
authority, even if fully applied to the North Sea, would cut across the
sea rather than encompass and integrate it. Norway's refusal to join
the EEC, as already noted, was founded to a significant extent on
fears that the EEC would seek control over shelf resources. Although
Norway's concerns about security of energy supplies and national
revenues should, it would seem, be well satisfied, the Norwegians
apparently wish to preserve their sovereign ability to conserve resources and pace development. In this way they hope to retain for as
long as possible their favored position in energy.

The outlook from the Community perspective for a greater
integration of North Sea policies and greater Community influence
over offshore activities is, thus, not bright. Yet if North Sea oil
would be able to make up only about 10 percent of the Community's
oil needs during the 1980s, as OECD now estimates, it is difficult
to see this as an issue of great material significance. To many, how-

ever, the issue seems important as a test of the political principles underlying the Community. Nevertheless, the weight of hard economic interests is on the side of national governments, making it seem all the more unlikely that the EEC will play a significant role in the shaping of future North Sea law.

In one area, there are undeniable advantages to greater political and legal integration of the regional level. This area is environmental management. Oil reserves are stationary; however, oil pollution created by offshore development is not. Pollution generated within the jurisdiction of one country can damage property within the jurisdiction of another. Interests at the regional level (now encompassing not the EEC but rather the North Sea littoral states) in creating a more integrated pollution control regime are significant. The North Sea littoral states have, in fact, taken joint action to define international liability for pollution damage and to provide a framework for the coordination of cleanup efforts (see in Chapter 4 "Substantive International Law Affecting North Sea Development.")

Finally, mention should be made of transnational relations operating at the regional level and beyond. The multinational oil companies operating in the North Sea naturally have a strong set of characteristic interests with regard to offshore development. They seek a legal environment in which the operations can be as free from both interference and uncertainty as possible. This implies a desire for a strong system of laws defining and protecting rights to offshore resources. Associated legal responsibilities—to pay taxes, to minimize onshore impacts, to permit government participation—are looked on as burdensome, if inevitable. Yet legal certainty appears to have a high intrinsic value to the corporate manager. Stiff regulations, defining, for example, minimum structural requirements for rigs, are often preferable to a vaguely defined legal liability for the consequences of rig failure. Comparatively high tax rates in whose stability companies may have confidence are often preferable to lower tax rates and the possibility of upward change. The trade journal Offshore reflected these interests in an editorial in 1977.

> Government, particularly that of Britain and Norway, needs to move now to assure the industry that the operating conditions won't be altered drastically again. . . . What's needed most of all is the assurance that private industry can operate in a stable economic environment. [24]

Without question, the oil companies have had a considerable influence over the evolution of North Sea law. They were consulted extensively by each of the North Sea states as the original laws and regulations governing the continental shelf were being formulated.

Particularly during the early, exploratory phase of development, the interests of the companies and the governments followed nearly parallel lines. Both had the desire to determine quickly the dimensions of offshore oil and gas resources and to initiate production. The involvement of the companies in the drafting of laws and regulations was an important factor underlying the strong similarities that exist among the legal arrangements governing the British, Norwegian, and Dutch shelves. (Another important factor was direct consultations between or among governments.) More recently, however, the interests of the governments and oil companies have become increasingly divergent, particularly on the issue of private versus public profit from offshore resources. This is due in part to the unexpected abundance of North Sea reserves and in part to changes taking place worldwide in the relationship between governments and oil companies. Although the precise involvement of the oil companies in the legislative or regulatory process has not been publicly documented, it would appear that recent changes in the legal arrangements enforced by the major North Sea states represent, at least in part, an effort to move in the direction of continental shelf laws that are oriented less toward industry.

NOTES

1. Jens Evensen, Report on Oil Policy Problems Viewed against the Background of Oil Legislation and Concession Policies of Other Nations, prepared for the Norwegian Ministry of Industry, Oslo, 1971.

2. The three-tiered model of the world political structure suggested by George Modelski is similar to the structure of categories used here. See George Modelski, Principles of World Politics (New York: The Free Press, 1972), esp. pp. 267-88.

3. United Nations, World Energy Supplies 1950-1974, Statistical Papers, Series J, No. 19 (New York: United Nations, 1976).

4. Ibid.

5. Neil Ullman, "NATO's New Nemesis, Europe Fears Growing Soviet Submarine Fleet Poses Future Threat to North Sea Oil Supply," Wall Street Journal, June 11, 1975, p. 32.

6. Ibid.

7. Norway, Ministry of Finance, Petroleum Industry in Norwegian Society, Parliamentary Report No. 25 (1973-74). Not everyone in Norway saw oil wealth as a source of menace. The conservative Oslo daily, Aftenposten, remarked in a review of the report:

With all due respect for the new problems and challenges facing us, it is hardly reasonable to regard the fact that we are about to become the only oil exporting nation in Western Europe as the source of great national catastrophies. Of course, it must be admitted that we have undeniable national traditions to live up to when it comes to finding gloomy prospects in an otherwise promising development.

Quoted in Peter H. Krosby, "Oil and the Environment: Norway's Enlightened Policy," Scandinavian Review, 4 (1976), p. 41.

8. OECD, OECD Economic Outlook, December 1976, p. 17.

9. United Kingdom, Parliament, Commons, First Report of the Committee of Public Accounts: North Sea Oil and Gas, (London: Her Majesty's Stationery Office, 1973), p. xxxi.

10. Ibid., p. xxxx.

11. United Kingdom, Department of Energy, Development of the Oil and Gas Resources of the United Kingdom 1976 (London: Her Majesty's Stationery Office, 1976), p. 11.

12. Norway, Ministry of Industry, Operations on the Norwegian Continental Shelf, Report No. 30 to the Norwegian Storting, (1973-74).

13. Ibid., pp. 54-55.

14. Offshore, February 1977, p. 70.

15. Diving is the most hazardous type of offshore work. The annual death rate on the United Kingdom continental shelf in 1975 was six for each thousand workers. The death rate among nondivers was one death for each thousand workers. United Kingdom, Department of Energy, Development 1976, op. cit., p. 14.

16. Pamela L. Baldwin and Malcolm F. Baldwin, Onshore Planning for Offshore Oil: Lessons from Scotland (Washington: The Conservation Foundation, 1975), pp. 19-30.

17. Ibid., p. 169.

18. Martin Saeter and Ian Smart, eds., The Political Implications of North Sea Oil and Gas (Oslo: Universitetsforlaget, 1975), p. 100.

19. Baldwin and Baldwin, op. cit., p. 112.

20. Clive Callow, Power from the Sea (London: Victor Gollane, 1973), p. 96.

21. Commission of the European Communities, "The Application of the Rome Treaty to the Continental Shelf" (Brussels: Commission of the European Communities, 1970).

22. United Nations, Treaty Series, Treaties and International Agreements Registered or Filed and Reported with the Secretariat

of the United Nations, vol. 294, "Traite Instituant la Communaute Economique Europeene," (Treaty of Rome, 1957), Art. 177, pp. 109-110.

(Note that an English translation of the Treaty of Rome, prepared in 1967 by Her Majesty's Stationery Office, is reprinted in Alan Campbell, Common Market Law (London: Longman's, Green, & Company, 1969).

23. Ibid., Art. 52, p. 54.

24. Offshore, February 1977, p. 41.

4

INTERNATIONAL LAW: THE
JURISDICTIONAL FRAMEWORK

The origins of international law pertaining to the continental shelf are comparatively recent. Four events in particular, may be cited as responsible for the shaping of the doctrine of the continental shelf recognized by most nations today. These events are the Truman Proclamation on the Continental Shelf of 1945; the first United Nations Conference on the Law of the Sea, 1958; the North Sea Continental Shelf Cases heard before the International Court of Justice in 1969; and the continuing Third United Nations Conference on the Law of the Sea. Obviously, the first three events noted were the most important in defining the international legal structure for the North Sea regime. However, the proceedings of the Third Law of the Sea Conference are suggestive of future trends in continental shelf law that may influence the development of offshore regimes around the world, including the North Sea regime.

THE LEGAL BACKGROUND TO THE TRUMAN PROCLAMATION

Perhaps the longest and most venerable tradition in the law of the sea is the doctrine of the freedom of the high seas. First articulated by the Dutch lawyer Grotius in the early seventeenth century, this doctrine held that the seas were not subject to the jurisdiction of any nation and were open for the use and benefit of all. As for the seaward limit of national jurisdiction, Grotius argued that "the empire of the sea is . . . belonging to a territory in so far as those who sail in that part of the sea can be compelled from there as if they were on land."[1] In those days, the effective limit of control over the sea exercised from land was the range of a cannon shot from shore, or about three miles. Despite improvements in weaponry, the extent of the territorial sea—that is, that part of the sea over which a nation enjoys territorial sovereignty—has generally been accepted by the major maritime powers as three miles from the low-water mark. A number of states have, however, claimed broader territorial seas extending out as far as twelve miles. A very few have claimed territorial seas extending beyond twelve miles. All of the North Sea littoral states claim three-mile territorial seas, except Norway, which claims a four-mile territorial sea. [2]

Derogations of the freedom of the high seas have traditionally been opposed by the major maritime powers because of restrictions that might result on the free flow of maritime commerce and on the movement of naval forces. However, limited derogations have been tolerated in special circumstances (for example, the British Colonial Act of 1811 asserted exclusive British dominion over Ceylonese pearl banks well beyond the three-mile limit). [3] The Treaty of the Gulf of Paria, signed in 1942 by Great Britain and Venezuela, is generally regarded as the first harbinger of modern doctrines in continental shelf law. [4] In that treaty, each signer agreed not to dispute any possible future claims of sovereignty by the other signer to the seabed or subsoil in the Gulf of Paria, which separates Venezuela and Trinidad (then a British colony). Such claims of sovereignty, by either nation, could not extend beyond a line, roughly following the median line, established by the treaty. Two aspects of this treaty are particularly important in light of future developments. First, the intention of the treaty was clearly to lay a basis for the amicable future apportionment of offshore petroleum reserves between the parties. [5] Second, the Treaty expressly denied that its provisions, which assumed at least the eventual possibility of national claims to the seabed, affected in any way the high seas character of the superjacent water[6]—a convenient distinction for a maritime power to draw.

Even before World War II, pressures emanating from the oil industry had begun building within the United States to extend American jurisdiction seaward to provide the stable legal climate necessary for the development of offshore petroleum. [7] This was in anticipation of technological advances that would make possible the exploitation of offshore areas beyond the three-mile territorial limit. Franklin Roosevelt died before he could sign a proclamation prepared jointly by the Department of Interior and the Department of State. On September 28, 1945, the document was issued by President Truman as the Truman Proclamation on the Continental Shelf. [8]

The proclamation asserted that the natural resources of the seabed and subsoil of the continental shelf contiguous to the United States would hence be regarded as "appertaining to the United States, and subject to its jurisdiction and control." The proclamation also stated: "The character as high seas of the waters above the continental shelf and the right to their free and unimpeded navigation is in no way thus affected." The proclamation did not define what was meant by the "continental shelf" or what its outer limits were. The White House press release that accompanied the proclamation noted, however: "Generally submerged land which is contiguous to the continent and which is covered by no more than 100 fathoms (600 feet) of water is considered as the continental shelf."[9]

The Proclamation cited no international legal precedent but argued that the action was reasonable on the following grounds:

1. There is a growing world need for new sources of petroleum.

2. Technological progress has made possible the exploitation of the U.S. continental shelf beyond the present limits of national jurisdiction.

3. Recognized jurisdiction is required in the interest of resource conservation and prudent utilization.

4. The effectiveness of measures to utilize or conserve these resources would be contingent upon cooperation and protection from shore.

5. The continental shelf may be regarded as an extension of the land-mass of the coastal state and thus naturally appurtenant to it.

6. Resources frequently form a seaward extension of a pool or deposit lying within the coastal nation's territory.

7. A coastal nation has a national security interest in keeping close watch over activities off its shores of the sort necessary for seabed resource exploitation.

Apparently the proclamation was thoroughly researched, for arguments heard in the ensuing three decades regarding extensions of coastal state jurisdiction over the continental shelf have tended to follow one or another of the lines suggested above. For coastal nations, however, the most persuasive argument of all remains the possibility of acquiring valuable offshore resources, with the economic and political benefits that this implies.

COASTAL STATE PRACTICE FROM 1945 to 1958 AND THE FIRST U.N. CONFERENCE ON THE LAW OF THE SEA

The Truman Proclamation met with no protests from foreign governments and inspired similar action on the part of a number of states. Mexico responded within a month to claim jurisdiction over the resources of its continental shelf out to its geographic limits.[10] Other nations adopted other formulas to define the limits of this shelf jurisdiction. Ecuador claimed sovereignty over its continental shelf to a depth of 200 meters (650 feet). [11] Israel claimed sovereignty over its shelf to such depth as admitted of the exploitation of seabed resources. [12] Many other nations chose, like the United States, not to define precisely the limits to the offshore areas over which they were claiming jurisdiction. To the chagrin of American authorities, certain nations did not rest content with claiming jurisdiction over their continental shelves but extended claims to the superjacent waters as well. Several South American nations claimed sovereignty to fishing resources out to 200 miles while El Salvador claimed a 200 mile territorial sea. [13] In extending their jurisdiction, these nations chose not to be bound by the exact provisions of the Truman Proclamation, which, from a South American perspective, seemed a self-interested document tailor-made to fit the United States' particular needs. Their actions were formally protested by the United States. Nevertheless, their claims to the continental shelf contributed, like the claims of other nations, to a growing international consensus that the coastal nation was entitled to some degree of seaward jurisdiction over, at least, the continental shelf. (Their further claims to resources of the superjacent waters have taken until the 1970s to receive international recognition.) In all, between 1945 and 1958, at least 26 nations officially announced claims to offshore regions that included the continental shelf. [14]

State practice thus seemed strongly to support an emerging international custom of broader states' rights to the continental shelf. On finer issues (for example, the definition of the continental shelf) there was little consensus, however. Figure 4.1 is an idealized profile of the seabed as it slopes away from the continent towards the deep ocean floor. The break between what geologists refer to as the continental shelf and the continental slope occurs worldwide at an average depth of 130 meters and is believed to correspond to the lowest level to which ocean waters have fallen in recent geologic history—that is, the sea level during the Pleistocene ice age. [15] The continental rise, which occurs at the base of the continental slope, consists of sediments deposited there by turbidity. The entire slope from the land to the beginnings of the deep ocean floor is referred to as the continental margin. Sediments that may be petroleum bearing occur throughout the continental margin. From a political and economic standpoint, perhaps the sharpest distinction between the continental margin and the deep ocean floor is that the floor generally contains no such sediments.

This idealized view of the geomorphology of the shelf does not suggest, however, the variety characterizing the real world. In some regions (for example, the western coast of South America) the shelf drops off to great depths almost immediately. In other regions (for

FIGURE 4.1 Report of the North Sea Continental Shelf Cases

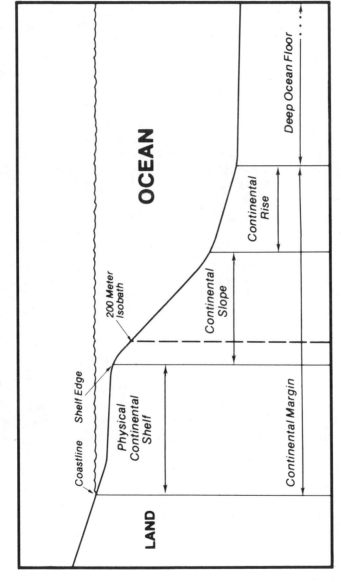

Source: Compiled by the author.

example, the eastern coast of South America and the Bering Sea) the shelf extends for hundreds of miles. In the North Sea both situations exist. The seabed slopes gradually away from Scotland, reaching a depth of 200 meters at a distance of 200 to 300 miles from shore. It then drops off sharply into a deep trench and rises again, reaching a depth of 200 meters as close as four or five miles from the Norwegian coast.

As the law of the continental shelf was emerging during the 1950s much discussion was devoted to the formula to be used in defining the outer limit of continental shelf jurisdiction. It became evident that some, more or less arbitrary, legal definition would be needed to supplement geologic definitions of the shelf. Even in shelves with classic contours, structural shifts—for example, from shelf to slope or from the continental margin to the deep ocean floor—take place gradually over a distance of miles, defining no clear line suitable for a legal boundary.

In 1949, the United Nations General Assembly instructed the International Law Commission to lay the groundwork for an international conference on the law of the sea. A draft treaty on the continental shelf released by the commission in 1951 defined coastal state jurisdiction as extending to all adjacent submarine areas that admitted of exploitation. [16] This flexible definition answered concerns, voiced in the United States and elsewhere, that advancing technology would soon render obsolete any definition of the shelf based on depth. However, there were concerns with the notion of a limit defined by exploitability—namely, that it was no limit at all. Several nations expressed fears that advancing technology would simply push the limits of the coastal states' jurisdictions outward until they met in the middle of the ocean.

The International Law Commission released a second draft of the treaty in 1953. In this draft the outer limit of continental shelf jurisdiction was defined as the 200 meter isobath. [17] Despite the fact that this closely resembled the United States' original though unofficial shelf definition of 100 fathoms, the United States expressed dissatisfaction with the new draft and in 1956 was joined by 19 other American states in adopting a resolution recommending that the exploitability criterion be joined to the 200 meter depth criterion. [18] The International Law Commission was persuaded by this resolution and released in 1956 a third draft of the treaty, which included this compromise. [19]

The United Nations convened its first Conference on the Law of the Sea in 1958. In attendance were delegations from 82 nations. Altogether 55 delegations participated actively in the committee that dealt with matters relating to the continental shelf. A number of delegations expressed the opinion that some degree of coastal state jurisdiction over the continental shelf was already a matter of customary international law. There was widespread feeling that, in any case, such jurisdiction would be appropriate.[20] After considerable debate over the legal delimitation of the shelf, the committee decided to adopt language virtually identical to that of the third draft treaty prepared by the International Law Commission (the treaty containing the dual criteria of 200 meters' depth and exploitability). An effort to excise the exploitability criterion through an amendment was defeated in one of the final acts of the conference by a vote of 48 to 20.[21] The Convention on the Continental Shelf[22] was signed on April 29, 1958 by 46 nations.

Article 1 of the Convention stated:

> For the purposes of these Articles, the term 'continental shelf' is used as referring (a) to the seabed and subsoil of the submarine areas adjacent to the coast but outside the area of the territorial sea, to a depth of 200 meters or, beyond that limit, to where the depth of the superjacent waters admits of the exploitation of the natural resources of said areas; (b) to the seabed and subsoil of similar submarine areas adjacent to the coasts of islands.

Article 2, section 1 specified that: "The coastal state exercises over the continental shelf sovereign rights for the purpose of exploring it and exploiting its natural resources." Thus only limited sovereign rights were granted. Articles 3, 4, and 5 of the convention discussed the duties of the coastal states not to interfere with other uses of the shelf (such as the laying of cables or pipelines) and of the superjacent waters (such as shipping and fishing). Article 6 established the means to be used in delimiting continental shelf areas adjacent to several states. Section 1 prescribed:

> Where the same continental shelf is adjacent to the territories of two or more States whose coasts are opposite each other, the boundary of the continental shelf appertaining to such States shall be determined by agreement between them. In the absence of agreement, and unless another boundary line is justified by special circumstances, the boundary is the median line, every point of which is equidistant from the nearest points of the baseline from which the breadth of the territorial sea is measured.

Section 2 prescribed exactly the same procedure for shelf areas shared by adjacent coastlines. As we shall see in discussing the 1969 ruling of World Court, however, the legal distinction between adjacent and opposite coasts is not entirely trivial.

COASTAL STATE PRACTICE FROM 1958 TO 1969 AND THE NORTH SEA CONTINENTAL SHELF CASES

The Geneva Convention on the Continental Shelf afforded coastal states the opportunity of extending their jurisdiction to potentially valuable offshore lands with a far greater appearance of legitimacy than had been possible before.[23] By 1969, "some three-score nations (had) given recognition to the principles of that Convention, 36 by ratifying it, the others by adopting major provisions of it in domestic legislation or in regional agreements."[24]

As we saw in Chapter 3, recognition of the principles of the Convention by the North Sea states came quickly. Denmark and the United Kingdom, both of which stood to gain wide shelves under either the 200 meter or exploitability criterion, ratified the Convention promptly. The U.K. ratification in 1964 was the twenty-second and thus the one to bring the Convention into force.

The Netherlands ratified the Convention in 1966 after the enactment of its first law governing mineral extraction activities on the continental shelf (The Mining Law for the Continental Shelf, September 23, 1965) but before the issuance, in 1967, of the royal decrees that set up and implemented the first round of Dutch offshore licensing.

Norway did not sign or ratify the convention but instead promulgated a royal decree (May 31, 1963) that asserted sovereign jurisdiction over the resources of the adjacent seabed and subsoil "to such extent as the depth of the sea permits the utilization of natural deposits, irrespective of any other territorial limits at sea, but not beyond the median line in relation to other states."[25] Omitted from the decree was, of course, the 200 meters depth criterion, since its application would have limited Norway to a narrow and barren shelf. In 1971, after its rights to the North Sea shelf out to the median line had been well established, Norway became a party to the Continental Shelf Convention.

Germany, though a signer of the Convention, did not ratify it. It declared its jurisdiction over adjacent shelf resources in a proclamation of the federal government of January 20, 1964.[26] The fact that it had not ratified the Convention was to prove important in its arguments before the International Court of Justice. Germany and Belgium remain the only North Sea nations to fail to ratify the Convention.

In the years before 1969, the delimitation of the North Sea shelf between the littoral states claiming jurisdiction was accomplished through the application of the equidistance line principle prescribed in Article 6, in a series of bilateral treaties. Three of these treaties are of particular importance.

The treaty delimiting the Norwegian and British shelves was signed in 1965. [27] Strict application of the principles contained in Article 1 of the Convention would have denied Norway a significant share of the North Sea shelf. Even the exploitability criterion was of little help because the exploitability of minerals at the lowest depths of the Norwegian Trench could not be demonstrated. On the other hand, Great Britain did not even have to demonstrate exploitability to gain most of the shelf—the 200 meter isobath was 200 to 300 miles off British shores. Yet Norway was a nonsignatory to the Convention and had not recognized its principles. Its royal decree of May 31, 1963 stated the government's view that it was entitled to jurisdiction over shelf resources as far out as the median line. Whatever the arena for dispute settlement in which the issue was eventually resolved, Great Britain might have succeeded in its claim if it had decided to contest the Norwegian position. Yet, at best, that would have meant a delay of several years, during which the ambiguous legal status of much of the shelf would have impaired offshore development. British authorities decided not to contest Norway's claim; the advantages of a prompt start for shelf development and continued good relations with Norway were judged to outweigh the advantages of a (possibly) greater area of British shelf.

The other, pre-1969 bilateral treaties of particular interest are the treaties delimiting portions of the shelf between Germany and the Netherlands (signed in 1964)[28] and between Germany and Denmark (signed in 1965). [29] These treaties defined partial boundaries for the German shelf extending less than 50 miles from shore. Further, tripartite negotiations held in 1966 to complete the division of the shelf were unsuccessful. In 1967, the three nations, in a protocol, agreed to submit the matter to the International Court of Justice for binding adjudication. The decision to resort to the Court reflected motivations similar to those that prompted Britain to seek a quick agreement with Norway. The gain or loss of a few thousand square miles of shelf was deemed less important by Denmark and the Netherlands than avoiding a lengthy period of legal uncertainty. The parties requested that the Court decide:

> What principles and rules of international law are applicable to the delimitation as between the Parties of the areas of the Continental Shelf of the North Sea which appertain to each of them beyond the partial boundary determined by the above-mentioned Convention. . . . [30]

The Netherlands and Denmark favored a line drawn by the equidistance method. Germany opposed the use of this method. Figure 4.2 illustrates the claims and their implications. Lines AB and CD are the lines established in the treaties mentioned above. Lines BE and DE represent the results of completing the delimitation of the German shelf using the equidistance method. Because the general shape of German coast is concave, while the general shapes of the Dutch and Danish coasts are convex, use of the equidistance method, because of geometric peculiarities, results in a small German sector and large Danish and Dutch sectors, even though the three nations have roughly the same length of North Sea coastline. Germany maintained that, as a nonparty to the Continental Shelf Convention, it was not bound to use the equidistance method and, moreover, that that method was not a principle of customary international law. Germany argued that, in this case, the shelf should be divided by more equitable means. Lines BF and DF represent roughly the resolution Germany sought.

A closely divided Court held, in a decision handed down in 1969, that Germany was not bound to abide by the equidistance principle. The Court maintained that the equidistance principle had considerable validity as a means for delimiting shelf areas between or among nations opposite one another because its application resulted in an equal split and had frequently been relied on. However, as a means for delimiting shelf areas between nations with adjacent coastlines, the equidistance principle could not be construed as a principle of customary international law because its application in areas with certain coastal contours would lead to highly inequitable results.

The Court articulated the basis for coastal state jurisdiction over the shelf as follows:

> [t]he rights of the coastal State in respect to the area of
> the continental shelf which constitutes the natural pro-
> longation of its land territory into and under the sea exist
> ipso facto and ab initio, by virtue of its sovereignty over
> the land, and as an extension of it in an exercise of sover-
> eign rights for the purpose of exploring the seabed and
> exploiting its natural resources. [31]

Beginning from this premise, the Court prescribed in its judgment that the parties negotiate continental shelf boundaries on the basis of the following principles and rules of international law:

> 1) delimitation is to be effected by agreement in accord-
> ance with equitable principles, taking account of all the
> relevant circumstances, in such a way as to leave as
> much as possible to each Party all those parts of the con-

FIGURE 4.2

Map Accompanying International Court of Justice Report

tinental shelf that constitute a natural prolongation of its
land territory into and under the sea, without encroach-
ments on the natural prolongation of the land territory of
the other;

2) if, in the application of the preceding subparagraph,
the delimitation leaves to the Parties areas that overlap,
these are to be divided between them in agreed propor-
tions or, failing agreement, equally, unless they decide
on a regime of joint jurisdiction, use, or exploitation for
the zones of overlap or any part of them. [32]

The Court further ruled that, in particular, the following factors would be taken into account in shelf delimitation negotiations:

1) the general configuration of the coasts of the parties,
as well as the presence of any special or unusual features;

2) so far as known or readily ascertainable, the physical
and geological structure and natural resources of the continental shelf areas involved;

3) the element of a reasonable degree of proportionality
which a delimitation carried out in accordance with equitable principles ought to bring about between the extent
of the continental shelf areas appertaining to the coastal
State and the length of its coast measured in the general
direction of the coastline, account being taken for this
purpose of the effects, actual or prospective, of any
other continental shelf delimitations between adjacent
states in the same region. [33]

The decision of the court thus generally favored Germany.

The Netherlands, Denmark, and Germany returned to the negotiation table and reached an agreement on complete continental shelf
boundaries in 1971. [34] The agreed boundaries were roughly those
Germany had been seeking throughout the hearing in the case. The
German-Danish border was adjusted to allow the recently discovered
Dan oil fields to remain in the Danish sector (see Figure 2.4), giving
the German sector its characteristic duckhead shape.

THE THIRD U. N. CONFERENCE ON THE LAW OF THE SEA AND
FUTURE CONTINENTAL SHELF LAW

In essence, the doctrine of the continental shelf, as it has
evolved since 1945, is that the coastal nations are the legal entities
to be invested with lawmaking authority over continental shelf resources. We would, therefore, expect the legal arrangements governing shelf resources to reflect strongly national interests. This, of
course, has proven to be the case.

The International Court, in its judgment, did raise the possibility of a regime of joint jurisdiction over portions of the area under
dispute. However, this suggestion was a suggestion only and was not
acted upon. As we have seen, there seems little chance, from a political perspective, that North Sea shelf resources will be governed
by a more integrated regime than presently is in effect. Not only is
the legal basis for a more integrated regime weak, but such a regime
would run sharply counter to the objectives perceived as most important by national decision makers in the North Sea states. While
the international legal framework for North Sea continental shelf law
is now well established, some insight into present trends in international law concerning the continental shelf may be gained by examining
the proceedings of the Third United Nations Conference on the Law of
the Sea. (A second conference held in 1960 produced no agreement.)
Such insight is useful in anticipating the development of law in other
offshore regions. Not surprisingly, the Third Conference on the Law
of the Sea has tended to affirm the international legal resolution arrived at in the North Sea.

The United Nations convened a first, preliminary session of
the Third Conference in New York in late 1973 to settle procedural
matters for the second, substantive session. This session was held
in Caracas, Venezuela during the summer of 1974. However, with
149 nations in attendance and over 90 issues on the Conference agenda,
procedural disagreements were not finally settled until midway through
the Caracas session. It was not until the third session, held in the
spring of 1975 in Geneva, that the conference was able to produce a
Single Negotiating Text as a basis for further negotiations. [35] This
text was revised several times in the course of subsequent conference
sessions. The latest text is the Informal Composite Negotiating Text,
which is the outcome of negotiations occurring at the sixth session,
held in New York in 1977. [36] This text was selectively revised at the
seventh session, held in Geneva in the spring of 1978. [37]

The negotiating texts have been prepared at the direction of the
conference president by the chairmen of the three conference committees. The President was careful to note that these "texts have been
prepared entirely on their (the chairmen's) responsibility and will

have no other status than that of serving as a basis for continued negotiation without prejudice to the right of any delegation to move any amendments or to introduce any new proposals."[38] However, the texts represent the chairmen's best efforts to capture such consensus as exists on various issues. The law of the continental shelf is not among the most contentious areas being negotiated at the Law of the Sea Conference (this distinction has been earned by the issues of deep seabed mining, scientific research, and marine pollution). In fact the last several sessions have resulted in only marginal alterations to the articles in the negotiating text concerning continental shelf law. Even if the Law of the Sea negotiations were ultimately to fail to arrive at a new Law of the Sea Convention because of irresoluable conflict over more controversial areas, the provisions of articles on the continental shelf could fairly be said to come close to reflecting a world consensus. Complete agreement has not been reached on these articles but the areas of controversy that remain are peripheral.

Article 76 of the Informal Composite Negotiating Text defines the continental shelf of a coastal state as the seabed and subsoil extending to the outer edges of the continental margin or to 200 nautical miles, whichever is farther. Article 77 confers upon the coastal state the exclusive right to explore for and exploit all natural resources of the continental shelf. Articles 80 and 81 explicitly confer on the coastal state the right to regulate all drilling on the shelf and the construction of all offshore installations. None of these provisions was officially revised or amended at the seventh session.

The obvious implication of these provisions is that the development of offshore petroleum resources falls under the jurisdiction of the coastal state. One finds in Article 82 the only accommodation in the area of the continental shelf to the internationalist spirit with which the Third Conference was originally conceived.[39] The article provides that a percentage of the proceeds accruing from the exploitation of mineral resources of the continental margin beyond 200 miles will be remitted to developing countries. This article was the subject of negotiations at the most recent session and a consensus on its provisions has not yet been arrived at.

The delimitation of areas of the continental shelf between adjacent or opposite coasts would be effected, according to Article 83, by agreement between the pertinent states in accordance with "equitable principles, employing, where appropriate, the median or equidistance line, and taking into account all the relevant circumstances." Deadlocked negotiations would be settled through mandatory dispute-settlement mechanisms provided for elsewhere in the text.

A section of the current negotiating text deals with the special problems of semienclosed seas. Article 123 calls upon coastal states bordering on semienclosed seas to coordinate their efforts, through appropriate regional organizations, in three areas of activity: the management and harvesting of living resources; the preservation of the marine environment; and the conduct of scientific research. The exploration for or exploitation of the mineral resources of a semi-enclosed sea are not mentioned in the article as pertinent areas for international or regional control.

The Law of the Sea negotiations have thus tended to confirm the North Sea experience. A consensus of nations would place the resources of the continental shelf within the exclusive jurisdiction of the coastal state. The delimitation of shelf areas between or among adjacent or opposite states, as provided for in the negotiating text, conforms to procedures used in the North Sea, including those set forth by the International Court of Justice in the North Sea Continental Shelf Cases of 1969. The three areas mentioned in Article 123 of Composite Texts as appropriate subjects of international coordination in semienclosed seas are all subjects of international agreements, either in force or awaiting ratification, among the North Sea states. There is, thus, strong evidence that law governing offshore development in other regions will be based on an international legal framework similar to that used in the North Sea.

SUBSTANTIVE INTERNATIONAL LAW AFFECTING NORTH SEA DEVELOPMENT

In general, international law prescribes little in connection with petroleum development in the North Sea aside from the establishment and delimitation of zones of national jurisdiction, discussed above. The significant exception to this generalization concerns pollution and pollution damage.

Until recently, international law governing pollution from offshore installations in the North Sea remained rudimentary. This was in sharp contrast to international law governing oil pollution from ships and tankers. Such pollution was the subject of a sophisticated convention which entered into force in 1958. [40]

Yet the need for international law governing pollution from offshore petroleum operations is obvious. While mineral resources are sedentary and can be expected to remain within the territorially defined jurisdiction of a single state, oil pollution is not sedentary and can drift across international boundaries, causing damage to foreign beaches and fishing areas.

A convention concluded in 1969, entitled the Bonn Agreement for Cooperation in Dealing with Pollution of the North Sea by Oil, [41] took a limited first step toward achieving regional cooperation on pollution matters. The agreement was signed and ratified by Belgium,

Denmark, France, Germany, the Netherlands, Norway, Sweden, and the United Kingdom. The agreement provides that parties will exchange information on competent authorities in each nation to receive reports of pollution, as well as on new methods for combating pollution. The North Sea is divided into eight zones of responsibility, six assigned to individual nations and two assigned jointly. Parties undertake to request that masters of ships and pilots of aircraft registered in their countries report accidents likely to result in pollution, and the presence of slicks likely to harm the coasts or other areas of interest to one or more parties. Each zonal authority is responsible for assessing the extent of pollution, as well as the direction and speed of drift; and it must immediately inform other parties of its findings and what actions it is taking. What the conventions do not require of parties is that they take any steps to deal with pollution. If a nation does, however, choose to deal with a pollution problem, it may call upon the assistance of other parties, who must use their "best endeavors" to provide such assistance.

A far more substantial step was taken with negotiation of a convention establishing civil liability for international oil pollution damage in the North Sea. Entitled the Convention on Compensation for Oil Pollution Damage from Offshore Operations, it was negotiated in London in 1976 and opened for signature in May 1977. Thus far, the Netherlands, Norway, Sweden, and the United Kingdom have signed it. In order for the convention to come into force, it must be ratified by four countries, and implementing legislation must be drafted by each of the parties.

The Convention provides for the strict liability of offshore operators for damage caused by oil released in the course of offshore operations. Parties to the Convention may set maximum levels of liability but the maximum may be no less than $35 million, rising to $45 million in May of 1982. Claims for damages may be brought in the courts either of the state in which the pollution originated or of the state in which the damages occurred. Offshore operators must be required to take out insurance necessary to meet their potential liabilities.

The Convention is the first of its kind anywhere in the world and is characteristic of the advanced legal arrangements now governing most aspects of North Sea operations. However, by far the bulk of these arrangements are national in origin and scope. This law is examined in Chapter 5.

NOTES

1. Hugo Grotius, De Jure Belli ac Pacis, 1625, quoted in L. John Colombos, The International Law of the Sea (London: Longmans, Green, 1962), p. 92.

2. Lewis M. Alexander, Offshore Geography of Northwestern Europe (Chicago: Rand McNally, 1963), pp. 64-65.

3. Zdenck Slouka, International Custom and the Continental Shelf (The Hague: Martinus Nyhoff, 1968), p. 72.

4. Great Britain, Foreign Office, British Treaty Series, No. 10 (1942), Cmd. 6400, "Great Britain and Venezuela: Treaty of the Gulf of Paria," February 26, 1942.

5. Slouka, op. cit., p. 72.

6. Treaty of the Gulf of Paria, op. cit., Article 6.

7. Lawrence Juda, Ocean Space Rights: Developing U.S. Policy (New York: Praeger, 1975), p. 13.

8. United States, Department of State, Bulletin, XIII, No. 327 (September 30, 1945), "The Truman Proclamation on the Continental Shelf," September 28, 1945, p. 485.

9. United States, Department of State, Bulletin, XIII, No. 327 (September 30, 1945), p. 484.

10. Slouka, op. cit., p. 44.

11. Ibid.

12. Ibid.

13. S. Houston Lay, R. Churchill, and Myron Nordquist, eds., New Directions in the Law of the Sea, 4 vols. (Dobbs Ferry, New York: Oceana, 1973), vol. 2, p. 843.

14. Slouka, op. cit., p. 44.

15. Grant M. Cross, Oceanography: A View of the Earth (State University of New York: Prentice Hall, 1972), p. 43.

16. International Law Commission, Yearbook (1951), vol. 2, p. 141.

17. International Law Commission, Yearbook (1953), vol. 2, p. 212.

18. "Resolution of Ciudad Trujillo (Inter-American Specialized Conference on 'Conservation of Natural Resources: The Continental Shelf and Marine Waters')," March 28, 1956, printed in the American Journal of International Law 50 (1956): 346.

19. International Law Commission, Yearbook (1956), vol. 2, p. 296.

20. Slouka, op. cit., p. 91.

21. Official Records of the U.N. Conference on the Law of the Sea, Vol. II, Penary Meetings, U.N. Doc. A/Conf. 13/38 (1958), p. 13.

22. United Nations, Treaty Series, Treaties and International Agreements Registered or Filed and Reported with the Secretariat of the United Nations, vol. 499, "Convention on the Continental Shelf, 29 April 1958," p. 343.

23. Roger Fisher stresses the importance of the appearance of legitimacy in prompting state action along new lines. Roger Fisher, International Conflicts for Beginners (New York: Harper & Row, 1970), pp. 151-77.

24. International Law Commission, Interim Report of the American Brand Committee on Deep Sea Mineral Resources, IX-X, 1969.

25. Norway, Ministry of Industry, Legislation concerning the Continental Shelf with unofficial English Translation, "Royal Decree of 31 May 1963," p. 9.

26. Germany, Bundestag, Bundesgesetzblatt II, 1964, "Proklamation der Bundesregierung, 20 January 1964," p. 104.

27. United Nations, Treaty Series, op. cit., vol. 551, "United Kingdom and Norway: Treaty on the Delimitation of the Continental Shelf between the Two Countries," p. 214.

28. United Nations, Treaty Series, op. cit., vol. 550, "Germany and the Netherlands: Treaty on the Delimitation of the Continental Shelf in the Vicinity of the Coast," p. 123.

29. United Nations, Treaty Series, op. cit., vol. 570, "Germany and Denmark: Treaty on the Delimitation of the Continental Shelf in the Vicinity of the Coast," p. 91.

30. International Court of Justice, Yearbook (1969), "North Sea Continental Shelf Cases," p. 7.

31. Ibid., p. 22.

32. Ibid., pp. 53-54.

33. Ibid.

34. Germany, Bundestag, II, 1972, "Germany and the Netherlands: Treaty on the Delimitation of the Continental Shelf under the North Sea, 28 January 1971" and "Germany and Denmark: Treaty on the Delimitation of the Continental Shelf under the North Sea, 28 January 1971," pp. 882-884.

35. United Nations, Third Conference on the Law of the Sea, Informal Single Negotiating Text and Text on Settlement of Disputes, May 9, 1975, A/Conf. 62/WP. 8.

36. United Nations, Third Conference on the Law of the Sea, Informal Composite Negotiating Text, July 15, 1977, A/Conf. 62/WP. 10.

37. United Nations, Third Conference on the Law of the Sea, Reports of the Committees and Negotiating Groups on negotiations at the Seventh Session contained in a single document both for the purposes of record and for the convenience of the delegations, May 19, 1978.

38. United Nations, Third Conference on the Law of the Sea, Revised [Informal] Single Negotiating Text, May 6, 1976 A/Conf. 62/WP. 8/Rev. 1/Part I, p. 1.

39. United Nations, General Assembly, 22nd Session, Resolution 2340, "The Pardo Resolution," December 18, 1967; also United Nations, General Assembly, 25th Session, Resolution 2749, "Declaration of Principles Governing the Seabed and the Ocean Floor, and the Subsoil, thereof, beyond the Limits of National Jurisdiction," December, 17, 1970.

40. United Nations, Treaty Series, op. cit., vol. 327, "International Convention for the Prevention of the Pollution of the Sea by Oil, 1954," p. 3.

41. United Kingdom, Foreign Office, United Kingdom Treaty Service, "Bonn Agreement for Cooperation in Dealing with Pollution of the North Sea by Oil, 1969" (Cmd. 4205).

5

NATIONAL LAW

Law relevant to operations on the North Sea continental shelf can usefully be broken down into five categories: licensing arrangements; taxation arrangements; safety laws and regulations; land planning laws and regulations; and environmental protection laws and regulations. These categories are roughly analogous to the categories used in Chapter 3 to define the dominant political interests associated with North Sea development that are operative at the national level. The licensing arrangements category has no obvious counterpart in Chapter 3, yet insofar as licensing arrangements are the principle determinants of the apportionment of shelf resources, it will be seen that they bear a strong relationship to national interests in achieving security of oil supply and maximizing private revenues to domestic businesses.

International law, as discussed in the preceding chapter, has placed the primary responsibility for the governance of continental shelf resources in the hands of national authorities. To only a very limited extent are the interests of authorities at other levels (the local and regional levels) influential in the governing process. As international law presently stands, local and regional authorities must generally work through national authorities to influence the shape of an evolving offshore regime.

It is the task of this chapter not only to describe the national legal arrangements governing North Sea petroleum resources, but to suggest the relationship that exists between these arrangements and the interests they were conceived to serve. The system of categories set forward in the first paragraph of this chapter will facilitate the examination of this relationship.

The subject of the chapter will be the legal arrangements governing resources in the British and Norwegian sectors of the North Sea. The bulk of presently known North Sea petroleum reserves has been discovered in these sectors and, consequently, the legal arrangements in force there are the most sophisticated and comprehensive of any in the North Sea. Moreover, the legal arrangements in force in other sectors tend to follow the pattern set by Great Britain and Norway. The most significant exceptions to this generalization are the shelf-wide concession policy of Denmark and the present hybrid policy (shelf-wide concession with pockets of block licenses) of Germany, as discussed in Chapter 2.

BRITISH CONTINENTAL SHELF LAW

The legal basis for British continental shelf law is the Petroleum (Production) Act 1934. [1] A simple piece of legislation, this act provides that petroleum resources in British lands are vested in the Crown, [2] that the Board of Trade has the power on behalf of the Crown to license persons to explore for and extract petroleum, [3] and that the Board of Trade has the power to regulate such activities. [4] The Continental Shelf Act 1964 applied the provisions of the Petroleum (Production) Act 1934 to areas of the continental shelf adjacent to the United Kingdom, the exact limits of which were to be designated by statutory instrument. [5] All rights to offshore petroleum were expressly vested in the Crown and authority to license and issue regulations was assigned to the Minister of Power. The Petroleum and Submarine Pipeline Act 1975 expanded the authority of the Secretary of State for Energy, the successor to the Minister of Power, to include powers to authorize and regulate the construction of pipelines and of refineries. [6]

Licensing Arrangements

By far the bulk of British law governing continental shelf activities pertains to the licensing of offshore activities. The latest regulations prescribing licensing procedures and license conditions are the Petroleum (Production) Regulations 1976, [7] which came into force on August 20, 1976 and were issued pursuant to the Petroleum (Production) Act 1934 as applied by the Continental Shelf Act 1964. The regulations provide for two types of licenses pertinent to this study, obtainable by application to the Energy Secretary: exploration licenses and production licenses.

Eligibility

"Any person" may apply for both exploration and production licenses. However, included among the circumstances listed as adequate grounds for the revocation of a license is "the licensee's ceasing in the case of a company to have its central management and control in the United Kingdom."[8] Previous regulations specified that licenses could only be issued to companies incorporated in the United Kingdom or to citizens of the United Kingdom. The modest retreat from this requirement instituted in the 1976 regulations (prompted by EEC pressure) apparently still makes necessary that foreign companies maintain a U.K. subsidiary. Such a requirement facilitates the assessment of taxes and the enforcement of regulations. The letter rather than the impact of the law appears to have been changed.

Exploration Licenses

Exploration licenses are issued at the discretion of the secretary. The application fee is 500 pounds. The regulations do not specify fees payable on exploration licenses after they have been issued, but recent licenses have required the holder to pay 1000 pounds per year. Licenses are valid for three years and are renewable. They cover areas designated in the license terms and may include major portions of the British shelf but not blocks for which current production licenses have been issued. Exploration licenses are nonexclusive—that is, similar licenses may be issued to other persons for the same areas. They entitle the holder to conduct passive physical and chemical surveys (such as seismographic, magnetic, gravimetric, and geochemical surveys) and exploratory drilling to 350 meters depth. Drilling for the purpose of extracting significant quantities of petroleum is, of course, prohibited.[9]

One provision of exploration licenses deserves particular note. As is not the case in, for example, the United States, the license requires the holder to provide "all information which the licensee has about the geology of the exploration area" to the secretary on request.[10] This affords government authorities a source of current geological information on the shelf. Through the discretionary licensing system the British government plays a considerably more active role in controlling the pattern and rate of shelf development than does the U.S. government. Accurate geological information is essential for the government to fill this role.

Production Licenses

The production license is the principal legal means for the assertion of government control over shelf activities. As it has been developed by Britain and Norway, it is an extremely flexible instrument for this purpose.

The production license confers upon the holder the exclusive right to drill for and extract petroleum in areas designated by the license. The term "production license" is something of a misnomer, since the most serious and expensive phase of exploration—exploratory drilling to depths at which petroleum might reasonably be expected to lie—is possible only under the terms of the production license. The basic licensed area is the "block," which is a rectangular area aligned north-south, bounded by lines of ten minutes latitude and twelve minutes longitude (roughly 100 square miles).

Like exploration licenses, production licenses are issued at the discretion of the Secretary, though here the exercise of discretion has considerably greater implications. In contrast with the auction system used in the United States to apportion offshore leases, the Secretary is under no obligation to issue a license to any particular company (for example, the highest bidder). All licensees pay the same license fees. The application fee is 1000 pounds; other fees are not fixed in the regulations. In the fourth round of licensing fees were as follows. In addition to a 12.5 percent royalty on any production, licensees were obligated to pay area fees. An initial payment of 45 pounds per square kilometer (or about 11,250 pounds per block) was due immediately. In the seventh year, an annual payment of 50 pounds per square kilometer was due, increasing to 80 pounds in the eighth year, and so on increasing in annual increments of 30 pounds to a maximum annual rate of 350 pounds per square kilometer (or about 87,500 pounds per block) in the seventeenth year and thereafter remaining at that level. [11] These area fees are not intended primarily as a source of revenues. Royalties are more significant and corporation taxes more significant still. Instead, they are intended to make carrying licensed areas an expense that increases with time (to a maximum of some $150,000 per block per year), to discourage companies from deferring exploration of areas—a practice that would be inconsistent with government interests in rapid shelf development.

Since a discretionary system rather than an auction system of tender bids is used to allocate licenses in Britain, a number of criteria are used to make choices among applicants competing for the same licensed area. For the fourth round of licensing (1971), the criteria noted in the official announcement of the round were:

1) where a body corporate incorporated in a country outside the United Kingdom holds a controlling interest in the applicant, the extent to which equitable reciprocal treatment is accorded in such other country;

2) the extent to which the applicant will further the thorough and rapid exploration of the . . . Continental Shelf, particular attention being paid to the financial and technical ability of the applicant to carry out an acceptable work program, details of which will be called for during the consideration of applications;

3) exploration work already done by or on behalf of the applicant for areas applied for;

4) where the applicant already holds a production license or licenses, his overall performance to date;

5) the extent of the contribution which the applicant has made or is planning to make to the economy of the United Kingdom, including the strengthening of the United Kingdom's balance of payments and the growth of industry and employment. [12]

In addition, for the fifth licensing round (for which the 1976 regulations were effective) the government made known that 51 percent participation by the British National Oil Company (BNOC) in any license issued was to be sine qua non. This and items two and five are generally considered to be the factors given the greatest weight in decisions on license allocation.

The work program proposed by the applicant is particularly important. Applicants are required to submit to the Secretary a program of exploration, including exploratory drilling they would be willing to carry out on a particular block if granted a license. [13] To a considerable extent, the discretionary licensing system, in the first five rounds, operated like an auction based on proposed work programs. However, the tender bid experiment conducted by the British in 1971 yielded in cash many times the value of the work programs that the government has generally considered reasonable and that companies have generally agreed to carry out. [14]

That the discretionary system of license allocation continued in use after the tender bid experiment is evidence of the high priority attached by the British to ensuring that the government have sufficient leverage over companies operating on the shelf to enable the government to effectuate its policies. The policy of rapid shelf development has been of overriding importance since the start of development on the British shelf (although the attainment of net self-sufficiency promises to temper this policy). The tender bid system simply could not guarantee rapid development and, argued British officials, could even retard development. They argued that the high initial costs imposed on companies by the tender bid system tended to limit interest in geologically unattractive or marginal blocks. [15] There has been sufficient experience in the North Sea of significant finds being made in blocks originally considered to be of marginal value that British authorities, intent on encouraging rapid and thorough exploration have favored the discretionary system because of the flexibility it affords the government in defining license terms. Britain has paid for this flexibility in foregone auction revenues, but continues to consider the exchange worthwhile.

In the sixth licensing round, the government is expected to encourage applicants for licenses to compete not only with respect to work programs but also with respect to terms for participation offered BNOC. Participation at a level of 51 percent is, again, considered sine qua non, but companies might offer BNOC a higher equity interest, participation on a carried interest basis, or other favorable financial terms. Thus, the sixth round, while not an auction based on tender bids, will reflect a move away from the previous strong emphasis on rapid exploration of the shelf and toward a greater concern for maximizing government revenues and control over crude oil supplies.

The discretionary system allows the government to pursue other national interests with respect to shelf development. The system allows authorities to discriminate in allocating licenses in favor of British corporations and in favor of foreign corporations that agree to make maximum use of British supply and service industries. That the discretionary licensing system is used in this way may be gathered from a close reading of item five of the criteria for selection listed above. Clearly, British firms will have an edge in demonstrating their commitment to advancing the economy of the United Kingdom. Moreover, in hearings held by the Committee of Public Accounts in 1972-73, a statement submitted by the Department of Energy explicitly stated as much:

> [The discretionary systems] enabled British-owned companies to be awarded a larger share of the territory . . . and, similarly, a larger share of the more attractive blocks . . .[16]

Of course, British industries cannot carry out the development of the British shelf alone. Inevitably foreign corporations, mostly from the United States, have played a major role. However, the discretionary system allows the authorities to favor those foreign companies with good records in making full use of British service and support industries. These government efforts are complemented by the Memorandum of Understanding signed by the United Kingdom Offshore Operators Association, which provides that operators (that is, companies physically as well as financially involved in offshore operations) will allow British industries a "full and fair opportunity" to compete for offshore service and supply contracts. One side effect of the discretionary system is that companies are given access to potentially valuable resources at comparatively little cost, creating a considerable incentive for speculation. In the absence of further government regulations, companies with no intention of eventually developing petroleum resources might apply for blocks in order to sell them at high profit to other companies. This abuse is controlled by government powers to regulate the reassignment of licenses. The Secretary must consent to all assignments of licenses or of rights conferred by licensees to new companies. [17] The Secretary may also attach conditions to his consent. [18] In several recent cases, the government has used this power to force new license holders to agree to accept substantial state participation.

Renewal and Relinquishment

After four years a license comes up for renewal. If the work program agreed upon by the licensee is being expeditiously carried out and other license terms are being adhered to, the license is renewed. If the license is, however, for any reason revoked, the licensee may still be held responsible for carrying out the exploratory work program agreed upon by him. [19] After three more years the license again comes up for renewal. The licensee must, at this point, delineate up to two-thirds of the licensed area (which may cover several blocks) to be relinquished to the government. [20] The effect of this provision is to minimize the amount of offshore lands out of the hands of the government. In the absence of such a provision, a licensee, upon discovering a significant petroleum reserve and completing his work program, might be content simply to hold the remainder of the block without continuing exploration efforts, speculating on higher future prices for oil. With the relinquishment provision the prospect of relinquishing two-thirds of the licensed area in seven years will generally encourage licensees to complete a comparatively thorough exploratory effort so as to avoid relinquishing valuable but undiscovered petroleum deposits. Relinquished areas can be and are relicensed by the government. Licensees are thus faced with the doubly unpleasant prospect of allowing valuable resources to pass out of their hands and into the hands of more energetic competitors.

Landing Requirements

Provisions encouraging rapid shelf development do not guarantee that the produced oil will necessarily be available to serve British national needs. This is provided for in part, by additional license requirements. All petroleum extracted from the British continental shelf must be landed in Great Britain unless written permission to do otherwise is obtained from the secretary.[21] This requirement helps ensure that Great Britain will obtain the maximum economic benefit from offshore oil through the expansion of domestic refining and petrochemical industries. If the Secretary consents to the landing of petroleum elsewhere, he may retain the balance of payments benefit by stipulating as a condition of consent that payment for petroleum be made to a person resident in the United Kingdom.[22] To bring crude oil directly under government control, the Secretary may stipulate that royalties be paid in kind.[23] However, participation arrangements are now the most effective means for obtaining direct government control over crude oil supplies.

Depletion Controls

The Secretary is given powers to control the rate of production in the license conditions. The Secretary may order a licensee to increase production if, in the opinion of the Secretary, such an increase will help the nation cope with a state of national emergency.[24] The Secretary is given broader powers to limit production. He may do so if, in his opinion, such a limit would serve the national interest.[25] This latter power is, in essence, a power to control the rate of petroleum depletion. Once Great Britain achieves self-sufficiency on oil, there will be a desire to maintain that favored position for as long as possible and thus a desire to limit increases in production. However, although the Secretary has the power directly to order production cuts, other less provocative means are available for controlling depletion. The rate of licensing has a strong if delayed effect on ultimate production rates. A more immediate decrease in activity can be brought about by the strict enforcement of environmental or safety regulations already on the books or the promulgation of new regulations pursuant to existing statutory powers. Such an approach would provoke a less negative response among companies than outright production controls, and would present less of a danger that investors would be frightened away from the U.K. shelf by the prospect of production controls or that foreign government would retaliate against British multinationals.

In any event, officials in the Department of energy have sought to reassure companies that depletion powers will not be exercised so as to endanger the economic viability of offshore operations. According to officially enunciated policy, the maximum production cut imposed on a field would be 20 percent. Production in fields discovered before 1976 would not be cut before 1982. Production in other fields would not be cut until four years after production had begun or until 150 percent of the original investment had been recovered, whichever is later.[26]

Unitized Field Development

Occasionally, oil fields are discovered that lie across block boundaries and thus are subject to development by two or more licensees. A scramble to pump as much oil as possible out of the field before the field is depleted by the other licensee or licensees could damage the field structurally and lower the ultimate recovery of oil. British blocks are smaller than, for example, Norwegian blocks. This smaller size ensures competition among a greater number of shelf explorers and thus promotes more rapid exploration. But it also increases the likelihood that block boundaries will cut across oil fields. The Secretary has the power to order that licensees with claims to such a split field join forces and establish a single operating committee that will develop the field as a unified entity. [27] British agreements with other North States establishing North Sea boundaries provide for the similar unitized development of fields crossing international boundaries. [28]

Pipelines

As already noted, the Petroleum and Submarine Pipeline Act 1975 broadened considerably the scope of the government's power to control the pattern of shelf development. Pipeline construction can now take place only with the authorization of the Secretary and under conditions that the Secretary may stipulate. Most importantly, the secretary may require the builder of a proposed pipeline to build a pipeline of larger capacity than he had originally intended. The Secretary further may require that the pipeline owner allow the pipeline to be used jointly by the developers of nearby fields at rates of compensation specified by the Secretary. [29] With these powers, government authorities hope to provide for more rational shelf development. Not only will the avoidance of parallel pipelines lower total capital expenses, but the existence of a nearby pipeline with excess capacity could render development of a newly discovered, small field commercially exploitable.

Participation and BNOC

The Petroleum and Submarine Pipelines Act also provides the legal basis for government participation as it is now being instituted in British licensing. The first section of the Act establishes BNOC as a wholly government-owned corporation with a mandate to carry out the government's commercial responsibilities with respect to petroleum and to provide expert advice to the government on oil-related matters. [30]

The range of activities BNOC may undertake includes exploring for and exploiting petroleum resources, refining crude oil, distributing petroleum products, and performing research functions. The corporation is subject to all the basic legal requirements effective for other oil corporations in Great Britain, with two notable exceptions. First, BNOC is not subject to the Petroleum Revenue Tax[31] (to be discussed in the next section). Second, BNOC is funded largely through a National Oil Account created by the Act.[32] The expenditures of BNOC are paid out of this account and receipts from commercial operations are paid in. In addition, however, all monies that the Secretary receives from oil production activities—including license fees, area fees, and royalties, but not including taxes—are paid into the account. The government hopes in this way to meet a large part of the expenses of establishing a fully integrated national oil company through revenues from the continental shelf. Thus far, however, BNOC has had to borrow considerable sums privately to meet its expenses.

In neither the Petroleum (Production) Regulations 1976, which prescribe the licensing procedure, nor the Petroleum and Submarine Pipeline Act 1975 is government participation actually mentioned as a license requirement. This again is illustrative of the flexibility afforded government authorities by the discretionary system. The Department of Energy made known, in announcing the fifth round, that license applications from groups that did not include BNOC as a 51 percent partner would not be considered. The sixth round is likely to be, effectively, an auction in which competitors bid against each other in offering BNOC the most favorable terms for participation. Some blocks will be issued to BNOC alone.

Government participation at a significant level in North Sea operations has now become an important objective of British offshore policy. Participation is an effective means to enable the national government to pursue its interests in offshore development. In those projects in which the government participates at a level of 51 percent or more, no major decision can be made without government approval. Majority participation can be used not only to bring crude oil supplies under direct national control and to increase government revenue, but also to increase the role of British industry in offshore activities, to institute higher safety standards, and to minimize social and environmental impacts. The constraints on this influence are defined by the hard economics of offshore development and by limits to the continuing willingness of private companies to cooperate with national authorities in shelf development.

Enforcement

Enforcement of conditions stipulated in licenses is provided for by granting to the secretary the power to revoke licenses. Such revocation may occur where there is a breach or nonobservance by the licensee of license conditions, where there is a failure to pay stipulated fees on royalties, where there is a breach or nonobservance of an agreed development plan, or for other reasons relating to the company's financial status. Such a revocation does not, however, absolve the licensee of any obligations or liabilities incurred under the conditions of the license. The licensee may not, for example, suddenly neglect the good order of installations.

Taxation Arrangements

Royalties payable directly to the Secretary of State for Energy (for deposit in the National Oil Account) provide a substantial portion of public revenues from offshore production. The largest source of such revenues is, however, the standard British corporation tax, which is assessed at a rate of 52 percent of net income and paid into the treasury.

Until 1975, oil companies were treated no differently for tax purposes from any other British corporation. However, as already discussed, because of skyrocketing oil prices the increasing profits accruing to oil companies operating in the North Sea outstripped even the rapidly rising costs of offshore production. This situation led to mounting political pressure from an increasingly vocal public. A substantial revision of the tax provisions applicable to offshore operations was enacted as the Oil Taxation Act 1975.

Two provisions of this Act are of particular importance. The first is the so-called ring fence provision, which prohibits oil companies from writing off against North Sea profits losses and taxes incurred other than in the course of North Sea operations. [33] Its most important effect is to prevent the international oil companies from deducting enormous taxes paid to the OPEC governments from taxes on North Sea profits under the double-taxation relief provisions of the Income and Corporation Taxes Act 1970. As will be recalled, these deductions could have enabled the companies to pay virtually no taxes on North Sea profits for an indefinite period.

The most important provision of the Oil Taxation Act 1975 created of a new tax, the Petroleum Revenue Tax (PRT), assessed at 45 percent of net income. [34] The PRT is deductible from the corporation tax, so that the additional drain on profits that it imposes is about 22 percent. This additional and, in a sense, discriminatory tax on oil operations was considered necessary because oil is not sold on a competitive market, and consequently rates of profit on oil operations are typically far above the norm for most industries. Nevertheless, assessing an additional tax on profits did pose the danger that fields

that were marginally commercial in the absence of such a tax would
not be developed once the tax had been imposed. Much of the Oil Taxation Act 1975, therefore, is devoted to defining the conditions under
which the tax may be assessed, so as to exempt marginal fields where
appropriate. The Act seeks also to reduce the tax burden for all fields
during the first several years of operations, when capital expenditures
are the highest.

Sliding scales were considered in the drafting of the Act as a
means for relieving the tax burden on marginal fields. However, the
solution actually adopted is more direct. The PRT will not be imposed
on a field where the rate of return on investment before the corporation tax is assessed at below 30 percent. Thus, the PRT could not
cause the after-tax return on investment to fall below 15 percent.
However, the PRT may not exceed 80 percent of the amount by which
the rate of return on investment exceeds 30 percent. [35] This causes
a tapering effect; the actual assessable PRT only gradually reaches
the full 45 percent level as field profitability increases. As a final
guarantee of the profitability of truly marginal fields, the Secretary,
under the Petroleum and Submarine Pipeline Act 1975, is given discretion to repay royalties to the licensee if he "considers it expedient
to do so for the purpose of facilitating or maintaining the development
of the petroleum resources of the United Kingdom." [36] Under the provisions of the Petroleum and Submarine Pipelines Act, this repay-
ment is to be disregarded for income tax purposes, multiplying its
effect.

Even for large and profitable fields an oil allowance of 1 million tons of oil per year, up to a cumulative total of 10 million tons,
may be deducted in calculating the PRT. [37] To cushion further the
impact of the PRT, capital expenditures that are deductible in the
calculation of the tax are uplifted by 75 percent. This has the practical
effect of delaying the onset of tax liability by several years. Since
companies typically calculate field profitability by discounting future
anticipated cash flows to the present, taxes late in the life of a project have a lesser impact on the overall calculation than do taxes
early in the project. This is not to suggest that companies are effectively being relieved of the responsibility to pay taxes. On the contrary, recent estimates indicate that under the present tax system
the government will siphon off 63 percent to 70 percent of total profits
from the average North Sea field. [38] Nevertheless, many in the industry are willing to concede that the present U.K. tax system reflects a sensitivity to the particular needs of the oil business.

In any event, whatever the harshness of the Oil Taxation Act
1975 and the Petroleum and Submarine Pipelines Act 1975, the British
sector of the North Sea witnessed a substantial increase in activity
following passage of these acts through Parliament. [39] Considerable

legal uncertainty had accompanied the drafting of the Acts and had de-
pressed offshore activity. The final outcome was, however, apparently
something the oil companies could live with, and activity resumed
once the outcome became known.

Safety Laws and Regulations

The Continental Shelf Act 1964 directed that the Secretary in-
corporate clauses in offshore licenses providing for the "safety,
health, and welfare" of persons employed in offshore operations. [40]
The Mineral Workings (Offshore Installations) Act 1971 empowered
the Secretary to draft safety regulations governing all aspects of offshore operations, including transportation to and from operations, the
use of vessels and aircraft in support of operations, undersea work,
and so on. [41] The Secretary was also empowered to draft regulations
regarding the structural fitness of installations, including regulations
requiring that installations be inspected and approved by competent
private certification authorities. [42] The breach of any duty imposed
by the Act or imposed by regulations issued pursuant to the Act not
only was established as a criminal offense but, if it resulted in a personal injury, was actionable under civil law. [43]

Regulations issued pursuant to the Continental Shelf Act through
early 1976 have provided, among other things, that offshore installations be registered with the Department of Energy, [44] that certain procedures be followed in appointing managers responsible for offshore
installations and that the secretary be notified of all appointments, [45]
that a log book to kept on each installation and all deaths be reported, [46] that installations be accessible to government inspectors
and all serious casualties be reported, [47] that installations meet
certain structural requirements and be approved by a private certification authority, [48] that public inquiries be initiated into any offshore
accident involving loss of or danger to life, [49] that diving operations
conform to strict operational standards, [50] and that an offshore employer maintain a minimum insurance of 2 million pounds to cover
claims made against him by employees injured in the course of work. [51]

Licenses issued in accordance with the Petroleum (Production)
Regulation 1976 establish, in addition, general duties to keep installations in good repair and carry out operations in accordance with "good
oil field practice." [52] Offshore work programs must be submitted to
the Secretary for his approval. [53] The Secretary may also give specific
instructions regarding the health, safety, and welfare of employees
on a particular installation with which the relevant licensee must
comply. [54]

It may be noted, particularly with respect to regulations issued pursuant to the Mineral Workings Act, that only in the past several years has the United Kingdom implemented a comparatively comprehensive code of safety regulations. The United Kingdom has been slower in this regard than Norway, for reasons that are not entirely clear. What can be said is that regulations now appear to be adequate. Major innovations in British offshore safety legislation are not anticipated.

Planning Laws and Regulations

The basis framework for planning decisions in Scotland is provided by the Town and Country Planning (Scotland) Act 1972. Detailing the provisions of this 300-page act is beyond the scope of this study. An outline of planning procedures will, however, at least suggest the nature of planning in Scotland as it relates to offshore development. Under the provisions of the Act, the dominant planning authority in Scotland is the Secretary of State for Scotland, a member of the British cabinet. There is no analogy in the United States for the planning powers vested in this office. Within his jurisdiction, the Secretary for Scotland has been likened to a combination of the "U. S. Secretaries of Transportation; Housing and Urban Development; Agriculture; Commerce; Health, Education, and Welfare; and the Chief of the Corps of Engineers."[55] The final appeal in planning decisions is to his office and much of planning in Scotland takes place at his discretion.

In theory, planning decisions are participatory. Local authorities—typically town councils and county councils—are given responsibility for preparing so-called structure plans for their jurisdictions, designating the sort of development to be permitted in a given area. After public discussion and review by the Secretary for Scotland, this plan, with amendments, becomes the development plan governing that jurisdiction. Those who wish to initiate development of a sort not anticipated in the plan (most oil-related development falls into this category) must apply to local authorities for an amendment to the plan. Such an amendment must be approved by the Secretary. A refusal to amend may be appealed to the Secretary. If, in the opinion of the Secretary, there is sufficient interest in the matter, a public inquiry may be held in which the various interested factions may testify and present evidence, much as is done in court. The ultimate decision, however, rests with the Secretary. The Secretary may, finally, bypass local authorities altogether in reaching a planning decision when he believes that the decision has serious implications.

Despite the Secretary's considerable powers, most substantive planning decisions have traditionally been made at the local level, with the Secretary taking a coordinating role, seeking to reconcile local plans with one another and with the basic national objectives being pursued by his government. The onset of oil development in 1970 has altered this pattern by accelerating the pace of development, particularly in coastal areas, and by engaging active interests at the national level in the results of local planning decision making. Local authorities, equipped with inadequate development plans, have been faced with planning decisions for which they are wholly unprepared. The Scottish office, for example, predicted in 1970 no significant growth for Aberdeen, now the focal point for Scottish onshore development. Such lack of awareness of the implication of offshore development for onshore areas was apparently quite widespread.[56] Nevertheless, strong national interests in rapid shelf development have demanded that decisions be made quickly. The result has been that the office of the Secretary has frequently been forced to fill the gap by making planning decisions over the heads of local authorities and by responding to appeals from would-be developers.

In 1975, Scotland was administratively reorganized into nine regions. Authorities at the regional level were given planning responsibilities within their jurisdictions.[57] One hope was that, while remaining sensitive to local concerns, regional authorities would be able to bring more resources and greater expertise to bear on the planning problem.

In two cases, local authorities acted in advance of regionalization to assume greater control over local planning decisions. Both Orkney County Council, governing the Orkney Islands, and the Zetland County Council, governing the Shetland Islands, urged and obtained passage of private parliamentary bills designed to strengthen their hands in making local planning decisions and in bargaining with the oil companies. As already noted, the Zetland County Council Act 1974 has been a particular success. On the basis of powers conferred by the Act, the Shetland Islands Council (successor to the Zetland County Council) has been able to sequester the development of a pipeline terminal and tanker-loading facility in a single tract in the north of the islands. Perhaps more importantly, the Council has obtained representation on the board governing the facility so that decisions with a direct impact on the islands can be made only with Council approval.

Despite individual local successes, however, oil development planning overall presents a picture that contrasts rather sharply with the sophistication of present licensing and taxation arrangements and the apparent adequacy of safety regulations. The swiftness and magnitude of oil development have created challenges that have strained seriously the present legal framework and led frequently to patchwork solutions neglecting local interests. The passage of private parliamentary bills to cope with particularly urgent local problems seems symptomatic of the broader inadequacy of present planning arrangements. These problems have been exacerbated by serious conflicts of interest within the governmental structure—that is, between local and national authorities. Problems such as these are not evident with regard to licensing, taxation, or safety.

Environmental Laws and Regulations

Whatever their limitations in controlling the flood of oil development activities, British land planning laws are, as already noted, more comprehensive than those in force in the United States. The opposite situation exists with regard to environmental protection laws. There is no British equivalent of the American National Environmental Policy Act of 1969 with its requirement that detailed environmental impact assessments be carried out for projects with significant environmental implications. There is, in fact, no comprehensive British environmental law; individual statutes and the common law combine to provide uneven degrees of environmental protection in different areas. In the area of oil pollution from offshore installations, legal protections are particularly inadequate.

Criminal liability for oil pollution caused by offshore operations is provided for in the Prevention of Oil Pollution Act 1971. The pertinent sections of this act replace section 5 of the Continental Shelf Act 1964, which made the discharge of oil or an oil-water mixture in the course of offshore operations in the British sector an offense punishable by a maximum fine of 1000 pounds. The 1971 Act raised the maximum fine to 50,000 pounds. [58] However, while this is by no means a prohibitive amount (it is equivalent to the gross value of less than an hour's work of oil production for a major North Sea field at present prices), fines actually imposed under the Act have been considerably lower. [59] An adequate defense, under the provisions of the Act, is demonstration that "neither the escape nor any delay in discovering it was due to any want of reasonable care and that as soon as practicable after it was discovered all reasonable steps were taken to stopping or reducing it."[60]

The Act has proven ineffective in regulating oil pollution from offshore operations. It is apparently impossible, given the present state of the technology for seperating oil from water, to eliminate all traces of oil from the effluent produced by offshore installations. An amendment to the Prevention of Oil Pollution Act 1971 was therefore included in the Petroleum and Submarine Pipelines Act 1975. The amendment granted the Secretary of State for Energy the power to grant exemptions for offshore installations. [61] Since no active installation can meet the requirements of the Prevention of Oil Pollution Act, all must have exemptions. The degree of environmental protection achieved thus depends entirely on the discretion of the Secretary for Energy. This does not seem an entirely satisfactory situation, since the Secretary for Energy has consistently been the most active promoter of rapid offshore development within the government. The situation contrasts with that in the United States, where general responsibility for environmental protection matters has been given to an independent official, the head of the Environmental Protection Agency. (The actual degree of his independence may be debated, yet not to the extent of undermining the basic contrast that exists between the two systems.)

Requirements relating to the structural fitness of installations and the use of safe equipment and procedures in offshore operations afford a degree of environmental protection. The Petroleum (Production) Regulations 1976 provide specifically that licensees shall take all steps practicable to prevent the escape of petroleum in the licensed area and shall comply with directives given from time to time by the Secretary in this regard. [62] The Secretary is given the power to review proposed programs of development, [63] and written authorization by the Secretary must be obtained before any drilling may be commenced or any well abandoned. [64] Here again, however, the decision on whether to delay development in order to ensure a higher degree of environmental security is left to the discretion of the official responsible, given present government policies, for the rapid achievement of energy security. More objective review of the fitness of installations for offshore work—including structural soundness and the use of safety equipment such as blowout preventers—is provided for by recent regulations (noted in the section on safety) requiring that installations be certified by approved private certification authorities. [65]

Preparedness for dealing with environmental emergencies resulting from offshore accidents, such as well blowouts, has been made largely the responsibility of the operators. The government, in discussions with the United Kingdom Offshore Operators Association (UKOOA), has sought to establish guidelines for dealing with oil pollution. All operators are expected to formulate contingency plans, including provisions for the cleanup of spills. The UKOOA has made available to its members supplies of chemical dispersants and spray gear stockpiled in important North Sea harbors. The government has expressed a willingness to assist with any incident that is beyond resources of the operators. However, the apparent government willingness to leave emergency preparedness for oil spills largely up to the oil companies presents a contrast with practices in other nations, including Norway.

British environmental law relating to offshore operations has been weakest where losses to the oil industry could be the greatest, that is, in connection with civil liability stemming from oil pollution. As has been mentioned, the Mineral Workings (Offshore Installations) Act 1971, governing the safety of workers, expressly provided that any breach of the requirements imposed by the Act and the regulations issued pursuant to it would be actionable under civil law if it resulted in personal injury. No such provision appears in the Prevention of Oil Pollution Act 1971 and it is doubtful that a British court would construe the act as creating not only criminal responsibility but a civil statutory duty. [66] This contrasts with the Merchant Shipping (Oil Pollution) Act 1971, which created a statutory tort placing nearly absolute liability on a shipowner for any damage in the United Kingdom resulting from an escape or discharge of oil from his ship. [67] The only defenses available to such a shipowner are that the pollution resulted from an act of war or an "exceptional, irresistible, and inevitable natural phenomenon;" or was due wholly to the actions of another person (not in the owner's employ), done with malicious intent; or was due to government negligence in the maintenance of navigational aids. [68]

Great Britain's recent signing and expected ratification of the Convention on Compensation for Oil Pollution Damage from Offshore Operations (see in Chapter 4, "Substantive International Law Affecting North Sea Development) will require the enactment of implementing legislation providing for the strict liability of operators for oil pollution damage to foreign waters and shores of up to, at least, $35 million. There seems little reason to suppose that legislation could not provide for similar liability with respect to damage to British waters and shores.

The civil liability gap that presently exists in the United Kingdom with regard to pollution from offshore operations has been filled by a voluntary agreement among offshore operators known as the Offshore Pollution Liability Agreement. Under this scheme 16 million pounds has been pledged to meet the expenses of cleanup and compensation for damages (up to 8 million pounds per incident) arising from oil pollution from an installation operated by a subscriber to the agreement. [69] In the absence of extraordinary circumstances 8 million pounds is, thus, the de facto limit on recovery obtainable in the United Kingdom for pollution damage resulting from offshore operations.

It may be remarked that unlimited civil liability is precisely the sort of legal uncertainty that the oil companies appear to view as the most threatening to the viability of their operations. Such liability creates a variable with considerable financial implications that could not be anticipated, even roughly, in the absence of expensive insurance schemes. Yet, if there is a risk of pollution from offshore operations, it would seem that this risk should be borne by persons other than those who occupy the coasts and suffer damages.

NORWEGIAN CONTINENTAL SHELF LAW

Norwegian continental shelf law bears strong similarities to British law. Yet there are contrasts between the two systems sufficient to make a review of Norwegian law essential for a reasonably comprehensive understanding of North Sea law.

To the researcher, the most gratifying difference between the legal systems of the two countries is linguistic. Norwegian statutes, in the simplicity of their language, afford a refreshing contrast to much British (and American) statutory law. The statute providing the legal basis for all Norwegian continental shelf laws and regulations, Act No. 12 of 21 June 1963 relating to Exploration for and Exploitation of Submarine Natural Resources, may be quoted in full:

1) This Act applies to exploration for and exploitation of natural resources in the seabed or in its subsoil, as far as the depth of the superjacent waters admits exploitation of natural resources, within as well as outside maritime boundaries otherwise applicable, but not beyond the median line in relation to other states.
2) The right to submarine natural resources is vested in the state.
The King may give Norwegian or foreign persons, including institutions, companies and other associations, the right to explore for and exploit natural resources. Specific conditions for such permission may be stipulated.
3) The King may issue regulations concerning the exploration for and exploitation of submarine natural resources.
4) Existing legislation shall not preclude the issue of regulations pursuant to Sections 2 and 3 of this Act.
5) The rights of navigation and fishing are not affected by this Act.
6) This Act shall enter force immediately.[70]

Licensing Arrangements

The latest regulations prescribing licensing procedures and license conditions is the Royal Decree of 8 December 1972 issued pursuant to the 1965 act. Under the provisions of the decree, three types of licenses are available: reconnaissance licenses, production licenses, and licenses for the emplacement of offshore installations and facilities other than production platforms.

Eligibility

Reconnaissance licenses may be granted to "Norwegian or foreign companies, foundations, or other organizations."[71] Production licenses may be granted to "companies, foundations, or other organizations established in conformity to Norwegian law and having their principal seat of business in Norway."[72] As in Great Britain, this provision facilitates the assessment of taxes and enforcement of regulations. There is apparently no similar concern with regard to the holders of reconnaissance licenses. No constraints whatever are stipulated for the granting licenses of third type.

Reconnaissance Licenses

Reconnaissance licenses are similar to British exploration licenses. They are issued at the discretion of the Ministry of Industry. License fees of 20,000 kroner (roughly $3700) are payable annually in advance, with the first payment constituting an application fee. Licenses are valid for three years and are renewable. They confer a nonexclusive right to conduct passive surveys of areas stipulated in the license terms. Reconnaissance licenses have not been issued for areas of the Norwegian shelf north of 62° N. (all surveys north of this line have been carried out by the government). Reconnaissance licenses do not entitle the holders to conduct drilling of any type.

As is true in Great Britain for exploration licenses, a condition of reconnaissance licenses is that the government be given access to all geological information obtained in the course of surveys. The Norwegian regulations specify that the company's interpretations of data shall also be made available to the government[73]—a point on which the British regulations are less explicit.

Production Licenses

Applications for production licenses are invited by the Ministry of Industry in a public announcement specifying which areas will be open for licensing in that particular round (although upon receiving applications the Minister is not obligated to license a particular block[74]). A fee of 15,000 kroner must accompany each application. The basic licensed area is a block bounded by lines of 15 minutes latitude and 20 minutes longitude (encompassing somewhat more than twice the area of British blocks).

As in Great Britain, production licenses are awarded on a discretionary basis. The same justifications for the use of the discretionary system rather than some other system are, in general, heard from Norwegian officials as are heard from British officials.

Licenses cannot be granted until a work program acceptable to the Ministry has been approved. However, competitive bidding in work programs is apparently less a feature of the Norwegian system than it is of the British. [75] Officials rely more on their bargaining position with the companies—that is, their ability to withhold licenses—to obtain satisfactory work programs. As in Great Britain, a licensee is responsible for the completion of his work program even if, for some reason, his license should lapse or be revoked. The Ministry may demand payment of an amount equivalent to the estimated cost of completing the work program in accordance with "good oil-field practice." [76]

The Decree provides explicitly that licensees shall use Norwegian goods and services insofar as "they are competitive with regard to quality, service, schedule of delivery, and price." [77] Norwegian contractors must be included in invitations for tender bids to the extent that they offer goods or services of the desired type. In weighing tenders, the licensee must take into account the extent to which each bidder would use Norwegian goods and services.

License fees are specified in the regulations. An initial payment for the license of 750 kroner for each square kilometer (or roughly $70,000 for each block) must be made, covering the first six years of the license. In the seventh year a fee of 1800 kroner for each square kilometer must be paid on all areas of the license remaining after relinquishment. The area fee increases steeply to 30,000 kroner in the seventeenth year (roughly ten times the British rate set in the fourth round). The cost of carrying a full Norwegian block after the seventeenth year is roughly $3 million per year. [78]

Royalties are assessed on a sliding scale that appears to be designed to protect the profitability of marginal fields and fields in the early stages of production, while taking a greater slice of the profits of medium and large fields. The royalties* are as follows:

Barrels per day	Percent of royalty
Under 40,000	8
40,000 to 999,999	10
100,000 to 224,999	12
225,000 to 349,999	14
Over 350,000	16

*Source: Norway, Ministry of Industry, Legislation Concerning the Norwegian Continental Shelf with unofficial English translation, 1973, "Royal Decree of 8 December 1972," section 26.

Norwegian royalties on natural gas production are assessed at a flat rate of 12.5 percent. The Ministry may stipulate a lower royalty on oil or gas production "if sea depth, capacity per well, or other conditions so require."[79] Alternatively, the Ministry may require payment of unspecified "production bonuses," that is, amounts payable when production reaches a certain level. [80] This gives the Ministry virtually unlimited powers to demand payments on oil production to the full extent that its bargaining position with the companies will allow. Thus far, the government has exercised restraint in this regard. A license issued to Mobil and Statoil in 1973 specified that a 25 million kroner bonus be paid when production reached 500,000 barrels a day (that is, less than two days worth of oil production at 1978 prices). [81]

The Norwegian government controls the assignment of licenses much as the British government does. [82] Conditions may be attached to ministerial consent to the transfer of licenses from one group to another. Since such transfers are generally made only in response to dire financial need there is usually little choice for the companies involved but to carry out the transfer and comply with the stipulated conditions. The government has used this power in several instances to impose substantial levels of state participation on licenses issued before such participation was a requirement.

Renewal and Relinquishment

The Royal Decree of 25 August 1967 provides that licensees who have completed their work programs and otherwise lived up to the terms of the license may renew the license for another thirty years upon the relinquishment of one half the licensed area. [83] This is one of the very few provisions in which Norwegian regulations appear to be less demanding than the British, which require the relinquishment of two-thirds of the licensed area (although the contrast may only reflect a British desire to keep area fees low while accomplishing the same purpose).

Landing Requirements

Petroleum extracted from the Norwegian shelf must be landed in Norway, unless the king upon application approves another landing point. [84] The regulations do not state that conditions may be attached to such approval, as is the case in the British regulations. The Norwegian Decree does, however, deal directly with the problem to which the British regulations seek a more roundabout solution. Section 34 of the Decree states flatly: "The King may decide that the licensee shall deliver petroleum from his production in order to satisfy national demand."[85] In cases of war or other national emergency, the

king may direct that all petroleum produced on the Norwegian shelf
be placed at the disposal of Norwegian authorities. [86] The Ministry
has the power to direct, at any time, that royalties be paid in kind. [87]

Depletion Controls

The Ministry may adopt measures aimed at controlling the rate
of depletion of reserves. [88] Thus far, however, the government has
sought to achieve resource conservation by maintaining a low rate of
development—particularly by limiting the number of licenses awarded.
The expectation generally has been that the government would allow
those fields already discovered to proceed through logical development sequence.

Pipelines

Although the Decree does not mention specifically any power of
the ministry to dictate the size of pipelines laid in the Norwegian
sector, a special license is necessary before pipelaying can be undertaken. [89] It would not be inconsistent with past government behavior
in other areas for the government to use its ability to withhold licenses to seek concessions regarding capacity from a pipeline builder.
The Decree does grant the Minister the power to order that a pipeline
or other offshore installation (with the exception of a production platform) be made available for utilization by other persons, if such
utilization would not result in any "unreasonable infringement of the
owners' requirements."[90] Compensation for such use would be determined by agreement or binding arbitration.

Participation

State participation in licenses is established in the decree as a
possible license condition. Since the third round of licensing, held in
1973-74, it has been the policy of the Norwegian government to require state participation of 50 percent or more on a carried interest
basis in all licenses granted. The government's chosen instrument
for carrying out its responsibilities in connection with participation
agreements is Statoil. Statoil was created on June 14, 1972, as a 100
percent government-owned, joint stock company, by a unanimous vote
of the Storting. The Ministry of Industry had requested that such a
company be established to take on broad responsibilities in exploration, exploitation, refining, transporting, and marketing. [91] The government is the principal source of capital for Statoil, and investments
in the company are seen as an excellent use for revenues from the
Norwegian shelf. There is, however, no Norwegian counterpart to
Britain's National Oil Account.

Enforcement

Enforcement of license conditions is provided for, as in Great Britain, by granting the Ministry the power to revoke a license. Licenses may be revoked in cases of "serious or repeated violations" of the provisions of the Decree. In the case of less serious violations, the license may be revoked if the violation is not corrected within a reasonable period. Specifically mentioned grounds for revocation include failure to pay fees or royalties and impeding a public inspector in his duties. In the event that a license is revoked, all equipment within the licensed area becomes the property of the state and the licensee is obligated to secure the good order of this equipment so as to ensure its continued use. [92]

In sum, the licensing arrangements established by the Royal Decree of 8 December 1972 are generally more demanding than the current British regulations, even though the latter were implemented some four years later. The overall congruence of the two systems in their basic scope and design is, nevertheless, notable.

Taxation Arrangements

The government's power to tax operations on the Norwegian continental shelf is provided for by Act No. 3 of 11 June 1965. Certain clauses of this act placing offshore operations in a slightly more advantageous position than other Norwegian industries were eliminated by Act No. 33 of 9 June 1972. Following passage of that act, offshore operations were taxed, like other industries, at a rate of 50.8 percent, broken down as follows: 26.5 percent to the central government, 21.3 percent to the municipality of the company's head office, 1.7 percent to the Tax Equalization Fund, and 1.3 percent to the Special Tax for aid to developing countries. [93]

Pressures similar to those that led to the adoption of the British Oil Taxation Act 1975 prompted the Ministry of Finance in late 1974 to propose to the Storting a new excess profits tax to be applied to offshore operations on top of the corporation tax. [94] Adopted in early 1975, the new special tax on oil operations was set at 15 percent, to be assessed on profit remaining after the corporation tax and royalties had been paid. The special tax is, thus, not deductible. The new taxation arrangements liberalized depreciation and investment allowances to delay the impact of the taxation on offshore projects.

The adoption of these new arrangements followed closely on the heels of the third round of licensing. A number of companies protested vigorously on the grounds that important financial conditions with which they had agreed at the time of the granting of their licenses were being changed retrospectively in apparent violation of the Norwegian constitution. Yet the fact that a matter of taxation was at issue complicated the question; governments have traditionally reserved to themselves the right to change prevailing tax rates and conditions even though such a change might force corporations and individuals to reassess their financial positions. In any event, the oil company protest had little effect on the Storting and was never taken to the Norwegian Supreme Court. Chevron, a company that was offered a license in third round, went so far as to seek a negotiation of the tax. The Ministry of Industry, noting past stipulations that a conditional acceptance of a license would be regarded as a refusal, retracted their license offer. Despite a subsequent change of heart by Chevron the license was awarded to British Petroleum. [95]

The total Norwegian government take, excluding government participation, is estimated to be from 55 percent to 68 percent of the profit from the average North Sea field. [96] This take is slightly lower than that of Great Britain but is compensated for by proportionately more extensive government participation.

Safety Laws and Regulations

Safety regulations have been promulgated as royal decrees pursuant to Act No. 12 of 21 June 1963, cited above. The right of the Ministry of Industry to issue "safety measures of all types" beyond those expressly provided for in the decree governing licensing (December 8, 1972) is provided for in section 38 of that decree.

A Royal Decree of 25 August 1967 provided Norway with its first comprehensive set of safety regulations designed particularly for operations on the continental shelf. These regulations, issued before any significant activity had begun on the Norwegian shelf, are now widely regarded as well conceived and farsighted for such an early stage of development. It will be recalled that the Mineral Workings (Offshore Installations) Act, which served as the basis for most of Great Britain's offshore safety regulations, was not passed until 1971.

Recently, the decree of 1967 was superseded by new regulations drawing on Norway's already extensive continental shelf experience. A royal decree promulgated October 3, 1975 now governs exploration and drilling work. A royal decree promulgated July 9, 1976 governs production activities. A royal decree also promulgated July 9, 1976 deals specifically with the safety of offshore workers.

The regulations provide for extensive supervision of all aspects of offshore work. Detailed work plans complete with technical data must be submitted to the Ministry for approval before, among other things, the commencement of geological survey operations,[97] the stationing of a drilling rig,[98] the commencement of any drilling,[99] the abandonment of a well,[100] the emplacement of a production platform,[101] the laying and routing of pipelines,[102] the use of divers,[103] and the assignment of working hours.[104] The Ministry is empowered to issue further orders as to the phases of production activities that may not commence without written consent.[105] During particularly hazardous operations, such as drilling, licensees have been required to make daily progress reports to the ministry by telex.[106] Inspectors may board installations at any time to inspect records, equipment, and the conduct of operations.[107] All deaths, serious injuries, and dangerous occurrences must immediately be reported.[108] Installations must be tested and checked "as the Ministry considers necessary" to ensure their structural fitness and compliance with safety regulations.[109] In practice, this has included the use of private certification authorities. Det Norske Veritas supervised the construction and installation of the Ekofisk platforms.[110]

In addition, the decrees now in force set forward a wide range of specific requirements with regard to the construction and equipping of rigs and the conduct of operations. These include requirements covering reconnaissance surveys, drilling platforms, drilling operations, contingency planning, electrical installations, fire prevention, use of explosives, telecommunications, air and water transportation, radioactive equipment, auxiliary systems, living quarters, hoisting gear, pipeline systems, and tanker-loading installations. Enforcement of the provisions of the decrees is provided for by making applicable fines under the Norwegian Penal Code of 22 May 1902[111] and by empowering the Ministry to halt operations or revoke the relevant license in the event of serious or repeated violations.[112] The ministry may, at any time, direct the licensee to post a guarantee sufficient to cover any liability related to his activity that incurred.[113]

In general, Norwegian safety regulations are more burdensome than British regulations, particularly in the degree of government supervision that they impose on all aspects of offshore operations. Moreover, Norwegian authorities have demonstrated a willingness to delay development significantly to ensure compliance with regulations, as was evidenced in 1976 when development of the Statfjord field was halted in order to enforce regulations governing safety in living quarters.[114]

Planning Laws and Regulations

Norway has a tradition in land planning that appears to be stronger even than that in Great Britain. Again, it is beyond the scope of this study to discuss in detail the relevant legal framework. However, an outline of procedures and policies should suggest the nature of Norwegian planning and its potential relationship to oil-related development.

Norwegian officials have noted that in Norway, as in other countries, industrial development tends to cause population and development clustering. The growth of urban centers attracts new industry, placing a demographic and economic drain on more sparsely populated areas. This process leads to regional inequalities and, in certain cases, to economic depression in rural areas. The central government has therefore adopted a national planning policy of so-called "localized," or decentralized, development. Jobs and facilities are to be placed in the least developed economic environments that can reasonably be expected to support them. [115] The division and dispersion of oil-related development in accordance with this policy presents a major challenge to Norwegian authorities. Yet the authorities appear determined not to exempt the oil industry, which, they anticipate, will pose some of the most serious problems to face Norwegian society in coming decades. [116]

Planning in Norway takes place at the municipal, county, and national levels. County plans are particularly important in determining the ultimate pattern of development on the scale that is likely to result from offshore operations. County plans set forth the basis objectives for development within the county, as well as important environmental constraints. They include employment budgets, which provide guidelines for determining the capacity of given areas to accommodate new development. County plans are reviewed annually and revised substantially every four years. They provide the basis for general plans drawn up by national authorities, which determine the actual use to which various areas shall be put. The central government has stated, in this regard, that it "attaches great importance to the work of decentralizing decisions in public administration—of moving public administration out of Oslo."[117] In furthering this aim, the government has recognized the need to strengthen the planning capacity of county authorities, particularly in technical areas such as pollution control and fisheries management. [118]

Because of the Norwegian Trench, Norway has yet to face development pressures on the order of those now evident in Scotland. Extensive development has thus far centered around Stavanger, which provides a base for offshore operations in the Norwegian sector but not a landing point for oil. However, the government does plan to make Norway a significant receiving point for oil by developing its refining capacity. The development of Norwegian support industries for offshore operations may also be expected to continue. It remains to be seen whether, given the present planning framework, development can proceed in an orderly fashion with due regard to local, as well as national, interests. Two factors, in particular, suggest that it can.

The first in that, for Norway, despite recent economic difficulties, rapid shelf development is not the overwhelming national priority that it has been for Great Britain. Norwegians exhibit a strong bias against unregulated industrial development. Serious conflicts of interest between local and national authorities, like those that have been evident in Scotland, are not so likely to occur. Consequently, there is a greater potential for adequate deliberation and coordination in planning.

The second is that the Norwegian government is demonstrating here, as in other areas, an exceptional ability to anticipate problems years before they must actually be faced. Central government authorities have directed the county planners in the north of Norway to include the potential impacts of petroleum development in the revisions of their plans. [119] Yet significant pressures as a result of development north of 62° N. will not be felt until the mid- to late 1980s at the earliest. This presents a strong contrast with British unpreparedness in the early 1970s for heavy onshore development in Scotland.

Environmental Laws and Regulations

The extensive supervisory powers given the Norwegian government under provisions of the licensing and safety regulations serve the dual purposes of ensuring worker safety and lowering the chances of environmental mishaps. In particular, provisions relating to drilling operations and the transferring of oil reflect the latter concern. The Ministry explicitly requires that before a well is drilled the licensee provide comprehensive information on the geologic strata to be encountered, potential high pressure zones, the placement of casings, the use of drilling muds, and all safety measures to be employed. The Ministry must consent before drilling can begin.

Inspections are exceptionally rigorous during drilling. Inspections may be conducted without prior notice and inspectors may request that emergency preparedness drills be carried out. Inspectors may be stationed continuously on board during particularly hazardous operations. [120] The licensee may be asked to bear the cost of such inspections.

The regulations also contain provisions regulating the use of environmental safety equipment, such as blowout preventers (hydraulic valves that seal the drill-pipe in the event of a sudden rise in pressure). [121] Current regulations require a stack of four blowout preventers for each well. [123]

Licensees are also required to draw up detailed contingency plans for a variety of emergencies, including oil spills. The plans must be based on the best available equipment. In addition to emergency equipment located on the platform, the licensee must ensure that he has access to adequate shore-based equipment for the clean-up of spills and for other emergencies. [123] The Norwegian government has favored strongly the use of mechanical devices to clean up spills rather than chemical dispersants, which may poison marine life. Mechanical equipment capable of working effectively in the harsh weather conditions encountered in the North Sea is only now being developed. The development of such equipment has been undertaken by the government because of the apparent dearth of development efforts in this direction elsewhere in the world. [124]

Contingency plans prepared by the licensee must be suitable for coordination with the national emergency preparedness plan provided for by the Oil Damage Defense Act, enacted in March 1970. Under provisions of the Act an Oil Protection Council was appointed, consisting of experts drawn from within the government. The Council is responsible for coordinating the nation's preparedness for an oil disaster. Every municipality that might be damaged by oil is required to maintain the personnel and equipment necessary to minimize such damage. An appropriation of 3 million kroner was made in 1975 for these purposes. Small spills could be handled by local authorities, while major emergencies would be dealt with under the direct supervision of the Oil Protection Council. [125]

Despite these measures, the government has recently concluded, on the basis of experience in cleaning up small spills resulting from shipping and as a result of the Ekofisk disaster, that present oil emergency preparedness is inadequate. [126] The government is willing to delay the commencement of exploratory drilling in the ecologically sensitive offshore regions north of 62° N. until a greater level of preparedness is achieved.

The causing of damage or inconvenience in the course of offshore operations is established as a tort under Norwegian law by the Royal Decree of 8 December 1972. The tort feasor, his employer, and the licensee, jointly and severally, bear unlimited civil liability for any claim for compensation as a result of such damage or inconvenience. [127]

The contrast with British law, thus, appears to be strongest in those areas of legislation that seek to mitigate harms resulting from offshore development. Nevertheless, there is a strong congruence between the two systems even in those areas, and the congruence will become stronger when Great Britain enacts a civil liability statute for pollution caused by offshore installations.

NOTES

1. All British statutes cited in this chapter are found in United Kingdom, Parliament, Public General Acts and Measures for the relevant years.

2. United Kingdom Petroleum (Production) Act 1934, section 1(1).

3. Ibid., section 2(1).

4. Ibid., section 6(1).

5. Continental Shelf Act 1964, sections 1(3) and (7).

6. Petroleum and Submarine Pipelines Act 1975, sections 20 (1) and 34(1).

7. United Kingdom, Statutory Instruments, 1976, No. 1129, The Petroleum (Production) Regulations 1976, section 4.

8. Ibid., schedule 5, clause 40(2)(g) and schedule 7, clause 21(2)(f).

9. Ibid., schedule 7, clause 3.

10. Ibid., schedule 7, clause 12(3).

11. United Kingdom, Parliament, Commons, First Report of the Committee of Public Accounts, 1972-1973: North Sea Oil and Gas (London: Her Majesty's Stationery Office, 1973), p. 157.

12. Ibid., p. 47.

13. United Kingdom, Petroleum (Production) Regulations 1976, op. cit., schedule 4, clause 14(1).

14. Kenneth O. Dam, Oil Resources (Chicago: University of Chicago, Press, 1976), p. 39.

15. United Kingdom, First Report, op. cit., p. 32.

16. Ibid., p. 32.

17. United Kingdom, Petroleum (Production) Regulations 1976, op. cit., schedule 5, clause 39(1).

18. Ibid., schedule 5, clause 39(3).

19. Ibid., schedule 5, clause 40(1).

20. Ibid., schedule 5, clause 5(1) and (2).

21. Ibid., schedule 5, clause 28(1).

22. Ibid., schedule 5, clause 28(2)(d).

23. Ibid., schedule 5, clause 11(1).

24. Ibid., schedule 5, clause 16.

25. Ibid.

26. Colin Robinson and Jon Morgan, "Depletion Control and Profitability: The Case of the U.K. North Sea," Energy Policy, September 1976, pp. 268-75.

27. United Kingdom, Petroleum (Production) Regulations 1976, op. cit., schedule 5, clause 26.

28. For example: United Nations, Treaty Service, Treaties and International Agreements Registered or Filed and Reported with

the Secretariat of the United Nations, vol. 551, "United Kingdom and Norway: Treaty relating to the Delimitation of the Shelf between the Two Countries," p. 214, Article 4.

29. United Kingdom Petroleum and Submarine Pipelines Act 1975, sections 22 and 23.

30. Ibid., sections 1 and 2.

31. Ibid., section 9(1).

32. Ibid., section 40.

33. United Kingdom Oil Taxation Act 1975, section 13, paragraphs (1) and (2). These sections must be read in conjunction with section 19(1).

34. Ibid., section 1.

35. Ibid., section 9.

36. United Kingdom Petroleum and Submarine Pipelines Act 1975, section 41(3).

37. United Kingdom Oil Taxation Act 1975, section 8.

38. "North Sea: A Comparison of Tax Systems," Petroleum Economist, May 1976, pp. 170-72.

39. Offshore, February 1977, p. 47.

40. United Kingdom Continental Shelf Act 1964, section 4.

41. United Kingdom Mineral Workings (Offshore Installations) Act 1971, section 6.

42. Ibid., section 3.

43. Ibid., section 11.

44. United Kingdom, Statutory Instruments, 1972, No. 702, Offshore Installations (Registration) Regulations 1972.

45. United Kingdom, Statutory Instruments, 1972, No. 703, Offshore Installations (Managers) Regulations 1972.

46. United Kingdom, Statutory Instruments, 1972, No. 1542, Offshore Installations (Logbook and Registration) Regulations 1972.

47. United Kingdom, Statutory Instruments, 1975, No. 1842. Offshore Installations (Inspectors and Casualties) Regulations 1973.

48. United Kingdom, Statutory Instruments, 1974, No. 289, Offshore Installations (Construction and Survey) Regulations 1974. The certification authorities appointed were Lloyds Register of Shipping, American Bureau of Shipping, Bureau Veritas, Det Norske Veritas, and Germanischer Lloyd.

49. United Kingdom, Statutory Instruments, 1974, No. 338, Offshore Installations (Public Inquiries) Regulations 1974.

50. United Kingdom, Statutory Instruments, 1974, No. 1229, Offshore Installations (Diving Operations) Regulations 1974.

51. United Kingdom, Statutory Instruments, 1975, No. 1289, Offshore Installations (Application of the Employer's Liability (Compulsory Insurance) Act 1969) Regulations 1975.

52. United Kingdom, Petroleum (Production) Regulations 1976, op. cit., schedule 5, clause 21.

53. Ibid., schedule 5, clause 15.

54. Ibid., schedule 5, clause 24.

55. Pamela Baldwin and Malcolm Baldwin, Onshore Planning for Offshore Oil (Washington, D. C.: The Conservation Foundation, 1975), p. 129.

56. Ibid., p. 134.

57. A. MacGregor Hutchison, and Alexander Hogg, eds., Scotland and Oil (Edinburgh: Oliver & Boyd, 1975), p. 113.

58. Prevention of Oil Pollution Act 1971, section 3.

59. M. M. Sibthorp, ed., The North Sea: Challenge and Opportunity (London: Europa Publications, 1975), p. 195.

60. United Kingdom Prevention of Oil Pollution Act 1971, section 6(1).

61. United Kingdom Petroleum and Submarine Pipelines Act 1975, section 45.

62. United Kingdom Petroleum (Production) Regulations 1976, schedule 5, clause 21.

63. Ibid., clause 15.

64. Ibid., clause 17.

65. United Kingdom, Offshore Installations (Construction and Survey) Regulations 1974, op. cit.

66. Sibthorp, op. cit., p. 201.

67. United Kingdom Merchant Shipping (Oil Pollution) Act 1971, section 1.

68. Ibid., section 2.

69. United Kingdom, Department of Energy, Development of the Oil and Gas Resources of the United Kingdom 1976, p. 15.

70. Norway, Ministry of Industry, Legislation Concerning the Norwegian Continental Shelf with unofficial English translation, 1973, "Act no. 12 of 21 June 1963."

71. Ibid., "Royal Decree of 8 December 1972," section 4.

72. Ibid., section 11.

73. Ibid., section 10.

74. Ibid., section 13.

75. Dam, op. cit., p. 56.

76. Norway, "Royal Decree of 8 December 1972," op. cit., section 17.

77. Ibid., section 54.

78. Ibid., section 25.

79. Ibid., section 26.

80. Ibid., section 81.

81. Dam, op. cit., p. 61.

82. Norway, "Royal Decree of 8 December 1972," op. cit., section 48.

82. Ibid., section 20.

84. Ibid., section 34.

85. Ibid.

86. Ibid., section 35.

87. Ibid., section 26.

88. Ibid., section 38(f).

89. Ibid., section 3(3).

90. Ibid., section 37.

91. Norway, Ministry of Industry, Operations on the Norwegian Continental Shelf Report No. 30 to the Norwegian Storting, p. 35.

92. Norway, Legislation, op. cit., "Royal Decree of 8 December 1972," section 57.

93. Norway, Ministry of Industry, Operations, op. cit., p. 52.

94. Norway, Ministry of Finance, Act Relating to the Taxation of Submarine Oil Deposits, etc., Odelsting Proposition No. 26 (1974-75).

95. Norway, Ministry of Industry, Activities on the Norwegian Continental Shelf, Report No. 81 to the Storting (1974-75), p. 22.

96. "North Sea: A Comparison," op. cit., p. 171.

97. Norway, "Royal Decree of 8 December 1972," op. cit., section 9.

98. Norway, "Royal Decree of 3 October 1975" (issued in un-official translation by the Ministry of Industry), section 7.

99. Ibid., section 48.

100. Ibid., section 66.

101. Norway, "Royal Decree of 9 July 1976 Relating to Safe Practice in the Production, etc., of Submarine Petroleum Resources," (issued in unofficial translation by the Ministry of Industry), section 7.

102. Ibid., section 111.

103. Ibid., section 7.

104. Norway, "Royal Decree of 3 October 1975," op. cit., section 110.

105. Ibid., section 7.

106. Norway, Ministry of Industry, Operations, op. cit., p. 29.

107. Norway, "Royal Decree of 9 July 1976," op. cit., section 37.

108. Ibid., section 19.

109. Ibid., section 11.

110. Norway, Ministry of Industry, Operations, op. cit., p. 31.

111. Norway, Royal Decree of 3 October 1975, op. cit., section 120.

112. Norway, Royal Decree of 9 July 1976, op. cit., note 102, section 129.

113. Norway, Royal Decree of 8 December 1972, op. cit., section 52.

114. Offshore, February 1977, p. 62.

115. Norway, Ministry of Finance, Parliamentary Report No. 25 (1973-74), Petroleum Industry in Norwegian Society, p. 83.

116. Norway, Ministry of Industry, Report No. 91 to the Norwegian Storting (1975-76), Petroleum Exploration North of 62° N, p. 74.

117. Norway, Ministry of Finance Petroleum Industry, op. cit., p. 85.

118. Norway, Ministry of Industry Petroleum Exploration, op. cit., p. 70.

119. Ibid.

120. Ibid., p. 45.

121. Norway, "Royal Decree of 3 October 1975," op. cit., section 28.

122. Norway, Ministry of Industry Petroleum Exploration, op. cit., p. 45.

123. Norway, "Royal Decree of 9 July 1976, op. cit., section 43.

124. Norway, Ministry of Industry, Petroleum Exploration, op. cit., p. 52.

125. H. Peter Krosby, "Oil and the Environment: Norway's Enlightened Policy," Scandinavian Review 4 (1976): 43-44.

126. Norway, Ministry of Industry, Petroleum Exploration, op. cit., p. 51.

127. Norway, Legislation, op. cit., Royal Decree of 8 December 1972, op. cit., section 51.

6

A NOTE ON IMPLICATIONS

The North Sea is presently one of a handful of continental shelf areas for which specific and detailed laws governing petroleum production have been drafted. Although offshore oil is being sought off every continent, large-scale development has thus far been restricted to the United States, the Middle East, and the North Sea.

There is every reason to believe, however, that the world is on the threshold of an explosion in offshore development activity. Whatever conservation measures consuming nations are able to impose on themselves, it is probably inevitable that the demand for oil will continue to rise, although more slowly, perhaps, than was anticipated a few years ago. Higher demand, dwindling land reserves, and rapidly improving offshore production technology: all these factors will contribute to a rapid rise in the percentage of the world's oil supplies that derive from offshore regions. Within the industry, estimates of 50 percent and higher by the mid-1980s are quoted. [1]

A successful Law of the Sea Conference would accelerate the pace of world offshore development by providing an accepted formula for the delimitation of national sectors and a mandatory mechanism for the settlement of disputes. At present, most continental shelf regions do not have agreed-upon boundaries, and at least 20 are the subject of active international disputes. [2] Yet even if the Law of the Sea Conference is not successful, international law, as it has evolved in the North Sea and elsewhere, now provides an adequate framework for the extension of national jurisdiction over continental shelf areas. The judgment in the North Sea Continental Shelf Cases set forth a reasonably flexible basis for negotiating zonal boundaries and demonstrated the utility of international arbitration in offshore boundary disputes. Moreover even if the Law of the Sea Conference is unsuccessful, much of what is now the subject of consensus will become part of customary international law. If the Law of the Sea Conference is unsuccessful, the work of the International Court and Arbitration Panel over the next few years can be expected to be devoted, to a considerable extent, to the determination of continental shelf boundaries.

Yet one of the important lessons of the North Sea is that the settlement of offshore jurisdiction, while a difficult and complex problem in itself, is only a first step. What benefits and harms are likely to flow from offshore development and how they are likely to be distributed is in large part a function of the offshore legal system that the coastal state institutes after jurisdiction is settled. Experience in the North Sea, if nothing else, demonstrates the intricacy of the task faced by national legislators. How are continental shelf mineral rights to be apportioned among private and public entities? How are these rights to be administered? In what form should public revenues be collected so as not to eliminate the financial incentives inducing private companies to undertake desired development? How can local industry be made to benefit without discouraging foreign companies whose efforts are essential to shelf development and without provoking retaliation by foreign governments? Is participation by the state in activities on the shelf appropriate? Is state participation feasible, technically and financially? If not, can the aid of private companies be enlisted to make it so? What level of safety in offshore operations should be sought through regulation and how can the state obtain the expertise necessary to ensure that the regulations are realistic? To what extent should benefits from the continental shelf be sacrificed to preserve the social and biological environments? The North Sea states have arrived at answers to most of these questions and embodied them in legislation and regulations. For a few of the questions, answers are still being evolved. Given the advanced stage that has been reached in the development of North Sea law, it is pertinent to inquire into the relevance of the North Sea experience to other regions. To what extent may North Sea law serve as a model for continental shelf legal systems evolving elsewhere?

No definitive answer to this question can be attempted in this study. However, one can briefly state several reasons for supposing that North Sea law may have considerable precedential importance.

It must be conceded that the regions of the world now considered to have a high potential for offshore petroleum development are numerous and diverse. Active exploration is currently underway off all continents, from the Arctic to the Antarctic, from the Indian Ocean to the Beaufort Sea, from Thailand to Greenland. The countries off whose shores petroleum is believed to exist can hardly be said to fall into a unified political or economic category.

Yet, for several reasons, the political, economic, and geographic diversity among states with substantial prospects for offshore petroleum need not imply the inevitability of diverse offshore
legal systems. First, as was pointed in Chapter 3, whatever diversity
may exist among coastal nations, the activity being regulated is essentially the same regardless of the coast off which it is being conducted. Since a limited number of companies are capable of extensive
offshore operations, continental shelf law is, in one sense, simply a
means of defining the state's relationship with these companies. Each
of the companies has expectations, some nonnegotiable, regarding the
sort of offshore legal environment in which it is prepared to operate.
Some hemogeneity in offshore legal systems is, thus, virtually inevitable.

Second, those national interests in offshore development that
in Chapter 3 were identified as characteristic of the North Sea states
probably have more general application. In virtually any modern
nation there are likely to exist strong interests in developing indigenous petroleum supplies (for internal use or to generate foreign
exchange), in maximizing revenues to the state from offshore development, and in channeling benefit to the local economy. Some concern is also likely for the safety of offshore workers and the environmental and social consequences of development, although these latter
concerns may be more attenuated in developing countries. To the
extent that the basic interests discussed in chapter three can be said
to be as characteristic of other regions undergoing offshore development as they are in the North Sea, to that extent North Sea law might
have international relevance as precedence. Moreover, Great Britain
and particularly Norway have pioneered legal devices for maximizing
the role of the state in shelf development while at the same time avoiding the alienation of the private oil companies. Given the economic
activism of most governments in the world today, the approach taken
in the North Sea is very likely to be favored over, for example, the
more laissez-faire approach taken by the United States on the American shelf.

This is not to suggest that all nations have identical interests
but merely that offshore development will tend to offer each nation a
similar combination of prospective benefits and harms. The extent
to which offshore development in other regions evokes national interests divergent from those that have been evoked in the North Sea
will, in large part, define the limitations on the relevance of North
Sea law as precedent.

Finally, offshore law typically evolves out of a delicate relationship between the state and private companies, characterized by a
blend of cooperation and hard bargaining. Where law is the product of
cooperation, North Sea law will function like any precedent, defining

a familiar path of lesser resistance for the conception of new law. Where law is the product of bargaining, the existence of the North Sea precedent will strengthen the hands of governments seeking concessions similar to those obtained from companies in the North Sea. Such concessions are likely to seem far less radical than they would have only a few years ago.

NOTES

1. Offshore, June 1976, p. 70.
2. Offshore, March 1977, p. 42.

INDEX

Arab oil embargo, 7; See also
  Oil price increase of 1973-
  1975

Balance of payments, 8; Impact
  of oil price increase of 1973-
  1975 on, 8
Bonn Agreement for Cooperation in Dealing with Pollution of the North Sea by Oil,
  13
British continental shelf law,
  Continental Shelf Act of 1964,
  84, 95; depletion control, 90;
  discretionary system of licensing, 86-88; eligi-
  bility for licenses, 85; enforcement of license conditions, 92; environmental
  laws and regulations, 98-101;
  exploration licenses, 85; landing requirements, 89; licensing, first round of license allocation, 24; second round of
  license allocation, 24; third
  round of license allocation,
  34; fourth round of license
  allocation, 34, 86; fifth round
  of license allocation, 40, 87;
  sixth round of license allocation, 40, 88; Mineral Workings (Offshore Installations)
  Act 1971, 95, 96, 107; Oil
  Taxation Act of 1975, 93, 94,
  95, 106; Offshore Pollution
  Liability Agreement, 100;
  participation, 92; Petroleum
  and Submarine Pipeline Act
  of 1975, 92, 94; Petroleum
(Production) Regulations
  1976, 92, 95, 99; Petroleum
  Revenue Tax, 93, 94; pipeline
  regulation, 91; Prevention of
  Oil Pollution Act of 1971, 98,
  99; production licenses, 85,
  86; renewal and relinquishment of licenses, 89; "ring
  fence," 39, 93; safety laws
  and regulations, 95, 96; taxation arrangements, 93; tender bid experiment, 36
British continental shelf development, Brent discovery, 37;
  Forties discovery, 37; Leman
  discovery, 24; margin of profit, 37; West Sole discovery,
  24
British National Oil Corporation
  (BNOC), 39, 91, 92
British planning law, Town and
  Country Planning (Scotland)
  Act of 1972, 96

Coal, effect of World War II on
  consumption, 2; erosion of
  production in Europe by cheap
  oil, 2-3; production subsidies
  by European governments, 2-
  3
Committee of Public Accounts
  (U. K.), 38, 50, 51, 88
Continental margin, 66
Continental rise, 66
Continental shelf, extension of
  coastal state claims, 64-70
Continental Shelf Convention,
  See Geneva Convention on the
  Continental Shelf

LAW AND OFFSHORE
OIL DEVELOPMENT:
The North Sea Experience

LAW AND OFFSHORE OIL DEVELOPMENT:
The North Sea Experience

David B. Keto

PRAEGER PUBLISHERS
Praeger Special Studies

New York   •   London   •   Sydney   •   Toronto

Library of Congress Cataloging in Publication Data

Keto, David B
      Law and offshore oil development.

      Includes index.
      1.   Offshore oil industry--Law and legislation.
2.   Petroleum in submerged lands--North Sea.
3.   Continental shelf. 4.   Territorial waters--
Great Britain. 5.   Territorial waters--Norway.
I.   Title.
K3918.K47   341.7'62   78-19745

ISBN 0-03-046646-6

PRAEGER PUBLISHERS
PRAEGER SPECIAL STUDIES
383 Madison Avenue, New York, N.Y. 10017, U.S.A.

Published in the United States of America in 1978
by Praeger Publishers,
A Division of Holt, Rinehart and Winston, CBS, Inc.

89   038   987654321

Printed in the United States of America